Clare Connelly was rai among a family of avid of her childhood up a tr hand. Clare is married t and they live in a bunga two children. She is frequently found staring into space —a surefire sign that she's in the world of her characters. She has a penchant for French food and ice-cold champagne, and Mills & Boon novels continue to be her favourite ever books. Writing for Modern is a long-held dream. Clare can be contacted via clareconnelly.com or at her Facebook page.

Susan Stephens was a professional singer before meeting her husband on the Mediterranean island of Malta. In true Mills & Boon style, they met on Monday, became engaged on Friday and married three months later. Susan enjoys entertaining, travel, and going to the theatre. To relax she reads, cooks and plays the piano, and when she's had enough of relaxing she throws herself off mountains on skis or gallops through the countryside singing loudly.

CROWNED FOR HIS DESERT TWINS

CLARE CONNELLY

FORBIDDEN TO HER SPANISH BOSS

SUSAN STEPHENS

MILLS & BOON

First Published in Great Britain 2021
by Mills & Boon, an imprint of HarperCollins*Publishers* Ltd,
1 London Bridge Street, London, SE1 9GF

www.harpercollins.co.uk

HarperCollins*Publishers*
1st Floor, Watermarque Building,
Ringsend Road, Dublin 4, Ireland

Crowned for His Desert Twins © 2021 Clare Connelly

Forbidden to Her Spanish Boss © 2021 Susan Stephens

ISBN: 978-0-263-28263-4

09/21

MIX
Paper from
responsible sources
FSC™ C007454

This book is produced from independently certified FSC™ paper
to ensure responsible forest management.
For more information visit www.harpercollins.co.uk/green.

Printed and bound in Spain
by CPI, Barcelona

CROWNED FOR HIS DESERT TWINS

CLARE CONNELLY

MILLS & BOON

To Trish Morey,
for your wisdom, kindness, and hours of fabulous stories.

PROLOGUE

THE ROOM SWARMED with exactly the sort of people Khalil had come to think of as 'the usual suspects' at such events. The ballroom of the elegant Manhattan hotel buzzed with America's elite, women in ball gowns and men in suits, chattering non-stop so the noise was like the buzz of cicadas droning on incessantly.

'Your Highness?' A waiter approached nervously, holding a stainless-steel tray and a single glass of Scotch.

Khalil's lips twisted cynically. Even here, across the other side of the world, his reputation preceded him. The Ruthless Prince, he thought with a sneer. Had he always been regarded as such? Or was it just after Fatima, when it had become easier to see people as they truly were, and therefore harder to hide his contempt? He lifted the glass with a dismissive nod, and the waiter scuttled away gratefully.

It was strong and spiced with citrus, just as he liked it. He took a sip, his eyes travelling the room, quirking a brow in greeting as he recognised a familiar face in conversation near the entrance, before his gaze continued to roam, his features unknowingly bearing an expression of bored impatience. This had never been his scene. He much preferred the important parts of ruling—policy, education, funding, policing. The frothy parties and socialising were a pointless waste of time, time he simply didn't have. Drawing himself to his full six and a half feet, he looked towards a set of wide doors, preparing to escape this pointless event, having at least made an appearance to appease international diplomatic relations.

And then, he saw her.

His gaze arrested, his body straightened unconsciously, something like adrenaline filled his mouth as he stared at the most beautiful woman he'd ever seen. Tall and slender with blonde hair that was pinned into a bun low on her nape, she wore a deep blue gown that demanded attention—not for the dress so much as for what it did to her figure. Curved breasts and hips, a slim waist and long legs were encased in a sheath of fabric that, while elegant enough to meet the dress code, lacked the puffy confection of the ball gowns the other women wore. Her smile was quick and transformed her face, showing dimples in either cheek, so her eyes looked as though they were filled with glitter.

Throwing back the rest of his Scotch, already poised to move closer, Khalil moved his attention to encompass her date almost as an afterthought. Whoever it was, it didn't matter. Such considerations were irrelevant to Sheikh Khalil el Abdul, ruler to one of the most prosperous countries in the Middle East. No woman he'd ever wanted had resisted him; it didn't occur to him she might be the first.

The blonde smiled again and Khalil's eyes narrowed, looking to the recipient of this beautiful gift. The man's back was turned to him, so all Khalil could tell was that he was fair and stood about a foot shorter than Khalil, almost the same height as the woman. He wore a tuxedo with tails, his shoes polished. But it was when the man angled his face in profile that a blade cut through Khalil's chest.

The recognition was instantaneous. He never forgot a

face, but this one in particular he had good cause to recollect—and despise. Ethan Graves, his one-time friend, a man he'd thought well enough of to introduce to his cousin—more like a sister, really—a man who'd then gone on to destroy Astrid's life. A familiar rush of guilt churned through him. He couldn't look at Ethan without seeing Astrid—the way their relationship had affected her. If only he hadn't set them up! If only he'd seen what was happening before it was too late...

Khalil squeezed the Scotch glass so hard it almost broke. He put it down before he cracked it, and eyed the pair with renewed interest.

His heart was beating hard, determination moving through his veins like steel. There was no one on earth he hated more than he did Ethan Graves. The man was the lowest of the low. He'd be doing this woman a favour by seducing her away from Ethan. Ethan wasn't good enough for the air he breathed, let alone for this woman to be giving him her attention.

Yes, she would benefit from this plan too but, mainly, Khalil wanted to make Ethan suffer. He wanted to hurt him; he'd been hoping for a chance to avenge his cousin, and fate had delivered that opportunity right into his lap. Adrenaline burst through him, determination wiping anything else from his mind.

He hated Ethan Graves, and there was nothing he wouldn't do to make the other man pay, including seducing his very beautiful lover...

CHAPTER ONE

'IN A ROOM full of peacocks, you are the only exotic bird.'

The voice whispered against her cheek, words murmured from behind, his accent spiced, tone deep. The flesh on India's arms lifted in a fine covering of goosebumps even before she'd turned around to see who was speaking to her. His appearance didn't help matters. She'd expected another boring banker type, dressed to the nines and swelled up with their own importance, and instead she'd come face to face with—

But it was impossible to put into words the effect of this man's beauty. He was tall and broad, with swarthy skin and dark hair that brushed his collar, a slight kick at the bottom. His brows were thick and dark, his bone structure symmetrical, his jawline square, covered with stubble, his lips generous and wide, his nose straight and long. He had eyes that were like never-ending tunnels, deep and fascinating, flecked with brown and black and gold, rimmed in thick, dark lashes that gave him the appearance of wearing eyeliner. She stared up at him breathlessly, completely unprepared for this, almost forgetting where she was and what she was doing.

But the amnesia was temporary.

India was working, and she couldn't afford to do anything to mess up this job—or any job—so she blinked, pushing her features into a politely dismissive smile. 'Thank you,' she murmured, turning her attention back to the bar just in time to see another woman—one of the peacocks this man had alluded to—sweeping in front of her and grabbing the barman's attention.

'Damn it,' she muttered under her breath.

'What is it you would like to drink?' His voice was like treacle—completely smooth and addictive. She bit back an irrational desire to suggest he could have a second career as an audiobook narrator, because if this man was here, at this thousand-dollars-a-head charity event, it was unlikely he was in need of a supplemental income.

'It's fine,' she dismissed. 'I'm next in line.'

'You were next in line before too,' he pointed out.

She slid him a glance. 'Yes, and if you hadn't distracted me, I would have ordered by now.'

In response, his lips curled in a smile of undisguised appreciation. 'Allow me,' he murmured, putting a hand in the small of her back and drawing her closer to him. Shocked, her body moved without her brain's consent, so her side connected with his, and she startled, her eyes leaping to his in surprise as sparks flared beneath her skin. Somehow, he found a small gap at the front of the bar and moved them towards it, lifting a hand at the same time.

To India's surprise, a waitress appeared immediately. 'Good evening, sir.' She dipped her head forward deferentially, so India's gaze flicked back to the stranger's face. 'May I get you a drink?'

'The lady would like to order,' he said, his fingers moving gently over her back now, the pattern he was drawing there rhythmic and distracting, so that when India opened her mouth to speak her voice emerged stilted.

'A mineral water for me, please, but in a champagne flute, and a glass of pinot noir.'

'And for you, Your Highness?' The waitress looked up at him.

India startled once more. *Your Highness?* The man's eyes caught hers, amusement in those never-ending depths, and embarrassment curdled her belly. Was he enjoying her surprise? The fact she had no idea who he was? No doubt he moved in these circles all the time, whereas India was an occasional guest, when the agency was in a jam and had to send her on a blue-chip date—usually reserved for the escorts who'd worked at the agency the longest. Her tenure was only new—twelve months ago the bottom had fallen out of her world, and she'd been doing whatever she could to make ends meet since then. She'd do whatever was necessary to keep her beloved younger brother in college. He'd already lost so much; she wouldn't allow him to lose his degree as well.

'A mineral water as well, but not in a champagne flute.'

'Your *Highness*?' India queried, while the waitress disappeared to prepare their drinks.

'Yes?'

She narrowed her gaze. 'You're royalty?'

'It would appear so.'

'Are you being deliberately secretive?'

'That's something I've never been called before.'

'Perhaps not to your face.'

He laughed then, a rich sound that had more than one head turning in their direction and which set India's pulse into overdrive. Not just her pulse. Every cell in her body was trembling with awareness, and she was secretly glad that the crowd pushing towards the bar meant they were being jostled closer together, her body shifting nearer to his big, broad frame until they were touching.

'Who are you?' she repeated, curiosity spreading through her.

'My name is Khalil,' he said.

'But should I call you "Your Highness"?'

'No, that would not be appropriate.'

Her brow furrowed in confusion. 'But if you're a king…?'

'I am not yet a king,' he said, half dismissively, so she wondered if she'd said the wrong thing somehow. But then he was moving closer, his head lowering to her ear, so he could whisper against her flesh. 'And I would like to hear my name on your lips, rather than my title.'

It was just a throwaway comment, and yet something about the way he'd phrased it and the timbre of his voice set her nerves jangling. A slick of heat flooded her body, low in her abdomen, so she was conscious of the way her nipples strained against the soft silk of her dress. She wasn't wearing a bra—she didn't possess one that worked with the lines of the dress—and so her breasts were crushed against the hard warmth of his chest, every nerve-ending tantalisingly aware of his proximity and raw charisma.

His eyes flicked to her mouth and her lips parted as if by magic, her heart rate as fast as if she'd just run a marathon. Her lips tingled all over. She was overcome with sensations she'd never known before. Surrounded by the crush of New York's elite and somewhere, only a few feet away, the date who was paying handsomely for her time, all she could think of was the man before her.

'Khalil,' she said, as if to stir herself from the strange dream that was wrapping tentacles around her.

His eyes flared with unmistakable desire. Her stomach swooped. 'And your name?' The question was said with a tone of command.

'I-India,' she stammered for the first time in years, since a speech pathologist had helped her overcome the childhood impediment.

'India.' His hand shifted to her hip, holding her close to him, promising things she desperately wanted to experience. 'It is a pleasure to meet you.'

'Here are your drinks, sir, ma'am.' The waitress's appearance was a welcome interruption. India's eyes flared wide and she would have stood back a little, if she could have. But there were too many people crowding around them, so India told herself she had no choice but to stay right where she was: for now—it was a convenient excuse, because she didn't really want to put any space between them anyway.

'Leave them on the bar.' He didn't take his eyes off India's face. She felt warm and desirable, and a thousand kinds of need. 'Tell me about yourself.'

India blinked, she'd never been asked this question, not on any of the agency dates she'd attended in the past year.

'I suspect it would be far more interesting if you told me about yourself,' she said truthfully, ignoring the glass of pinot noir to her right—due to be delivered to her date at any moment.

'Why is that?'

'Well, you're the first royal I've ever met,' she said with a lift of one shoulder. It drew his gaze downwards, and from the creamy flesh of her shoulder sideways, to the exposed decolletage and valley between her breasts. India sucked in a sharp breath, butterflies colonising her belly. His interest was unmistakable, but her own physical response bowled her over.

'And you are the first woman named India I have ever met. What is your point?'

Her cheeks flooded with warmth. She was heart-stoppingly attracted to him, and that was a disaster. Or, at the very least, hugely inconvenient, because she was on a date with a client and she wasn't being paid to flirt with another man. She could imagine the complaint Ethan—who seemed as if he had definite jerk potential—would make to the agency if he saw her locked in intimate conversation with another man—particularly one like this. She couldn't say why she knew that *this* man in particular would be incendiary, except that he was so hyper-masculine. She suspected he was intimidating to all other males.

And very likely knew it.

'My point...' she pulled away from him with difficulty, curling her fingers around the drinks '...is that I should think your life story would outdo mine any day.' She offered him a small smile. 'But unfortunately, I can't stay to hear it. I'm here with someone.'

His eyes flashed with an emotion she couldn't decipher. Annoyance? Impatience? Irritation?

She understood all three. But her work was hugely important—she'd already spent tonight's pay cheque three times over, and the very thought of the college-fee notice stuck to the fridge door had her breaking out in a cold sweat.

'Someone you'd prefer to be with?' he prompted with easy confidence. What must it have been like to be so self-assured? Oh, he was right, of course. She'd have given anything to swap out her dates, but this was business, not pleasure, and so her own needs had to take a back seat.

It wasn't a fair question. 'I came here with someone else.'

'It does not follow you must leave with him, *azeezi.*'

'Actually, it does.' She flicked a glance downwards, regret in her heart. On this night, of all nights—her twenty-fourth birthday—what she wouldn't have given to indulge her own wants, just for once! The day had been so lonely, in stark contrast to the way her mother, stepfather and brother used to make a fuss each year. Oh, Jackson had still called, and they'd spoken for almost an hour—his happiness had lifted her heart for a time. But beyond that, it was just India in a big, empty home, thinking of the family she'd used to have, the way things used to be. Flirting with this incredibly handsome stranger would have been the perfect present to herself, but what she needed, more than anything, was the payment for tonight. She couldn't do anything to risk the job. With true remorse, she offered him a parting smile. 'It was nice to meet you, Your Highness.'

But he wasn't ready to let it go. 'I asked you to call me Khalil,' he reminded her softly. His thumb pressed beneath her chin, lifting her face to his, so their eyes locked and the world seemed to disappear, tipping away, leaving just the two of them on a precipice of time and space.

'I can't call you anything,' she said, her voice lacking the firmness she needed despite her resolve. 'I must go.'

'Is it what you want?'

'Don't keep asking me that.'

'Have I already?'

'More or less.' She sighed, but didn't look away. 'My date will be waiting for me.'

Now his lips curled with unmistakable derision. 'A date who sent you to the bar to get his drink? Is such a man really worthy of your time?'

'I offered,' she said. 'He was in an important business conversation.'

'No conversation is more important than your time. If you were here with me, you would know that.'

Her lips parted; a reply was impossible.

'A man lucky enough to secure a date with you should make it his life's mission to keep you happy, not send you scurrying to the bar whenever he develops a thirst.'

Her breath escaped in a hot rush. 'It's not—like that—' she insisted. Her pulse was thready and her lips were tingling. Even as she acknowledged that Ethan had, in fact, pointed to the bar and given her his order, treating her like the paid companion she, in fact, was.

'Would you like to hear what a date with me would entail?'

'I have to get back,' she groaned huskily, without making any attempt to free herself from his proximity.

'First, I would send you the address of a Fifth Avenue boutique, so you could go and enjoy choosing what you would wear—lingerie, a dress, shoes, jewellery, anything your heart desired. My driver would then take you to the presidential suite at the Carlisle, where you would spend the afternoon preparing, pampering and, most vitally, enjoying a nap to be sure you were well rested.'

A frisson of desire ran the length of her spine at the image he was painting. It was a far cry from the life she currently led.

'I would collect you at eight. We would go for dinner, but I would book the entire restaurant to be sure we each had the other's full attention. Alone, we would dance with no eyes on us, and then, before midnight, we would return to your hotel room, where I would enjoy hearing my name on your lips over, and over, and over again.'

Her eyes closed as imagery flourished in her brain, his body naked, hers, entangled in billion-thread-count sheets at the impossibly prestigious hotel. The night sounded like perfection, and if India hadn't learned for herself how fleeting men's interest would be, then she might not have known to ask the next question. But once bitten, twice shy, was a motto that had served India well for years.

'And in the morning?' she whispered, the thickness to her voice betraying how tempted she was by his words.

Her eyes glanced at his, just in time to see a spark of something like surprise in their depths.

'The morning would be a new day,' he said quietly.

'And without you in it.'

His head dipped forward. 'I am never in America for long. My life is in Khatrain.'

Ah! Khatrain. She knew of the country instantly, of course. Prosperous, modern, politically important, perched on the edge of the Persian Gulf with a capital city that was one of the modern wonders of the world.

'The date sounds wonderful,' she said wistfully. 'But I make it a rule not to get involved in one-night stands.' Now she pulled backwards, but not quickly enough.

'Even when it's what you want?' he prompted silkily.

Her heart began to slam into her ribs. She stared up at him, lost in his eyes, his nearness, her breath burning. 'How do you know what I want?'

'I don't. I'm guessing. Am I wrong?'

Yes. Say yes. But India was honest to a fault. She shook her head once, her body swaying forward.

'I didn't think so,' he said simply, his head dropping slowly to hers, his eyes teasing her, tempting her. He intended to kiss her, and even when India knew she should pull away, her body moved of its own volition, her feet pushing her higher, willingly submitting to his passionate kiss, his outright possession, so her ability to think was blown completely to smithereens.

His hand stroked her hip, and one leg shifted, moving forward to brace her, forming a sort of cage around her body, holding her just where she was, totally wrapped up in him. 'It would only be one night, but the night would set your soul on fire, *azeezi*, I promise.'

It was like being doused in ice water. She jerked her face away, quickly looking towards the crowded bar. Ethan's back was turned to her—thank God. Her fingertips quivered with the flood of sensations and the rush of anxiety over what had just happened. She'd be fired for sure if

Ethan reported this to the agency, and she couldn't live with that. Where else would she get a job like this? Warm Engagements was an escort agency with a difference—no sex between client and staff. It was a hard rule, and it meant India felt safe accepting bookings without worrying that her client was going to expect a little 'added service' at the end of the night, and it paid ten times better than anything else she was even remotely qualified for.

'I can't,' she said, her eyes awash with anguish because, oh, how she wanted to! 'Please, just, forget we ever met.'

CHAPTER TWO

ETHAN'S VOICE HAD been droning on for a very, very long time. India nodded and smiled—it was pretty obvious he didn't require much more than that. The few times she'd attempted to interject her own thoughts, he'd given her a condescending look, as if to imply, 'what would you know about it?' and then waffled on some more. His companions didn't seem to mind, which led India to believe that Ethan Graves was either seriously rich or seriously important. There was no other reason for so many people to be intent on sucking up to him. Oh, he was handsome, in that movie star way, but he was clearly so full of himself that India was beyond bored.

Unfortunately, that left her brain with way, way too much run time, and it was occupied on a singular task: overthinking the experience she'd had with Khalil—she didn't even know his last name! And yet he'd almost kissed her as though she were his dying breath, and he had—for that moment—been all she was aware of. She tried to think of other matters. Her conversation with Jackson this morning, for example, and how happy he'd sounded, his placement at college coming at a time when he'd been besieged by grief—they both had been—after the sudden, tragic loss of their parents. Her life's purpose had become, in the last twelve months, about maintaining the status quo for him.

She owed that to her mother and stepfather. She'd loved them so much, and they'd worked so hard to give their children a great life. She'd do anything she could to honour them, and working out a way to cover Jackson's expensive tuition so he could take up his place at the prestigious institution seemed like a good place to start. They'd been so proud when he'd got his acceptance letter. Jackson's degree had meant the world to them. She had to make sure he was able to complete his studies.

But was it tenable? Could she keep this up for another three years? Panic rose in her chest, as it always did when she contemplated the future, the financial obligations around her neck tightening until she felt as though she were going to black out. Unfortunately, there were only so many ways an unqualified twenty-four-year-old could make money in this economy, and the amount of money India required meant she'd had no option but to turn to a job like this. Escorting wealthy men to fancy functions wasn't exactly her dream career, but it paid well. And Jackson was worth it.

She would have done anything she could to be with him today. It was her first birthday without her parents. They'd died three days after she turned twenty-three. She hadn't stopped to think about that, but this morning, she'd faced this milestone without them, and it had brought all the grief and loneliness and missing them back so she'd wished the day away, simply so she could get this 'first' day over with. Christmas had been the same. Jackson had come home though, so at least they'd been together, but it had been hollow and haunting, their parents' absence making the holiday heavy with sadness.

Ethan's companions laughed at something he'd said, dragging her back to the conversation. She faked a laugh, before lifting the mineral water to her lips and taking a sip.

It wasn't intentional, but her eyes shifted sideways and it was like being electric-shocked.

Khalil stood across the room, in a conversation he clearly wasn't listening to. His eyes bored into her in a way that sent her pulse into overdrive. She didn't—couldn't—look away, and a moment later his lip lifted in a knowing smile, before his eyes dipped lower, undertaking a slower, more thorough inspection. Her body's response was immediate. Her stomach squeezed and her breasts tingled, her nipples taut. She knew he realised, and heat bloomed in her cheeks. India sipped her drink again then forced herself to listen to Ethan, dragging her gaze back to her client.

He knew nothing about economics. He clearly thought he did, but India had finished two years of her degree and, beyond that, economics had long been a passion of hers. She knew that he was fudging numbers and his understanding of trade relationships was deeply warped. Did the others in the group realise?

On he went, for at least another twenty minutes, before turning to India. 'Darling, would you mind fetching me another from the bar?'

Heat flushed her cheeks for a different reason now, and a quick glance confirmed that Khalil was watching, a look in his eyes that knocked the breath from her lungs.

'Of course not,' she said, embarrassed, but all too aware she was being paid to be the perfect date.

'Anyone else for a drink?' he offered the group.

'A beer,' one of the men said with a grin of appreciation.

'Same,' another agreed.

India smiled through gritted teeth as she turned and walked towards the bar.

'You know, there are waiters here who would happily take care of his needs for you.' Khalil was behind her, his voice caressing. 'Why does he send you like a little servant?'

The moment he spoke, she realised she'd been hoping he would pursue her. 'I'm his date and I'm happy to make him happy.'

'Is this what you think a date should be like?' Khalil murmured, making a tsking sound of disapproval. 'What fools you must have been wasting your time on.'

'You don't know the half of it,' she muttered, before she could stop herself.

'Then let tonight be the night your poor taste in men stops,' he said with a lift of his brow.

'We've already discussed that. I'm not going home with you.'

'Because you'd rather go home with him? Or because I was honest about what would happen the morning after?'

Her heart felt as though she had a stitch. 'A little of both.'

'I don't believe you. Not on the first count. I have been watching you all night and there is no spark between the two of you. Not like when I touch you.'

India swallowed quickly. She'd never felt *anything* like she had when Khalil had touched her, let alone when he'd moved in to kiss her, as though her lips had been designed to dance with his.

'I wish you'd *stop* watching me,' she murmured quietly, except it was a lie. Even his eyes, from across the room, had the power to turn her blood to lava.

'I can't. For as long as you are in this room, I will watch you, and I will want you.'

It was so direct! India's eyes leaped to his, all the breath whooshing out of her. 'Khalil,' she moaned. 'You have to stop this.'

'When it is so obvious that we both want the same thing?'

She couldn't deny that, so she stuck with the line she'd already given him. 'I'm here on a date. I'm not going to ditch him for someone I've just met, okay?'

His response was to reach down and put an arm around her waist, drawing her away from the bar.

'Hey,' she protested. 'I have to order their drinks.'

'Drinks, plural?' He swore under his breath. 'You are retrieving beverages for the entire group?'

'Just a few, it's no big deal.' She waved her hand in the air. 'I offered.'

It was obvious he didn't believe the lie. His lips compressed in an angry slash as he lifted a hand and beckoned another waitress with enviable ease.

'What is your order?' he commanded, and for a moment she was struck dumb by the sheer authority he exuded from every pore of his body, his comfort with command unmistakable.

'India,' he insisted.

She nodded, regathering her wits. 'Um…a pinot noir, and two beers, please.'

'Deliver them to that group, over there. With the arrogant blond man holding forth on matters about which he knows little.'

Her eyes flew to Khalil's face. How did he know? Had he had the misfortune to be stung by Ethan in the past?

She didn't get a chance to ask. Order handed over to a waitress, Khalil was whisking her further away from the bar, towards the edge of the room. There were floor-to-ceiling windows here, bracketed on either side by a plush velvet curtain made of gold damask. Security guards, indiscernible from the tuxedo-clad guests, except for the little earpieces they wore, stood at each window.

As Khalil approached, one of the guards bowed before stepping back. Another pressed the windows, so India realised they were actually French doors, opening onto a narrow balcony that formed a perimeter around the Manhattan high rise.

The view was eye-watering. Picture perfect, showcasing the glittering city in all its postcard glory. Even now, as someone who'd seen the view many times, she felt a rush of emotions as she contemplated the beauty of the outlook.

'That's better,' he remarked, right beside her, his body so close they were almost touching.

She shivered, not because she was cold but because alone out here she experienced a rush of feelings and they were sending her nervous system into overdrive.

Nonetheless, Khalil shrugged out of his jacket, handing it to her on autopilot, so some part of her responded to his ingrained good manners. It reminded her of her step-dad, and the way he'd always treated her mother. But she couldn't think of her parents now—it was too sad. Even a year on from their sudden deaths, and the fallout from that tragedy, tears were still too quick to moisten her eyes.

'I can't stay long,' she said, and heard the acquiescence in her voice as he did. She was fighting him as best she could, but it was a losing battle, given that he was right: she wanted to go home with him, to hell with the fact it would never be more than a one-night stand.

'Why are you so adamant you want to be with him? Is it serious between the two of you?'

She hesitated a moment. 'No, it's not.'

'Surely you can see he's not worth your time?'

'That's none of your business.'

'Isn't it?'

'Khalil.' Her voice was lightly pleading. 'You seem to be forgetting we've just met.'

'I'm not forgetting that. Nor am I forgetting how much I'm looking forward to getting to know you properly.'

Her skin flushed all over. 'You're talking about sex.'

His laugh was a warm reward. 'I'm talking about a long, beautiful night together.'

Desire flashed through her—she wanted that. Oh, she wanted it more than she'd ever wanted anything in her entire life. But how could she? It was so outside her experience... 'I'm sure you do this kind of thing all the time, but I really don't,' she said, brutally honest. 'I know that being here, dressed like this, you might think I'm the kind of woman who...who...'

'Who what?' He pushed, but the smile on his face was teasing her innocence and she hated that! She squared her shoulders and fixed him with a cool glance.

'There's no need to laugh at me.'

He sobered, shaking his head. 'I'm not, I assure you. It's only that I find your honesty refreshing.' An emotion crossed his eyes, a look that made no sense. Guilt? Regret? 'Come home with me.' His voice was gruff. 'We can have coffee, sit and talk if you would prefer. This does not need to be about sex.'

Her lips parted in surprise at the offer. She rejected it instantly. 'Coffee' wasn't enough. She wanted so much more.

'Kiss me properly.' She blurted the command out. Foolish? Definitely. But when he kissed her, she saw things with a blinding clarity—or perhaps it was simply that she stopped overthinking everything, and could truly comprehend what she wanted.

Khalil did not need to be asked twice. He stepped forward, his powerful frame pressing hers back against the brick wall, his body dwarfing hers despite the fact India wasn't short. He was all hard planes and angles, the weight of him against her a pleasure she could barely process. Just like before, he stared into her eyes and dropped his head slowly, giving her time to rethink this, to change her mind, but India had already decided what she wanted.

He sensed her acquiescence, his kiss relentless, his tongue lashing hers as his mouth moved, so she could

barely breathe, and yet she kissed him back just as hard
with a matching urgency, her hands curving around behind him, her nails digging into his suit jacket with the
strength of her desperation.

The dress was a fine silk and his fingers caught the hem,
lifting it at one side, so the flimsy evening air brushed her
bare legs, creating the perfect contrast to his warmth and
hardness. Higher and higher he drew the dress, until his
fingers were on her hip, the dress bunched in his palm,
and she moaned, low in her throat, because she wanted
now to be naked for him, to be all his, just as he'd promised he'd make her.

The thought should have been sobering and yet it wasn't,
it was the exact opposite. An erotic fever had overtaken
India completely, she was subject to its whims completely.

Higher and higher his hands went, until the dress was
at her breasts. She moaned, lights bright behind her eyelids. He broke their kiss so he could stare at her nakedness, his eyes fixated on her in a way that sent a rush of
power through her limbs, before his dark head swooped
down and his mouth drew one of her nipples in. His teeth
clamped down and she cried out, the sharp pleasure too
much to bear, more than anything she'd ever experienced.
Her body was quivering with needs; the heat between her
legs demanded attention.

'Please,' she whimpered, tilting her head back to stare
at the sky.

'Say my name,' he demanded, transferring his mouth
to her other nipple. She groaned, the touch so perfect, the
first breast he'd lavished with attention enjoying the contrast of the cool night air, sending her pulse into overdrive.

'Please, Khalil,' she said instinctively, not even sure
what she was asking for, only that her life might very well
depend on it.

His wolfish grin when he looked up at her was all the confirmation she needed. Her heart thumped and her stomach rolled with desire. She wanted him; she had to have him.

But it wasn't so easy. There was Ethan to consider—not for himself, but for the fact he was a client and she desperately couldn't afford to lose her job.

'How long are you in town for?' She whimpered, as his hand found her inner thigh and teased the flesh there, tantalisingly close to—and yet desperately far from—her sex.

'Why?' He moved his mouth back to hers, kissing her once more, so answering was impossible. The dress fell back down and she moaned, because the silk against her taut, overly sensitive breasts was a form of torture.

Now his knee wedged her legs apart and she pressed down, her most intimate cluster of nerves seeking gratification, needing a pleasure only he could give her. His laugh was a rumble in his throat, and his fingers worked her hair, loosening it from the bun so it fell in waves down her back.

'Tomorrow night,' she said breathlessly, unable to think beyond the words she was trying to get out. 'A date.'

'No. Tonight.'

'I—'

'Do not tell me you can't,' he said firmly, and she heard his regal authority and knew that, in his country, Khalil would be obeyed by all he met, without question.

'I can't,' she whispered.

'And yet you will, if you want me to make love to you.' And with that, he stepped back, the ultimatum delivered at the same time he put space between them, the distance between their bodies a form of torture for India. She groaned as she straightened, staring at him with disbelief.

'Why?' It was thick with surprise. 'Why does it have to be tonight?'

'Do you think I would accept you going home with another man now?' he said seriously, but with such a sense of possession that her stomach burst into flames. 'You will be mine tonight, India. Not his.'

India knew better than to tell him she wasn't 'anyone's' to claim—she was a sentient human being with her own will and desires—but he knew that already, because he'd stoked her desires to a fever pitch and was currently demanding she exercise her own free will by choosing him over Ethan. He was making her acknowledge their connection, but she was under no illusions: this decision was hers. He was waiting for her answer.

'But how?' she said with a shake of her head. 'I don't want to offend Ethan.'

His eyes narrowed. 'A man who treats you as little more than a waitress deserves to be offended,' he said with firm disapproval, so she smiled despite the precariousness of her situation.

'I'm serious,' she said after a beat. 'We can't be seen leaving together.'

He shrugged. 'Fine. Then tell him you are not well and make your escape. I will follow a short time later.'

Her breath grew thin, as though the altitude were affecting her. Yes, *that* was an option. She could make her excuses via text message, apologising and saying she'd suddenly become unwell. It was hardly a glorious way to conclude the evening, but it also wasn't likely to get her fired.

'Okay,' she said with a quick nod, before she could change her mind. 'Where shall we meet?'

His smile was pure arrogance—as though he'd known all along it would reach this point.

'My car is out the front. I'll let my driver know to expect you.'

A tremor ran down her spine as their plans took a firm shape. There was no turning back; this was happening.

But India didn't want to turn backwards anyway. For this night, and just this night, she wanted to look forward, at the man opposite her, who'd promised to make love to her until she couldn't think straight.

'Fine, I'll meet you soon,' she said.

She turned to leave but he grabbed her hand, pulling her abruptly back to him and kissing her soundly, so her senses were in overdrive all over again.

'Be quick, India. I don't want to wait.'

India nodded, then slipped through the glass doors, into the buzzing ballroom. It took on an almost psychedelic quality now: the world was tilting at an odd angle; her experience with Khalil had sent her into another dimension. She made a beeline for the restrooms, ignoring the queue of Manhattan socialites waiting for a stall to free up and instead heading for a mirror. She braced her palms against the marble counter and stared at her flushed reflection and wild hair. There was no way she could face Ethan like this—even if she wanted to. Surely anyone would take one look at her and know exactly what she'd just been doing!

Pulling her phone from her bag, she loaded up a text message. She'd exchanged a few messages with Ethan to arrange the date, so had his number.

I'm so sorry, but I'm not feeling at all well. I didn't want to interrupt your conversation, nor to risk making you ill. Thank you for a lovely evening.

'Holy hell, what are *you* doing here?'

Khalil couldn't hide the sneer from his face. He hated this man but, until now, he hadn't realised that he'd been waiting a long time for the perfect opportunity to take his revenge. He had fantasised about making Ethan pay for what he'd done to Astrid, he just hadn't known the perfect plan would land right in his lap. He curled his hand into a fist, dug deep into his pocket. For Astrid, he would have liked to punch him hard in that arrogant, pretty-boy face. For India, he wanted to shove him out of the nearest window. What the hell had she seen in this guy?

Khalil clenched his jaw, staring down at the inferior specimen, as the men Ethan had been standing with ebbed away, sensing an impending dispute.

'I was invited,' he drawled. 'And you, Ethan? Looking to find the next wealthy heiress you can sink your teeth into?'

'There's no need.' Ethan's smile was the last word in smarmy. 'My divorce settlement from your cousin was more than enough to set me up for life. I must thank you again for introducing us. You really made all this possible for me.'

Khalil's temper was rock steady, except where his cousin was involved. Orphaned at only a few months old, she'd come to live with Khalil and was more like a little sister to him. There was nothing he wouldn't do to protect her, and, in this instance, avenge her. And appease your own guilt, a little voice reminded him, and of course that was true.

'Now, if you don't mind, I'm going to go and find my date.' Ethan's leering smile at Khalil was the last straw.

'Do you mean India?' For the briefest moment, he regretted the words. India deserved better than this—to become collateral damage in his need for revenge. But he was also saving her from a future with this bastard. Maybe she'd even thank him one day.

Ethan stopped walking, his back straight, as he turned slowly to face Khalil. 'How did you—?' Ethan frowned. 'Do you know her?'

'We've just met, but I intend to know her a lot better.'

'You can't be serious,' Ethan demanded, looking around, his face puce with outrage. A moment later, his phone buzzed and the blond man drew it from his pocket, his eyes darting with unmistakable anger as he read the text message.

She'd messaged him, rather than said goodbye? A small smile touched Khalil's lips at the slightly anxious gesture. Ethan was disappearing into the recesses of his mind, barely worth his time.

'I'm very serious,' Khalil murmured, leaning closer, his expression showing exactly why the press had nicknamed him the Ruthless Prince. 'So while you are alone tonight, you can imagine India and me, together. Believe me when I tell you she won't be missing you at all, Ethan. I'll make sure of that.'

CHAPTER THREE

'MADAM.' A SUITED driver stood waiting, the door to a black car with darkly tinted windows held open, his eyes focussed behind India.

She bit down on her lip, a hint of apprehension at what she was about to do assailing her. But it was too late to turn back, and besides, she didn't want to. Sliding into the car, she realised that it was far larger than an ordinary vehicle, though not quite as big as a limousine. A bench seat was at the back, and, directly opposite, two large chairs faced her, with a shiny black box between them. She took a seat on the bench, knowing it was because she hoped he would sit beside her, wanting to pick up right where they'd left off. The door clicked shut and she sat, hands clasped in her lap, waiting, her heart pounding, her breath burning with the desire he'd invoked.

Her phone beeped and she pulled it out of her bag, guiltily reading the response from Ethan.

I hope you feel better tomorrow, India. Sleep tight.

She winced, not liking how it felt to lie, the unusual turn of events pushing her to act in a seriously uncharacteristic manner. Before she could slide her phone away, it beeped again. A text from Jackson.

Hope you're having a great birthday. Wish I could have been there.

Her heart skipped a beat, because she *was* having a great birthday, and with a hint of disloyalty she realised she was now glad Jackson hadn't come back to New York. She was glad she'd been here tonight, that she'd met Khalil.

Having a great night, miss you. Thanks for checking in. x

She pushed the phone into her bag as the car door opened once more and Khalil stepped in, his frame instantly making the enormous vehicle feel smaller.

'Hi,' she murmured shyly. His cheeks were slashed with colour and his jaw was locked, as though angry or stressed. But as he looked at her he smiled, a smile that sent a kaleidoscope of butterflies into her stomach and pulled an answering smile across her own lips.

'I believe you promised me a life story,' he reminded her as he took the seat beside her, just as she'd hoped.

He pushed his arm up behind the seat, making no effort to keep any kind of space between them.

'I'm not sure you're remembering accurately.' The car's engine throbbed to life. A moment later, a dark screen slid between the back of the car and the front, offering privacy.

'Are you keeping secrets?'

She shook her head, wide-eyed, and lifted a hand to his chest. 'No, I just—'

But he understood. His eyes flared as he dipped his head lower. 'Don't want to talk?' He finished the sentence for her, brushing his lips over hers.

She shook her head.

His laugh was husky, uneven, and somehow, despite

her lack of experience, she knew he was as surprised by
the strength of their desire as she was.

His kiss was slow and explorative at first, but that wasn't
enough. This time, it was India who deepened it, hungrily
demanding more of him than he was giving her, her body
cleaving to his as the car moved through Manhattan. She
groaned, the kiss nowhere near enough to satisfy her, so
she moved swiftly, unclicking her seat belt and pushing
up, her dress lifting over her thighs as she straddled him,
rolling her hips in a silent, eager invitation to his mascu-
line strength. His arousal was firm between her legs, with
far too much fabric blocking him from her, so a wild kind
of desperation overtook her. As she kissed him, her fingers moved, thrusting his belt apart, then his zip, needing
more than she could put into rational thought and words
to feel him inside her.

'Please, Khalil,' she said, because she knew how it
drove him wild to hear his name on her lips. She rolled
her hips again, kissing him more, and then, she lifted her
dress over her head, needing to be naked. There was flame
burning within her, a flame he'd lit, and she needed him
to control it, to feed it, to eventually extinguish it—but
not for a long time, yet.

He swore at her nakedness, and then his hands were
cupping her breasts, his fingers plucking at her nipples
until she saw stars. Her back arched and she cried out as
he moved one hand between her legs, brushing against
her sex almost by accident as he reached into his pants
and freed his arousal from the confines of his clothing.

She kissed him hard then, lifting up on her haunches
so his hands could dispose of her underpants, pushing
them low enough for her to kick them off. It was instincts
that were driving her, not experience. India had barely
any of that, certainly nothing that would guide her in the

way of men and pleasure, and yet she moved back to his lap and welcomed him, taking his length deep on a long, slow breath, pleasure exploding as he filled her completely, her muscles stretching to accommodate his generous size.

It was impossible to be aware of the lights that were streaking past their window, the city a shimmering blur in the distance as he rocked his hips and India thrust down on his length, pushing them towards an inevitable, almost immediate climax, tipping her over the edge at the same time he exploded, drawing her close to him, kissing her hard as their bodies united in rapture and joy, their mutual release punctuated by India's frantic cries.

Afterwards, only the sound of their breathing was audible in the back of the car—no sounds of New York permeated the vehicle's bulletproof steel. Even if it had, India wouldn't have heard it. Her ears were full of the rushing of her blood and the exhalation of her breath, her heart turning over at the suddenness—and rightness—of this.

'That was—' She searched for the right word, but Khalil beat her to it.

'Just the beginning.'

Her eyes flared and she smiled, lazy, warm pleasure spreading through her completely. She didn't move; not at first. She didn't want to be parted from him. It was far nicer to feel their bodies melded together, to experience his breath through her chest, to be able to kiss him as she wanted, as the car snaked through the city. But eventually, Khalil ran his fingers lightly over her back, his voice husky. 'We're here.'

She lifted her head to see they were in an underground parking garage.

'Allow me.' As she wriggled off his lap, Khalil retrieved her dress, lifting it over her head then letting it cascade down her body. 'I am already looking forward to removing that all over again.'

Anticipation squeezed all of her organs, so India could barely breathe.

Khalil watched her sleep as the dawn light filtered across Manhattan, resisting a selfish urge to wake her with a kiss. She was exhausted, and with good reason. He'd made love to her for hours, sensually exploring her body with his mouth, his hands, before taking possession of her once more, this time with him calling the shots, drawing her to the brink of orgasm before pulling back, then pushing her close again and again, almost tormenting her with his mastery of her body. All for a good cause, though— her eventual release, when he moved with the intention of gifting it, caused her to cry out so loudly he paused for a moment to ensure she was okay.

His ego was still riding high. They'd swum together in the infinity pool, before making love again, wet and tangled together on the terrace floor, then lain beneath the sky, talking until her eyes grew heavy and she'd fallen asleep, her head heavy on his chest. He'd carried her here rather than disturb her, and still she slept, her face angelic, her body far too beautiful to belong to a mere mortal.

Their night together had exceeded all of his expectations. His libido was impressive, his stamina renowned, and he'd never known a woman to be such a match for him. Her excitement was a thing of perfection; he wanted more of her. It was the first thought that occurred to him, and he grappled with it, frowning. More?

He didn't do more.

One night was all he took from a woman, all he gave of himself. Fatima had made sure of that. His ex-fiancée had ensured he'd never again allow his heart to believe it was anything so foolish as 'in love'. One night was easy. Sex was simple. Chemistry determined the trajectory, the terms were clear, as though spelled out in black and white. Physical pleasure, no promises, no line-crossing, just sex.

But with India, the sex had been enough to lure him to want more. His mind told him it wasn't possible even as his body was taking control, trying to discover a way that he could enjoy more of her company without risking any emotional complications. His own heart was safe—it had been turned to stone by Fatima's actions—but India wasn't like him. There was a gentleness to her that reminded him, strangely, of Astrid, so that he wanted to protect her even as his body yearned for more.

He left the room before he could weaken, pressing a pod into the coffee machine and watching as golden liquid poured into his cup. He always drank it black and strong, a shot of energy to give mental clarity and to remind Khalil that he could achieve anything.

He carried the cup towards the balcony, his eyes landing on the hotel they'd been at the night before, just able, at this distance, to make out the hint of the balcony they'd moved onto, when he'd wanted to be sure they were alone. Remembering the way they'd kissed then, as though there were a ticking time bomb and only their intimacy could avert its explosion, brought a smile to his face and a hardness to his cock. He sipped the coffee, relishing the bitterness and warmth, the immediate buzz firing through his brain.

A noise sounded across the room and he looked over his shoulder, half expecting to see India. Only it was his phone, in the kitchen, buzzing. Frowning, he strode towards it, an immediate wave of disgust forming in his belly when he saw Ethan's name on the screen. Last night had started out as a revenge plan, but it had very quickly morphed into something else. He no longer saw India as a means to an end; had he ever?

'What do you want?' he demanded in his most scathing tone—the kind of tone that would ordinarily turn his enemies into jabbering messes.

'Oh, nothing. Just to see how your night went.'

Khalil's brows lifted heavenwards. 'Do you really want to know?'

'Sure. Why not?'

But Khalil shied away from sharing any details—even when he knew they'd drive the other man crazy. He was already regretting the implication he'd made, all for vengeance—India had deserved better. 'I'm sure you can imagine.'

'Yes, you're right about that. I suppose you spent the night together?'

Khalil's hand formed a fist again. He hated this guy with all his heart.

'It's none of your business.'

'Business is an interesting choice of words.' Ethan didn't sound remotely concerned. If anything, he was happy...? Something wasn't adding up.

'What are you getting at, Graves? Spit it out or get the hell off the phone.'

'I presume you know she's a prostitute?'

Khalil was not often blindsided, but the other man's words hit him with all the strength of a knockout punch. He could hear Ethan's smug smile, the delight he had in saying the vulgar lie.

'An expensive one, obviously, or I wouldn't have hired her. But she's very, very good at her job, don't you think?'

It couldn't be true. Nothing about what Ethan was saying tallied with the woman he'd spent the night with. He didn't believe it. This was just Ethan's way of getting his own revenge.

'You are a disgusting excuse for a human being,' Khalil ground out.

Ethan laughed, a cackle that set Khalil's blood raging.

'Her name is India McCarthy, and she works for Warm Engagements Escort Agency. Search online and you'll see her profile.'

Khalil was holding the phone in a fist. He couldn't speak.

'And don't be put off by the wording that says "no sex". I've booked loads of their girls before, using darling Astrid's money, of course, and they're always more than happy to put out—for a small extra fee. I hope you're tipping her as well as I'd planned to, Khalil.' He laughed as he disconnected the call.

Khalil stared at the phone, knowing he'd regret it even as he loaded up an Internet browser and typed in the name Ethan had given him. He was doing it to prove Ethan wrong, not because he believed that bastard.

Her face appeared as soon as he hit 'search'.

Nausea rode through him. It was obvious that Ethan had played Khalil at his own game—and won. Not only had he brought a prostitute home, he'd kissed her at the bar, in full view of Manhattan's social elite, an army of spies armed with cell phones, who would be all too happy to sell this picture to the tabloids. It was Fatima all over again. Fatima's lies, Fatima's trickery, Fatima's mercenary ability to wrap men around her little finger purely for financial gain, her cold-hearted devotion to money the only thing she cared about. And India was just the same! But she wasn't. Was she?

He ran his mind over the night, trying to connect the dots of Ethan's words to the woman he'd bedded. Surely that passion hadn't been faked? No, their chemistry was genuine, of that he was sure, but that didn't mean she wouldn't be willing to exploit it. He'd told her he was royal almost as soon as they'd met. He had no way of knowing if her interest from that point on had been genuine or motivated by his endless coffers, as Fatima's actions had been. But her relationship with Ethan suddenly made so much more sense. It wasn't a relationship. She was too smart for him, too beautiful. She was being paid to be at his side, to laugh at his jokes, to fetch his damned drinks. It was why she'd hesitated to leave Ethan, her current pay cheque, why she'd questioned the fact he only wanted one night with her. If she was going to give up Ethan, it had to be worth it. Everything suddenly made so much sense! It was why she'd wanted to let Ethan down gently, to feign illness, rather than being honest with him. She wanted to have her cake and eat it too! Had she thought she could sleep with Khalil one night and Ethan the next? Disgust chipped at his gut.

He slammed his palms into the kitchen counter, staring at it with a rising sense of outrage. After Fatima, he'd thought he'd protected himself against women like this! He'd thought he could spot them a mile off! How had India managed to get under his skin so thoroughly?

Was there any chance this wasn't true? Was there any possibility? He groaned at his gullibility. What kind of escort agency offered dates with no sex? Not any that he'd ever heard of! Admittedly he had very little experience with such matters, but he was sure a happy ending was a guaranteed part of the night.

With every minute that passed, he began to see India as the second coming of Fatima, to see her as a very beautiful, manipulative, dishonest, scheming woman. Old pain was exposed, bitter and fierce. He stared at her photograph on the phone; the confirmation of her vocation stared right back at him. Damn it! How had he been so foolish?

He put down his phone and straightened his spine, renewed determination firing in his veins. He'd made a mistake, but at least there were no lasting consequences this time. He would wait until she was awake and then he'd throw her out of this apartment, and out of his life. He never wanted to see her again.

'So what exactly is the going rate?'

She frowned, still sleepy, her body on fire, her nerves sensitive, her stomach hungry and mouth dry, and, most of all, her heart blessedly, completely content in a way she'd never known before. Khalil stood in the hotel kitchen, dressed in an expensive bespoke suit that fitted him as though it were moulded to his frame. Naked he was glorious, but like this he was the embodiment of power and success, so a thousand and one sparks went off beneath her skin. Given his formal state of dress, India was glad she'd paused long enough to wrap a sheet, toga-style, around herself.

'For coffee?' she prompted as the fragrance reached her nostrils. 'I'd pay about a thousand dollars right now.'

He didn't smile. 'I meant, for a night of your…company.'

India stopped walking, frozen to the spot. Her smile dropped to her toes and her blood turned to ice. 'I'm sorry?'

'Oh, apologies are definitely warranted,' he said with a cutting tone to his voice.

'That's not what I—what do you mean?'

'Now I understand why you were trying to move our arrangement to tonight,' he said, throwing back half of his own coffee without shifting his eyes from her face. 'You were already booked last night. I suppose you expect me to compensate you for two nights of business?'

Her eyes swept shut as the true horror of the situation became clear.

'I'm just surprised you didn't negotiate your price and ask for payment before you climbed into my bed. Surely that's better business practice?'

India felt sick. 'Don't,' she snapped, slicing her hand through the air. 'Don't you dare suggest that I slept with you in exchange for '

'Oh, that's rich,' he interrupted. 'Acting outraged when the whole world can see who and what you do.' He lifted up his phone, showing her Warm Engagements profile picture. She felt the sharp sting of tears at her eyes and in her throat, but refused to give in to that weakness now.

'That's a legitimate escort service,' she insisted, but of course she could see how damning the facts were, on the surface.

'Sure it is,' he said in a way that made it obvious he didn't believe a word she was saying. 'Legitimate prostitution.'

'No,' she ground out. 'You're wrong. It's not that kind of agency. We specialise in dates for out-of-town business-people, who need someone on their arm for one night and don't want the complication of a romantic entanglement. That concept is the *only* reason I agreed to work for them. I have *never* slept with a man for money, and it definitely isn't what last night was about.'

'That is not what Ethan said.'

Her jaw dropped. 'Ethan?' She groaned, lifting a hand to her forehead and pacing across the room, towards the kitchen. 'You do know him, don't you?'

'Yes.'

'But what did he say? How did he—? He didn't know about you. And us. I mean, he didn't know I left with you.'

'I made sure he did, actually.' Khalil glared down his nose at her. 'It turns out, you weren't the only one telling lies last night, *azeezi*.' Now when he used the term of endearment she flinched, impossibly hurt by the tone of his voice, the obvious accusation.

'You used me,' she whispered, the words sticking in her throat. But it was the truth, of course. What other explanation was there? Was that why he'd pursued her so relentlessly? Overpowering her very minuscule defences, all because he wanted to hurt the other man? Was that all last night had meant to him? 'Why?'

'You use men for money. Is that any better?'

She stormed across to him without thinking, shoving his chest as a primal, animalistic rage overtook her. 'Damn it, I'm not going to stand here and listen to this! I would *never* sleep with a man for money—never. If you think me possible of that, then you're a terrible judge of character.' Anger made the words vibrate and she clung to that emotion rather than allowing sadness to take over.

'Then don't stand here,' he said, quietly, his words cutting her like glass. 'Our *business* is concluded. Please leave.'

She bit down on her lip, his scathing dismissal undoing a part of her soul. She stared at him, trying to find a trace of the man she'd spent the night with—and failing. He was cold, completely unfamiliar. Part of her wanted to run out of the room immediately and never think of this night again, but at the same time she couldn't live with him believing what he did of her! She'd only slept with one other man—her boyfriend at the time. She was just about as far from being a call girl as it was possible to get.

'I work for an escort agency, yes, but the work is strictly professional. Events like last night, that begin with the client meeting me in the lobby and end in the same way.'

His eyes flashed with contempt. 'Unfortunately, I know Ethan better than that. I have no doubt that if we had not met, you would have spent the night with him instead of me.'

'You're wrong,' she said, numb. 'Being with you was
a spontaneous, out-of-character thing for me. I don't go
home with men I've just met. I don't make love to people
I barely know.'

'And yet you were so very comfortable with it.'

Because you were different, she wanted to scream at
him.

'The innocent act worked last night, but I know better now,' he pointed out with quiet, stupid logic. 'All I can
hope is that no one managed to catch that ill-conceived
kiss at the bar on their cell phone. If it were to go viral
that I took a woman like you home, it would be the death
of my father.'

'Then it's just as well I have every intention of forgetting this whole night ever happened.'

His lips were a grim line. 'As do I, believe me.'

The dress she'd worn was discarded on the floor. She
scooped it up and pulled it on quickly, scanning for her
shoes and handbag—which were blessedly near the front
door. She slid her feet into the heels, swallowing back a
sob, and thrust her handbag under her arm. She didn't even
turn around and look at him; she couldn't. Her mind was
all over the place, her pride in tatters. She waited until
the door had slammed shut behind her before breaking
into a run, sprinting the length of the hallway and pressing the button for the lift. India desperately wanted to put
the whole sordid ordeal behind her, but even as she swore
to herself she'd do exactly that, she felt terrified of how
difficult it would be. Last night hadn't been an ordinary
event—it was the kind of night that imprinted on a person's soul, and she knew, even as she desperately pushed
him from her mind, that she would never forget Sheikh
Khalil el Abdul.

* * *

He watched her leave with a sinking feeling in the pit of his stomach. He was so angry with her! So angry with Ethan! So angry with the world, if he were honest. But he was especially angry with India, because she'd made him forget every promise he'd made himself after Fatima. When he was with India, he'd felt as if the world was good again, he'd felt as if he could smile, for the first time in years. He'd enjoyed himself, and his grief and loss had been so far away.

Discovering it was all part of her job description chipped away at an essential part of him, so he didn't—couldn't—stop to think if there was even a chance he was wrong.

Would he have felt so vehemently if not for Fatima? Would his rage have been so quick to spark? Or might he have given her more of a chance to explain herself? He couldn't say, but with every minute that passed in the wake of her departure, he felt a mix of shame and disappointment, frustration clipping through him.

Ethan had thrown her identity in his face, and the other man had his own reasons for wanting to hurt Khalil. But what about the website? What about the fact she did in fact work for an escort agency? Was there any chance she was telling the truth?

He ground his teeth together, throwing his head back and staring at the ceiling.

And what did it matter? Even before he knew this, they'd agreed it would simply be one night. His life was in Khatrain, and it was time for him to get on with it. He simply had to forget India McCarthy ever existed.

CHAPTER FOUR

'OH, GOD, NO.' She stared at the pregnancy test with a sinking feeling in the pit of her stomach, her worst nightmares confirmed. Six weeks after rushing from the penthouse apartment she'd shared with Khalil, India finally had an explanation for all the strange symptoms she'd been experiencing. The exhaustion, nausea, sore back and rioting emotions had been easy to explain on their own, but her skipped menstrual cycle was the final straw. It was only when writing overdue bills in her calendar that suspicion had formed.

It couldn't be true. Surely fate wouldn't be so desperately miserable as to throw this complication into her already careening out of control life? She looked around the home desperately, as the future seemed to twist away from her completely.

'Pregnant?' She groaned, shaking her head and laughing at the same time—this couldn't be true!

The realisation hit her that she was alone. No, she corrected herself. She'd have Jackson, and, even though their finances were in a parlous state, somehow, she'd cope. Her parents would expect that of her, and for them, she'd do this.

On autopilot, she strode into the kitchen and opened the top drawer, where she'd stashed the envelope, the morning after returning from Khalil's hotel room. He must have put it in her bag while she slept; she hadn't discovered it until she'd returned home. She'd been too numb to do more than reach for her bus pass at first, but then, she'd needed her keys and that had required a more detailed rifle through her bag. It was only then that she'd identified the envelope with thick black lettering on the front.

You earned this.

Her heart had thudded to a stop as she'd opened the envelope to discover a cheque—grey in colour with gold lettering and the intricate emblem of the Khatrain royal family. The cheque was made out to her, for an absurd amount, more than she earned in a month—or had earned, before losing her job.

'*This is a reputable agency, India. I will not have the name of this business dragged into disrepute by young women who are looking for an extra way to earn income. You will no longer be listed on our books. There are several other...businesses...that deal in the kind of work you do.*'

She had been mortified and offended, and then terrified. Keeping her younger brother Jackson at college was all her responsibility, and on top of attempting to maintain her parents' mortgage, so that she didn't lose their family home, India already struggled to make ends meet. Without the booking fees from Warm Engagements, she had no hope.

Why hadn't she cashed the cheque sooner? Because she *hadn't* earned it. And to cash it would be some sort of tacit acceptance of his accusations. Now, though, the cheque took on a new meaning, as she imagined all of the expenses involved in carrying out a pregnancy and then delivering a baby. Courtesy of her mother's cancer treatments, India was no stranger to hospitals and what they charged—there were some bills still outstanding. There were also the baby's needs once it was born. She could thrift shop a lot of things, but certain items would have to be purchased new, and there would be a period of time when she was unable to work altogether. What would she do for childcare? There was no one who could help her.

How was she going to do this, and all on her own?

But she *had* to. For the sake of their baby, she had to find a way to manage. And the cheque Khalil had written was a good place to start. To hell with her pride; there was a baby to consider.

Khalil had truly hoped she wouldn't cash the damned thing. He didn't realise how much he'd needed that assurance until his bank in New York called to advise him that the cheque had been brought in that morning. It was all the confirmation he needed—not that it had been necessary. A cursory investigation by his security team had shown that she was a popular employee of the agency, going on multiple dates a week. They'd been unable to confirm her assertion about meeting men at the events, however society photographs had captured more than enough images of India being held tight by her dates, the intimate nature of the pictures making it impossible to believe that things were as innocent as she claimed.

Why had she waited six weeks to cash the cheque? It was a question that barely mattered. She'd lived up to what he'd thought of her, it was time to stop remembering the night they'd shared. It had been the worst mistake of his life; he could only be grateful his father had been spared the mortification of tabloid speculation about it. Their kiss had not gone public.

It was not appropriate that he continued to think of her, that she played such a part in his fantasies night after night. Somehow, her betrayal stung almost as much as Fatima's. When he looked back, there was a part of him that had, on some level, always known Fatima for what she was: mercenary and opportunistic. He'd fallen in love with her quick wit and fun-loving attitude, but there had been something in her eyes that had been appraising, always, something that had held parts of him back from her as well. But with India, he'd been completely fooled, her innocent act so easy to buy into.

He scraped back his chair, pacing towards the windows that overlooked the capital city of Takistan and, in the distance, the Persian Gulf—which, today, sparkled as though a net of diamonds had been cast over its surface.

At twenty-nine years of age, he knew he could delay no longer: his country required him to marry before his thirtieth birthday, when he would become King of Khatrain. It was necessary to choose a suitable bride—he could no longer think about India. She didn't deserve it.

Only his mind was not obeying him today, and India continued to flash before his eyes, as she'd been in the car on the way back to his suite. She was an excellent actress, he'd give her that. His lips twisted in a mocking smile as he reached for his phone.

'Have my horse readied. I intend to ride west.' He gripped the receiver more tightly. 'I do not know,' he responded to the question of, 'for how long?' and then disconnected the call. The desert was an essential part of his soul, and it was there that he could clear his mind of the American call girl—an obvious mistake—once and for all.

'He is still unavailable, madam.' India stood like a flamingo in the kitchen, one foot propped against her opposite knee, her hand resting on the bench to her left. The other pressed to her still-flat stomach as she tilted her head to catch the phone between her ear and shoulder. It was a warm day and pregnancy hormones—in full flight despite the fact she was only eight weeks along—were making her tired, nauseous, anxious and cranky. She had been attempting to contact Khalil for over a week, ever since she'd decided he deserved the courtesy of the information at least.

Only contacting a royal was no mean feat.

'Well, when will he be available?' she snapped, although it wasn't this low-level staff member's fault that Khalil had disappeared into thin air.

'I cannot say, madam. My apologies.' The line went dead.

India made a deranged laughing sound as she placed her cell phone on the bench. Was he dodging her calls? Or truly unavailable? She suspected the former, and it made her furious to think that he wouldn't even give her the courtesy of a conversation after that night. But then, she'd seen his anger when he'd accused her of being a prostitute. She'd left his hotel with no question in her mind that he hated her—and truly wished to never see her again.

'Well, tough,' she said softly, patting her stomach. 'I know what it's like to be abandoned by your dad and I'm not going to let that happen to you, little one. At least, not without a fight.'

She knew a little about Khatrain—bits and pieces garnered through her life, and studies—but most of her knowledge related to their economy. It was dry, black-and-white information about their oil industry and burgeoning tech sector with their headquarters in the then fledgling city of Takistan. Only Takistan was now a stunning metropolis, a sprawling construction of steel and glass that burst from the earth. The dusk sky gave it a perfect backdrop, the gradient colours spreading from purple to gold and orange highlighting the twinkling lights of the monoliths in the foreground. She craned her neck to see the city better, admiring not just its modernity but also its proximity to the ocean, which curved around it like a ribbon, and had been diverted, at some point, to create several canals that ran as veins between the buildings.

'Beautiful,' she said with a shake of her head, earning an approving nod from the man beside her. Their elbows had been engaged in a silent battle for the duration of the flight, the too-small seats and narrow armrest far from ideal for the number of hours she'd had to spend cramped between her neighbour and the portal window. But it had all been worth it to secure this exceptional vantage point of the city as they descended.

The plane was climate-controlled. It was only once the doors were opened that a rush of hot air blasted into the cabin and India had to brace herself against the seat in front. Nausea rose in her chest. She grabbed a mint from her purse and sucked on it—this was the only thing she'd been able to discover that helped with the waves of sickness that assaulted her occasionally.

Their aircraft had been towed to a distant terminal— the budget airlines' designated space—and there was no air-conditioned aerobridge leading inside. Instead, there were stairs, wheeled to the doors of the plane, and a large, sweeping route around another aeroplane before they were ushered through security doors and passport control.

India stifled several yawns as she shuffled along the queue, grateful when at last she was beckoned forward.

'And the purpose for your visit?' the woman, stunning with her dark eyes and lips that had been painted a deep red, murmured as she scanned the passport.

To tell your bastard of a sheikh he's going to be a father then get the heck out of Dodge, she imagined saying, a tight smile curving her lips. 'To see an old friend.'

'Social.' The woman nodded, ticking a box. 'How long do you intend to stay?'

'Twenty-four hours.' And though it wasn't necessary, she flashed the printout of her return ticket, her escape route already planned. She would do whatever she could to give the Sheikh this information, and then she would leave. If he still refused to see her, then at least she could tell their baby that she'd tried. She knew first-hand the importance of that. And if he refused to let her leave? The idea flashed into her mind suddenly, so she froze, her eyes wide, before she discounted it. He'd be as glad to see the back of her as last time.

'Such a short visit. It is a shame. There is much in Khatrain to see—many wonders to enjoy.'

'I'm sure there are. Unfortunately, I have commitments back home.'

The woman reached for a stamp, clicked it onto India's passport, then slid it across. 'Enjoy your brief trip, then, madam.'

Again, India was buffeted by the heat when she stepped out of the airport, so she lifted a hand to her face, waving it rhythmically. There was a long queue for taxis, and she waited with depleting energy. Her plan had been to go to her hotel first and freshen up, before attempting to contact Khalil, but now that she was here, she simply wanted to get this over with.

When she finally slipped into a taxi—with at least some air conditioning—it cooled her rising temperature. She stared at the hotel's information, opened her mouth and then closed it again. 'The royal palace, please.'

The driver met her eyes in the mirror and India was

grateful she had over a year's experience attending glittering social events in Manhattan. If she'd learned anything, it was how to act as though she belonged anywhere. 'Is there a problem?' Her tone was stiff, her demeanour imposing.

'Of course not, madam. Right away.'

The car pulled into traffic and India allowed her head to drop backwards, against the leather seat of the car. For a moment, she closed her eyes, needing to restore a little of her energy.

Only Khalil was there, as always, his face haunting her, so there was no real respite. She woke with sweat beading her brow, just as the car drew to a stop.

'This is as close as I can get,' the driver said, gesturing to the large golden gates in the foreground of, without a doubt, the largest and most magnificent building India had ever seen—whether in real life or photographs. Her jaw dropped and the magnitude of what she was about to do sent a tremble down her spine.

Her baby was a part of all this. And she'd had no idea just quite what that entailed—she had been imagining Khalil and Khalil alone, without quite realising what his title meant. He was going to be King, and their child would be—what? His heir? Or an embarrassment? Was she making things worse by coming here? What if he refused to acknowledge their baby? Was it worse if she'd told him and Khalil made that decision? Was it better for the baby to believe its father had never known? Could she do anything to make this better?

But what if he *did* want to know the baby and be a part of his or her life? India had barely known her father—he'd blown into her life when it had suited him, then disappeared for months or years, so she'd never been able to count on him. What if Khalil wanted to be a real part of their child's life, to see him or her regularly, to call and ask how their day went? India would have given her eye teeth for that, and she would fight for the chance for her baby to know that kind of love.

Even though there was a real risk that it could backfire.

'Thank you.' She paid the driver before opening her door. She was prepared for the heat this time, though it still dried her eyes out. She pulled her sunglasses into place and hitched a small backpack over one shoulder, standing and staring at the palace as the taxi driver sped off.

Turrets of white stood high in the sky like puffs of cream atop large round towers. Some were golden, others pale, and there was a large open courtyard lined on all sides by palm trees that cast spiky shadows across the marbled floor. A fountain stood in the very centre, spurting water in several directions, before landing in a large oval-shaped pool. Her mouth went dry at the very visage. She turned her attention to that barrier, scanning it thoughtfully, until her eyes landed on the security guard nearest to her. There were several, standing every ten feet or so, staring out at the road, ever watchful. The man in front of India had his eyes on her, so she smiled—it was not returned. His hands were at his sides, but at his hip he wore a pistol and a large rifle was holstered diagonally across his back. Though his uniform was ceremonial, she had no doubt he had full military training. Fear shifted through her, but India had come this far; she wasn't about to be turned back now.

'Excuse me,' she said, when she reached the man.

He didn't say anything, but his eyes met hers, curiosity in their depths.

'How do I get inside?'

He regarded her with evident surprise. 'Do you have an invitation?'

She thought quickly, playing out multiple scenarios in

her head. If she said that she didn't, she would likely be turned away immediately. There was no guarantee that any words she uttered would even make it to Khalil's ears—except for one sentence.

'I do, yes. His Highness Khalil el Abdul sent for me.'

The man's expression changed immediately. He lifted his walkie-talkie—propped on the hip that lacked a gun—and began to speak in his own language, harsh words that she didn't understand.

'Your name?' He switched back to English. Butterflies burst through her.

'India McCarthy.'

He repeated her name into the walkie-talkie.

'Documentation?'

'It was a phone call,' she lied. 'He asked me to come over the phone.'

'Identification documentation,' he clarified.

'Oh.' Heat stained her cheeks as she reached into her bag and lifted out her passport. 'Here.'

She held it up for him but he took it, turning away from her and moving to another guard. That guard left with the passport, and the original returned to his post.

Something like anxiety tightened in her gut. 'Where's he going?'

The original guard didn't answer. She was grateful that the sun was low in the sky, as she stood waiting for a long time—at least twenty minutes. Already fatigued, weary and emotionally exhausted, she wanted to cry, but wouldn't give the guard—or anyone—the satisfaction. Eventually, Original Guard's walkie-talkie began to crackle. A brow shot up, before he gestured about three hundred metres down the fence. 'There is a gate. Go to it; someone will take you from there.'

India nodded her thanks. It was a long walk, and, given

the heat, she didn't rush. Eventually, she reached the gate, where several guards were waiting. Anxiety grew.

'This way, please.' A woman gestured without smiling towards the marble courtyard. India followed behind, aware of the two guards who came to flank her. As they passed the fountain she stopped walking, giving into temptation despite the certainty it would earn the disapproval of her companions. She moved to the water and quickly lowered her hands, splashing some onto her forearms and neck, instantly refreshing. The female guard stood waiting, her face impassive. No, not impassive, India realised. There was almost something like sympathy in her beautiful eyes.

'It has been particularly hot this summer,' the guard said, slowing her pace a little.

India could have wept for the small kindness from this random stranger. To be spoken to with something approaching civility was beyond her expectations—and it was badly needed!

'I had prepared for heat, but this caught me unawares.'

'Tourists find it hard to bear at first.'

Whatever reply India had been going to make died on her lips as they swept through a set of double doors— each several metres wide, and at least four times her height. The foyer they were in was clearly a 'nuts and bolts' part of the palace— with security apparatus and a minimum of décor—and yet it was still impossibly grand, with high ceilings, chandeliers, marble floors, and artwork adorning every bare space on the walls, so that her eyes were almost overwhelmed with the visual feast.

'You will need to pass through security,' the woman said, gesturing to the large scanners, the same as India had passed through at the airport.

'Okay.' She bit down on her lip, placing her bag on the

tray so it could be whisked along a conveyor belt, then stepping through the frame. Just as at the airport, the scanner
did not register any problems.

'Good.' The woman even smiled, so India's butterflies
were somewhat allayed, momentarily. With that hurdle
crossed through, there was now the task of telling Khalil
he was going to be a father—a conversation she was utterly dreading. If only she could have sent a text or email,
but she had no direct way of contacting him.

'Will you take me to Khalil now?'

The woman's expression was startled. 'His Highness
Sheikh el Abdul has been informed of your arrival. I am
not yet aware of when he will see you. Please, take a seat
while you wait.'

India's nerves were on the brink of fraying. *Are you kidding me?* She shook her head as she moved towards the
seat the guard had indicated, easing herself into it. She was
too wound up to relax, though, far too coiled to enjoy the
comfort of the armchair. She fidgeted with her fingers in
her lap for the first hour, before frustration got the better
of her and she moved towards the man behind the com-
puter screen, who'd scanned her handbag.

'Excuse me, sir, are you able to get an update on the
Sheikh's schedule for me?'

The guard looked at her as though she'd asked him to
swim to Mars. 'His Highness will see you when he can.
If he decides to see you at all.'

If? India hadn't even thought of that. What if, even now,
he refused to meet her? Tears sprang to her eyes and she
turned around quickly, before the man could see her. Odi-
ous, horrible person!

Thirty minutes later and a door opened, so she stood,
apprehensively, but it was just a servant wheeling a trol-

ley. She came towards India before stopping, lifting the lid off the top tray.

'Some refreshments, madam.'

India stared at the food and felt instantly sick. She dug her fingernails into her palm, trying to control it, but the waves of nausea were growing stronger. 'Is there a restroom?' she demanded urgently.

The woman nodded and gestured to a purple door. India broke into a run and just made it, heaving over the toilet until her stomach was empty and her hairline moist with perspiration. When she emerged, the servant had gone but the tray remained. India was able to pick over it now, choosing a plain bread roll with some butter, and draining the glass of iced tea far too quickly. She sat down again, frustrated and angry.

Another hour passed. She approached the guard once more, her mind made up. 'I'd like to leave. Would you help me organise a taxi to the city?'

The guard met her eyes, shrugged, then spoke into his walkie-talkie. She bit down on her lip, the reality of her situation landing squarely between her eyes. She'd wasted money she couldn't afford on flying to Khatrain, all because she'd believed there might be a shred of decency in Khalil. Why had she even thought such a thing after the way he'd spoken to her the last time they'd met? The things he'd said to her, the look of hatred in his eyes—she should have known better than to hope.

She pulled tighter on her handbag strap and waited, her arms crossed. It was only minutes but, given India had already been waiting for several hours, she was ready to burst something when, finally, another door opened. This time, three guards swept through, and behind them, Khalil. But not as he'd been in New York. Then, he'd been spectacular-looking but somehow familiar to her. Now, he was so fascinating and majestic that, even though her heart was flooded with hate, she found that all she could do was stare at him as he stormed towards her. He wore long white robes that breezed behind him with the speed of his stride, and his body was broad and powerful, even more so dressed like this. His eyes bored into hers and she felt the same rush of anger she'd known on that last morning, the hatred and disrespect. Her heart flip-flopped. 'Khalil,' she said as he drew close, and one guard gasped.

'Your Highness,' he corrected coldly, without breaking his pace. 'Follow me.'

The lack of courtesy was surprising even after all that had passed between them. Nonetheless, she had come here with one thing in mind, and she intended to carry out her objective. She scooped up her bag and fell into step behind him, but she had to half run to keep up. He moved away from this pragmatic entranceway and into a corridor—though, really, it was as wide as at least four corridors, and decorated with ancient-looking furniture on both sides, including enormous vases of flowers that were totally unfamiliar to her, exotic and spiky, like something out of a fairy tale. Their fragrance was sweet, and, in her current state, India's nausea returned with a vengeance.

'Will you slow down a bit?' she asked, slowing her own pace accordingly, pressing a hand to her hip.

Khalil stopped walking and turned to look at her, exasperated. But as his eyes scanned her face there was, for a moment, something like concern. Perhaps there was a hint of humanity in the man after all?

'You are ill?'

'Well.' She put her other hand on her hip, glaring at him with undisguised irritation. 'Let's see, shall we? I've endured a cramped plane trip, a hot taxi ride, a stand-off out the front of your palace with an armed guard who was clearly hostile, and then hours in a room waiting for Your Royal Highness to decide to see me. How do you think I feel?'

If India had been less angry, she might have noticed the blanching of the guards' faces at her tirade to their Prince, but she was in her own bubble, completely incapable of thinking clearly or acting calmly.

Khalil was used to his guards and didn't mind their presence in any respect. He paced towards her, his eyes sparking with hers. 'You arrive unannounced and expect what, India? That I might roll out the red carpet? And what exactly in our interaction gave you any idea I would be glad to see you again?' He leaned closer, lowering his voice. 'We agreed we would both forget what happened.'

She looked away, wondering if he'd been able to do that so easily. For India, Khalil had been burned into her mind, so she saw him all the time, dreamed of him, woke up reaching for him...

'Believe me, I don't particularly relish being here, but you gave me little choice. Had you accepted any of my attempts to contact you, then we could have dealt with this over the phone. You left with me no choice.'

'On the contrary, I left you with a very clear choice— to stay out of my life.'

Her lips parted and now she saw the guards, their faces carefully blanked of emotion, and embarrassment swept through her. 'Is there somewhere more private we can speak? I just need a few moments of your time, Your Highness.' She imbued his title with as much scathing cynicism as she could, easily matching a tone he had employed in the past when speaking to her.

'I was taking us somewhere more private when you demanded that we stop.'

She compressed her lips. 'I asked you to slow down; that's not the same thing.'

It was obvious that Khalil was not used to being contradicted—and she enjoyed that fact. He deserved nothing better than to be strenuously put in his place. If it weren't for the conversation that was to follow, she could almost have enjoyed the awkwardness of their interaction. But this was just the prelude to what would necessarily follow, and India could see quite clearly that it was not going to be as simple as informing him of her pregnancy. She'd run straight into the lion's den and she would need to think fast to get out alive.

CHAPTER FIVE

'So?'

Her stomach was in a constant cycle of loop-the-loops. She wasn't sure if it was deliberate or not, but the room he'd led her to was impossibly intimidating. Vaulted ceilings with a wall made of glass on one side, framing a view of the city that now, given the lateness of the hour, twinkled against the black of the sky. The floor in here was mosaic and very old, and at the front of the room there were two large thrones, gold and marble, imposing and grand. The flower arrangements in the corridor had given way to enormous trees in golden pots, some wrapping tendrils around the marble pillars that stretched like limbs towards the ceiling. His voice echoed in the room and she shivered, an unintentional response to the emotions of that moment.

'You have come to my palace and demanded to see me, yet now stand mute. Are you here simply to waste my time?'

Outrage fired through her, finally slotting her brain into gear. 'I just hadn't expected your palace to be quite so... palatial,' she finished lamely, crossing her arms over her chest, then regretting the gesture when his eyes dropped to the hint of cleavage exposed by her simple white linen blouse. She wore it tucked into her faded jeans, with cream sliders that revealed pale pink toenails. It was a simple, elegant outfit but under his inspection she felt as though she were wearing lingerie. Desire stirred in her stomach, catching her completely off guard. How could she feel *anything* but revulsion for this man?

'Why don't we cut to the chase?' he murmured. 'Tell me how much you want.'

She frowned, not understanding.

'You cashed the cheque I gave you; I presume you want more? Is it blackmail, India? Are you demanding money in exchange for your silence?'

Heat fired behind her eyes. 'How dare you?'

His smile was cynical. 'I'm sure you can understand why I think you capable of this.'

'No, actually,' she muttered. 'I have wracked my brain for anything that happened between us that night that would justify your harsh opinion of me, and drawn a blank. At no point did I say or do anything to give you the impression I sleep with men for payment. That you would think me capable of that says more about you than it does me.'

For a moment his eyes flashed with uncertainty, but it was gone again almost immediately, harsh contempt usurping it. 'We have already discussed the matter of your employment. Frankly, it's none of my business. You can do what you want with your life, but do not involve me again.'

'And that's it? Case closed?'

'There is no case. I have no interest in debating this matter with you. If you need more money, tell me how much and I will have my aid cut you a cheque.'

Her lips parted in surprise. Of course such a thing would be easy for him, but it still made her head spin to imagine the ease with which he was making that offer. After all, India had spent the morning looking under the sofa cushions for loose change, to be sure she could cover her bus fare to the airport.

Take the money and run! Get out while you still can...
'Are you so afraid of people finding out you slept with me that you would effectively offer me a blank cheque?'

'I would prefer to keep news of our liaison private, yes.' His lips compressed and India felt there was more he wasn't saying, something serious and sombre. 'It would be far from ideal to have this story breaking in the press right as I am due to announce my engagement.'

'Your engagement?' She froze to the spot, her eyes scanning his face. She'd thought he couldn't hurt her more than he already had, but those simple words pulled at something deep in her soul, so she spun around, looking for support—and found none. Her knees were trembling, almost unequal to the task of supporting her. He was engaged? Had he been engaged that night? She hated to think she'd been so wrong about him...

'I am to marry before my thirtieth birthday. It is required in order to assure my ascendence to the throne.'

'I see,' she mumbled, numb, moving towards the windows purely so she could prop her hip against something steady.

'Your father has remarried, darling. He won't be able to make it to your party after all.'

Soon Khalil would be married, and shortly after that he would have children of his own, children who were his true heirs, children he would actually want. Her brow broke out in hot and cold, memories of her own childhood horribly close, the feeling of rejection that had surrounded her again and again as she'd grappled with the fact her father had made a very deliberate choice not to know nor love her. Was history going to repeat itself?

'So you might understand why I would offer any amount of money to ensure your continued cooperation. Name your price, and I will willingly pay it.'

Oh, how tempting it was! She could simply state an amount—an exorbitant amount that would see Jackson through college and clear all her mother's medical debts, an amount that would mean she could stay home with their baby for the first year of his or her life, with no worries or stress, and then afford childcare afterwards when she was ready to return to work. Heck, she could ask him for enough to cover her own college fees and she could finish her beloved economics degree, and get the kind of job she'd known she wanted ever since she was a schoolgirl!

And what would she tell their baby? Oh, it wouldn't matter for years, but one day the baby would be a child and then an adolescent, and they would look into her eyes and ask her about their dad—would she ever be able to meet their questions if she'd lied to Khalil, and prevented him from having a part in their child's future?

Panic spread through her, because she knew she could accept his money and walk out—not exactly with her head held high but with her needs met, at least—and yet she would never take that option. It was the coward's way, and if her epic journey here today had proven anything, it was that India was no coward.

'Thank you for your offer, but that is not why I'm here.'

He was silent, and she kept her gaze averted, her eyes focussed on the distant city, its shimmering lights offering solace and reminding her of Manhattan. She tried not to think about the view from the balcony, when he'd led her outside and kissed her as though he were drowning and she his sole lifeline.

'Perhaps you could get to the point, then. I do not have all night to stand here with you.'

She turned slowly, keeping her back pressed to the glass. He spoke as though he had plans, and perhaps he did. Maybe he'd been with another woman, making love to her, driving her as wild as he'd driven India. Jealousy spiked through her and she dug her fingernails into her palms to control her heated flashbacks.

'It is a shame that you believed Ethan,' she said quietly, her voice softened by hate. 'I don't know why he lied to you, but he did. I'm not what he accused me of. I'm not what you think.'

Impatience sparked in his gaze, but his voice rang with cool control. 'Why does it matter? That night was a mistake—not the first of my life, but one I have learned from. If I could undo it, I would. As for your request for money, it could have been made from America; there was no need to arrive at my palace gates so dramatically.'

Her jaw dropped at the unfairness of that. 'I beg your pardon, Khalil, but I *tried* to speak to you over the phone and you were always "unavailable". If there had been any other choice, I would have avoided coming here, I promise.'

'I don't believe you.'

'What a surprise.'

His eyes narrowed. 'If your goal is to blackmail me, then arriving like this, inspiring gossip and interest from my palace staff, would only serve to provide me with the necessary motivation to silence you.'

'Then it's just as well blackmail isn't the point of my trip.'

'Then what is?'

She ground her teeth together, sadness washing over her. It had been a single night in a lifetime of nights, and yet, for all their time together was brief, she had felt an undeniable connection to this man. Beyond a connection, she'd felt a sameness, an understanding, as though in some vital way they had been forged from the same elements.

She'd been wrong.

'Come on, India. Name the amount you want so we can both move on.'

She thrust her hands onto her hips and straightened off the glass, but without its support she was instantly woozy, swooning a little before she caught herself. He moved quickly, instincts no doubt firing to life because if he'd paused to consider his actions, he might have chosen to stay where he was and let her drop to the cold hard floor. But instead, he crossed to her quickly, catching her behind her back, holding her to him. From a distance he'd seemed so cold and in command, but like this, she felt it—his warmth and fire, the harsh ructions within his chest as he controlled his breathing, his anger, and something more, barely contained within him. All she could do was look up into his eyes, desire storming through her, the night they'd shared a memory that was so fresh for India she almost felt as though they were travelling back in time.

Kiss me. The idea flared in her mind and terrified her. India pulled away, still unsteady, but needing space before she did something stupid and actually *begged* him to kiss her for real.

'I'm fine,' she lied as exhaustion and nausea threatened to swallow her. 'I just want to get this over with.'

'On this, we are in agreement.'

'I have a flight booked for tomorrow afternoon, and accommodation arranged at a hotel in the city. As soon as we have had this…conversation… I will leave this palace, and shortly thereafter your country, with no intention of coming back. I am not here to threaten you, nor to blackmail you. I am not here to ask you for money—at least, not directly.' He lifted a single, mocking brow. 'I came because I needed to tell you something about that night.'

India was at a crossroads, on the brink of moving in a direction from which she could never return. Once she'd told him about the baby, there was no going back: he would know that he would be a father, regardless of what he chose to do with that information.

'I'm listening.'

'I know.' That was part of the problem. He was staring at her as though he could pull her apart, piece by piece, and examine her until he was satisfied. Anxiety pulsed in her veins.

'I'm not asking you for anything, nor am I expecting anything of you. I'm telling you this because I—well, for personal reasons—feel it's very important that you should have all the information.'

'I have never known anyone to prevaricate to this degree.'

She looked across the room and her gaze inadvertently landed on the thrones. Thrones that belonged to his parents and would soon pass to Khalil and his wife, and then to their children. Biting back a small sob, she pressed her hand over her stomach, sympathy for the little person who would surely grow up being unwanted and unacknowledged by their father landing in her gut like a rock. It was a pain she knew far too well.

'I'm getting to it.' Her tongue darted out, licking her dry, lower lip, and while her gaze continued to rest on the thrones, his eyes were squarely on her face, following the movement of her tongue as though he couldn't look away.

'The thing is, Khalil, there's no easy way to tell you this,' she whispered, her voice almost lost in the cavernous room. 'I'm pregnant.'

The dropping of a pin would have been easily audible. He said nothing for so long that she wrenched her eyes back to his face, trying to read how he might be feeling. Except it wasn't possible. There was a look of steel in his eyes, his features set in a mask of cold rejection.

'And?'

She frowned, her heart plummeting. 'And, I thought you should know. I—didn't see a lot of my birth father growing up. I wish… I just thought…' but this was going to be a case of history repeating itself. He was clearly showing no intention of acknowledging their baby.

'I just thought you should know,' she finished weakly, unable to believe he would be so callous in the wake of her news. 'And now, I'd like to go to my hotel, please.'

He stood more still than the marble columns that ran through the room, his body held tight with a tension radiating from his gut to his brain. Her words were detonating inside him, tiny little bombs, going off again and again. She was watching him, waiting for him to speak, and yet he didn't trust himself to say anything just yet.

'Goodbye, Khalil.' Her features crumpled in her beautiful face—how could he still find her so stunning after what she'd proven herself capable of? What he knew her to be? She was every bit as bad as Fatima, exploiting her power with men for financial gain. That should make him despise her on every level, but when he'd held her a moment ago, he'd been so tempted to kiss her, to claim her just as he had that night. What the hell was wrong with him?

He watched her slow movements towards the door—she seemed fatigued and ill and, despite what had happened between them, he found it impossible to ignore her obvious suffering. Clenching his hands into fists at his sides, he moved to catch her, his stride easily doubling hers, so it was only seconds until he was with her.

'Stop.' He spoke with easy command.

She didn't. At no point had she acquiesced to his wishes. Not before she knew who he was, and not now, even when surrounded by this palace and an army of guards.

'India, do not take another step.'

She whirled around to face him then, her face so pale his worry spiked. 'Why not, Khalil? Do you need to insult me a little more for my apparent lifestyle? Or are you going to tell me you need a paternity test before we can discuss this further?'

The reality of her words began to crack through his frozen brain, and for the first time it occurred to him that she was telling the truth. That India was pregnant—and with his baby? Or another man's she was looking to foist on him? Perhaps the paternity test was a wise place to start. 'Could you blame me, given your vocation?'

Her skin paled but she tilted her chin, her gaze defiant even as her lips were trembling. 'I haven't slept with anyone else in a long time, so there's no doubt in my mind that this child is yours. But if you don't believe me, I don't even care any more. I did what I came here to do—I told you about our baby. Now I can go home with a clear conscience.'

He felt hot and cold at once, as Fatima morphed into his mind, the way she'd thrown her abortion at him at the same time as ending their engagement. The baby he'd been unable to protect had been a dagger in his side ever since. There was no way he'd allow this baby to come to any harm. He would die to protect it. Who knew what India would do when she left here?

But he needed to act with care—this was a delicate situation and, despite the fact he could block her from leaving the country, he didn't want to strong-arm her into anything unless it was absolutely necessary, and only because he would do whatever it took to protect this baby.

His expression was grim as he regarded her, his body strong and unyielding even when his heart was thumping into his ribs so hard it was like an anvil. 'This is not the place to have this discussion,' he said, after a moment, looking around the room. He'd brought her to the least comfortable place he could think of, intentionally seeking to inspire awe of his position, but she was clearly not well, and he wasn't so barbaric that he didn't feel a responsibility to protect her—pregnant or not.

'You think?' she snapped, moving away from him. 'I'm not sure there's any place to discuss this that would make a difference, though, to be honest. You've made up your mind about me and nothing I say or do is going to change it. I'm glad I told you, but now you can go back to ignoring me. I don't need anything from you.'

He didn't bother arguing with her—there was no point. He had a pretty clear idea of what her pregnancy would mean for them both, it was simply a matter of working out the finer points of the arrangement. 'You will spend the night here. In the morning, we can speak about this further.'

Her lips parted. 'I will do no such thing. Do you honestly think I would ever go near you again?'

It took him a moment to understand what she'd meant. That he was propositioning her to join him in his bed? 'One night with you was a mistake—and I do not intend to repeat it,' he said firmly, even as desire stirred, tightening his body, making him ache for her. 'I meant for you to sleep in a guest bedroom.'

'I have a hotel room booked,' she demurred, stepping backwards.

'It is too late to be travelling into the city on your own.'

'And whose fault is that?' she demanded with a stamp of her foot. 'I was kept waiting for hours.'

He crossed his arms. 'Let us not lay blame now. The past is irrelevant. We need to focus on the baby, and what is in their best interests.'

She nodded, but her eyes were wary, looking for a trap. 'That's exactly what I think. I despise you after the way you treated me but that doesn't change the fact you're going to be this baby's father. And so long as you can treat him or her with respect and love, then I don't see why you can't be a part of the baby's life, in some way or another.'

He instantly rejected the picture she painted—that he would be the kind of father who flew in and out of his own child's life, a temporary, transient parent that the child never really got to know.

'We can discuss the details in the morning. Come, I will show you to a guest suite.'

In truth, India was so exhausted, she would have much preferred to simply go along with his suggestion, but a warning beacon blared, so she shook her head again. 'I have a hotel room booked. All I need is a ride into the city. We can meet for breakfast and discuss this further. The hotel has a nice restaurant—'

'If we were to meet at a hotel restaurant, everyone would know our business,' he snapped. 'And as you seem unaware of the importance of your pregnancy, allow me to spell it out for you: the baby you claim to be carrying if true—is the heir to the throne of Khatrain. As such, for the duration of your pregnancy, you are one of the most important people in the kingdom and your security is my responsibility. I will not have you wandering through a hotel lobby in the middle of the night, understood?'

Her lips parted on a rush of breath. 'But…no one knows about us and no one knows about the pregnancy! There is no risk to me.'

'That is a decision I will make.'

'You cannot make decisions about my life with such unilateral authority,' she insisted, and he felt it again, that sharp spurt of desire, like an electric livewire—just the same as the night they'd met, and often since. What was it about this woman that made his body burn?

'Actually, I can,' he said with a shrug, as though it barely mattered to him. 'You are in Khatrain, pregnant with my child. That makes you my responsibility. Furthermore, here my will is absolute, and I will not allow you to leave the palace given your situation, and the political importance of this pregnancy. So you might as well stop arguing and simply accept the hospitality I am offering.'

'Hospitality?' she spat with a flash of her eyes. 'You are turning me into a prisoner!'

'Don't be so melodramatic.' He half laughed, even as tension of a different sort cut through him now, a tension that was born of his own behaviour, and the choices he was now making to protect the baby she purported to know was his.

'Ha,' she said with obvious sarcasm. 'You think my freedom is melodramatic?'

'It is one night,' he lied, 'and from a practical standpoint, it makes sense. You say you are flying out tomorrow. Why waste time in transit?'

India stared up at him with a sense that she was lost at sea, no rescue in sight. She was so angry with him, and it was making her lash out and argue over every small detail, when some of what he said had merit. Besides, she was so tired, the idea of being able to be asleep within minutes was what finally tempted her to concede.

'Fine,' she muttered. 'If you insist.'

His response was to place his palm in the small of her back and guide her towards the door. It was a gesture that meant nothing and yet little lightning bolts of need speared through her, as though her body, filled with a portion of his DNA now, were genetically programmed to recognise and want him, even when her brain was shouting at her to pull away from the man. Only she was tired, and his touch gave her a strength and support she badly needed. At the door, he reached across and took her handbag, hooking it over his shoulder instead, relieving her of the burden of its weight.

She allowed him to do that, because it meant nothing, and it was temporary. In the morning, they'd talk about how this would work, she'd stick firm to the ideas she had for the kind of role that would work for her and their baby, and then she'd leave—putting him, this country, and the whole thing behind her.

But with every step they took, doubts began to plague her. She'd been so sure this was the right thing, but she acknowledged now that she'd given up all of her power by coming here to his country, right into the heart of his palace. Only her fears went way beyond that. Because irrespective of the fact that he was a sheikh and she was not, there was something between them that scared India to death.

She wanted him.

Their bodies were close, brushing as they moved, and it took all of her concentration to remember that she hated him, when her traitorous fingers were itching to reach for his chest, spin him around and feel his warmth against the palms of her hand.

It was all the more reason she had to get this over with and leave. One night with Khalil had been dangerously addictive, any more than that and she wasn't sure she'd ever be able to get him out of her head, and, for the sake of her sanity, she *had* to move on.

CHAPTER SIX

INDIA COULDN'T REMEMBER the last time she'd slept so well. It didn't make sense, with all that loomed over her head, and yet the previous day's exertions, the heat, the mental stress had all combined to mean that as soon as her head hit the pillow, she was in another world. She was not aware of stirring at all through the night, and in the morning, it wasn't nausea that woke her, but the sound of a door clicking across the room. She blinked open her eyes, disorientated by the sight that greeted her. This wasn't her bedroom. It took her a moment to remember exactly where she was, and a moment longer than that to push up to a sitting position and realise that Khalil was standing just inside the door to her enormous guest suite, his arms crossed over his chest, his eyes trained on her with the sort of possessive heat that definitely skittled her ability to think straight.

He wore a suit today, dark trousers, a crisp white shirt and a jacket that reminded her of the night they'd met. Her mouth felt dry; she looked towards the bedside table, then reached for the glass of water there.

'Good morning.' His voice was like treacle against her nerves.

'What time is it?' she asked, still disorientated.

'Nine o'clock.'

'Nine o'clock?' she repeated, jackknifing out of bed

in surprise before remembering that she'd slept in under-pants and a singlet top in deference to the desert heat. His eyes skimmed her body and little flames leaped beneath her skin. Oh, how she wished she were less aware of him on a physical level! It would be so much easier to have this conversation if her body weren't willing to betray her at every opportunity. She glared at him to compensate for the direction of her thoughts, then, as an afterthought, dragged the sheet off the bed, wrapping it around her shoulders like a superhero cape.

His smile made her feel like a ridiculous toddler; her expression grew defiant.

'And?' she prompted. 'Is there a reason you've barged in on me?'

His face sobered but she had the sense he was conceal-ing a smile, and that angered her more. 'The doctor will be here soon. I thought you would appreciate a chance to eat something, and dress, before she arrives.'

'What doctor?'

'The gynaecologist,' he said, as though this were some-thing they'd discussed time and time again.

'I don't have a gynaecologist.'

'You do now. Did you want to shower?'

She compressed her lips. 'I don't need to see a doctor.'

'I beg to differ.' He crossed the room, gesturing to the table. It was laden with trays of food and a pot of steam-ing hot coffee. Her stomach gave a little roll and a hint of nausea spread through her; she looked away again.

'I just want toast or something simple,' she said, then, aware it sounded ungrateful, she explained. 'I've had pretty bad morning sickness. I find it hard to eat much.'

'That explains why you have lost weight, rather than gained it.'

She dipped her head. 'I know people talk about morning sickness being bad, but I had no idea. And it's not just in the mornings, either, it's all day.'

'And that is common in the first trimester?'

'Yes.' Then, suspecting he was actually asking a different question, she expelled a sigh. 'I really don't know how I'm going to convince you that this is your baby.'

His eyes bored into hers, and she wished, more than anything, that he would simply believe her. But Khalil mistrusted her with every fibre of his being, that much was obvious, and this was a pretty important thing to have faith about. She moved to her backpack and lifted out the change of clothes she'd brought.

'I'll shower first,' she said, moving towards the en suite bathroom. Hovering just inside the door, she turned to face him. 'Are you still going to be here?'

'Of course.'

She lifted a brow. 'Great.' If he detected the sarcasm, he didn't react. She took her time showering—the steam felt impossibly good, and the products were the most luxurious, fragrant things she'd ever seen. A far cry from the simple bar soap she used at home for the sake of economy. The rest of the bathroom was just as well appointed, with moisturisers and a hairdryer, even a small selection of nail polishes and face masks. No convenience had been overlooked.

Not for her, obviously.

There had been no notice of her arrival, and certainly no expectation of her being accommodated. This was clearly how guest rooms at the royal palace were kitted out. If India were prone to bitterness, she might have experienced a wave of it to contemplate the disparities and inequities in life. She had become so good at making her toiletries stretch, cutting the bottom off the tube of toothpaste, to squeeze every last bit out, mixing moisturiser with kitchen

oil to make it last longer—what must it be like to live in
such obvious wealth? Without a care in the world, at least
not a financial one. Her head swam when she thought of
the bills she had back home—with no way to cover them.
But pulling Jackson out of college wasn't an option. She
had to work out a way through this.

Her hand moved over her stomach in a habit she'd de-
veloped. Though she was only eight weeks along, she felt
a fierce connection to her baby already, and she knew she
would do anything to give them everything she could in
life. How was she ever going to be able to care for her
brother and her baby?

The dress she'd brought was a simple blue linen sun-
dress, cut on the bias so it was floaty around her slender
body, with sleeves that covered just the tops of her arms.
She wore minimal make-up when she wasn't working;
India applied a hint of lip gloss and mascara now, then, in
concession to a face that was pale from the ravages of her
hormones—she had no idea when the 'glowing' stage of
pregnancy began but she was far from it!—a light dust-
ing of blush on her cheekbones. Her blonde hair she left
down, pulled over one shoulder to keep her neck cool—
even now, the sun was high and the day's warmth could be
felt penetrating the ancient glass of the palace's windows.

Khalil was sitting at the table when she emerged, his
legs spread wide, a large phone in front of him. His face
bore a scowl, so she paused, wondering if he would prefer
to be left to read whatever was giving him such displeasure
alone? Except he'd come to *her* room, and they had only
the morning to deal with their situation—she was already
counting the minutes to her flight. Escape was imperative.
Only once she lifted off the tarmac would she be able to
breathe easily again.

As she drew near to the table he looked up, his dark

brown eyes lancing her, so she almost lost her footing and tore her gaze away, her breath uneven. What kind of joke was God playing to make this man the only person she'd ever been attracted to?

'Is everything okay?' She nodded towards the phone, taking the seat furthest from him—across the table.

A slightly mocking look in his eyes convinced her that he understood and was amused by her efforts. Heat flushed her face.

'Fine. Just checking over a contract.'

'Is that part of your…job?'

She reached for what looked to be a muffin, sniffing it first and finding that she could tolerate the sweet fragrance— a good sign! It had pieces of fruit and something like cinnamon stirred through it, and it was still warm from the oven. Cutting into it, India added a generous whip of butter, watching as it melted through the middle.

'My job involves many things,' he said with a lift of his shoulders.

'Such as?'

'In less than a year, I will become the head of this state. Already I undertake a great many political tasks on my father's behalf; that will increase once I am crowned.'

Again, India wondered about his father's health, and somehow, she understood what he wasn't saying. She had experience with that particular type of stress, and the euphemisms one used, the words employed to skate about the subject and avoid deeper questioning. The truth was, it was very difficult to discuss a parent's mortality. She didn't push him on the subject.

'I suppose there have been many expectations on you since birth,' she said, wondering what that must have been like. He was born to a unique position, and must have been raised with an awareness of that.

'I have never known any different,' he said, his eyes regarding her with an intensity that took her breath away. 'And what of you, India? What is it in your life that made you decide to enter into your...vocation?'

Heat stung her cheeks, and she understood the meaning beneath his quietly voiced question. 'I needed a job that was flexible, that paid well. It ticked the boxes.'

She felt his disapproval coming off him in waves but at least he didn't disparage her any further. How could a man with all this understand the position she'd been in?

'I was lucky to find Warm Engagements,' she said, biting into the muffin and swooning a little as the flavours spread through her. It was the first food she'd genuinely enjoyed in weeks, and she took a moment to have a little silent celebration. She washed it down with a whole glass of water, thirsty from the heat of the night, then poured another. 'I had done a little work for them in the past—my best friend's been there for years. I knew it was an agency of quality, the kind of place that didn't stand for what you accused me of,' she insisted. 'And that was important to me. Plus, the pay is really great.'

His expression showed he didn't believe her. She sighed, but what did it matter in the scheme of things? She didn't have to win Khalil over. They weren't going to be friends, or anything to one another whatsoever—they were simply two people who would have a child in common. And surely he'd lose interest in their baby once he'd married and procured legitimate royal heirs right here in Khatrain?

'Anyway, I really just came here to tell you about the baby. I'm happy to see your doctor, if that's important to you, but then I'd like to leave.'

'Your flight is not until the afternoon,' he reminded her softly.

He sounded like himself, but there was an undercurrent to his words that set the hairs at the back of her neck on end. It all seemed…too easy. She'd come to Khatrain to tell him the truth, because she knew the importance of that, but she'd expected him to respond differently. Without fully acknowledging the fear to herself, she realised now that she'd had a niggling worry he might insist on holding her in the country for longer, perhaps until the baby was born, so he could be assured of his parentage. His calm acceptance of her departure didn't ring true. Which meant… She gulped past a lump in her throat, knowing she needed to play it cool, and act totally calm.

'I don't mind hanging around in the airport.'

'Tell me this, then.' His gravelled voice drew her attention back to his face; her stomach swooped. 'What did you expect me to say, when you dropped this bombshell in my lap?'

She took another bite of the muffin to buy time. 'I wasn't sure. I just knew that it was the right thing to do.'

His eyes widened and yet she couldn't understand even a hint of what he was feeling. He was a completely closed book to her.

'And if I say I want nothing to do with you or the baby?'

India dropped her eyes to the table, her father's rejection spearing her sharply, so for a moment she couldn't speak. The idea of their baby, still just a little cluster of cells but growing bigger and stronger every day, having to be born into a world where that kind of rejection was their reality?

'I would accept that, and do everything in my power to shield my child from the pain of your decision.'

She wasn't looking at him, so didn't see the way his jaw tightened, his eyes flashing with surprise.

'What pain might that be?'

Her laugh was hollow, a weak, tremulous sound. 'The

pain of knowing their father didn't want to be a part of their life.' She shook her head, reaching for the juice.

Silence prickled around the room, so that when she put her glass on the table and it knocked the edge of her plate, the noise was almost deafening.

'And financially?' he prompted.

Pride kept her silent on that score—he didn't need to know how dreadful her situation was. 'I'll cope,' she promised through gritted teeth. And even though the idea of child support was something she knew to be fair—and certainly given their relative positions—the thought of taking anything from this man, who thought so little of her and might not even want to know her child, was painful to think about.

'You have support?'

Her heart felt heavy. She had no support, but again, she kept that to herself, not wanting to reveal anything more to Khalil than was necessary. He wasn't on her side. Whatever she thought she'd felt in him that first night they'd met, he'd shown his true colours since then, and she would give him only the bare minimum details—details that would show him she had no intention of being pushed around nor dictated to by him. 'I'll be fine,' she reiterated firmly. 'There is a hospital near me; I've chosen to have the baby there. Obviously, I will keep you updated as the pregnancy develops and if you want to come and see the baby once he or she is born, then I'll understand.'

'How good of you.' He lifted a coffee cup to his lips and took a drink, his features like stone. The cup was too small and fine for his enormous hands—it looked ridiculous.

'So having a baby without being married means nothing to you?'

A warning siren blared in the back of her mind. Marriage was a topic she saw no sense in discussing. 'Life has a habit of dispensing curve balls.' She pressed a finger into a crumb on the edge of her plate, lifting it to her lips with no idea of the way the small, thoughtless gesture affected the Sheikh. 'I know that I'm not afraid, and that I am resourceful and determined. Our child will *never* lack for anything it needs. I'll make sure of that.'

'That's what I'm afraid of,' he muttered, refilling his coffee.

'What does that mean?'

'I have already seen the lengths you are prepared to go to in order to make a living. What will you do once there is a baby to support? What kind of environment will this child be raised in?'

'A loving one,' she responded, fear snagging in her throat. She had to get out of here. She stood, gripping the back of the chair in both hands, needing the support. 'I will not sit here and be judged by you for having made decisions you cannot possibly fathom. I came here as a courtesy but let me be clear: this is *my* child. I have done my duty and informed you of the fact they exist, but that's where I'm drawing a line. You don't need to be a part of their life and you sure as heck don't get to sit there and lecture me and act as though you're so damn morally superior to me. I will love this baby with all my heart, and that is enough.'

'Except it isn't enough,' he interjected quietly, something sharp in his gaze that stood as a warning to India. The warning siren was blaring louder now. She dug her fingers into the chair back, seeking strength.

'Babies are expensive, and they require care. Who will look after this child if you are working nights? Or is your plan to find some other man and stooge him into marrying you, to help you care for our baby? Because if you think I am having my son or daughter raised by another then you are frankly delusional.'

'That hadn't even entered my mind,' she denied hotly. 'But, as a point of fact, I was raised by my stepfather from the age of four and he is so much more of a father to me than my biological dad ever was. So if I should choose to marry, at some point, that has nothing to do with you.'

'I disagree.'

'You disagree as a matter of habit,' she snapped.

'A habit we share.'

'There is a difference between disagreeing and defending—I am forced to do the latter with you at every turn.'

'If you are defensive of your lifestyle then that is a question for your conscience.'

She ground her teeth together. 'I'm not defending my lifestyle, damn it! I am defending what you *believe* my lifestyle to be; there's a difference.'

He held up a hand, in a clearly authoritative manner. 'Let us not discuss your—profession. It is clearly upsetting to you and, given your condition, that should be avoided. Besides, it doesn't matter now. You are pregnant, and whatever happened before is irrelevant to the future of this baby. Okay?'

No! It's not okay! She wanted to scream the denial at him, to tell him she didn't want to live in a world where he thought her capable of what he'd accused her. Where he could reduce what they'd shared down to a financial transaction. Her pride hurt with the knowledge that she hadn't been able to simply tear up the cheque he'd written her, but without that money, she could never have afforded to come to Khatrain and tell him the truth.

A knock sounded at the door, making any response impossible, as Khalil stood and moved with his long, confident gait towards it. He drew it inwards and a woman entered, followed by a male with a large trolley.

'Your Highness.' She bowed towards the Sheikh, and the man behind the doctor did the same.

'This way.' His voice was grim as he gestured towards India. She felt like a naughty schoolgirl, being dragged before the headmaster. At the same time, even this brought her a hint of pleasure, because seeing a doctor in America was a luxury beyond her means. She'd done an at-home pharmacy test to confirm her pregnancy, then another to confirm the confirmation, but she had been waiting until closer to twenty weeks to book a hospital appointment for a scan.

'Dr Abasha.' Khalil gestured to India. 'India McCarthy.'

'How do you do?' Dr Abasha's smile was kind, and India warmed to her immediately.

'Thank you for seeing me,' India murmured.

'Of course, it is my honour.' She turned to Khalil. 'Is there somewhere private I can speak to the patient?'

India had to hide a smile; it was clear Khalil didn't like being excluded, but after a moment's hesitation, he exited the room.

'I take it you've done a home pregnancy test?' the doctor asked, reaching into her briefcase and withdrawing another such test.

'Yes. Two of them.'

'Well, they are almost always accurate, but this one is a little different—it will tell me the amount of hCG—the pregnancy hormone—in your system at the moment. It's useful for many things, including dating the pregnancy.'

India's heart dropped to her toes. This woman knew what her job was: to confirm—or maybe even to deny?—that the baby was the Sheikh's. The idea of a protracted fight over paternity made her stomach ache—she would never do it. There would be too much risk of publicity, and she couldn't have her baby ever discovering that India had needed to fight for the father to acknowledge their life.

'Okay,' she said. 'No problems.'

When she was finished with the pregnancy test, she carried it out to the doctor, who regarded it with a smile at first, and then a small frown. 'You say you are eight weeks along?'

India nodded. She knew the exact date of conception, of course. But the doctor's countenance gave her some cause for concern. 'Yes. Why? Is there a problem?'

'Could there be some confusion with dates?'

'Definitely not.'

Dr Abasha took the pregnancy test and placed it on the trolley, then switched the light on so a monitor on the top tray came to life. 'Come and have a lie-down. Let's do a scan to see what's going on.'

India's eyes grew wide. 'Isn't it too early?'

'We'll see. At eight weeks, a dating scan should be possible.'

Under different circumstances, she might have felt excited, but there was a look of concern on the doctor's face that made India hold her breath.

Her dress had buttons down the front so she undid several in the middle and lay on the bed as Dr Abasha moved the trolley closer. 'Would you like me to get His Highness?'

'No,' India denied quickly. 'Let me see first, please.'

Dr Abasha hesitated a moment before nodding, applying a cold, wet goo to India's belly. 'Lie still,' she said. 'This will be a little uncomfortable.'

She moved the wand around, her eyes on the screen as she shifted positions, her fingertips clicking buttons before she peered closer at the image.

'Is there a problem?' India asked, after what felt like for ever.

Dr Abasha's eyes met India's. 'Stay here, madam.'

India's heart was racing, worry clutching at her, as Dr Abasha left the room and returned, a moment later, with

Khalil. His eyes met India's and she felt her own worries reflected in his.

'Please, just tell me what's going on,' India begged, pushing up onto her elbows, uncaring that her belly was still exposed and covered in translucent blue syrup.

'The dating scan confirms that you are eight weeks pregnant, madam, congratulations.'

Khalil's eyes bored into hers, and India's heart tripped over itself, the triumph of that moment dwarfed by something else entirely. She swallowed past a lump in her throat, turning back to the doctor. 'And the baby's okay?'

'I was interested by your high levels of hCG—much higher than one would expect at this stage of a pregnancy, hence the dating scan.'

'Do high levels of hCG indicate a problem?' India asked, panic overtaking her now.

'Not in this case,' Dr Abasha said with a smile. 'Tell me, do twins run in your family?'

India's jaw dropped and she shook her head, trying to make sense first of the doctor's implication and then of her question.

'My mother is a twin,' Khalil said. 'And her mother.'

'And your children,' the doctor said with a grin, as though this were purely good news.

'Oh, my God.' India sat up straight now, staring at the wall opposite. 'Twins?' She squeezed her eyes shut, her first reaction of sheer delight quickly being overtaken by stress. One child had been scary enough, but two? On her own? And all her bravado seemed to crumple at once, so she had no faith in herself and her resourcefulness, she saw only an enormous, insurmountable wall.

'Thank you, Doctor. What do we do now?'

'You've really already done the important thing,' the doctor said with a wink, then apparently sensed the tone of the room and sobered. 'I will bring some pregnancy vita-mins to you later today, as well as information on diet and lifestyle habits to support a healthy pregnancy. Twin preg-nancies are generally considered higher risk than single, though in someone of your age and obvious good health, I am not concerned. I'll schedule another scan for you at twelve weeks.'

'Higher risk as in…something might go wrong?' India asked, latching onto the question, feeling Khalil's eyes on her.

'There is a slightly higher risk, yes,' the doctor said gently. 'The first trimester is when a miscarriage is most likely—but you are already eight weeks. It is also likely the twins will be born early—anywhere from thirty-six weeks, sometimes even sooner.'

Perspiration dampened India's brow and she pressed a hand to her stomach, a fierce need to do whatever she could to protect her babies rushing through her.

'What can I do?' she asked.

'Nothing.' Dr Abasha smiled kindly. 'Eat well, get plenty of rest, avoid stress, relax. And wait.'

India closed her eyes, because such simple instructions were almost impossible for her to follow. Her life back home was not relaxing, stress was a constant companion, she wasn't sleeping and as for eating well—it depended on what she could afford.

'Okay, sure,' she said, fighting back tears. 'I can do that.' For her babies, she'd find a way. And she knew what that would mean. Selling the family home. She'd been de-termined to hold onto it for Jackson, and when she'd found out that she was pregnant, the idea of raising her babies in the home she'd lived in with her parents had made her feel that they would be a part of the baby's life, but it was more important to take care of her pregnancy in the here and now.

By selling the home, she could free up enough cash to buy a small apartment that she'd own outright. That would alleviate some worries. But what about the medical bills and Jackson's college fees? It would quickly chew through the capital, so whatever she had to spend on an apartment would quickly diminish.

She was conscious of Khalil walking the doctor out, thanking her for her time before closing the door, pressing his back to it. Once they were alone, she realised, belatedly, that she hadn't corrected the doctor on something.

'I won't be here this afternoon,' India said quietly, standing on legs that were so full of adrenaline and surprise they wobbled a little. She had to get out of Khatrain, and fast. Something about the discovery she was carrying twins made everything seem more urgent—and dangerous.

Khalil's brow lifted in a silent encouragement for her to continue.

'The doctor said she'd bring some vitamins and information to me, but I won't be here. Do you think she could come back sooner?'

'I think,' Khalil said, his voice quiet yet determined, 'that your place is now in Khatrain. Not only will you be here this afternoon, India, you will be here from now on.'

CHAPTER SEVEN

IT WAS HER worst fears—fears she hadn't fully acknowledged to herself until this moment—confirmed. She stared at him, shaking her head, even when she knew there had always been a risk of this. Why had she thought she could give him this news and then leave again? What kind of fool was she?

He crossed his arms over his chest, everything firming into place with the strength and certainty of lightning, bolting towards the earth

'You're pregnant with my *children*. Clearly you cannot go back to America.'

'I'm sorry, that is certainly *not* clear to me. What difference does it make that they're twins?' She stared at him in that way she had, as though he were so far beneath her, her blue eyes narrowing scathingly. 'Or is it simply that you believe me now that a doctor has confirmed their gestational age?'

'The doctor's confirmation was important,' he said unapologetically. 'Anyone in my position would seek the same assurance.'

'And my word wasn't enough?'

Strangely though, Khalil hadn't questioned the honesty of her statement until she had suggested that he might doubt her. Then, it had been easy to believe she was lying to him—after all, Fatima had already greased the wheels there, her dishonesty and ultimately viciously mercenary behaviour making it impossible for him to trust women, particularly when it came to children.

'I have the confirmation I wanted,' he said, as though that was all that mattered. 'And now we must focus on the future.'

Indignation fired in her eyes so he was tempted to sweep her into his arms and kiss it away, reminding her that before there was this anger between them, a different kind of passion had flared.

'I *have* been focussing on the future,' she said through gritted teeth, looking around the room with a hint of panic in her eyes then striding towards the sofa, where she'd discarded a shirt at some point during her stay. She lifted it up and stuffed it into her backpack, then disappeared into the bathroom, returning with a small, zipped bag that she also added to the backpack. 'I've been focussed on nothing but the future since I learned of this pregnancy, but that future is not here in Khatrain. I'm going home.'

'The sooner you start to think of this as your home, the better.'

Her lips parted and she stared at him as though she couldn't fathom this response—as though it had never occurred to her that he might fight to be a part of the children's lives.

'You said you would do whatever it took to give your child everything you could in life; are you surprised to discover I feel the same way?'

'Yes, frankly,' she said with a shake of her head, as if to dispel the very idea. 'I'm not here because I want you in their lives! I came because—'

'You thought I should know. Yes, you have said this, many times. But what did you think I would do with that knowledge, *azeezi*?'

'I—don't know.' She zipped up her backpack and lifted it over one shoulder, but the gesture—while valiant—lacked certainty, and her trademark defiance was nowhere to be seen. The truth was, she'd feared this response, but she'd told herself it wasn't possible. She'd lied to herself, because a desire to do the right thing had outweighed her self-preservation instincts. Or was it something else that had motivated her to fly to Khatrain? Had she actually hoped—but, no. India would not allow her thoughts to go in such a mortifying direction. She didn't want any part of what he was suggesting!

'I will be Sheikh of Khatrain—did you think I would allow my child to be raised in America? That I would simply visit from time to time, when I happened to be in the area? Did you think this pregnancy would mean so little to me that I would not turn my life on its head to accommodate it—and you?'

Her lip trembled and he felt, unmistakably, pity for her.

'I thought you wouldn't want it,' she said softly, and shock split through him.

'I thought you'd be angry at me for having conceived. I thought you'd offer money for me to disappear, and that you'd marry someone else soon enough and have royal heirs all of your own, so that you wouldn't want the embarrassment of our illegitimate child hanging around your neck.'

He stared at her in shock. 'Nothing you have described is what I feel, believe me.' His eyes narrowed though as he replayed her statement in his mind. 'Did you want money? Is that why you came?'

Sadness shaped her features. 'No.' Her voice was hollow. 'And I wouldn't have taken it, even if you'd offered it.'

'Even for the baby?'

'Not unless it was a matter of life and death,' she said

emphatically. 'Children don't need much beyond love and that I am well able to provide.'

Admiration flared in his gut, and something else too: gratitude. Because the most important trait he could ask for in the mother of his children was that she would want to protect them with her life, and India clearly felt that in spades.

'This is a decision you no longer have to make.'

'You mean it's a decision I no longer *get* to make,' she corrected, fidgeting with her fingers. 'If I stay in Khatrain, it will be because you've forced me.'

'How about we try a different word?' he said as he crossed towards her, lifting the backpack off her shoulder and placing it on the floor. 'What if we speak of persuasion instead?'

'You have not persuaded me. You've dictated to me.'

His look alone silenced her.

'You cannot afford one baby, let alone twins. Your debts are monumental, and you lost your job at the agency shortly after our night together.'

Her eyes were like saucers in her face, her skin blanching pale. 'How did you know?'

'That doesn't matter.'

'It matters to me! Have you been spying on me?'

'Naturally I did my research,' he said. 'I thought someone might have taken a photograph of us kissing at the bar, remember? I wanted to be prepared if the story broke in the papers.' He raked her face with his eyes, his expression grim. 'You are in no position to fight me.'

'And yet I would, with all that I am.'

'It would never be enough.' He moved closer, near enough to touch. 'You are in my country, where we play purely by my rules. Even if we weren't, I have the means— and motivation—to pursue custody of our children through the highest courts in your country. And I would win, India. Your vocational choices make that a given.'

'Damn it, Khalil, I'm not what you think I am.'

'Even if that is true, working as an escort is still enough to put doubt into a judge's mind.'

Her lips parted on a whoosh of hurt and he felt a stirring in his gut, a yearning that spread through him like wildfire, so he caught her face in his hands and held her right where she was.

'But beyond that, there is a part of you that doesn't want to fight what I am suggesting. There is a part of you that wants to stay here with me, isn't there, India?'

Her eyes were like pools of doubts, but they were also awash with desire, so much he could swim in it. He stroked her lower lip, and felt her tremble beneath his touch, the pulse point at the base of her throat visible beneath her translucent skin.

'I found it impossible to resist you that night, and that same desire flashes through me now, even after   ' he shook his head. 'What kind of fool does that make me?'

He saw hurt in her eyes right before he kissed her, and he blanked it from his mind. He didn't want to wound her. He was only being honest And in that moment, all he honestly wanted was to kiss her until he felt sane again.

She was breathless with the pleasure of his kiss, its unexpected nature catching her off guard, so she was completely lost to him, her knees sagging her body forward, and it was the most natural thing for his arm to clamp around her waist, holding her to him.

Fight him. Fight this!

Her brain was screaming at her, warning her that within pleasure lay the potential for so much pain, and yet they were bonded, the two of them; bonded by babies and some-

thing else, an undeniable force that held them together, so
that when he lifted her and carried her to the bed, she didn't
even think about saying anything to resist him.

She didn't want to. It was selfish and short-sighted but
India's craving for Khalil usurped everything else. He undressed her quickly, pausing only to undo his own belt and
trousers before he separated her thighs with his knee then
pushed into her, kissing her as he possessed her body. She
groaned at the immediate sensation of relief then white-hot
pleasure, his possession of her swift and urgent, the same
need rushing through them both, overpowering them, making speech and sense unnecessary. There was only this.

His fingers weaved with hers, pinning her hands above
her head as he moved, trapping her. His other hand roamed
her breast, cupping it as he kissed her and thrust deep and
hard, faster and faster as their need grew to the point where
neither could bear it, neither could fight it: they clung to
one another as they exploded, pleasure a burst of light that,
for a moment, pushed aside the dark.

Khalil's body weight on top of hers was blissful, but
only for a moment. Reality began to push against her and
regrets were not far behind. This situation was complicated enough without having brought sex right back into
it. India's breathing slowed and his weight became impossible to bear, so she pushed at his chest, rolling out from
beneath him and standing, lifting a hand to her forehead
and shaking her head.

'That shouldn't have happened.'

There was no regret in his face, only determination.
Had he planned to seduce her? To prove a point?

'No,' he said simply, so she realised she'd asked the
questions aloud.

'Then what the heck…?'

'I meant what I said. Whatever drew us together that

night still exists between us. Nothing that happened since has changed our desire.'

'But it has for me! Everything is different now.'

She had the satisfaction of seeing his eyes darken with something like doubt, but it was gone again almost instantly, arrogance back in place.

'The fact we have this chemistry is a bonus, India. Our marriage needn't be a disaster—we can share this, and our children. Many people have wed for much less.'

Her jaw dropped, her mind too spongy to make sense of what he was saying. 'Did you just say—our marriage?'

'Of course. What else did you think I meant when I said you would stay in Khatrain?'

'I thought you meant until I'd had the babies.'

'And then what?' he asked, sitting up. 'Did you believe I would pack you off to America, out of our babies' lives?'

'You'll forgive me if I don't give you much benefit of the doubt,' she responded, her eyes devouring his naked form even as she tried to pull away from him.

'You were wrong.' He ignored her barb. 'I meant for you, and the children, to remain here. Obviously we must marry, to ensure their place in the line of succession.'

It was all too much. India shook her head, looking around for the time. She could still make her flight. She just had to convince Khalil that was in everyone's best interests—she needed him to see sense.

'You believe that I've been engaged in the kind of career that no one in your kingdom would *ever* accept. What if we were to marry and your suspicions hit the papers? You were worried enough when it was a simple kiss in a bar, but marriage?'

'That is a consideration,' he said seriously. 'But it's a risk we must take.'

'What about your father?' She pushed, desperate.

His lips tightened. 'There is no option but to marry—for the sake of our children.'

'You're not listening to me. I don't need your help. I can raise my children in the States, on my own.'

'But they are my children too, India, and I will fight for them with every last breath in my body. I will not allow them to be raised away from me. So what option do we have then?'

Consternation struck her in the middle. She looked around for her clothes—discarded at the foot of the bed—and pulled on her dress, preferring not to have this conversation while she was stark naked, her body still covered in red patches from his stubble and touch.

'Let me put it this way instead,' he said slowly, once she was dressed. 'The line of succession in Khatrain is quite specific. On my thirtieth birthday—in a matter of months—I am to inherit the throne. I will be crowned Sheikh, but only if I am married. It is a peculiar requirement of our country's constitution. I have known for a long time that I must choose a bride and marry swiftly. If we were to do this your way, and not marry, I still would not permit you to leave Khatrain until the children were born, at which point I would demand that they remain here. In the meantime, I would be forced to marry one of the women my advisors have urged me to consider, and that woman, my wife and Sheikha, would be a stepmother to our children. Is that the future you want?'

She gasped, hot, bright lights flashing in her eyes at the awful picture he painted.

'Or,' he continued, his voice husky, his accent thick, 'you could accept my proposal. Marry me and we will raise the children together. You would live the life of royalty, my kingdom would be your kingdom, the homes I have around the globe yours to enjoy, a fleet of jets at your disposal to travel home and see family any time you wished. And there would be this,' he reminded her, standing and placing his arms on her hips, holding her tight against his taut body. 'A marriage that meets both of our needs, yes?'

'No,' she whispered, shaking her head, even as the strength of his argument was impossible to fault. How could she deny what he was offering? And what he was implying would happen if she didn't agree? He was carving out a place for her in his life, in royal life, and, most importantly, in their children's lives. The alternative was not hard to imagine: she would be sidelined at first and excluded eventually, her children raised without her.

But marrying a man she didn't love? Who despised her? Since she'd watched her mother fall in love with her stepfather, India had known she wanted exactly that for herself—true, everlasting love. A proper family. That certainty had only solidified as she'd continued to witness her parents' happiness over the years.

Marrying for love was a luxury no longer open to her. She wanted—more than anything—for her children to be near to her. That had to override everything else.

'And what will you tell your people about me? More importantly, your parents?'

'My parents will be so glad to know I'm engaged. They will not ask questions beyond that.'

He made it sound so simple, but it wasn't. Marriage to Khalil was paved with danger. If the last half-hour had taught her anything it was that she was monumentally weak where he was concerned. What would it be like when they were husband and wife?

It was all too much to consider—she needed more time, a chance to breathe and think this through. But Khalil was staring at her, his mind made up. And on one score, he was perfectly right. She was in *his* country. His word was law.

'Getting married is extreme,' she said, her voice juddering.

'On the contrary, it is sensible.'

She analysed their situation from every angle, trying to see her way through this, to imagine a different future. But all roads led back to the truth: they were tied together already. Was there any harm in formalising it? And yet, still she clung to the idea of more time, a chance to be sure she wouldn't live to regret this decision. Lost in thought, she didn't notice as he moved closer, his hand lifting to her cheek, cupping it. 'And it is not as though our marriage won't have a silver lining. It's clear we share this desire.'

She bit down on her lip as her body responded to his nearness, his touch, overriding her momentary uncertainty. His eyes probed hers and she bit back a sigh, because she wanted to lift up and kiss him, but as soon as she did that, she knew what would happen—again. They couldn't simply tumble into bed together every time they got close. This conversation was too important to be overpowered by their very mutual desire. India forced herself to step back, away from him and temptation, but it did nothing to tamp down on the slick of heat between her legs. She looked away, frustrated at her body's response.

'You don't understand,' she murmured. 'My parents loved each other. I've always wanted that.'

His eyes sparkled, a hint of challenge in their depths. 'It's unrealistic.'

'A loving marriage? You're kidding, right?'

'It's unrealistic for us, in this circumstance.'

She clamped her lips, biting back whatever she'd been intending to say.

'You should be aware that our marriage contract will include a financial arrangement. It's standard for royal marriages.'

Sadness welled inside her—a sadness born of his beliefs. Why didn't he see who she really was? Why didn't he accept her version of events? She wanted to shout at him that she didn't want his money, that he could take his fortune and run straight to hell with it, but the truth was, if she remained in Khatrain, she would need access to funds immediately to cover costs back home. There was a small amount left in her account, which would pay for upcoming utilities, but Jackson's college fees were due before long and India would need... She dug her fingernails into her palms to stop tears from filling her eyes. She would need to accept his payment, again. Her pride was stripped to pieces.

'How much?' The words were whispered, sadness thickening the consonants.

'And now I have your interest?'

'I'm just curious,' she lied, as though it weren't vitally important to her.

'Naturally. What amount do you think would be fair?' he prompted, arms folded over his chest. 'It would help, of course, if I knew your going rate—then we could simply multiply that out to cover a lifetime.'

'Don't.' She squeezed her eyes shut, anguished. She hated what he thought of her! And worse, that she was now living up to it, by accepting any kind of marriage settlement.

'Why not?' He sighed heavily. 'Why can't you at least own your decisions, India?'

Her stomach looped. He couldn't possibly think any worse of her. The truth was, she knew exactly the amount she needed—enough to cover Jackson's degree. She would sooner sell the house than ask this man for a cent more—as much as that would pain her. It was her family home, but her mother would have understood. She wouldn't debase herself for a physical possession, but for Jackson? So he could stay at college, even when she was over here? She couldn't leave him stranded. He had to be taken care of; her parents would have expected that of her.

'I need one hundred thousand American dollars,' she muttered, without meeting his eyes, so she didn't see the surprise that flashed in them—surprise, because his marriage contract with Fatima had stalled at the point she'd sought ten million dollars on the day of their marriage, and a generous annuity thereafter.

'I know it seems like a lot.' She continued to stare at the ground, hating this situation with all her heart.

'And what do you need this sum for, India?'

Her skin grew pale. She looked away, the awful truth of her financial situation like a lump in her throat.

'It's…personal.'

'So personal you cannot share it with your fiancé?'

Fiancé…! She squeezed her eyes closed. Was she really going to do this?

'Does it matter?' she murmured eventually.

'No.' Contempt fired in the word and her stomach dropped. 'Was there anything else?'

She was on a sinking ship, unable to find a life vest. She looked around, panicked, her mind in a spin. But yes, there was one other consideration, the most important one of all perhaps.

'I think we should wait another month to announce our engagement.'

'No. We must marry immediately; within days.'

'Let me finish,' she insisted. 'You heard what the doctor said. The first trimester carries a higher risk of miscarriage. I hope and pray with all my heart that we are blessed with two healthy babies in seven months' time, but if we're not, if anything happens, then there's no point in…the marriage between us…wouldn't make sense.'

'I also heard the doctor say that your risks are low,' he reminded her.

'Low, but not nil. It's a simple precaution. You've made it perfectly clear that I'm far from the ideal bride. Why risk upsetting everyone if it's not necessary?'

His expression was inscrutable, his handsome, symmetrical face as still as if it had been carved from granite.

'It makes sense,' she said softly. 'We'll wait a month, and then, if everything looks good, and this still makes sense... I'll marry you, Khalil.'

CHAPTER EIGHT

KHALIL LEANED LOW to the stallion's mane, his eyes focussed on the waving lines of the horizon, the early morning sun already beating down on his back. He rode hard, the wind rushing past him a balm he needed, the freedom of the desert one of the few things that could bring him a sense of relief.

Every day since India had arrived, he'd done this—pursuing the dawn in a fruitless attempt to catch it, pitting his power and strength against the elements of the universe. He wasn't seeking victory though, so much as attempting to outrun his thoughts.

His engagement to Fatima had been a disaster. For one thing, he'd believed himself in love, which was, he realised now, just about the worst reason one could have for getting married. Particularly a wedding of this sort. He didn't need a wife he loved, he needed one who would provide him with heirs, and in this way, India was perfect. Two children already on the way meant the order of succession would be protected.

But he had been careless with Fatima—because he'd loved her. He'd trusted her and believed her: mistakes he would never make again. It was the only explanation for why he'd palmed off the arranging of the marriage contracts to his lawyers rather than overseeing negotiations himself. He'd presumed Fatima would want nothing—that she would know that, as his wife, she could have whatever she wished. It hadn't been enough, though. Her greed had known no bounds, and as her list of demands had grown more and more outrageous, his legal team had sought to protect him, with no idea that she had something in her belly he would have paid his entire kingdom to keep safe.

He leaned lower, murmuring quietly to the horse so his ears pricked and he began to move faster, cooperating with the Sheikh's commands.

A week ago, India had arrived in Khatrain, and since she'd provisionally agreed to marry him, he'd steered clear of her. But that, he realised, was a mistake. If he'd been more involved in the negotiations with Fatima, he might have been able to prevent what had happened. He should have been able to save their baby. He would never forgive himself for the fact that his carelessness had led to that tragedy—he had to do whatever he could to protect *these* babies, here and now.

He would care for India, he would manage their marriage negotiations personally, and then, on the day of the deadline she had imposed, they would marry.

Discomfort pressed against him. He had never imagined he'd be in this position. He was a highly sought-after bachelor, his bed never empty for long, the prospect of marrying him something many princesses and heiresses had made clear they wished to fulfil. India was not one of them.

And that bothered him.

What was he expecting? That she'd jump at the chance to marry a man who'd scorned her the morning after they'd slept together? That she'd ignore the way he'd spoken to her, ignore the fact he'd treated her like—

He made a low growling sound, his frustration bursting from him. He hated how they'd met. He hated that he'd used her, and that she'd used him. He hated the way he'd spoken to her the morning after they'd slept together, but, more than that, he hated the idea of her using her beautiful body to seduce men purely for financial gain.

And yet, what if Ethan had lied?

The question had been hammering away at him since he'd left America. What if he was wrong? What if she was telling the truth? The sun shifted, rays of warmth beating across his back. He clamped down on his naïve desire to believe her, or even to set aside what he knew of her career. He'd believed in Fatima, and it had cost him the world. He would never be so stupid again. India was to be the mother of his children, but he could never allow himself to trust her. Too much was at stake.

But that didn't mean he could keep ignoring her either—or pretending to ignore her. No purpose was served by running away from her—if he wanted to get her out of his mind, he needed to keep her in his life, in his bed, so that he no longer spent every waking minute craving her to the point of distraction... They were to marry, and the sooner he found a way to live with that—and her— the better.

India disconnected the call with Jackson, a frown on her face. She hated lying to her little brother, but it was for the best. Until she was absolutely certain that she was marrying Khalil, and staying in Khatrain, she didn't see any point in bringing him up to speed. It was just easier to pretend she was still in New York, that life was continuing as normal—or in their new normal, at least.

A knock sounded at her door, startling India out of her thoughts. She put down her phone on the tabletop and stood, just as the door opened and Khalil strode in—but not as she'd ever seen him! He wore loose linen pants, long to the ankle, and his chest was bare, moist with perspiration. His hair was damp, and there was an intensity in his eyes that spread fire to her core. India hadn't seen him in a week, and her body ached for him, so seeing him in her room, dressed like this, was enough to shoot her pulse into overdrive, big time.

'Khalil.' Her voice was hoarse. She stood exactly where she was, even as he began to move towards her and her first instinct was to jolt her legs into action and touch him. The instinct shocked her; she mentally bolted her feet to the floor. 'Is something the matter?'

'Yes.'

Was it possibly he was regretting their arrangement? She stood perfectly still, watching as he strode towards her, but with every step he took, an answering thud landed in her heart, so her pulse was thick and thready by the time he reached her. His eyes furrowed, as though he were lost in thought, his expression inscrutable. He had six freckles across his cheeks, barely recognisable because of the depth of his complexion, but up close she could see them and they mesmerised her.

'This isn't working.'

She swallowed hard. 'What's not?'

'Ignoring you. It won't work.'

Her pulse jumped.

'If we're going to get married, we need to act like it.'

She ignored the torrent of adrenaline and desire that tore through her, aiming to keep a restrained, cool expression on her face. 'Meaning?'

'Meaning we have to be seen together.'

Disappointment seared her; she blinked away, and he made a throaty sound of understanding. Damn it, why was she so easy to read?

'Publicly, but also we must be together privately. It's the only way.'

'We can wait three weeks. Until we know for sure—'

'Can we?' His lips formed a grim smile. 'Is that what you want?'

He scanned her face, not waiting for an answer.

'Or have you been thinking of me this week as I have you? Have you been tortured each night, wanting me to kiss you, to touch you? Have you touched yourself, imagining it was me?'

Heat exploded in her cheeks. She looked away from him, even as her body leaned forward, traitorous, needy body. Her nipples tingled, silently begging for his touch, and, as though they were connected in some way, he lifted his hands, cupping them, catching their weight and brushing his thumbs over her nipples. She tilted her head back, stars dancing against her eyelids.

It was madness, but a madness she had wanted all week, a touch she needed, even when she hated herself for that.

'We are not marrying for love, but that doesn't mean our marriage need be empty.'

She blinked, his words like a hammer against ice, so she straightened, staring at him, but he moved quickly, kneeling before her, catching the hem of her skirt in his hands and pushing it up as his eyes met hers, taunting her, teasing her, challenging her to reject him. But she didn't— she couldn't. She was spellbound, desire throbbing in her belly. He drew her underpants down slowly, the feel of his palms on her legs sending shock waves of need through her, so she tilted her head back again.

When he kissed her sex, she cried out, the touch so personal and perfect, so unlike anything she'd ever known, that she almost couldn't bear it. Her fingers drove into his hair, tightening around its lengths, a whimper in the base of her throat as his tongue lashed her most sensitive cluster of nerves until she was tumbling into an abyss of delight, her cries ringing out in the room, loud and fast, her hands wrenching his hair until the waves of torturous release eased and she could breathe once more. He stood, something like satisfaction glinting in his eyes, and then he scooped her up, carrying her through the enormous suite and into the bedroom.

'This was real,' he said, and it made no sense, but she didn't have time to question him, because he was undressing, staring at her, as though she were a puzzle he needed to understand. A moment later, his knee separated her legs and his arousal was pushing into her warm, moist core. She arched her back, calling his name out, the taste of it in her mouth perfection, everything about this moment perfection.

His body played hers like a maestro. His mouth tormented her nipples as he thrust into her, hard and fast, then slowly, pulling her pleasure back so that it built to an ultimate, unruly crescendo, each time such pleasure pain in the nearness of her release. He was prolonging their mutual release, and frustration at his mastery clipped through India, so suddenly she pushed at his chest, rolling him onto his back. His eyes caught hers for a moment, surprise obvious, and she grinned as she straddled him, moaning at the delight of it, moving her hips to her own tempo, moving her hands over her breasts as the wave built and built and she rode it towards the crest. His hands dug into her hips, moving her faster, holding her lower, and he bucked as she moved, so their bodies morphed and exploded as one, their cries mingled, the air in the room explosive with the pleasure they felt.

India could barely think afterwards. She stayed where

she was, focussing on her breathing, on the tingling that ran through her body, the throbbing between her legs, the beauty of the man beneath her, the rightness of what they'd just done, even when everything else was such an abject mess, and she realised she didn't feel the regret she had thought she might. She was sure it would come, but for now she wanted to glory in being with him, with the fact she'd taken control and driven him over the edge, with how perfectly their bodies worked together.

'See, India? Whatever else happens in our marriage, we have this. It is enough.'

She wished he wouldn't talk. Their bodies spoke fine for both of them; words ruined everything.

But he *had* spoken and her brain had clicked back into gear, so she had no choice but to respond. 'Is it? I always thought marriages were about love and respect.'

'A childish fantasy,' he murmured, indolently running a hand over her breast, his eyes following the gesture with possessive intent.

'How can you say that?' She shook her head, thinking of her parents' marriage, or everything she knew to be true. 'Haven't you ever been in love?'

'That's irrelevant. *We* are not in love, and never will be, but it doesn't matter.'

She opened her mouth to argue with that, but his finger brushed the flesh between her legs, sparking a bolt of lightning in her belly. She stared at him, and he moved his fingers again, his gaze locked to hers.

Damn it, he knew exactly how to pleasure her, and he did so now, stirring her to fever pitch all over again, before rolling her onto her back, kissing her as he moved his fingers, so when she crested over the wave this time, she was breathless and exhausted, and totally absorbed by sensual pleasure.

* * *

She looked like a woman who'd been made love to so thoroughly she could barely speak. He stood, scanning her beautiful body, stepping away from the bed with regret. He'd thought sleeping with her would ease the ache in his gut, the ever-present need, but having opened the floodgates, he simply wanted more of her. He wanted to shower with her, to run the sponge over her body, feeling her soapy and wet beneath his hands, to kiss her, naked, as water ran over them both…

'There is an event tonight. I usually take a date. Come with me.'

She flipped her head to face him, a frown on her lips. He moved towards her, kissing her quickly, so the frown disappeared. 'It's a formal affair. I'll send a stylist to help you prepare.'

He dressed, watching her, waiting for the inevitable argument, because India so often liked to find a flaw in his plans. But she stayed silent, her eyes on him, for so long that it didn't make sense.

'Okay?'

She nodded, but something was clearly wrong.

'What is it?'

Tightness began to coil in his gut. Guilt. They'd both wanted needed the release of their coming together, but was she regretting it now? It was a doubt he'd never felt with a woman before.

'It makes sense,' she said eventually, her eyes latching to his. 'If we're going to marry in a few weeks, it will be less… dramatic…if there's some evidence that we actually knew one another prior to the wedding. A date is a good idea.'

'I'm glad you agree.' Even when he'd half been looking forward to convincing her a little more…

'And in private,' he said, moving closer to the bed, his

whole body craving her, wanting to lie at her back and hold her close, to simply feel her pressed against him. 'At night, you will be mine, India. We'd be fools to ignore the one good thing this marriage has going for it.'

She swallowed and looked away, so he couldn't tell how she was feeling. 'Three good things,' she said, eventually, when he was about to turn and walk to the door. He waited for her to continue, his breath held.

'The babies,' she reminded him. 'If it weren't for them, we'd never have seen one another again. It's because of them that we're marrying.'

He nodded, and left the room, wondering at the hollow sensation in his gut that simply wouldn't quit.

'Who will be there tonight?' she asked, as the car slowed down at traffic lights, anxiety thickening her blood.

'Dignitaries, film stars, politicians, some diplomats and artists.' He spoke with cold detachment, as though they hadn't made love earlier, as though they were strangers who barely knew one another. 'The gallery is renowned throughout Europe and the Middle East.'

'Are these people your friends?'

'Some are,' he said, but she had the feeling he wasn't being completely honest with her. 'My cousin will be there—Astrid el Abdul. She is a few years younger than me, and a woman of great integrity. I will introduce the two of you. If I am busy, she will take care of you.'

Her smile was lopsided. 'I don't need to be taken care of—you might have forgotten but I'm quite experienced at mingling with strangers at fancy events.'

'The kind of mingling you indulged in in the past will not be tolerated here, remember?'

She looked away from him, her smile dying. 'So Astrid is actually some kind of babysitter for me?'

'If necessary, she will be.'

India bit down on her lip. 'I don't know what I can do to make you believe me,' she said softly, shaking her head at the futility of that. 'I was never that kind of escort.'

He stared at her, his eyes probing hers, and she waited, because for a moment it almost seemed as if he believed her, or wanted to believe her, and she desperately needed that. She didn't know how they could really make their marriage work if he bought into such lies about her. But after a moment, he shrugged, a careless, throwaway gesture, and looked to the window beyond her. 'It doesn't matter any more. We've put the past in the past. Our children are the future.'

But it did matter! India reached across to touch him, and his eyes dropped to the gesture, consternation on his face, so she withdrew her hand abruptly. Were there rules for this too? That they could touch in the bedroom, but not beyond it? Ice filled her heart. She looked away, nodding once, just as the car pulled to a stop outside a modern building on the edge of one of the canals she'd spied from the plane. It was illuminated by red spotlights, and enormous posters were hung from the windows proclaiming the benefit. A score of paparazzi stood waiting, roped off the event, kept separate from the guests.

His hand on her chin surprised her, and as he drew her face back to his she didn't resist. 'I have never wanted a woman as I've wanted you.'

'Is that supposed to make me feel good?'

'It's a start,' he said, with a frustrated jerk of his head. 'We're both working this out as we go along. I don't want to hurt you, but nor do I want to lie to you. I'm not going to pretend to feel something for you that I don't, I won't act as though I care for you or am falling in love with you, simply to placate you. I'm offering a relationship that works for me; you have to decide if it works for you.'

CHAPTER NINE

INDIA THOUGHT SHE'D attended fancy balls before, but she very quickly realised that nothing within her experience prepared her for something of this magnitude. The modern façade of the high-rise was exactly that—a façade—behind which a centuries-old building stood wrapped in a lush, overgrown courtyard, the gardens of which had been strung with fairy lights overhead, and, on the ground, covered in a delicate carpet of tea lights, so it looked like something out of *A Midsummer Night's Dream*. An orchestra played and, while their song was unified, they stood throughout the gardens: a cluster of three violinists here, a pianist there, an ensemble of flutists and a clutch of harpists, so that the delightfully ethereal music wafted and breezed on the wind—both all-consuming and delicate at the same time. The details took on a new importance to India as a sort of coping mechanism, and she immediately understood why Khalil had presumed their kiss at the bar in New York might have been photographed.

Here, he was the star of the ball, every eye on him at all times—which meant that every eye was also on her. It wasn't simply about attention, but also appraisal, as dozens of women eyed her with barely concealed envy.

So he was considered to be that much of a catch, huh? Well, she could see why, from the outside at least. He was devastatingly handsome, wealthy, powerful, and on the first night they'd met, he'd been charming—if, oh, so arrogant. But he was the last man on earth she would have chosen to marry if it weren't for their situation! She had to remember that. Only, when Khalil offered his arm, she placed hers in the crook of it, and a blade of desire pressed hard to her breast, so she forgot, for a moment, that she wanted to dislike him…

'I'm suddenly regretting the impulse to bring you here,' he muttered *sotto voce,* so her eyes skittled to his.

'Oh?' Her lips, painted red for the occasion, formed a perfect 'O' and his eyes dropped to them with obvious desire.

He swore softly, drawing her close. 'We won't stay long. It's only a matter of being seen together, then we can leave.'

'What if I'm having fun?'

'I promise you will have more fun alone with me.'

She smiled, and, despite the tangle of emotions pulling at her, surrendered to the sheer sensuality of being near him, of his words, and the power that came from knowing how much he wanted her. It was—for that moment—enough.

'We'll see,' she teased, and he laughed, a soft, throaty noise that made her ache to turn on her heel and slide right back into his car, to leave the crowds behind and be alone with this man. All night, just the two of them…

He caught her hand and lifted it to his lips, kissing the back of it as though he couldn't help himself. Flashes went off—not the paparazzi lenses that had snapped them outside, but the flashlights of phones every guest at the event carried.

'In New York, that would be considered very bad etiquette,' she said under her breath.

'The kiss, or the photos.'

'Both.' She slid him a sidelong glance. 'But I meant the photos.'

'Here too,' he agreed. 'Under ordinary circumstances, but you are the first woman I have been seen with publicly since my engagement ended, so it is natural that your appearance has sparked a flurry of fascination.'

India stared at him, his words not making sense at first. 'I'm sorry, did you just say...you were engaged?'

'Was, yes.'

'What? When? To whom?'

He lifted a brow at her numerous questions. 'Our engagement ended six months ago. It was a mistake.' His voice was stony suddenly, as though he were pushing her away physically. 'And this is not the place to discuss it.'

'Six months ago? So the night we met, it had only been four months—or just over three and a half, in fact,' she clarified, nodding slowly.

'So?'

So, she was a rebound girl. That night had been meaningless to him, even before Ethan had informed him of what he believed India to be. Until that moment, she hadn't realised how hard she'd been clinging onto the spark of what they'd shared, as though it stood in a little box outside normal time, just him and her and a connection that had formed spontaneously and urgently, that had actually meant something.

But it had been nothing. A chance to push his ex-fiancée from his mind, nothing more.

'Dance with me,' he murmured.

'Now?'

'Why not?'

'Because no one else is dancing.'

'We want the world to see us together, do we not?'

'I think your kiss accomplished that.'

He laughed, softly drawing her into his arms, the moon-light above cutting a pale silver swathe through the garden, so her dress sparkled like fairy dust.

'It was barely a kiss,' he reminded her. 'Just a chaste sign of affection.'

'Nonetheless, it will be all over Twitter by now.'

'Perhaps.' He shrugged, beginning to move in time to the music, his body's rhythm captivating hers, so she was dancing along with him even before she realised it. His eyes were the most fascinating shade of brown, and she found her gaze drawn to them, her mind solely occupied in the cataloguing of the flecks of gold. It was tempting to relax into the moment completely, but there was danger in letting down her guard with Khalil, so she forced her brain to keep working, her mind focussed.

'Why did you break up?'

He stiffened, his movements stopping for a moment, earning India's fascination. But at least he didn't ignore the question.

'It would never have worked.'

'That tells me precisely nothing.'

'As I intended.'

India considered that. 'Why? Is it a secret?'

'It is something I prefer not to think about, let alone discuss. And it is part of a past that doesn't affect us— nothing good can come of bringing it out into the open.'

It was India's turn to miss a step, so Khalil's arm tight-ened around her waist, offering necessary support.

'I believe most things benefit from being brought into the open, in fact.'

'Then let's talk about you,' he quietly cajoled, his words just a whisper in her ear. To anyone looking, they would have seemed like a couple so in love they couldn't stand to have any distance between them whatsoever, but for

India, their proximity was a convenient necessity—only at this distance could they speak so frankly without risk of being overheard.

'My response hasn't changed since the first night we met, you know. My life story isn't particularly interesting.'

'Let me be the judge of that.'

'Fine,' she sighed. After all, they were getting married. Of course they should spend time talking, getting to know one another better. Except, India had the strangest feeling that she already knew Khalil, even when there were clearly still so many secrets in his past. 'What would you like to know?'

His response was lightning fast. 'How did someone like you end up doing what you do?'

'A woman like me?' His hand lifted to the flesh at the top of her back, his fingers trilling over her spine slowly, so every cell in her body began to quiver with awareness.

'You are smart, India. You are clever, too, and yet because you are beautiful, you took a job that trades solely on your looks. Why?'

'That's a mischaracterisation, for a start. Making conversation with strangers from varied walks of life is not easy,' she responded with a tilt of her head.

He swayed her sideways, and though there was a crowd of people at the event, she was conscious only of Khalil; his overwhelming charisma absorbed her completely.

'For you, I think it would be.'

'Why do you say that?'

'For the reasons I enumerated already. You are smart and clever.'

Pleasure spread through her, the compliment disproportionately pleasing. She had to remind herself that tiny compliments from Khalil did nothing to erase his enormous insult.

'Thank you,' she murmured, her fingers toying with the hair at his nape on autopilot, so she wasn't even aware she was doing it.

'Who were you going to marry?'

He lifted a brow. 'I thought we agreed not to discuss my ex-fiancée,' he said with quiet determination.

'No, you decreed that we wouldn't discuss her, and because you are used to saying one thing and having it be obeyed, you think that counts as "agreement",' she said calmly, unaware of the way his lips curved in a quick, appreciative smile that he flattened almost immediately. 'But I didn't mean her, anyway. You have to marry before your coronation. I presume there was someone else you had decided to propose to, before this situation...unfolded?'

'No.' He moved his hand lower, down her spine, to the curve just above her bottom, his fingers splayed wide, holding her close to him so she was aware of his strength and hardness, so that she was aware of all of him. 'There was a shortlist.'

India couldn't help smiling at that, but it was a sad smile, pricked with remorse. 'I see,' she murmured. 'No wonder you're so...'

'So?' he prompted.

'Arrogant.' She lifted her shoulder unapologetically. 'You have a queue of women desperate to marry you. It wouldn't even occur to you that some women don't value marriage to you as the highest prize imaginable.'

'On the contrary,' he responded, and she couldn't tell if he was amused or annoyed. 'You made it very clear that this marriage is the last thing you want.'

'I feel sorry for the women who were hoping you'd turn to them,' she said. 'They'll be heartbroken.'

'I'm sure they'll get over it.'

Silently, India disagreed. If she had loved Khalil, and

thought he might want to marry her, she would have had a hard time moving on. He was incomparable. But she didn't say that to him—his ego didn't need any more stroking. His certainty spoke more of his belief that women were fickle and unfeeling. As though he couldn't comprehend true, unfaltering love. Why? What had happened to him? Was it because of his ex-fiancée?

'As for being arrogant,' he said, 'I think that has more to do with how I was raised than anything else.'

Curiosity had her gaze sharpening. 'And how were you raised?'

'With the certainty that I would be master of all I survey.' He said it in a jocular tone, yet India detected a hint of something beneath the surface.

'Specifics, please,' she murmured.

'What would you like to know?'

She cast about for one of the many questions that were swimming through her. 'Well, did you live at the palace, even as a boy? Or did your parents have somewhere a little less…intimidating…when you were younger?'

'The palace has always been my home.'

'So your parents live there now?'

'They do.'

'Where?'

'In the East Wing.'

'Of course.' She narrowly avoided rolling her eyes. 'So you see them often?'

'I see them as infrequently as you likely see your parents.'

Her step faltered, and her hand on his hip dug in a little, as though grabbing hold of something tangible. 'My parents are dead.' She offered a tight smile to put him at ease, as most people would feel regret at having made such a *faux pas.* Her heart ached, as always, because she missed her parents so much it was like a physical injury.

'When?'

Most people would also choose to sidestep the issue, but not Khalil. His insatiable need for answers overrode everything. And yet, despite her first reaction, India realised she wasn't upset to discuss her parents with him. If anything, she felt that talking about them now was a way of bringing them into her life. 'A little over a year ago. It was a car accident,' she forestalled his next question. 'They died immediately.'

'I'm very sorry to hear it. Were you close?'

India stopped dancing, pain lancing her now. 'Very.' Her voice was croaky; she looked away. 'I think we've done what we needed to here, don't you?'

But a muscle jerked low in his jaw and he didn't release her. 'My cousin Astrid lost her parents,' he said, stroking her back, the comforting touch almost kind, except 'kind' wasn't a word she would use to describe Khalil. 'She was much younger, so it is not really a comparison—she never really knew them actually, so it's more the idea of them she misses. It's a pain that doesn't seem to get easier.'

'No.' India nodded gently. 'It doesn't. At least, not in my experience.' She found herself pressing her cheek to his chest. Not looking at him made it easier to talk. 'My mother had actually been sick for a couple of years before the accident. Cancer. It was aggressive, so we were prepared for the worst. Though she'd been granted special permission to take a drug that wasn't approved for treatment, and it was helping. I thought I'd made my peace with losing her, but I hadn't. It was an awful time in my life.'

He kissed the top of her head and butterflies spread inside her, buzzing through her limbs. It was just an act, he was playing a part, but the effect of his attention was very, very real. She lifted her face to his, and when their eyes locked, it was as though nothing existed beyond them. Their past no longer mattered. Except it *did*, her brain interjected swiftly. Nothing about what she'd just revealed to Khalil changed a damned thing.

'Before my mother married my stepfather, we were alone, and I was lonely. Then, overnight, I had a father— a real one, who truly cared about me—and soon enough, a little brother for me to dote on.' Her smile was ethereal, so Khalil's gaze dropped to her lips.

'You have a brother?'

'Yes. I was very lucky. I had, for a while, the most perfect family.' She pulled her lips to the side, lost in thought.

He ran a finger over her cheek, saying nothing, promising nothing. What could he offer, anyway? He'd been completely honest with her. Love would have no part in their marriage, and it was love that had made her family perfect. Love between her mother and stepfather, and both parents and children. They had been a team. She and Khalil would never be that, but with luck, they could love their children enough to compensate. She had to cling to that hope because she had always sworn she would never get married unless she could find someone who made her as deliriously happy as her stepfather had her mother.

'Excuse me, Your Highness.' A servant appeared as if from nowhere. 'The Prime Minister is asking for you.'

A scowl—unmistakable and fierce—crossed Khalil's face. 'I'm sure he can wait until tomorrow.'

'He says it's important.'

'It's fine.' India took a step back, the appearance of the servant offering her a reprieve from their play-acting.

Khalil's frustration was palpable, though, and she understood it: he didn't like to be interrupted. 'Tell him I'll be a moment. There's someone I'd like to introduce India to first.'

* * *

Astrid was a very kind and thoughtful companion. She spoke flawless English, courtesy of having attended university in London, and while beautiful and immaculately dressed, she was also friendly enough to set India completely at ease.

'It's a whirlwind, isn't it?' Astrid laughed as India's eyes skimmed the crowd, mesmerised by the beautiful dresses and elegant guests.

'It really is. I don't know if I've ever seen anything so beautiful.'

'Then you should ask my cousin to take you to see the fireflies of the Athani Caves. They will captivate you more than you can imagine.'

'I've never seen a firefly.'

'At Athani, you will see thousands. They are blinding in their beauty.'

'I'm sure they are,' India said, almost wistfully, because she suspected Khalil would have little interest in taking her to some caves to see the insect life. After all, what would the point be? There was no chance of being photographed to substantiate their relationship somewhere so remote, and that was what this dating charade was all about—giving his people a chance to adjust to the idea of his girlfriend before she became his wife.

'Khal seemed to enjoy dancing with you. It's nice to see him happy again,' Astrid said with a gentle smile, flagging down a passing waiter. 'Would you like a champagne?'

'Just a juice would be great, thanks.'

Astrid gave the order to the waiter then turned her attention back to India.

'Was he ever unhappy?' India asked, feeling a hint of guilt for prying. After all, if Khalil didn't want to discuss his break-up then she shouldn't try to extort information from his cousin.

'Has he told you about Fatima?'

India hazarded a guess that this must be the name of his fiancée. 'His fiancée,' she said with a soft nod. 'He's mentioned her, in passing.'

'I see.' Astrid's manner changed, her expression growing more circumspect. 'It was a messy break-up. He wasn't himself afterwards. I was worried he might suffer the effects of her…choices…for a long time. But you seem to have brought him back to life, India, and for that I am most grateful.'

The waiter returned with two glasses of juice. India thanked him in his own language, having been listening to tutorials since arriving. After all, her children would speak this as their native tongue, so naturally she needed to learn the language also.

As their conversation moved on, India found herself dwelling on Astrid's final remark, surprised to realise how much she wished that were true—that she could have been responsible for bringing Khalil back to life. The truth was, though, he was still as cold as ever before; he was simply acting out a role tonight.

CHAPTER TEN

'I LIKED ASTRID very much.'

'You want to talk about my cousin, *now*?' he drawled, propping up on one elbow, feathering his fingers over her breast so she sucked in an uneven breath. And yet she smiled, and the dawn light filtering into his bedroom washed over India, bathing her in almost pure gold so her hair shimmered and her eyes shone.

'She's sweet,' India said. 'And funny.'

'Correct on both counts. She must have liked you too, because usually she is reserved with people she doesn't know well.'

'She wasn't at all reserved with me.'

'As I said, she must like you.'

India felt immeasurably pleased by that.

'She came to the palace when she was only a few months old; she is like my annoying younger sister,' he said with a grin that showed he wasn't serious. India thought of Jackson, and how much their sibling relationship had shaped her life. Even now, every decision she made was with him in mind. 'Her life has not been easy,' he continued quietly, his brows knitting together as he concentrated on his thoughts. 'She was bullied as a little girl, by some children at her school. My parents didn't realise at first. It was only after I read Astrid's diary—I was twelve—' he defended, 'that I understood what was going on.'

'Astrid was bullied?'

'She was different,' he said. 'She was royal, an orphan, and naturally quite shy. It was easy for her to be picked on.'

Indignation fired in India's belly. 'Children can be so horrible,' she said with anger.

'Yes.'

'What happened? Did she change schools?'

'No.' His lips curved into something like a grimace. 'I started taking her to school, walking her to class. I suppose I saw myself as her bodyguard. There was one particularly cruel little girl who used to call her—the equivalent in English would be "loner"—and I...had a word with her, about the wisdom of continuing to taunt Astrid in this manner.'

'You defended her,' India said, her heart fluttering at this show of character. It didn't surprise her—she could tell that Khalil had a form of moralism that was black and white—and yet imagining him as a young boy storming into Astrid's school to look out for her made India's chest swell.

'Until she learned to defend herself. And she did. Astrid grew strong at school, because she had to be.'

'You said she was married, but I noticed last night she wasn't wearing a wedding ring.'

'No.' His lips were grim and now when he looked at India, she had the sense he was holding something back.

'What happened?'

'She married the wrong man.' He hesitated a moment, an uncharacteristic pause. 'Her husband was charming at first. We were friends, I introduced them, so she trusted him from the start. It was a whirlwind romance, and Astrid fell in love hard and fast. They married months after meeting, but it was a disaster. Astrid fell pregnant quickly, and he began screwing around behind her back, sleeping with half of Khatrain's elite.'

Indignation burst through her. 'That's terrible!'

'So you can see why, when I had a chance to take something precious from him, I did not hesitate,' he murmured, his finger tracing an invisible circle over her shoulder, his eyes holding hers meaningfully.

It took India a moment to understand, and then realisation slammed into her like a stack of bricks. 'Are you saying Ethan Graves is her ex-husband?'

'Yes.'

India flopped onto her back, her brain exploding, her mind needing to process that without the intensity of his watchful gaze. 'And that's why you threw it in his face that you were taking me home,' she said with a quiet nod, her brain still making connections. 'Is it *why* you took me home?' she asked, angling her face back to his. His jaw was square in his face, his eyes darkened by emotions she couldn't comprehend.

'It was a part of it.' Hurt split her heart in two.

'I see,' she said unevenly, pushing back the sheet and standing, her pulse in overdrive. She had come to his room straight from the ball, and her gown was the only item of clothing she possessed here. She lifted it off the floor, shaking it so the skirt fell straight and she could step into it more easily.

'What are you doing?'

'Getting dressed.'

'Why?'

'Because it doesn't seem appropriate to walk through the palace in just my underwear.'

'Then stay here.'

'No.'

'Why not?'

'Damn it, stop interrogating me. Isn't it obvious? Do you really need to ask?'

'You are angry. For what reason?'

She bit down on her lip, shaking her head with impatience. They were so disconnected, her emotions nowhere near in tune with his.

'Because,' she blurted out, staring up at the ceiling. 'You—' but she clutched the rest of that close to her chest, something holding her back from answering him too honestly. 'It doesn't matter. I just want to be alone.' She yanked the dress on, pulling her hair over one shoulder so that the zip at the back wouldn't get caught. She could only get it halfway up in her anger, but she didn't care.

'Allow me.' His gravelled offer was the last thing she expected.

She shook her head. 'No. I don't want you to touch me right now.'

He lifted a sceptical brow, which only made her fury grow. She strode towards the door, hands balled into little fists.

His harsh laugh erupted through the room. 'Stop.'

She didn't.

She heard the rustle of sheets and his feet on the floor behind her, and as she reached the door he was there too, his palm pressing down on it. 'Don't run away from me.'

'Don't tell me what to do.' She whirled around to face him.

'Then stop acting like a child and tell me why you are upset.'

'You just admitted you used me to hurt Astrid's ex-husband, and you actually have to ask why that bothers me?'

He frowned at her, still clearly not comprehending.

'Forget about it,' she snapped. 'I don't want to discuss this. I knew you were callous and heartless when I first arrived here, I don't know why I let myself start to think that you were different.'

'Talk to me,' he demanded, his hand on the door forming a sort of barrier, enclosing India. She stared at a point beyond his shoulder.

'You have said worse things to me than anyone in my life. You have hurt me, you have demeaned me, and you have insulted me.' She looked at him square in the face now and had the satisfaction of seeing something fleck in the depths of his eyes. But was it guilt? Remorse? 'But that night...' She shook her head sadly. 'That night was... before all this. I know our babies weren't conceived out of love, but I had been telling myself they were at least conceived out of intense attraction, and some kind of spontaneous affection. I *liked* you, Khalil. I went home with you because I really, really liked you. I actually—'

She swallowed back the words but he leaned closer, his voice gravelled. 'You actually what?'

Forcing her eyes to meet his, she spoke honestly. 'It was my birthday that night. It was my first birthday since losing my parents and I was struggling. Then I met you and everything just lit up. I actually joked to myself that you were some kind of gift from me to me.' She rolled her eyes at the stupidity of the very idea. 'I didn't care that you were royal; I just wanted to be with you.' Emotions clogged her throat. 'I wasn't thinking about anything that night except for that. Liking you. But you were just using me for revenge.'

Her skin blanched, her eyes closing. 'And then you had the nerve to accuse *me* of being mercenary? You have been hanging that over my head since I got here, as though I was the one who turned that night into something sinister and cynical, but you're the one who chose to seduce me because of who I was with. You're the one who threw it in Ethan's face, even when we'd agreed I would make up an excuse, lie to him, to avoid insulting him. You did that because you wanted to hurt him, and instead, it hurt me. I lost my job because of what you did, and you didn't even care. You have all this, you wouldn't have any idea what it's like to need to work, to go from pay cheque to pay cheque. And all for what? So you could avenge Astrid? Do you think that's what she would have wanted? If she knew what you did, do you think she'd be proud of you?'

'She was devastated by their marriage breakdown.'

'As I am devastated by our marriage agreement,' India whispered. 'But I guess that doesn't matter. I'm no one to you, and never will be, right?'

He stared at the closed door for several seconds, her words slicing through him with all the intensity of a fierce sandstorm, and then he wrenched it inwards, striding to catch up with her. Of all the accusations she'd hurled at him, each had merit, but there was one that was pulling at him, so he found it hard to move. It had been her birthday. She'd chosen to spend it with him. It was such a sweet, lonely admission; how could it fail to touch something deep in his chest?

She went quickly, and was a long way down the corridor, yet he could have reached her easily if he'd wanted to. He let her go ahead, his heart pounding as he followed after. Even in anger, she exuded a classic elegance that was impossible not to notice, or admire.

She turned into the corridor that housed three guest suites, passing two guards stationed there as she went. They kept their eyes forward-facing, but as Khalil passed they bowed.

He strode past them without acknowledgement, reaching her door just as she went to close it.

'Wait,' he said gruffly, pressing his forearm against it, holding it ajar.

'Why? Is there anything more to say, Your Highness?'

He hated it when she used his title; it put distance between them, a distance he didn't want. 'Let me in.'

For a moment, he wondered if she was going to refuse—and what he would do if she did! Every bone in his body wanted him to speak with her some more, but he wasn't going to strong-arm his way into her suite if she was determined to keep him out. He stood where he was, something strange gripping his chest, a sense of concern he couldn't comprehend. Even when she stepped back to open the door wider, the worry didn't evaporate.

'Thank you,' he said, pacing into the room and putting his hands on his hips.

'What do you want?' She matched his gesture, hands thrust on hips, eyes glaring through his.

'I noticed you before I saw him,' he said, before he could stop himself—it was something he'd never wanted to reveal to her. And yet, faced with her obvious devastation, and the reasons for it, he knew he couldn't lie to her, even when some form of self-preservation was pushing him to. It would be better if she believed it had all been a ruse to make Ethan sweat, but that wasn't the sum total of why they'd come together.

'I saw you across the room and felt like I'd been smacked in the gut. I wanted you and I swore I'd have you, regardless of who you were with. Seeing it was Ethan was a way to kill two birds with one stone, I suppose. But that's not why I wanted you.'

She didn't respond, but her body was taut, her spine straight, shoulders squared. There was a defensiveness about her that made him ache, and it was all the worse because he'd done this to her. It was late in the day to realise how much he liked seeing her smile.

'Whether you were with Ethan or not, I would have wanted you, India. I would have done everything I could to take you home with me.'

The admission was wrenched from deep inside; he felt as though he was giving away a part of himself he had wanted to keep firmly boxed up.

'It doesn't matter,' she said softly, the words rich with sadness. His gut twisted.

'It clearly *does* matter. You are upset.'

'Yes.' She nodded curtly. 'I am. And a half-hearted explanation that, actually, you *were* kind of attracted to me after all doesn't change the fact that you used me. What other explanation is there for the fact you told him we were going home together?'

'I have already admitted I wanted to take something from him, something of value. I had no idea then that your date was simply an…arrangement.'

She closed her eyes.

'No, you didn't. You thought we were a couple, and you decided to take me from him. But it was never actually about me. It was about you and Ethan and Astrid.'

'You're not listening to me. I'm saying—belatedly—that I wanted you *before* I knew he was your date.'

'And I'm supposed to be flattered by that?'

'You're supposed to see that you're right—what we shared that night was about you and me, not him. No one else.'

'You waved our leaving together in his face!' she shouted. 'You hate this man. He has shown himself to be the worst of the worst, yes?' she demanded fiercely. 'What he did to Astrid was an abomination, I understand that.

But nothing excuses what *you* did to *me*. I didn't ask to be a part of any of this.'

'If my sole purpose was to hurt him, I could have bragged about taking you home and then dropped you back at your place. Spending the night together was unnecessary to finalise that part of my intentions.'

'Come on, Khalil. You're still a red-blooded man. You were hardly going to look a gift horse in the mouth, especially one giving themselves to you so freely.' She paused angrily, shaking her head. 'Not so "freely", of course. You believed there would be a charge at the end of the night.'

'Don't,' he ground out, irritation and impatience and anger all snapping through him. 'I'm trying to say that before Ethan sullied what we shared with his…revelation, I had one of the best nights of my life. Our babies were conceived out of something good. Something that was special to both of us, at the time.'

'But it wasn't.' She shook her head. 'It was brought about by hate. And if you don't believe me, let me show you how I know this to be true.'

His breath exploded from his lungs, angry and fast. His words were being twisted, and he had only himself to blame. Hadn't he intentionally misled her about that night? He had wanted to protect himself, and so he'd misled her as to the true reason he'd taken her home, but it had backfired, spectacularly. He would do anything not to have India feel like this.

'You have told me what Ethan did to Astrid. He is a horrible man, I agree. Despicable, untrustworthy, and mean.'

He dipped his head at her accurate assessment.

'And yet you believed him, about me,' she whispered.

His eyes narrowed as he recognised the devastation on her face.

'He told you I was a prostitute, and it didn't once occur to you to doubt his word.'

Khalil was not used to feeling in the wrong. His arrogance was born, primarily, from the fact he had excellent instincts and used them wisely. Her logic was, however, flawless.

'He sent me the agency listing,' Khalil pointed out, his voice ringing with a certainty he no longer felt. 'It wasn't only his word, but also the evidence.'

'Evidence,' she snarled, crossing her arms hard across her chest. 'That was no evidence. Not of what you're accusing me of, at least. I worked for an escort agency, yes. I went on dates with people who, for whatever reason, needed a companion for the evening. One of my favourite clients was an eighty-two-year-old man whose wife died ten years ago. We would go to the theatre together once a month. Do you think I was having sex with him, too?' She shook her head angrily. 'Only you could take what is a perfectly legitimate job and turn it into something else.'

'I had you investigated, after that night.'

'I know. You spied on me. I remember.'

'I wanted to know if it was true. I hoped—I wanted to believe—'

But she didn't let him finish. 'If you had me investigated then you must know that I do not go home with the men I date.'

'There was no evidence of that,' he said warily. 'But there was plenty of evidence that many of the women who are hired out by Warm Engagements do in fact bed their clients.'

India gasped. 'That's against the rules.'

He stared at her, the response more telling than anything else could be. Light blinded him, and he turned away, so that she wouldn't see on his face the comprehension that was dawning—the realisation that he might have seriously misjudged her this whole time.

'And you didn't know that then,' she reminded him softly, her voice trembling as she returned to the original point with effortless focus. 'The morning after we slept together, you had only Ethan's word and my agency listing to go off. You wouldn't let me explain myself. You wouldn't believe me.'

No, he wouldn't. Because everything she'd said had reminded him of Fatima. He'd been fooled once, badly, and he would never forget what that had cost him. The idea of being duped all over again had made him react harshly—more harshly than he should have.

'You believed that horrible man over me, and I will never forget that. Not ever. Not when we make love. Not when we marry. Not when we become parents.' Tears sparkled on her lashes and he stood perfectly still, because the alternative was to go to her and pull her into his arms, hold her against him and beg her to forgive him. To forgive him? Khalil's compass no longer faced in a recognisable direction. Confusion swamped him. 'I really, really hate you right now, Khalil. Please, just leave me alone.'

CHAPTER ELEVEN

STANDING BESIDE HIM and not speaking was a form of agony, so too their obvious desire to avoid touching. The horse race was well attended, reminding her of news footage she'd seen of Ascot or Australia's Melbourne Cup, well-dressed men and women piling into the racecourse, prepared for a day of fun and adventure.

In other circumstances, India might have enjoyed the day, but the argument she'd had with Khalil—several days ago now—was still festering in the back of her mind. She'd tried to make her peace with what had happened, but the more she thought about it, the angrier she became, the more hurt.

That he would trust someone like Ethan Graves over her!

Hearing him speak about the other man's conduct, she could perfectly understand why Khalil had wanted to hurt him, but to allow her to become collateral damage?

'After the morning's events, I will have to leave you for a time. It's tradition for me to ride a lap of the course.'

She nodded without looking at him. One of the servants who'd helped her dress for today had already explained the procedure. 'Fine.' She didn't look at him.

'India,' he sighed. 'This has to stop.'

She compressed her lips.

'The doctor said you are not supposed to be upset.'

She fidgeted her fingers at her sides. 'I'm fine.'

'You have not been fine for days.'

It was true. They'd seen each other multiple times and she'd barely spoken to him. She wasn't trying to prolong their argument, only she had no idea what to say. Her heart was in tatters, her mind furious. She hadn't realised how desperately she'd been clinging to the idea that their first night together had been about something else, something completely separate from all of this.

She'd been wrong.

She'd been a pawn to him, a dispensable, worthless tool to inflict pain on a man who didn't even deserve his consideration.

It was impossible to forgive.

'Do you blame me?' she asked, looking up at him finally.

He swallowed hard. 'No.' Surprise stirred in her eyes. 'I don't blame you at all, India.'

She looked away quickly, emotions rioting. They were just words, but they moved through her in a way that was terrifying, so she needed to remember why she was so angry with him, why this was all such a disaster.

His fingers curled around her cheek, turning her to face him. 'We can leave.'

'We *can't* leave,' she demurred. 'We are in a royal box with cameras trained on us. You have to ride your lap of honour or whatever. We're stuck.' And she didn't just mean here, at this fancy horse race. They were stuck in every sense of the word, trapped by one night, for the rest of their lives.

He shook his head. 'We can leave.'

She didn't respond this time. Aware of the cameras, she lifted her hand to his, removing it from her cheek. To the outside world, it was a moment of shared affection, but for India, she simply needed him to stop touching her. She felt too much, even then, swaying towards him as though there were an inevitability to their being together, when that wasn't—couldn't be—true.

'And then what, Khalil?' She let the words fall between them, rock boulders into choppy water. 'Tomorrow there'll be another event, and another the day after that. This is my life now.' She swallowed hard, but a lump in her throat made it almost impossible to breathe. 'There's no sense trying to run away from it.'

He wanted to ride his horse as he did in the desert. He wanted to lean low to the stallion's mane and whisper words of urgency, to kick his side three times, fast, so that the beast took flight, carrying him as though he would make for the horizon at any moment. He wanted to ride far away from here, and this. But not all of this. His eyes sought her without his permission, landing on the royal box and scanning the seats until he found her. She was still standing, as they'd been together, her eyes trained on him. Even at this distance, he could feel her tension, her stress and strain.

There's no sense trying to run away from it.

He turned the corner, so his back was to her now, and he resisted—just—a desire to cast a glance over his shoulder.

She was right. They couldn't run away. Though the desert beckoned him, there were no answers there. It was no longer an escape path for him. Khalil's place was here, with her. They were having children together, and she had agreed to marry him. In a matter of months, he would be crowned Sheikh of Khatrain and all the responsibilities of ruling this great country would fall to him.

They would live together as man and wife and they

would need to forge a path that didn't involve so much recrimination.

He couldn't hurt her again.

He sat up straighter, the clarity almost blinding. He hated himself for what he'd done to her. More clarity. He didn't want her to feel as she did now. He wanted to make her happy. He wanted a fresh start.

Everything exploded inside him at once, so now, with renewed purpose, he did speed his horse up, dismounting as soon as he'd finished the lap. He lifted one arm into the air in a gesture of acknowledgement; the crowd roared their applause. He barely heard it. He took the steps two at a time, pushing past his security into the private enclosure, taking the next staircase until he reached the royal box.

It was empty.

'Are you better?'

He stormed into her room without so much as knocking, but India had expected that. She turned to face him slowly, her face pale.

'India?' His voice was tortured. 'Are you okay? Is it the babies?'

A sense of guilt formed in her gut. It hadn't even occurred to her that he'd be genuinely concerned, nor that he'd think the note she'd left pleading 'a headache' might indicate anything more severe.

'I'm fine,' she said with a shake of her head.

'"Fine" again?' he demanded, crossing to her and pressing his palm to her forehead. She pulled away, but he put a hand on her hip, holding her close. 'What is it? Do you need the doctor?'

She shook her head. 'It was just a headache. From the heat, I think. I feel better now. I've had some water and rested a little.'

His eyes scanned her face with care. 'I'm glad to hear it.'

She swallowed, looking away from him. 'You shouldn't have come back early. I didn't mean to spoil your fun.'

'I wanted to check on you,' he explained slowly, as if lost in thought.

'It wasn't necessary.'

He sighed with exasperation. 'Actually, it is perfectly necessary. We need to talk.'

Her eyes swept shut on a wave of dread. 'What about?'

'This marriage.'

She felt as though she were approaching a precipice with no idea if she were to be thrown off it or not. 'What about it?'

'This won't work.'

Her heart stammered almost to a stop.

'I don't want to see you like this. I don't want to make you miserable. You don't deserve this.'

Her eyes flared wide. 'Are you…saying…you don't want to get married?'

He stared at her, silent, shocked. 'No,' he said, firmly. 'I don't mean that.'

She frowned. 'So, what?'

'The fact that you're pregnant means we must marry. There's no other way. I can't order the twins into the line of succession if they're born out of marriage. We've discussed that.'

'Then I don't understand what you're saying now.'

'I want this marriage to work. More than that, I don't want to fight with you. It has to stop. Neither of us can live like this.'

Her heart stammered, because he was right, but it was still so clear that he thought the worst of her. Even after all that she'd said to him, pleading with him to accept her version of events, he still didn't. And he never would.

'I want us to start over. I want us to focus on the good between us—the babies we are to raise—and nothing else. I want us to remember that there is chemistry here and that we can make whatever future we want for ourselves. But most of all, I don't want to see you sad and miserable and to know that I am the cause of that.'

His words, on some level, were important—she needed to hear them. But at the same time, they were just a further reminder of how false all this was.

'I want you to be happy.'

Her smile was weak. 'That's very kind of you.'

'Damn it, it's not kind. I have been the exact opposite of kind, please don't say otherwise. But I do want to fix this, India, and I have every intention of succeeding.'

Her stomach squeezed. 'Why?'

Silence fell, thudding around them, and finally, he spoke. 'Our children deserve that we at least try, don't they?'

'But how do we do that? After everything that's gone between us?'

'Have dinner with me tonight.'

'We have an event.'

'We'll skip it. It doesn't matter. This is more important.'

Something fluttered in her chest. But hope refused to settle. 'I don't think a dinner is going to solve this.' Whatever good he claimed lay between them, there was bad, too, and it stretched unendingly.

'Isn't it worth, at least, the attempt?'

Her eyes probed his, her heart frozen in her chest, her nerves firing disjointedly. Was he right? Did they owe it to their children to at least attempt to form a truce of sorts?

'Where?' she said, after a beat.

Satisfaction arranged his features. 'Leave the details to me. I'll meet you here, at eight.'

* * *

In the end, he sent a servant instead, a man dressed in a suit who greeted India one minute after the hour. India wore a simple dress—the same one she'd brought with her from America—and teamed it with a pair of sandals. She'd left her hair out, flowing loose down her back in voluminous waves. The servant took her away from the guest suites and through the palace, a circuitous route that she would have no hope of backtracking if she were forced to make her own way. Eventually, they emerged into a courtyard, and, beyond it, a large open space that housed a gleaming black helicopter.

Khalil stood beside it, his arms crossed, his eyes watchful.

She was a mix of nerves and anticipation, but it was anticipation that was at the fore as she moved towards the vehicle, the servant forgotten, nothing penetrating her mind now but this man and her awareness of him.

'Good evening, India.'

His voice wrapped around her, warmer than the night air. 'Khalil,' she responded in kind, dipping her head in a nod, earning a smile from him.

'After you.' He gestured to the rear doors of the helicopter.

She hesitated.

'Is there a problem?'

She sent him a sidelong glance. 'Well, I've never been in one before,' she said with a slight laugh.

'There's a first time for everything.'

He was right, and their marriage would be like this too. It would be a first for them both, and they would need to learn a lot as they went. Screwing up her courage, she stepped into the helicopter. And though she was braced for it to be luxurious, the sheer decadence of the interior nonetheless took her breath away. From the plush white leather seats to the wood grain details, to the bar fridge in the centre that boasted an array of expensive champagne, she felt as though she'd entered the twilight zone.

'Would you like a drink?'

'Mineral water?'

He nodded, indicating that she should take a seat on the long bank of three at the rear of the helicopter. She did so, fastening her seat belt while he retrieved a couple of bottles of water.

A moment after he took the seat beside her, the rotor blades began to spin, and the door was slammed shut by a servant.

She jumped, so he laughed softly. 'Relax, *azeezi*.' He leaned closer to her. 'It's perfectly safe.'

'It's probably very normal for you,' she murmured. 'But this is a big deal for me.'

He put his arm along the back of the chair, his fingertips casually brushing her shoulder. 'Try to enjoy the experience.'

As it turned out, her nerves settled as the helicopter lifted into the air. Or perhaps they just became focussed on another element of the night. His fingers moved softly over her skin, sending little sparks and shock waves through her, so that within moments she'd forgotten that they were in the air in a machine that could hardly be described as aerodynamic. A moment later, the view drew her attention, so she shifted, closer to the window, her eyes chasing the incredibly beautiful city, so that Khalil stared at her, his eyes observing every shift on her face, all the fascination and wonder dancing in her features.

The helicopter ride took twenty minutes. They passed the city and tacked further south, before moving inland, covering a vast expanse of desert that finally gave way to a gentle mountain range.

The helicopter set down at the foot of it, and then the doors were opened.

'This is...the middle of nowhere,' she said with an uneven laugh.

'Not quite.'

'Where is it, then?'

'The Athani Mountains.'

She blinked, excitement bursting through her. 'The fireflies?'

'Astrid suggested it.'

India grinned. 'I've never seen them before.'

'She said that too. I thought a new chapter in our relationship required a new experience.'

'Two,' she corrected. 'The helicopter and the fireflies.'

'Even better.' He kissed the back of her hand, his eyes holding hers. 'I want to make this work, India.'

Her heart pounded hard against her ribs, and she nodded. 'I know that.' A sigh whooshed through her, as finally she reconciled herself to this decision. 'I do too.'

It felt more meaningful than when she'd agreed to marry him. That had been logistical, this was more. It was a statement of intent, a promise to make this work, to be good to one another, to find a way to parent their children together that didn't involve navigating a warzone; to be a family.

She slipped her shoes off as she exited the helicopter, transferring them to her other hand, so that it was easier to walk across the cool desert sand. Khalil did likewise, catching her hand in his, lacing their fingers together. She blinked up at him then wished she hadn't, because the moon was shining on him like a spotlight, making him appear larger, and like the only person in her world.

A new start was good, but it was a mistake to get too

carried away. This was still essentially a business arrangement. He needed a wife, he needed heirs, and she was pregnant with his twins. She wanted her children to grow up in a family, she wanted his support, and, yes, she needed his financial help. There were reasons for them to enter into this marriage—a marriage neither would even be contemplating if it weren't for the unique circumstances that were playing out.

This wasn't love.

It wasn't special.

It was—

'Oh, wow.' She stopped walking about twenty yards from the entrance to the caves. A swarm of fireflies danced past them, their delicate, ethereal beauty shimmering in the night sky, their little bodies aglow with what looked like embers. 'They're—incredible.'

'Wait for it,' he said, squeezing her hand and drawing her with him, nearer to the caves. Once inside, she saw what he meant. Here, they were everywhere, flying through the tunnels, creating enough light to easily see by. They ignored India and Khalil, exploring the ancient cave walls instead.

'They are spread throughout the kingdom, but this is the most numerous collection. It's the perfect environment for them, the right climate and light, the best food source.' He hadn't relinquished her hand. 'When I was a young boy, it was my favourite thing to do with Astrid. We would come to these caves whenever we could, and watch them fly around. I would try to catch them, but as soon as I did their lights would go dim, as though they were hiding from me. I found it hard to reckon with that, at the time. Admiring them so much I wanted to grab some, to take home with me, but realising that if I did so, I would lose what I had loved.'

'A predicament,' she murmured, imagining him as a child. 'Was there no way to bring some to the palace?'

'Perhaps, but my parents did not encourage it. They reminded me that everything has a place and theirs was here.'

'Your parents sound very wise.'

'They are.'

'You didn't answer me, the other night. I asked how often you see your parents. Are you close to them?'

'I admire them very much.'

She pulled a face. 'That's not exactly an answer.'

He laughed. 'You're right. We are as close as we can be, given the circumstances.'

'What circumstances?'

'I was sent away to school when I was thirteen. I finished high school as a boarder. I missed them, and I changed a lot, in the time I was gone. Afterwards, I went to university, then did a rotation in the military. So for many years there, I hardly saw them. But they're good people, and my father has been an excellent sheikh.'

'Is it tradition for royal children to be sent away?'

'Yes.'

She stopped walking. 'How strong a tradition?'

He grimaced. 'Strong. But not unbreakable. If you do not wish for our children to leave home, then we can arrange an alternative.'

Her heart split. There was so much in that sentence to unnerve her! 'Our children', 'home', and his willingness to be flexible, to accommodate her needs. It was beyond what she'd expected.

'I can't even think about it yet,' she said with a shake of her head. 'It sounds like the last thing I would want. I know that I could never have been separated from my parents at that age.'

'Did you enjoy high school?'

'Yes.' She smiled. 'I had a good group of friends and I loved studying.'

'Was it not something you wanted to pursue, after high school?'

'What?'

'Studying.'

'Oh.' She frowned. 'I did. I went to college for a couple of years.'

It was obviously something he hadn't expected her to say. 'What degree did you undertake?'

'Economics. I dropped out before I could finish.'

'Economics?' His brows shot up.

She laughed. 'What? You don't think it suits me?'

'I just— had no idea.'

'I've always loved economics with a crazy passion.'

'Why?'

'Because it's so visceral. People think it's dry and boring, but they don't understand that it's the framework of our civilisations. Societies are made and shaped by economic policy, all of our programmes for social justice are made possible by the economic forethought of the government. Economic strategies have the power to save lives, enrich whole societies and make fundamental differences to the world—from lowering crime rates in traditionally impoverished areas to expanding healthcare.' Her eyes grew shimmery as she spoke and her cheeks were flushed. 'It's the cornerstone of all societies, it's the underpinning of who we are. I am fascinated by it.'

'Then why did you leave your degree?'

She contemplated not answering, but it was no big secret. Her eyes flicked to his, then away again. 'My mom got sick. I wanted to be closer to her.' She toyed with her fingers. 'And college is expensive.'

'They couldn't afford it?'

'Not really. Not that they ever said that, but I knew what her treatment was costing. I didn't want to risk that she would walk away from her medical needs to keep me in school. The bills were enormous. They needed to dip into our college funds to pay for them.' She lifted her shoulders defensively. 'I came home and helped out around the house, got a job doing secretarial stuff so I could contribute—it wasn't much but even just paying for groceries relieved some of their stress.' India didn't see the way Khalil's expression changed, the look of pity that softened his features. 'And then they died, and there was just Jackson and me, and a mountain of bills—'

'Your brother?'

'Yes.' She smiled as she thought of him. 'He was offered his college placement, right before they died. They were so happy. Medicine's all he's ever wanted to do. Even as a boy, he used to walk around with this little toy med kit, asking to listen to our heartbeats all the time.' Her expression was laced with nostalgia, her eyes sparkling with the warmth of her memories. 'Then Mom got sick and he became even more determined. All he wants to do is help people get better.' She shook her head wistfully. 'I swore I'd do whatever I could to send him through school.'

His eyes closed as he stopped walking. 'And let me guess. His degree will cost one hundred thousand dollars?'

She nodded. 'I should have told you that's what I needed that amount for.'

'You were under no obligation to tell me anything.' He looked away again, so she barely caught his muttered oath. 'But I should have asked.'

'Would it have changed anything?'

He turned to face her, lifting his hand and catching her hair, his eyes on hers. 'It would have helped me understand you better.'

* * *

It was such a specific—and low—amount, given her bargaining position. All this time he'd been thinking of her as mercenary, just like Fatima, when she'd given him incontrovertible proof that money was not—and never had been—a driving force for her. Why hadn't he queried that at the time? Why hadn't he asked her why she needed precisely one hundred thousand dollars? Why hadn't he pushed her, when he'd asked about her job, and her reasons for doing what she did?

She hadn't said she 'wanted' one hundred thousand dollars—she'd said she 'needed' it. He'd pushed that aside at the time but now he saw the desperation behind her plea, and the embarrassment she felt at asking for such a paltry sum, and was furious with himself for being so thoughtless. Anger had blinded him and he'd failed to see her predicament. Or had he simply not wanted to see it?

He had taken everything at face value because it had suited him to think the worst of her. It had suited him to see her as another Fatima, to believe she was just the same, driven purely by money, when the more the heard from India, the more he wondered if, actually, everything she did was driven by love.

CHAPTER TWELVE

'TELL ME ABOUT your parents?'

She considered that as he reached up and held back a particularly long and spindly branch of the pomegranate tree.

'Thank you,' she murmured, inhaling the intoxicating fragrance of the citrus grove as they walked, early in the morning, before the sun was too high, through the kitchen gardens. In the distance, a team of servants had scattered, carrying out their work separately but in harmony—some picking fruit, vegetables and herbs for the day's meals, others tending to the garden. Yet despite their presence, India and Khalil were virtually alone. This walk had become a habit of theirs in the week since visiting the wonders of the Athani Caves. Neither had discussed it, but it seemed to happen regardless, and it had become a highlight for India. She relished these opportunities to be alone with Kahlil, to speak with him, to brush her hand against his, to feel his nearness and to realise that they were walking side by side—into a future they would share. It was a different togetherness from what they shared in bed. That was primal and animalistic, driven by an insatiable chemical need to come together. This was slower, more exploratory, as though each were walking a tightrope towards trust and acceptance, trying to find their way to solid ground without falling.

'What would you like to know?' She plucked a lemon blossom from a tree, bringing it to her nose. The aroma was delightfully sweet.

'What did your mother do?'

'She was a teacher,' India said. 'And very passionate about it.'

'And your stepfather?'

'A librarian.'

'Did they meet at school?'

'No, at our local library, actually.' She swished the lemon blossom between her fingertips before passing it to Khalil to appreciate. 'After my father left us, we moved around a bit. Mom struggled with rent, and work—I was only little. It was a very hard time in our lives. I was too young to remember much of it. I know there were times when we were living in a car, eating from food banks.' She shook her head, oblivious to the way Khalil stared at her, his features frozen, hanging on her every word, painting the picture of the life she described. 'Then, one day, we settled, for a while, in Brooklyn. She had a friend from school who lived there—Juanita—who was going to Australia for a year's work. She offered Mom the house on really cheap terms—basically no rent, just the upkeep. It was such a gift—a real opportunity for Mom to claw her way out of poverty. We didn't have much, just a suitcase, and I was an avid reader, even at that age. So Mom would take me to the library, almost every day. And while I was checking out the books—'

'She was checking out the librarian?' he prompted, lifting a thick, dark brow.

'Something like that.' India laughed. 'Dad—I call him "Dad", because he raised me—was so kind. The opposite to my biological father. And he doted on us. He helped Mom get a contract with a local school, even though her work experience had been patchy for a few years. I enrolled in the same school, which meant childcare was easier. And before Juanita came back from Australia, they were married, so we moved in together. They were such a great couple. Anyone who knew them adored them. They were so much fun to be around. Dad was a total dork. He had theme songs for our family, and he'd randomly burst into song when we were out in public, like at the mall. I used to be mortified, but now, that's one of my favourite memories.'

'He sounds unique.'

'Yeah, he was.'

'And your biological father?'

'A total non-event.' She shrugged, the pain in her chest ever-present, even though her birth father didn't deserve that. 'He blew in and out of my life from time to time, when it suited him, but never for long, never with any reliability, and the older I got, the less he knew how to be with me, how to speak to me. Eventually, he stopped coming altogether.'

'And I take it he did not support your mother financially?'

She poked out her tongue. 'Not even a little. He was the worst.'

He stopped walking, a frown on his face. 'India...'

'What is it?'

'I'm very grateful that you came here, to tell me about your pregnancy. I can see how hard it must have been for you, not knowing how I would react, not knowing if I would be like your biological father or your actual father.'

Her heart lifted at his distinction. Despite the fact English was his second language, he had understood the nuance perfectly.

'It *was* hard,' she agreed with a nod, moving towards him and linking their fingers. Sparks flew through her and her heart lifted, but there was always a dark spot within it, a weight that pressed her down to earth. Knowing what he believed her capable of sat like a stone in her gut. She closed off her mind to it, ignoring the threat of an aching pain, wanting to feel only the good and warmth of the morning. 'But worth the risk, I think.'

'I think so too.' His smile blasted light into her world; she returned it without hesitation. 'What about your parents?'

He reached for a flower as they passed by a tree that India didn't recognise. Fragrant with a small blue fruit, the blossoms a pale pink.

'What about my parents?'

'When will you tell them about all this?'

'When you have agreed to marry me.'

She blinked slowly. 'Haven't I agreed?'

'Provisionally.'

India's hand curled over her stomach as she remembered the negotiations they'd had when she'd first arrived in the country. Back then, she'd pushed for a delay, and part of that had included reminding Khalil that the first trimester was a high-risk time in gestation. But the idea of anything happening to the twins made her feel as though she were going to pass out. She couldn't bear it.

'So after twelve weeks,' she said slowly, 'you'll tell them.'

'And we'll announce our marriage.' He nodded. 'If my calculations are correct, that's next week.'

Her cheeks flushed with warmth. 'Yes. Wednesday.'

He nodded, turning away from her, resuming their walk, but at a gentle pace so India found it easy to keep up.

'The wedding will take place Friday evening. Is there anyone you'd like to invite?'

She thought of Jackson, and how strange it would be to marry without him, and yet, at the same time, she didn't want to make a big deal out of what was essentially a convenient arrangement.

'No. No one.'

'Not your brother?'

She glanced at Khalil, wondering how he knew exactly what she was thinking. 'It would feel like lying to him. I don't think I can do that. It's not real.'

'Lying how?'

She sighed. 'We grew up in the same home. We saw what our parents were like, how madly in love, and what a perfect pair. He wants the same things I do—love, happily ever after, you know, the whole deal. I don't know how he'll…when I tell him…'

Khalil frowned. 'You haven't told him?'

'No. We were waiting, remember?'

'But now?'

'Soon.' She nodded. 'I'll have to tell him soon.'

Khalil stared at her as though there were a thousand things he wanted to say, his brows drawn together with obvious non-comprehension, but he let it go, relying on her instincts. She was glad. She didn't want to explain about Jackson, and how she'd always been protective of her younger brother; she didn't want to go into the details of why she didn't want to worry him. She knew he'd be disappointed in her, and for her, and she couldn't bear that.

'Then we will keep the ceremony small: just us, my parents and Astrid.'

'What was your other wedding going to be like?'

A muscle jerked in his jaw, and she could see the topic gave him little pleasure. 'Big.'

'As in, lots of people?'

'Yes.'

She lifted a brow, her tone lightly teasing. 'You're being evasive.'

'Am I?'

She laughed, despite her frustration. 'Obviously. If you don't want to talk about it, just say so; I'll understand.'

He expelled a harsh breath. 'I will talk about anything you wish. But do I need to elaborate?'

The problem was she'd asked simple, 'yes' or 'no' questions. She changed her approach. 'How many people would have come to that wedding?'

'Two thousand.'

She gasped. 'You can't be serious?'

'Yes.'

She bit down on her lip. 'Is it going to be a problem that our wedding is so understated? Perhaps your parents will expect something more substantial?'

'The size of the wedding had nothing to do with my parents.'

She considered that. 'Nor with you?'

'No.'

'So your fiancée wished to invite all those people.'

'Yes.'

'What happened with the two of you? Why did you break up?'

Khalil stopped walking, his hands on his hips as he stared directly ahead. Tension radiated off him in waves. India studied him, knowing she should give him a way 'out', tell him it didn't matter. But curiosity was burning through India, eating her alive.

Finally, he spoke. 'Fatima is very beautiful, sophisticated, clever, and witty. She made me laugh effortlessly with her dry commentary on our mutual acquaintances. My experience with women, before Fatima, was limited to brief affairs. It had never occurred to me that I might fall in love with a woman, because that is simply not how it's done for us. My parents' marriage was arranged by their parents, as was their parents' before them.'

India could barely breathe, and pricks of light filtered through behind her eyes.

'She is also very, very ambitious.'

'And that's a bad thing?'

'No, of course not. But her ambition was solely for wealth and power.'

'Then I suppose it's fortunate she fell in love with a sheikh.'

'She didn't love me.' The words were spoken quietly, but with all the force of a freight train barrelling towards her. 'And she taught me an important lesson about love that I will never forget. Love made me weak. Believing myself in love with her blinded me to all her flaws. I stopped seeing her as a real woman. I idealised her. If I hadn't, I might have anticipated her behaviour. I might have at least known what she was capable of.'

India's lungs were filled with a rush of hot air. She tried to expel it, drawing breath from deep within. He was speaking about another woman but his indictment of love was like a weight on her chest. 'What did she do?'

'What Fatima cared about most in the world was money.' He spat the word with derision, and even though he was speaking about another woman, her tummy swirled. She knew instantly that she'd been tarred with the same brush the morning after they'd slept together—what else could explain the level of his venomous anger? 'My personal wealth is no secret. Separate to the royal income, my family has several businesses and holdings abroad. When it came time to negotiate our marriage contract, she asked for a king's ransom.'

Just as India had.

Heat stung India's ears and she felt nausea spread through her. She pressed a quivering hand to her brow, nodding, silently encouraging him to continue even when a wave of guilt at having asked him for *anything* made it difficult to think straight.

'I had no interest in the negotiations. To me, they were a triviality. Because I was in love.' He spat the word scathingly. 'I left the work to my lawyers; that was a mistake. If I was too emotionally invested, they were not nearly enough. They refused many of her requests, argued over things I would never have cared about. The negotiations stretched on and things between Fatima and me grew tense.'

India pulled her lips to the side in a gesture of deep thought. 'But surely you and she could have talked about it—'

'She would never have showed her hand to me. She wanted me to think our wedding was all about love for her too. And fool that I was, I believed that. If the wedding had happened, she would have had access to anything she wanted. It wasn't necessary for her to do it.'

She didn't need to prompt him. It was obvious that he had disappeared through a time tunnel; he was back in the past, reflecting on the events as they'd happened.

'Negotiations soured. She presumed I knew and had done nothing to salvage them. To punish me, she had an abortion.'

India's lips parted on a noise of shock and horror. 'No.' The word drained out of her.

His face was ashen. 'At least, that's what she said. I don't know if she made it up to wound me. She certainly hadn't told me she was pregnant, but that doesn't mean...' He shook his head, as if that could wipe his grief and worry. 'I have been tormented by guilt. If her claim is true, then the negotiations were responsible for the death of my baby. I couldn't protect my own child.'

But I'll protect these.

A frisson ran down her spine, as understanding shifted in her mind. It was why he'd fought so hard for her to stay in Khatrain, why he needed to see and be near her, to ensure nothing happened during this pregnancy.

'Your fiancée was responsible, no one else.'

'I would have walked over fire to save that baby.'

The sadness in his statement was gut-wrenching. She nodded slowly, tears making her eyes sparkle. 'I know that.' Because that was exactly what he was doing this time around. From the moment he'd heard of her pregnancy he'd done everything he could to draw her into his life, to be sure these babies were cared for. Ultimately, that was what he cared about—making sure history didn't repeat itself, in any way, shape, or form.

'You must hate her.'

He made a sound that was halfway between a gruff laugh and a sigh of disbelief. 'I do. She is the worst of the worst.'

Love had turned to hate; he'd never love again. He'd said that, over and over, and she'd wondered if it was truly possible to live without love, but now it was as if he were whipping her with his words, the very idea tearing something vital and irreplaceable apart inside her, because she understood. She understood *why* he couldn't contemplate loving someone again. He'd loved, he'd trusted, and he'd been burned—the kind of burned from which one didn't recover. What he'd been through was too much. He was broken.

Only, she desperately didn't want him to be. Her mind was spinning too fast, trying to make sense of a conundrum, but attempting to reach the answer was as difficult as catching soap in the bath. Her brain wouldn't work.

'I was so angry with you that night.' He stopped walking, staring at her. 'After Ethan called me, and said what he did, all I saw was Fatima. I swore I'd never be fooled by a woman again and, in that moment, it was so easy to believe the worst. I was furious—with myself, with you, with the world.'

India's lungs were expanding and contracting without catching air. She felt faint.

'I get it,' she said, slowly, her voice thick. 'I didn't then, but knowing what you went through—'

He lifted a hand, as if to touch her cheek, then dropped it. 'What I went through with Fatima was a nightmare, but it was with Fatima, not you. I should have given you a chance to explain. I should have believed you. God knows I wanted to.'

She looked away, wondering at the mixture of pleasure and pain that was lancing her.

'I have been fighting myself ever since you arrived in Khatrain—for longer, if I'm honest—wanting to believe you, wanting to listen to you, but knowing that listening is a fast track to being lied to.'

It made sense, and, more than that, it showed her how awful his heartbreak must have been, the first time around. She lifted a hand to his chest, sympathy colouring her eyes. 'I'm so sorry for what she did to you.'

'When you told me about your pregnancy, all I could think was that I had to act to protect our baby. I think about that every day, wondering if I missed some vital sign, if I had paid more attention, would things have been different? I don't mean that I wish to have married her, only that for her to have gone to the lengths she did...what did I miss? What could I have done differently?' He lifted his shoulders at the rhetorical question. 'So when you arrived, I swore I would miss *nothing*. I had to keep you here, to know that you were safe and well, that our baby, or babies, as it turned out, were fine. Fear drove me to act in a way I'm not proud of, India.'

His admission pulled at something in her chest. She blinked up at him, her heart exploding with love. She wanted to wipe away his guilt, his worries. She wanted to make him smile.

'From the moment I got to Khatrain we have been in agreement about one thing: that our children are our priority. That's how you've acted. Even when you have made me so mad I wanted to scratch at your eyes, I have always, *always* known that you were fighting for our kids. And I love that.' Her voice cracked a little as she said the final sentence, her heart begging to be unleashed, to be freed by her admission.

He growled. 'You gave up university to care for your mother, you work a job you are overqualified for to support your brother, and now you make excuses for me. At some point, your heart of gold is going to become a liability.'

'Is it?' She moved closer, so their bodies brushed, and she felt a rush of heat between them, a sensual awareness that she now understood was so rich and urgent because it was driven not just by sex but also by love. 'I think it's going to guide me pretty well, actually.'

He furrowed his brow, not understanding.

'Khalil, listen to me,' she murmured urgently. 'I'm not Fatima. I'm not going to use you, I'm not going to hurt you, I'm never going to lie to you. What I will do, if you'll let me, is be your wife.' She brushed her thumb over his lower lip then pushed onto the tips of her toes, kissing him slowly, savouring the feeling of their mouths dancing together. 'In every way, your real wife.'

'You know that's what I want,' he growled, deepening the kiss, his hands against the small of her back, holding her to him, so stars burst through her and desire ran rampant. He took a step forward, pressing her back against a broad, ancient tree with a wide canopy, so they were shaded from the sun, mostly hidden from view. He found the waistband of her shirt and pushed at it, his fingertips connecting with her bare flesh. A moan was trapped low in her throat, and she succumbed to it, to him and to this perfect moment. But it wasn't simply a moment. It was one moment in a thread of moments, a lifetime of memories they would make together, side by side, just as she'd always wanted.

'I will never get tired of this,' he promised, pushing at her skirt, finding her underpants and guiding them down as he freed himself from his trousers. He lifted her easily, wrapping her legs around his waist and pushing into her, kissing her as he possessed her, as his body moved with hers. She held onto him for dear life, pleasure usurping everything else; every single one of her senses was in overdrive, so the sky, the grass, the warmth, the fragrance of the blossoms that surrounded them, all took on a startling clarity. She dug her nails into his shirt-clad back, her heels interlocked, holding him deep inside until they reached a euphoric, shared release.

It was so perfect, and she knew then that she was right. She loved him. And she had to tell him. That was terrifying, but it was also important—how could she marry him and keep that secret? She'd just promised him she wouldn't lie to him—what was that if not a lie?

'You are incredible.' He kissed her hard, his tongue flicking hers as he lowered her to the ground.

'I need to ask you something.'

He lifted his brow, focussing on straightening his clothes, so he wasn't looking directly at her. 'Right now, you could ask me for all my worldly goods and I'd happily comply.'

She pushed aside his assurance. Wealth, when you were Sheikh Khalil el Abdul, was easy to part with. His heart, on the other hand, was likely under far tighter lock and key.

'We'll see,' she murmured.

'What is it?'

'I'm just wondering how sure you are about the whole love thing.'

'What "whole love thing"?'

'The whole "you'll never love anyone again" thing,' she said, forcing herself to meet his eyes. She saw nothing in his that gave her reassurance.

'I'm very sure,' he said simply, but she knew it was a veneer. He was treading carefully, his hackles rising, his concerns shifting so he was seeking to minimise risk.

But she'd come this far. She couldn't walk away now. 'Because, the thing is, I just wonder if maybe love doesn't have ideas of its own.'

'What exactly do you mean?'

'Don't you think there might be something more here than either of us realised?'

He stared at her without speaking. Only his chest moved, rapidly, so she dropped her eyes to it for a moment, before looking at him once more.

'I think our marriage is based on a pregnancy that was an accident. That's not love.'

She pulled a face, hoping the grimace would hide the waves of uncertainty that were rolling through her. Was he right? Or was she? 'And what about everything that came after? This last month has been so much more than I expected. Getting to know you, spending time together...'

'Yes, it's defied my expectations too.' He spoke gently, almost sympathetically. 'But that's sex, *azeezi*, nothing more.'

Her heart stammered; she shook her head. 'I don't agree.'

'You do not have much experience,' he pointed out softly.

'And you do, but that doesn't make you right and me wrong.'

'In this, it does.' All so gentle! So compassionate! That made her want to break something! She didn't want to be treated like a fragile glass vase.

'So you're saying we can't have great sex and also fall in love?'

'Yes.' He nodded his head to underscore his verbal response.

'Are the two mutually exclusive?'

'No. But love is out of the question for me.' He lifted a hand to her face, but she jerked away from his touch on autopilot—she couldn't bear the kindness, it made her want to cry, and she wouldn't show her vulnerabilities like that. 'I've been honest with you about this. I have never wanted you to care for me. I should have thought it impossible, after the things I said...'

'Initially, perhaps. I didn't fall in love with you because you're perfect.' She sighed. 'If anything, I fell in love with your imperfections, with the way you fought yourself, fought me, fought for our children. I fell in love with you and I needed you to know that, before we got married. I told you I wouldn't lie to you, so I'm not going to. When I say those vows, I'll mean them.'

'India, no.' His features tightened and he stepped backwards, panic radiating from him. 'Listen to me.' There was a new kind of urgency in his tone now. 'This is impossible. You're mistaking lust for love. I understand that— our chemistry is off the charts, but there's nothing more between us than sex. And one day that will fade, we will no longer want each other like this, and you will forget all about loving me. Trust me, this is fiction, fantasy, not fact.'

If it weren't for the tree at her back, she might have stumbled. His words were so completely the opposite of what she'd expected that she didn't know how to respond to them at first.

'Let me get this straight,' she murmured distractedly. 'You think the only thing we share is sex?'

He compressed his lips, dragging a hand through his hair. 'Obviously it's a huge part of it.'

India sucked in a breath that didn't begin to fill her lungs. 'Did you ever stop to wonder why?'

'No.' He crossed his arms over his chest. 'I get the basics of sexual attraction. I don't need to analyse things further than that.'

She rolled her eyes. 'By your own admission, you've never wanted anyone like you've wanted me. Haven't you stopped to ask yourself why that is? Maybe, just maybe, our chemistry is because of our connection, our compatibility.'

'I wanted you the first night I met you, when I knew nothing about you. That wasn't love, it was desire, plain and simple.'

'And revenge,' she remembered with a shudder.

'No, we've dealt with that. I saw you and wanted you before I even knew you were with Ethan. The revenge thing was just convenient.'

'Not for me,' she pointed out, then shook her head, refusing to be drawn into an argument they'd already had out. 'But that's beside the point now. Since I've arrived here, since we agreed to get married, things have changed between us. Like you just said, you've seen beyond your first impressions, you've got to know the real me.'

'Yes,' he agreed. 'But again, that is not love.'

That hurt. She blinked away from him, a frown line forming between her brows. 'Can you really say that everything we share is just sex?'

He hesitated and for a moment, she had hope. But then he nodded, once.

'So how come we walk like this together each morning? How come we talk about anything and everything that comes to mind? How come you took me to see the fireflies?'

He ground his teeth together, his eyes pleading with her. 'Again, treating you with decency is not love. If I wanted to atone for the way things started between us, then that should be seen as an attempt to improve our relationship, for the sake of our children, nothing else.'

Her lips parted. 'So all of this is, what? Guilt?'

He expelled a harsh breath. 'I wouldn't have put it so crudely.'

She closed her eyes as pain washed over her. 'I'm not asking you for a declaration of love. I just need to know that you're not so broken by what Fatima did that you will never love. I need to know that you're open to loving me.'

He didn't answer. She opened her eyes, trying to read his face, and understanding nothing.

'And that's what I have been trying to tell you all along. I'm not open to loving anyone. Nor do I believe it's necessary. As I have said, numerous times, we can have a great marriage without that sort of emotional complication.'

'Because of sex,' she whispered.

'Sex, yes. Children. Shared interests. Respect.'

'But not love?'

'No.'

'Never love,' she repeated, for her own benefit more than his, wrapping her arms around her chest and stepping out of the shade of the tree. It didn't improve her temperature; she felt iced to the core.

'I'm sorry.' His voice was soft, coming from right behind her. 'I should have been clearer.'

'You were plenty clear,' she corrected. 'I just didn't believe you.'

They were silent, staring at each other for several long moments.

'This is the last thing I want,' he said, taking a step towards her. 'I don't want you to be hurt any more. What can I do to fix this?'

Her smile was a ghostly impersonation. 'Nothing. You feel as you feel. I just need to learn to accept it.'

She went to walk away but he caught her wrist, spinning her back to him. 'You'll realise that I'm right soon enough. You'll realise that your love for me is an illusion. And I'll be glad when that day comes.'

She nodded awkwardly, tears filming her eyes as she spun away. She knew he was wrong—she would never stop loving him. But she also knew he'd never return it, and suddenly the future seemed desperately bleak. They were getting married, and she faced the prospect of walking down the aisle towards a groom who would never be able to give her the one thing she'd always known she wanted. Leaving him was not an option. Not because of the babies, not because of sex, but because she did love him, with all her heart, and she would do anything to be with him, even if there was torture in that togetherness, because he'd never love her back.

CHAPTER THIRTEEN

THE FACT THAT their wedding was to be intimate did not, as it turned out, mean her outfit was correspondingly plain. In fact, the wedding dress was utterly magnificent. Made of white silk, the gown was fitted to the waist where it flared in a confection of skirts and tulle. Tiny diamonds were stitched into the hemline, giving it a weight that prevented it from flaring too much. There were also diamonds along the neckline, small at the shoulders and decolletage, then enormous at her cleavage, so India balked at even wearing the thing for fear of what it must have cost. Though the dress's opulence was dwarfed by the tiara she was presented with—the diamond in its centre was the size of a large button, shaped like a teardrop, and it was bracketed on either side by equally flawless, shimmering jewels. The weight of it was significant so a team of servants braided her hair to catch the clips, giving it more support. She watched with an awe that almost edged out her sadness. But not quite.

Her overarching emotion as she prepared for her wedding day was grief. Grief that her mother wasn't with her, grief that her groom didn't love her, grief that she was marrying for practical reasons rather than the fairy tale she'd been foolish enough to hope for.

But it was enough—it had to be. She couldn't change

their situation and if she'd had any doubts about Khalil's feelings, his silence since their conversation had shown her the truth.

Nervousness flared through her as a servant appeared at her door. 'It is time, madam.'

India nodded, apprehension tightening every muscle in her body.

'The ceremony is to take place in the Court Rooms,' the servant said, and India appreciated that she didn't refer to it as a wedding. 'Ceremony' felt far more appropriate. This was a simple formality—the legal binding of a man and woman for the sake of their accidental children's future. The more she thought of it in those businesslike terms, the better. Except it wasn't businesslike. She loved him, and, having admitted that to them both, she was plagued with doubts.

There was the sensible solution—marrying him for the sake of their children. She could easily make herself see the points in favour of this plan. It was right that they should be parents together—that was what they both wanted.

But at the same time, her fragile, aching heart was beating her, begging to be heard. Because marrying someone who didn't love you was guaranteeing disaster, wasn't it? What would her mother—who'd struggled with a small child on her own rather than living in an emotionally abusive and hurtful relationship—say about India's choice? Would she understand that India was doing this for love? Or would she remind India that marriage was an important partnership that demanded work and respect, a lifetime of commitment?

A lifetime!

Her knees wobbled as she stood on the threshold of the Court Rooms, shifting to the side suddenly so she could press her back to the wall and stare up at the ceilings. In-

side, her fate awaited her. But it was a fate that would require all of her courage to pursue and, suddenly, India
wasn't sure if she was brave enough.

'Calm down, Khal. You look as though you're about to
fall over.'

He shifted a sidelong glance at Astrid, catching his
parents' disapproving glances from their seats a little way
across the room.

'She's late.'

'Yes, well, that is a bridal traditional, at least in America. And this is a very big palace. It is quite possible she's
wandering a corridor, looking for us, completely lost...'

'Someone was sent to collect her thirty minutes ago.'

'Then she is simply finishing getting ready. Calm down.
She'll be here.' Astrid put a hand on his arm, her eyes
warm and comforting—neither emotion did anything to
reassure Khalil. 'Believe me, Khal. I have seen the two
of you together, and I have spoken to India at length. That
woman would walk through the desert at midday for you.
She'll be here.'

Khalil was very still; even his heart slowed to a heavy,
uncertain thump in his chest. 'What?'

Astrid frowned. 'What do you mean, "what"?'

'Why do you say that about India?'

Astrid's expression was quizzical. 'Because she's in
love with you. And gathering by the way you're burning
holes in the door, and intermittently shaking your watch
to ensure it hasn't stopped working, it's quite clear you
feel the same about her.'

Anxiety isn't love.

And he was anxious. He realised now how foolish he'd
been to ignore her in the lead-up to the wedding. Except
'ignoring' her wasn't exactly accurate. She'd plagued him,

head and heart, every minute of every hour since last he'd seen her. Only he'd resisted going to her. He'd avoided seeing her, even when she had somehow become a part of him anyway. Was it possible she would refuse to marry him after all? And then what would he do?

Whatever it takes to make her happy.

Even if that meant letting her go.

He looked around the room with a growing ache in the pit of his gut.

She wasn't coming.

'Why did you marry Ethan?'

Astrid frowned. 'Why does anyone get married? I loved him.'

'Do you regret that now you know what he's like?'

'How can I? I have Romeo. But, more than that, loving Ethan taught me a lot. It's like your experience with Fatima—you went through hell with her, but it made you all the more equipped to recognise true love when you found it.'

He looked away, his throat feeling thick and textured, as though he had razor blades stuck there.

'Love is a huge leap of faith, Khal. It never comes with a guarantee, you know. But look—how beautiful and serene your bride looks.'

His head whipped around, his eyes pinpointing India immediately as she entered the room. Astrid was right; she was beautiful, but he knew the woman in question better and he saw much that Astrid had missed.

India was strained. Tired. Exhausted. Stressed. Scared. *Terrified.* She also looked completely and utterly…alone.

It was wrong for India to be walking down the aisle like this. Someone should have her arm. Her brother should be here.

It would feel like lying to him.

It's not real.

His heart slammed into his ribs and he stepped forward, instincts stirring to supersede anything else. Everything about this was wrong…

'Excuse me a moment.' He was conscious of his parents' attention on him as he strode down the aisle, aware when his father stood, but Khalil didn't stop. He walked quickly towards India as though she were her own gravitational pull, and he powerless to resist it.

India's stomach was in knots. Her panic attack had receded, but she was still light-headed and uncertain, the enormity of what she was about to do cascading through her like a tsunami. It wasn't helped by Khalil's approach. Was this some custom she hadn't heard of? Was the groom supposed to meet her?

His eyes seemed to lance hers and the intensity in their depths had her steps faltering.

'Is something the matter?' she whispered, when he was right in front of her.

'Yes.' He reached out, touched her hands lightly then immediately withdrew again, angling his face away, his gaze deliberately averted, as though he couldn't bear to look at her. Was the idea of this marriage so terrible to him?

'We need to speak.'

Her heart tripped into her throat. Only minutes ago she'd balked at the idea of marrying him, but now that she stood on the cliff-face of not doing so, she was awash with remorse. It took the spectre of losing him—this— to know without a doubt what she really wanted, regardless of the pain she knew would follow. Some pain was worth enduring.

But what if that wasn't the case for him? What if nothing about this marriage made it worthwhile after all? It was patently obvious that he was having doubts.

'What is the meaning of this?'

His father's voice was booming, a noise that resonated through the room. Khalil reached for her hand now, interlacing their fingers.

India closed her eyes as something like a sense of completion wove through her.

Guard against it. It's not real. Nothing about this is real. He doesn't love you.

'A moment.' Khal responded in the same voice, terser though, as though tension were overtaking him.

'Come with me.' He drew her with him, through a row of seats towards a door at the side of the room, carved from dark, heavy wood. He pushed on it and it creaked a little as it opened to reveal a room that was smaller in size, but no less sumptuous. This had a large red carpet square in the centre, and the furnishings around the room were gold. There was only one window, but it was large and pushed out from the walls, creating a seating area with a view of the rose garden.

He dropped her hand as soon as they entered, then swept deeper into the centre, his back to her, hands on hips. Her heart dropped into her toes. It was clear that whatever he wanted to discuss was negative.

'Khalil,' she murmured, her voice throaty. 'Why don't you just say it?'

He was silent, but slowly, oh so slowly, he pivoted, his eyes unreadable as they locked to hers.

'I mean it. Whatever you're thinking, whatever it is, just say it. I'd rather hear the truth than stand here not knowing.' But she did know. She could see the intent in his expression and was simply waiting for the execution-er's axe to fall.

His eyes narrowed, his expression carefully muted of feeling. 'This wedding is a mistake. We cannot marry.'

She'd feared this was coming, but hearing the words shattered a part of her. 'Because I love you?'

'Because you're miserable,' he responded, dragging a hand through his hair. 'Because despite my best intentions I will never be able to make you happy—and I promised that I would try. But I can't. You love me, and I can't give you that. There is no happy ending here for you. You're already miserable—marrying me is only going to make you feel a thousand times worse. We can't do it.'

His words swirled around her, wrapping her into knots, so she didn't know which way was up. 'I'm not miserable,' she contradicted quietly.

'You are. I can see it in your eyes. Marrying you was a simple equation when I didn't know you. Then you were just a woman I'd slept with.' He frowned, a line forming between his brows. 'No, you were never just that to me. I don't know what I'm saying. It was easier when I still thought you capable of—'

'When you didn't care about my feelings,' she said with a tight lift of her lips.

'Yes.' He was arrogant enough to cross his arms over his chest and stare at her unapologetically, but a moment later he grimaced, shaking his head. 'What a monumental ass that makes me. As though I had any right to dictate this decision to you.'

'You didn't dictate, you persuaded.'

'I persuaded by employing threats. That is no different from dictating. If I had given you a true choice, would you have made this one, India?' He didn't wait for her to respond. 'Of course you wouldn't.' The words were grim, and it was obvious that he was angry with himself.

'You don't know that.' She paced slowly towards him,

but then changed direction, moving across the room instead. Space was needed. 'I have always known I wanted a family.'

'A true family,' he interrupted gruffly, shaking his head. 'A husband who loves you, children who were created out of that love. Not this.'

Her heart stammered. 'I do love you. So far as I'm concerned, our children are born of love, even if it's not mutual.'

'That's not a good enough reason to marry,' he said firmly, loudly, his voice shaking her so she flinched, and he groaned. 'Damn it, India, this isn't enough for you. Any fool can see you deserve better than what I can give you. This marriage was a mistake, but, fortunately, not one I will live to regret.'

Pain seared her. She stared at him, struggling to draw breath.

'I will take legal advice on the line of succession,' he said quietly. 'As I should have done from the beginning. I understand the importance of ensuring their birthright. If needs be, we may marry purely for their birth, and dissolve the marriage almost immediately. I appreciate that is still far from ideal—'

'Stop.' Anger shifted through her; the word emerged as a roar. 'Just, stop this.'

Surprised by her outburst, he did so.

'You just said you persuaded me into this marriage, rather than giving me any real choice, and now you're doing exactly the same thing about cancelling our marriage. Don't you care what I want?'

'All I care about is what you want!' he responded with strange determination, so an odd, uncertain suspicion began to flicker to life in the recesses of her brain.

'And you think I want this?'

'Yes. Clearly.'

'Why is it clear?'

'Because I can see the fear in your eyes. The hesitation in your steps. A bride should glow with pleasure, and you do not.' He moved closer and she sucked in a deep breath, bracing for his nearness. 'You deserve to marry a man who makes you glow.'

'And how will you feel then, Khalil?'

He stopped walking and stared at her, his eyes a stormy grey with flecks of gold showing uncertainty.

'If we don't marry now, and in a year's time I meet someone else. How will you feel?'

'Relieved,' he said, but that flicker of doubt burst into a full flame. Her heart began to pound.

'Oh, yeah?' she whispered. 'Then why do I only see fear in your face? Is that what all this is about, Khalil? You're afraid?'

He stared down at her, his nostrils flaring. 'Of what?'

'Of loving me! Loving someone is an act of faith. You have to trust them not to hurt you, and Fatima betrayed that trust, so you're afraid to trust me, even though you know I'm different. But more than that—and here's what you really need to understand—loving someone isn't a choice. Do you think you can end our engagement and whatever feelings are in here—' she jabbed her finger into his chest '—will simply go away? Do you think you'll stop thinking about me? Do you think you'll stop wanting me?'

'I think you'll be happy.'

'I won't be, because you're the man I love. Like I said, it's not a choice. I can't simply box away those feelings and move on to some other guy. I don't *want* to move on.'

'Even if I can never give you what you want?'

Flames overtook her. 'Oh, Khalil, you *can* give it to me. In fact, you already have. What you've done just now is incontrovertible proof—not just of your decency, but of your love for me. You care about me—to the point you'd break with your constitution to ensure my happiness. What is that if not love?'

'Respect,' he muttered. 'Fairness.'

Sadness washed over her. She knew she was right, but he was determined to fight her. 'Are you really so afraid of this?' she said gently, because now her pain was a shared pain.

'If I'm afraid, it's of hurting you. Of seeing you live a lifetime, broken by our marriage. I cannot bear it.'

'And why do you think that is?' She allowed the rhetorical question to fall between them, watching him, waiting for him to speak. He didn't, and the weight of his silence grew heavier and heavier until India sighed, tears stinging her eyes. 'Is this really what you want?'

He stared at her, a pulse working overtime at his temple. 'It's the right thing to do.'

She nodded, a single tear falling down her cheek. She brushed it away quickly. 'That's strange, because it feels the opposite of right, doesn't it?'

She stared at him for a moment, waiting for an answer that didn't come, and then, on a huge gasp of air, spun away, moving back to the heavy wooden doors. She wrenched them open and startled to see Astrid in a close conversation with Khalil's parents, across the room. For a moment, she stood perfectly still, pale-faced and frozen to the spot, and then she turned, moving quickly away from them, away from the flower-embellished altar at the head of the room, back to the golden doors that had marked her entrance to the ceremony.

Her breath was burning, coming in shallow spurts, just as it had before, but this was for another reason. She wasn't panicking now, so much as struggling to get enough oxygen—grief had swollen inside her, forming an organ of sadness, and it had overtaken the space previously occupied by her lungs. Once she'd cleared the room, she broke into a run, lifting the heavy silk skirts of her dress, holding back a sob until she'd rounded the corner. Then, she pressed her back to the wall and gave into her tears, letting them fall unchecked, perfectly aware in that moment she'd never know true happiness again.

He swore to himself as he followed her, ignoring his father's commands that he stop, his mother's pleas for him to come back and explain himself. He was aware, vaguely, of Astrid's hushed tones urging patience and calm, but nothing—no one—could prevent him from going after India. Hell. He'd wanted to fix things for her, to make her happy, and he'd failed miserably.

He cursed again as he came out of the Court Rooms and looked left and right, the empty corridors filling him with a sense of panic and dread that defied logic. He knew she couldn't leave the palace without his knowledge and consent—a fact that filled his mouth with tart acidity, for what that said about her living conditions this past month. She'd been his virtual prisoner, and still she believed she *wanted* to marry him?

He thrust his hands onto his hips and looked left once more, but this time, a palace guard caught his eye and with the simplest shift of his head nodded further down the corridor, and around a corner. Khalil stood right where he was for all of two seconds and then moved quickly, his long legs carrying him with haste through the ancient hallways and then to the left.

And when he saw her, his heart ceased to function as he'd known it. It no longer beat, but burst. It was no simple organ in his body, but a creation of something more, something that was intrinsically linked to India. Seeing her in tears immediately pulled at him, so he groaned, striding towards her so fast she didn't realise he was there until he put his hands beneath her elbows and drew her to him, pressing her sobbing body to his. She was stiff, resisting him at first, and his heart squeezed again, recognising her rejection and knowing it was the least he deserved.

But he moved a hand to her back, stroking her there, each touch lighting a part of him with intuition and understanding—an understanding he would never have found if India had been less courageous, and less wise. She'd been prepared to fight him—to fight for him—even when he'd pushed her away again and again with his stubborn insistence that she meant nothing to him. He couldn't even imagine how ferociously she would fight for their children!

His heart swelled to overtake his whole body and he pulled away from her just far enough to look into her eyes for several long, vital seconds.

'You're right,' he said finally, moving his hands to cup her face, loving the feel of her there, the goodness and beauty and wisdom and strength that fired through her eyes filling him with all the strength he needed to face the truth. 'I love you. And the idea of that terrifies me. But a life without you in it scares me so much more—a fact I didn't fully appreciate until I watched you walk away from me just now. My God, India, how did you do this to me? Somehow, when I was not paying attention, you dug in here and I know now that you will always be there—a part of me. The best part of me.'

Her lips parted and her eyes, awash with sadness, met his. 'I don't know why you're saying this. If it's because you feel bad, please don't. I always, always appreciate honesty—'

'Then I am glad I can finally give that to you. In my defence, I have not been honest with myself either. I fought this so hard. I wanted to keep you in a neat little box, a wife of convenience who would never mean more to me— yes, I hear how absurd and stupid that is, after everything we've shared. And it is not, in any way, something I could ever have achieved with you, my darling, beautiful India.'

She blinked, each flutter of her lashes seeming to clear the sadness away. He expelled a breath he hadn't realised he'd been holding, releasing tension and pent-up angst from deep within his gut. She sparkled once more. But there was still something in the depths of her gaze that held him back. He hadn't convinced her yet.

'But this wedding today is still wrong,' he said gently. 'I do not want to marry you in a hushed, hurried affair. When—if—we marry, it should be worthy of the love I feel for you.'

Her eyes flashed away from him. 'I'm not Fatima,' she said firmly. 'I don't *want* a big wedding. That's never been what this is about.'

'Not a big wedding, no, but a wedding that celebrates our love, with our loved ones present. All of them. How can we marry without your brother here, India? Without me even having met someone who is so important to you?'

Her gaze flickered back to his, and his heart soared. He could see that he'd expressed a hesitation she herself felt.

'But it's more than that.' He scanned her face slowly. 'I do not want to marry you until you believe the truth of my words. When you walk down the aisle towards me, I want you to be floating on air. I want you to glow with happiness and certainty. I want you to glow with the knowledge of my love for you and trust in you.' He caught her hands in his, lifting them between their bodies. 'I love you. I have loved you, I think, for as long as I've known you, since I first saw you. I knew I wanted to make you mine, but it was so much more than physical. I felt that if I didn't take you home that night, a part of me would wither into nothingness. And then, that night we shared was like something out of time and reality. It was like a dream. You were unlike any woman I had ever known.'

'Until the morning…'

'And I reacted so harshly, because already you had come to mean so much to me. I think, if I was truly honest with myself, I would admit that a part of me had begun to build a fantasy about our future. So when Ethan told me such a vile lie about you, I clung to it, because it was proof of something I'd come to believe—not about you but about love, lies, and about all women.'

'You were protecting yourself,' she whispered softly, her heart so gentle even then that she rose to his defence.

'That doesn't make it okay. I pride myself on my instincts and, with you, I had it so completely wrong. If you had not conceived the twins, I shudder to think of what I might have lost.'

'Might have?' she said with a lifted brow.

'You have no idea how I had to fight from coming back to New York. I thought about you, India. I thought about you often. You were like a fever in my bloodstream and I have no doubt I would have realised, at some point, that things between us were unresolved. If only I could have realised that I loved you—imagine how much simpler this would have been.'

'Simpler, perhaps, but do you know, Khalil, I'm not sure I would change a thing about what we've shared. Our love has been forged in fire, tested at many points, and I know, without a shadow of a doubt, that it's the kind of love that will survive anything. Anything. So long as we live, and love—'

'And trust,' he finished, dropping his forehead to hers before brushing their lips together.

Thirty minutes later, after more reflecting on their love, and the circumstances that had brought them to it, they returned to the Court Rooms, hand in hand.

The three guests were still there, and as the doors opened they turned, as one, to the couple.

'The wedding is off,' Khalil said, with a broad grin, which brought a corresponding frown to the faces of his parents and Astrid.

'What? Why?' Astrid looked from one to the other.

'Because, my dear cousin, when you love someone with your whole heart, as I do India, it is not enough to marry like this. I want to shout it from the rooftops. I want a wedding that the whole kingdom hears of.' He turned to face India then, his voice ever so slightly uneven. 'I want everyone in the world to know that I have fallen in love with the woman I intend to spend the rest of my life attempting to deserve.' He squeezed India's hand, before turning back to Astrid. 'And we will count on you to help us organise it.'

Astrid beamed as she swept towards them, pulling India into her arms in an enormous hug. 'Of course! This is a far better idea, cousin. I'm glad you are not completely brainless after all.' She drew back and winked at India, in time for Khalil's parents to appear.

'Your Highnesses.' India pulled free of Astrid and Khalil and dipped into a low curtsy.

It was Khalil's father who laughed, a gruff noise, before putting a hand on India's forearm. 'My dear girl, please stop that at once.'

She shifted an uncertain glance at Khalil.

'You are to marry our son. You clearly make him happier than we have ever seen him. We're family now. We do not need to stand on ceremony.'

And then, Khalil's mother hugged her, and India fought back more tears, but the kind that were drawn from the happiest wellspring a person could possess. Somehow, she'd found her way to family, to home, and every single part of her was whole again. She smiled, and wondered if she'd ever stop.

EPILOGUE

'YOU COULD SKIP the meeting,' he murmured, squeezing her hand.

India el Abdul slid her husband a sidelong glance. 'And say what? That our two-and-a-half-year-old twins kept me up all night? I don't think that's an excuse anyone will appreciate.'

'Or that the baby in your belly has you running for the bathroom every five minutes,' he said with a sympathetic grimace. Khalil had wished, many times, that he could do more to relieve the burdens of pregnancy, but, beyond running warm baths, offering back massages and foot rubs at any time of day, he was relegated to the role of silent witness.

'It's fine,' she said, patting a hand over her gently rounded stomach. 'I'm looking forward to this. I've worked hard on the proposal.'

'I know you have.' Khalil's face stretched with pride. India's economic forecast for Khatrain was detailed, innovative and, in his opinion, brilliant. But that wasn't just the bias of a doting husband—India had collaborated with economics professors the world over, pulling together a strategy that would take Khatrain forward, not just economically, but in terms of social development too. The investment in schooling and childcare centres meant their people would continue to live in one of the most prosperous and fair countries in the world.

'I'm proud of you,' he said, quietly, as the doors to the economics chamber were opened. India blinked up at him, smiling, a smile that made it appear as though the sun were filtering through her face, warmth and enthusiasm exuded by every pore. 'Almost as proud as my parents are of you.'

She laughed. It was a running joke between them that Khalil's parents loved India more than they did Khalil. They thought she was utterly perfect and could do no wrong. They were also incredibly supportive grandparents, spending as much time as they could with the twins.

'I know you are.' She squeezed his fingers, looking directly forward. 'Thank you.'

He dropped her hand as they entered, purposefully walking a step behind his wife. This was her moment. She had worked hard, channelling her innate abilities and passions into the last eighteen months of work, developing a report that was thorough, achievable and inspired. She deserved every accolade that was laid at her feet.

And though Khalil had expected that to be the case, even he could not have prepared for the rapturous response her report would garner. From even his oldest and most cynical advisors there was only praise, and the room hummed with the kind of enthusiasm he wasn't sure he'd seen in his lifetime.

'Did that just happen?' India asked, eyes wide, when they were alone again.

Khalil nodded. 'It's fair to say, you were a hit.'

India laughed, relieved. 'I knew the report was good, but I hadn't expected—'

'You deserve it,' he interrupted, brushing his lips to hers. 'I think you are incredible.'

She sighed, lifting up onto the tips of her toes to kiss him back.

'What time is it?' she asked against his lips.

'Just past noon. Why?'

'We have several hours before the dinner.'

She flashed a wide-eyed glance at him, a smile playing about her lips. Jackson was due to fly in that afternoon, and, as per their tradition, that meant a big, happy dinner with all of them—Khalil and India, Khalil's parents, Astrid, the twins, and Jackson. It was always loud, fun, with a lot of lively conversation about anything from politics to Broadway shows and economics initiatives.

'Then I guess we'll have to think of a way to kill time.'

'Exactly what I was thinking. Do you have any ideas...?'

He pulled back, a smile crossing his lips as he saw the glint in his wife's eyes. 'Many, many ideas,' he said with mock seriousness, earning a pout from her.

'Such as?'

He scooped down and lifted her easily, cradling her to his chest. 'Plans that are better discussed anywhere but here.'

'Like our bedroom?'

'The perfect venue, Your Highness.'

She laughed as they swept from the room, the bright afternoon sunshine crossing their paths like a golden blade, bathing them in warmth and optimism, paving the way for a future that would be blessed. Light shone, and love grew, as it always would.

* * * * *

FORBIDDEN TO HER SPANISH BOSS

SUSAN STEPHENS

MILLS & BOON

For my reader friends across the world, this is for you.

Susan xx

CHAPTER ONE

*A beachside wedding party on a private island
off the coast of Italy, owned by Raffa Acosta's
polo-playing friend Prince Cesar*

'COME TO BED with me.'

Rose Kelly's jaw dropped. If it hadn't been a familiar voice that just husked in her ear, she'd have retorted with something unprintable. As it was, she swung around, ready to make light of it. 'Are you tired, *señor*?'

'Tired?' Her boss laughed and ramped up the infamous Acosta charm. 'Not even slightly. I decided to take pity on you, standing here, looking lost in the shadows.'

'Pity?'

Rose's defensive tone of voice made him look twice, but they were both off duty, and Raffa Acosta had broken his own golden rule first. 'Never fraternise with the employees' was rumoured to be branded on his buttocks, if tack-room gossip was to be believed.

'Joke?' he prompted with the worst attempt at looking penitent Rose had ever seen.

Was it, though? Raffa Acosta carried such a punch of testosterone, it was hard to believe anything he said in relation to the bedroom could in any way be regarded as a joke.

'I'm not lost, and there's no need to pity me. I'm just taking it all in,' she said with a sweeping gesture. 'The closest I usually get to this sort of thing is when I'm racing past the champagne tent to the pony lines during a polo match.'

'You're not missing anything, Rose.'

Rose took a fresh look at her boss. Raffa Acosta was enough to addle any woman's brains, but there was a new note in his voice. Accustomed to hearing him barking orders on his fabulous ranch in Spain—where, after three challenging, glorious years of proving that a five-foot-two Irishwoman could work the pants off any man, Rose was Head Groom in his polo stables—Raffa's confiding tone just now had surprised her. Was he as relieved as she was to be out of the post-wedding mayhem? When people had a few drinks, everything could change from decorously happy and polite to rowdy and increasingly wild. The wedding itself had been a fabulous occasion, but the pressure to chat and smile had been unrelenting.

His penetrating look raked her from head to toe. 'I didn't realise you and my sister were that close, until I saw you in the role of bridesmaid.'

'Oh, we've been good friends for some time.' Since around nine o'clock that morning, but she wasn't going to drop Sofia Acosta in it by admitting Rose had been drafted in at the last minute to fill out a dress. Sofia always made time to chat to the grooms, and it had been a complete surprise, as well as an absolute pleasure, when Sofia had asked Rose to help her out on the morning of her wedding to Cesar. It was also a unique opportunity to experience the sort of high life a groom normally only witnessed from a distance. 'I hope you don't object to me being here.'

'Why should I?' Raffa queried, frowning.

Because she worked for him? And was supposed to be in the Prince's stables? Raffa had brought over a team of grooms to help with the horses he'd flown over to the island so the Prince and he could enjoy a few chukkas of polo. Rose had no right to be swanning around at anyone's wedding, and had switched around schedules to be here. If Sofia hadn't been so popular, she doubted that would have been possible. 'I'll make up the time,' she promised. 'And please don't worry about the ponies. I'd never leave them without organising proper cover for them first.'

'I don't doubt your reliability, Rose. Since the day you started work for me, you've been one of my most capable grooms.'

Capable? Coming from a sinful delight like Raffa Acosta, that was more a blow than a compliment. Shrugging it off, she concentrated on reassuring him. 'My colleagues have me on speed dial.' Producing a phone from the front of her dress, she flourished it in front of him, which, on reflection, was perhaps not the best idea. The bridesmaid's gown was skimpy, and Rose could be described as well built.

'I am reassured,' Raffa said, with a look that swerved her frontage, and landed squarely on her eyes. 'My sister couldn't have picked a better bridesmaid.'

'Well, thank you, kind sir.'

'Don't mention it.'

It was impossible not to laugh and relax when the great Raffa Acosta made a mock bow. He was a towering colossus of impossible good looks, with pheromones firing off the scale; it was growing harder by the second to remember that she worked for him, and her job meant everything to Rose. So much depended on her keeping it. Ponies had always been her life, and the money she earned went straight home to Ireland to pay for her father's keep.

'Best guess? My sister asked you to be a bridesmaid last minute.' Raffa's dark eyes burned into hers. 'Am I right? I'm thinking you took the place of the bridesmaid who breakfasted on sex and champagne—the woman who wasn't fit to be seen, according to my sister. I'd say Sofia got a lucky break, ending up with you.'

'As a sub,' Rose reminded him. 'I'm not a real guest. And, on that note—'

'Not so fast—'

Electricity streaked through her as she stared at his hand on her arm. 'People will talk.'

'Let them,' Raffa dismissed with a shrug.

'Don't you care that we're already attracting interest?'

'Do you?'

'No,' Rose admitted, 'but you should.'

'Why is that?' Loosening his grip, Raffa stood back.

'The god of polo getting off with his groom?' she said bluntly. 'How will that play in the society press?'

'I really don't care, and neither should you.'

'I'm only trying to protect you,' she protested.

One sweeping ebony brow lifted. 'Do I look as if I need protecting?'

'You look...'

Like every woman's dream lover—tall, dark and handsome, with more than a hint of danger about you. A gold hoop in your ear and that thick, unruly black hair, which, together with your deep tan and formidable build, makes you look more like a gladiator than a tech billionaire with a talent for playing polo.

'Well?' Raffa prompted.

'You look fine to me,' Rose teased with a one-shouldered shrug.

'Fine? Is that all you can find to say about me?'

'What more do you expect?' Rose frowned through a grin as Raffa's lips pressed down in the most attractive way.

'As we're clearly not going to bed, will you dance with me, Rose?'

The gladiator and the stable maid? That could work. If she could stretch her imagination for the span of a dance. Angling her chin, she stared up into his ridiculously handsome face. 'You really don't care what people think, do you?'

'Correct.'

The expression in her boss's eyes and the little tug at the corner of his mouth were all it took for heat to surge from Rose's toes to her belly with long stops in-between.

'The sun's going down,' Raffa observed, glorious eyes narrowed as he stared out to sea. 'We'd better dance, Cinderella, before you disappear.'

'Cinderella?' Rose queried with an ironic look.

Raffa held her gaze in a way that made everything riot inside her. Countering that feeling, she made up her mind and lifted her chin. 'Why not? Let's give them something to talk about.'

Rose led the way, but Raffa's hand was in the small of her back like an incendiary device for the senses. When they reached the dance floor, he dipped his head to murmur in her ear, 'There goes the bride and her new husband, so your duties are officially over. You've no excuse not to dance with me now, and, as I'm giving you the rest of the evening off, you're free to enjoy yourself any way you like.'

'Monopolise the chocolate fountain?' she suggested. 'Joke?' she added dryly in answer to Raffa's narrow-eyed stare.

'Okay, so you paid me back,' he conceded. Tilting his head, he regarded her in a way that made the heat in her body rush upwards to join the heat in her face. 'There's a lot of life left in this party,' he commented. 'Unless there's some other way you'd like to enjoy yourself?'

'Safely?' Rose suggested pointedly. 'Shall we dance?' Before this situation gets any trickier. 'Take care of my toes. I kicked off my shoes,' she warned. And then some devil got into her. 'I'd easily tower over you if I'd kept them on.'

Raffa laughed. 'Yeah, right. You'd still fit under my chin.'

The borrowed shoes had killed her, so Rose had ditched them as soon as she could, but now it felt as if she were about to launch herself into the arms of a giant. 'One dance only,' she stressed. 'If you can brave the curious and green-with-envy brigade, so can I.'

'Am I so popular?'

'I'm talking about me,' she shot back teasingly. 'Do you know how lucky you are, to be dancing with Rose Kelly, when everyone knows I prefer the company of horses?'

'I'm honoured you're making an exception, in that case.'

Raffa's second mock bow made everyone stop and stare. Rose hid her smile at the thought of the great Raffa Acosta dancing with Rose Kelly from a small farm in Killarney. The four Acosta brothers and their sister, Sofia, were known the world over for their brilliant minds, skill on horseback and the capacity for accumulating wealth, second to none. And here she was, flaunting herself with the best-looking brother. It seemed incredible. Maybe it was. 'Are you using me?' she asked suspiciously.

'For what?' Raffa demanded with a heart-stopping frown.

'To put off some annoying woman who's been chasing you.'

When he laughed, the blinding flash of strong white teeth only emphasised the depth of his tan. How gorgeous he was. A fact not lost on their fast-growing audience. 'If that's what you're up to, you could do better than me with my red hair and freckles. What about one of these sloe-eyed beauties over there, drooling over you?'

'Where?' He made as if to look around.

'I'm being serious,' she insisted. 'Or I'm trying to be, but you do make it hard.'

'Only because no one here compares to you.'

'You can take that tongue out of your cheek right now,' she scolded lightly.

'I'm being serious,' Raffa insisted with a perfectly straight face that threw her for a moment. It was one thing joking with the boss, and another when their stares met and held. 'Off-duty Rose has been a revelation to me,' he continued. 'You make me laugh.'

For the space of a dance, Rose thought, but as the banter continued she wondered if her boss was enjoying it as much as she was. Electric moments passed as they stood facing each other, waiting for the music to begin. Anticipating the touch of Raffa's hands on her body was almost as startling to Rose's senses as she was sure the real thing was going to be. At least, that was what she thought until they started dancing.

For a moment she couldn't think, breathe or exercise any of her faculties. It was a miracle her legs agreed to hold her up, let alone obey the rhythm that seemed to flow so effortlessly between them. Glancing around was another eye-opener. 'I was perfectly happy in the role of spear carrier, or place-filler, or whatever you want to call it, but I'm not so keen on every other woman at this party hating me.'

'I wouldn't trust you with a spear, and I certainly wouldn't call you a place-filler,' Raffa argued.

'What would you call me, then?'

'An entertainment.'

Was that bad or good? Look on the bright side. The women watching them had no cause to be jealous. Raffa couldn't have made it clearer that Rose's sole purpose was to lessen the tedium.

Was this really happening?

Rose didn't have a hand free to pinch herself as they danced on, as one was locked in Raffa's big fist, while the other was tentatively resting on what felt like a mountain of muscle. Grooms didn't get cosy with their employers, yet here she was, causing comment as she danced with Raffa Acosta, as if she belonged in his world.

Which she did, for tonight, at least, Rose reminded herself. Lifting her chin, she blocked out the jealous glances and silently dedicated this dance to all the wall-flowers out there.

'Problem?' Raffa queried when she exhaled happily.

'Homesickness,' she lied. Admitting to the bliss of the moment would give him entirely the wrong idea, and she could always rely on the small farm in Ireland where she'd been born and grown up to make her feel wistful. Raffa's ranch was beyond fabulous, but there were times when Rose missed the old, ramshackle farmhouse, even with all its mixed-up history, cranky heating and creaking stairs.

'Are you sure?' he pressed when she frowned.

Those eyes could prise the truth from the Sphynx, but she could hardly tell him that along with wholesome dinners in front of a roaring fire, she was remembering her father drunk and her mother frightened he'd kill himself one day with the contents of a bottle. Dancing with Raffa Acosta was the most wonderful thing that had ever happened to Rose, but nothing would ever banish those memories.

'I'm sorry, I can't ease the homesickness for you, Rose.'

'I'll be fine in a minute.'

It might take several minutes. She wasn't used to caring comments, or tears stinging her eyes. She'd always had to be strong for her father. When her mother died, he'd gone to pieces, sinking ever deeper into an alcoholic haze. When he was sober, he mourned the wasted life he'd spent in a bottle, when Rose's mother had needed his support. Rose's father was a good man, a kind man, a gentle man, but he was weak. Sometimes Rose thought it was always the women who had to be the backbone of a family. They were the true warriors, the ones who never complained or gave up.

She would never give up on her father, and she would save enough money to find him a treatment. Having given herself a stiff talking-to, she blocked out the past and smiled.

'I should thank you,' Raffa commented in response to the change in her manner.

She was surprised. 'For what?'

'For pricking my ego,' he explained. 'Why should I expect to have all your attention?'

'Because you're my boss? And you do have my attention. Ask any of the women here, and they'd say I'm lucky to be dancing with you.'

'That sounded dangerously like flattery to me.'

'And you get enough of that, I imagine?'

'Flattery is sweet food for those who can swallow it, but I'm more of a cheese and pickle man.'

Rose pinned a theatrical frown to her face. 'Are you saying I'm a navvy's wedge of a sandwich?'

When Raffa laughed she couldn't help noticing yet again that his teeth were perfect. He was perfect. It was dangerously easy to imagine that mouth and those lips creating havoc on her body. She shouldn't even be thinking like that, but nothing suited a man better than a sense of humour, in Rose's opinion.

'You're the only woman worth dancing with at this party,' he assured her as he twirled her around and around.

'Are you sure you're not just trying to make me dizzy?'

His answer was to yank her even closer.

There was a lot to be said for feeling light-headed. Raffa Acosta, who could have anyone he wanted, and capable Rose, who resembled one of those little dolls in an Irish gift shop, pleasantly plump and agreeably smiling, only short of wearing her red hair in plaits, dancing as if they belonged together.

'Tell me, why haven't we done this before tonight?' Raffa demanded. 'I had no idea what I was missing.'

'Honesty?' she suggested.

The smile on his face was something else to take away and store in her memory box. When they were working together on Raffa's ranch, he was all grim concentration.

'I didn't know what I was missing, either,' Rose confessed. 'I'd no idea you could loosen up to the point where you'd dance with a groom.'

'Don't tell anyone,' Raffa confided with a glance at all the avid faces watching them. 'Let this be our secret.'

'I promise not to say anything to tarnish your formidable reputation,' Rose pledged, enjoying the joke.

'You're lucky to have such an attractive accent, Rose Kelly, or I'd be forced to scold you severely for your cheek tonight.'

That could be nice.

No. No! She mustn't even think that way. This was one pity dance for the wallflower at a society wedding. Cinderella would soon lose her glad rags and don her work clothes to finish off mucking out the stables. But the music was upbeat, her heart was racing and Raffa didn't seem to care that they had become the biggest talking point of the night. 'Who has the accent?' she challenged, raising a mocking eyebrow.

'Are you daring to criticise my impeccable English accent, *señorita*?'

'No. I love the way you talk,' Rose admitted frankly. That sexy Spanish accent was the icing on an already delicious cake.

'Shall we dance on?' he suggested.

'Yes. Let's—but, there's something we need to get straight first.'

'What's that, Rose?'

'I won't sleep with you when the dancing stops.'

'I didn't have sleep in mind.'

'You're every bit as bad as they say you are,' she scolded, unable to help laughing out loud.

'Worse,' Raffa confirmed, with a look that scorched her from the inside out.

When the music finally stopped, neither of them seemed eager to part. Rose knew she had to make a move. 'Well, this has been wonderful, but I should be going—'

'If that's what you really want?'

'It is.' It was the last thing she wanted.

'Why am I not convinced?' Raffa murmured as he drew her into his arms.

Rose's heart pounded with a mix of excitement, at feeling Raffa's body so intimately pressed against hers. Tonight had turned out to be unexpectedly exciting, and reckless. That said, she didn't try to break free again. They were two people enjoying a party. What was wrong with that? Yes, they were causing gossip, but Raffa didn't seem concerned, and by tomorrow the gossipmongers would have something else to talk about. She was almost tempted to grab the mic to reassure the glitterati that Rose Kelly, without a penny to her name, let alone a title, would not hold Raffa's interest beyond tonight, because Rose was, as ever, determined to be herself, which left her with no place in Raffa Acosta's glamorous world. Whatever they said about Rose would be water off a duck's back, because she had no harsher judge than herself.

CHAPTER TWO

DANCING WITH THE most beautiful woman at a party was nothing new. Dancing with Rose Kelly was a revelation. He hadn't expected Rose to be dynamite off duty, or to feel so voluptuous in his arms. During his sister's wedding she'd unfurled like a flower, but it was the way Rose challenged him and made him smile that was the real surprise.

Alert as ever, she stared up at him. 'You seem distant. Is there a problem?'

'Beyond waiting for the band to start playing again?' He shook his head. 'No.'

That was a lie. Smiles had been in short supply since he'd witnessed the tragedy. Guilt had been his constant companion ever since. What was it about Rose that allowed him to hold the memory of his parents perishing in a plane crash and accept it as a scar surrounded by healthy tissue, rather than a wound that would never heal?

'Are you sure?' she pressed.

'I'm sure.' The concern in Rose's eyes threw him. He was the fixer, the one people looked to for answers. And he didn't disappoint—except himself, one time, on one memorable occasion, when even his strong will had been incapable of preventing a tragedy.

'Okay, then.' She smiled faintly, obviously unconvinced.

Rose's luminous quality soothed his troubled mind, *and* attracted jealous glances, he noticed now. The urge to protect her was strong, but Rose was used to paddling her own canoe. She was the person people went to with their problems on his ranch. This was no milksop princess or society flitter-bug, but a strong, resourceful woman with a mind of her own. More than ever tonight, Rose had proved that appointing her Head Groom was one of the best decisions he'd ever made. 'I should apologise,' he found himself conceding.

'For what?' Her green eyes flared with interest.

'My shabby start with you this evening.'

Disentangling herself from his arms, she stood back, amusement dancing in her eyes. 'I've heard a lot worse. Six brothers,' she reminded him. 'And your charm won't work on me now. Nothing you say will persuade me to let you have your evil way with me. I've got too much to lose.'

'Your job?' he guessed.

'My self-respect,' she corrected him.

Tension crackled between them. Identikit women, boasting the same breasts, lips and overbleached hair, paled by comparison to an understated woman who could amuse him with nothing more than the thoughts that came out of her highly kissable mouth.

'Is it bedtime?' she teased, when a couple next to them exchanged a meaningful look before leaving the dance floor.

'If I thought *you* were serious.'

She laughed. 'You wish.'

Rose's cheek was unparalleled, but she inflamed his desire. Feeling her body against his when they danced had proved that by some mysterious alchemy they fitted together perfectly. Lust tormented him.

But lust would have to wait. For the first time in his life, it seemed more important to get to know a woman. The cold hard facts provided by his team about each member of staff didn't come close to describing Rose Kelly, who was right in thinking they were causing a stir. He could practically read people's thoughts.

Who was this woman?

Where had she come from? Was she a close family member?

She must be, or why was she a bridesmaid?

He drew Rose to him on the thought that she was more than a hard-working employee. She was brave and tough, and tender too. The substitute bridesmaid standing in the shadows, keeping her thoughts to herself as she watched everyone else have a good time, was almost certainly a lot closer to the real Rose Kelly than Rose would have him suppose.

She was playing with fire, just by dancing with Raffa. The way her body was responding to his was ridiculous. She wanted him in a way that wasn't safe—not for her job, not for Rose. Had she forgotten the reputation of the unmarried Acosta brothers? Notorious for landing, conquering and moving on, they were hardly the safe option for a dance. Their sister, Sofia, was different. The seeds of friendship had been sown between the two of them that morning, when Sofia had confided in Rose that she was creating retreats for those who needed healing beyond the scope of conventional medicine, and Rose had immediately thought of her father.

'You're very quiet,' Raffa commented, so close to her ear that it tingled.

'Just thinking...'

'A dangerous recreation at the best of times. Good thoughts, or bad?'

'Mostly good,' she admitted, lifting her chin to meet the stare of a man who could easily muddle her thinking.

'You're not usually lost for words, Rose,' he prompted.

'I'll blame those six brothers again,' she admitted on a laugh. 'Bantering with them tends to hone your conversational skills.'

'Sofia would agree with you, I'm sure.'

'Then, you know what to expect from me,' she stated bluntly.

'Trouble?' Raffa proposed.

'As much as you want,' she offered wryly.

The hand in his was small, but strong, while the woman beneath the couture dress was as lovely as any here, but Rose had the edge in his eyes, because she was never afraid to speak her mind. His sister's friends were generally marked out by their manicured appearance, but, even on this most important of days, he could tell Rose's preparation had been rushed. He could imagine Rose devoting all her time to helping Sofia look perfect and doing little more than pelting in and out of the shower herself, leaving her womanly body smelling of soap. A mere slash of eyeshadow enhanced the emerald in her eyes, while the gloss on her lips begged to be devoured—

'Do you like the gown?'

'Do I...?' He laughed as she sucked in her stomach. 'You don't need to do that.'

'Oh, but I do,' she insisted. 'I was the closest to the original bridesmaid in build, but it's still a dress size too small for me. It's couture, you know.' She gave a twirl. 'And I was determined to get into it. I've never worn anything like it before. Talk about silk purse and sow's ear—'

'Don't you dare,' he warned. 'The gown looks lovely

on you.' How could it not, when the silk and lace show-cased a figure any woman would envy?

'Sofia said I can keep it,' Rose confided as they started dancing again. 'I feel bad, because I'll never have the chance to wear it again.'

'You don't know what life holds.'

This evening had made up his mind. He had a tour of business appointments coming up that required the use of his yacht, the *Pegasus*. It was the easiest way to move around Europe while entertaining in style. Rose would come with him. Her work in the stable was exemplary, leaving only one question: Could she handle the social aspect of the job?

There could be no hiding in the shadows on his yacht. Rose hadn't held the post of Head Groom for very long, and it called for mixing with royalty and celebrity alike to discuss the merits of his various ponies. What bet-ter training ground could there be than a week on the *Pegasus*?

'It's time to go,' Rose announced as the band gave way to a DJ. 'I'll check on the ponies first, and then I'm off to bed. My own bed,' she stressed with a grin. 'We've got an early flight in the morning.'

'And if we didn't?'

'I'd still go to bed on my own.'

He couldn't help laughing. 'What about a drink first?' he suggested, reluctant to let her go. 'The ponies are safe, and you of all people know how important it is to remain hydrated.'

'Sensible me?' Rose suggested dryly, before cheekily adding, 'Or, capable me?'

'You got me,' he admitted wryly, hand to chest.

Not at all offended, she was laughing as they walked

to the beachfront where a bar had been set up. A waiter quickly found them some seats.

'This is nice,' Rose murmured as she dabbled her feet in the water.

'You're a force to be reckoned with, Rose Kelly.'

'I'm glad you think so.'

'School, college, equestrian training—top of the class in every arena.'

Every arena except one. The romance she longed for had so far eluded Rose, and she doubted tonight would put that right. It was her own fault. She'd been too busy striving to be the best, to earn enough money to find her father some effective treatment, to spend time on relationships. 'Forged in steel and horse muck,' she agreed.

'And a great deal of hard work,' Raffa argued.

'Nice of you to say so...' Turning her face to the sky, she closed her eyes to drag deep on the scent of ozone, laced with the heady perfume of warm, clean man at her side. 'And now, look at me, reaping the benefits,' she teased, sitting up straight to smile into his eyes. 'Who'd have thought I'd find myself here?'

'You've earned this opportunity,' Raffa said firmly. 'Don't let anyone tell you any different. Your gift with horses is second to none, and you've got heart, Rose. The horses know it.'

But did he? She doubted it.

'You *have* been forged in steel, Rose Kelly,' he asserted. 'I've read your CV.'

'It was that, or crumble when my mother died. I'm sorry,' she jumped in, desperate to right the wrong. 'We've both suffered loss. I should have been more sensitive. Loss either breaks you or makes you, doesn't it?'

And now she'd made things worse. Raffa's stare was dark and long. Rose fell silent too. Everything had been upbeat until she'd taken them both to a place of grief. She knew little about the death of his parents apart from what she'd read in the press, that the plane crash had affected all the Acostas, even Sofia, who'd been very young at the time. Whatever Raffa's torment, she couldn't leave him in that dark place on his own.

'I'm sorry for your loss.' As she spoke, she impulsively covered his hand with hers.

'As I am for yours, Rose,' he murmured, pulling his hand away.

'I still have my father,' she said lightly to cover her embarrassment. 'Just.'

'Just?' Raffa queried, dipping his head to interrogate her with one of his penetrating black stares. 'Is there something I don't know that I can help you with?'

'No. Nothing.' *Everything.* But she wouldn't ask Raffa for help. What would he think of her? Didn't everyone go to him for some sort of assistance—usually financial? This was Rose's family problem, and she would sort it out. By herself.

Seeing Raffa still brooding, she went in with a dis traction. 'Tomorrow, this magic will all be over. You'll be back to riding the pants off the competition and running your billion-dollar corporations, while I'll be mucking out your horses.'

He laughed, but not before she'd seen the well of grief behind his eyes—grief that mirrored her own. 'If you ever want to talk?' she couldn't help adding.

He stiffened. 'I'm not in the habit of discussing personal matters.'

That response should have been enough for Rose to keep her mouth shut, but she'd never been good at that. 'Why not? Talking helps. Why is talking about you off limits?'

'I'm your boss?' Raffa suggested with a look that warned Rose again to back off.

'Thanks for reminding me.' She also silently thanked six argumentative brothers for prepping her well for this type of combat. 'For a moment there, I thought we were two human beings sharing experiences on an equal footing.'

She held her breath, uncertain as to how Raffa would respond. And had to stop herself exclaiming with relief when the same humour that had attracted her when he'd come out with such an outrageous opening statement to her at the wedding crept back into his eyes. 'What if I told you your boss is considering your next training programme, to advance your career?'

Rose's heart leapt out of her chest—or felt as if it had. Each module she'd embarked on so far at Raffa's prompting had been equivalent to an advanced course in equine care. The thought of another thrilled her to the bone—but not to the point where she wouldn't be honest with him. 'I'd still tell you the truth.'

'That's what I hoped you'd say.'

Rose's head was spinning. She loved her job. All good things sprang from it. Her career was not just the bedrock of Rose's self-belief, but the means by which she hoped one day to pay for her father's treatment. On those rare occasions when he was sober, and she saw the man he could be, Rose redoubled her determination to live up to the pledge she'd made to her mother to take care of the family. Any advancement in her career would help her to do that.

'I'll see you receive the details as soon as possible,' Raffa was saying.

'I'd appreciate that.'

'Goodnight, Rose.'

Dismissed, she stood, recognising that tomorrow was already here. Reality had been stalking them, and the magic was now well and truly gone.

'Goodnight, Señor Acosta. And thank you once again for everything.'

He sat in the same chair for almost an hour after Rose had left. The moon beamed down like a spotlight on the ocean, while he turned a spotlight on himself. He'd never opened up to anyone. Not even by the smallest hint had he revealed the wounds Rose had uncovered with her words. To protect his brothers, and most especially his sister, Sofia, he avoided talking about the past in case he intruded on their grief. So why tonight, when accompanied by this young woman who worked for him, with whom he'd enjoyed some low-level flirting, had he been prompted to lay bare a part of himself that was as raw today as the day he had stood watching in helpless horror as his parents' plane crashed in flames on the runway in front of him?

Impatient to be thinking about the past, when there was nothing to be done about it, he sprang up. He'd seen the sadness in Rose's eyes and had done something about it. Workwise, she was a worthy candidate for advancement, and he'd give her every chance.

In other ways?

There were no other ways where Rose was concerned. He'd seen how emotional involvement led to disaster. If he'd diverted that plane—insisted his parents travel on a regular flight, rather than taking their small private jet with a drunken pilot at the controls—they could still be alive today.

The pain that thought brought him was warning

enough to keep his feelings in check. He was a man of business, a man of polo, a man who...

Would never have a family of his own?

He braced his shoulders against the truth. The man who, on his last polo tour, had looked at his brothers and Acosta cousins with envy, as they'd played with their children and laughed with their partners. Good luck to them! They'd been lucky. He had more sense than to tempt fate to smile on him where love, luck and family were concerned.

Having thanked the wedding organisers for giving his sister a wonderful day, he headed back to the palace. He never went to bed without checking on the ponies first. The grooms travelling with him were more than capable of doing this, but there was always the possibility that they might need something, or one of the horses had refused to settle. The fact that Rose could be carrying out the same checks was irrelevant to him, except that nagging part of him that insisted they weren't done yet—and not just in the professional sense.

When he reached the palace stables the grooms were changing shifts. One sleek, spotless, air-conditioned interior of a top-class polo stable was much like another, and Prince Cesar's facility made him long for home. In that, he and Rose weren't so dissimilar, he reflected as he entered the security code to gain entry. Rose might enjoy her job, but he suspected that part of her heart would always be in Ireland.

Once inside the stable block, he shed his jacket and rolled up his sleeves.

'Raffa!'

'Lurking in the shadows again?' he reprimanded, though Rose's voice had caressed his senses like a welcome embrace.

'Working, not lurking,' she assured him.

Rose was smiling when he walked up to her, holding an armful of kittens. She'd changed out of her gown into an old pair of jeans and a shapeless top, with a pair of serviceable muckers on her feet. 'You call that work?' he challenged.

'Tell that to the kittens,' she said as she buried her face in soft fur.

Work lights illuminated her face, making Rose appear more radiant than ever.

'Do you want to hold one?'

He declined. 'Better put them back with their mother. She'll be missing them.'

'You're right,' Rose agreed reluctantly. 'I found them in one of the stalls, making a break for freedom.'

Animals were a great leveller, and a great indicator of character too. 'You don't have to make up your time for attending the wedding by working late,' he made clear as they went to find the mother cat's nest.

'You're here,' Rose pointed out. When he didn't reply, she added, 'And while you're here, I should ask—did I go too far with the cheek tonight?'

He raised a brow. 'Just put the kittens back in their nest.'

Rose seemed reluctant to part with them, and turned to give him an imploring glance. 'If you even hint at the fact that rescuing kittens has been the best part of your night, I will take offence,' he warned.

He received an amused glance. 'I'm sure you won't stop teasing me any time soon,' Rose declared. 'So, yes, if you must know, the best part of tonight was dancing with you.'

Her frankness disarmed him. 'But you're more comfortable with animals?' he guessed.

'It would be rude to admit that.'

'But it's true?' he pressed.

'They're not as dangerous as some of the humans I've met,' she admitted.

'I hope you don't count me amongst those threats?'

'You'd better be one of the good guys, or I'm in trouble,' Rose countered, humour brightening her eyes. 'Although you certainly don't look like one of the good guys to me.'

'To prove my credentials, I'll escort you to the door of the grooms' quarters.'

'That's very good of you, but it doesn't prove a thing,' she pointed out. 'Do I have cause to worry?'

'Not tonight.'

'Well, that's honest enough. You have my permission to walk me to the door—but no further.'

'Thank you, *señorita*,' he mocked lightly. 'I'm hugely honoured to end my evening with such a crushing blow to my ego.'

'You'll get over it,' Rose assured him.

The verbal banter between them was entertaining, but reality had landed with a bump, Rose mused with a twist of her lips. Cinderella would quite literally be returning to her garret at the top of a palace tower, while he would spend the night in supreme luxury in one of the Prince's best suites. 'After you,' he invited.

As Raffa politely gestured she should go ahead of him, Rose tried to squeeze past, but the mother cat had made her nest in a narrow passage where space was extremely limited. This made it inevitable that they brushed against each other. Instead of apologising and moving on, which was what she should have done, she paused and stared up at him. In that moment, she could have sworn Raffa wanted to kiss her.

He didn't kiss her.

It was amazing what the body could drive the mind to believe. 'Excuse me,' she said politely.

'Of course.' He took a step back.

Not that it wasn't a joy to move past him and feel those hard muscles resisting the press of her softly yielding body, but that would be the only thing yielding tonight. She'd do nothing to risk the advancement of her career, because there was so much at stake—not just Rose's career, but her father's future hung in the balance too.

CHAPTER THREE

LONGING WASN'T SO much a state of mind as a real physical ache, Rose concluded as Raffa, true to his word, escorted her back to the grooms' quarters. Of course she wanted him. Her body demanded she sleep with him, but too much hung on keeping her job.

She'd settle for a lifetime of wondering *What if?* because that was far safer. Hadn't she seen an excess of emotion taking her parents on a roller-coaster ride, with far too many downs and not nearly enough ups? When emotion was in the mix it wasn't just sparks that flew, but whisky bottles and teacups, and anything else that came to hand.

When they reached the old oak door that marked the entrance to the grooms' quarters, she held out her hand to shake his. 'Thank you for a wonderful evening.'

'Thank *you*, Rose. I've enjoyed myself immensely.'

The touch of Raffa's hand was shockingly arousing, and she had to quite literally remind herself to let him go. 'Have a great night's sleep—'

'You're not turning me down again, are you?' Raffa teased.

'That I am,' she confirmed.

Who was this woman to keep him up all night? With a disbelieving shake of his head, he stood beneath an ice-cold shower the following morning, wondering why the freezing water was having no effect. It wasn't subduing his interest in Rose—his body was straining at the leash.

Once he'd prised her from the shadows, Rose Kelly had proved more intriguing than he could possibly have expected. Even Rose's cold shoulder was the hottest thing to have happened to him in quite a while. Her lilting Irish accent and those sparkling emerald eyes, combined with her quick wit, and a body to die for, might have seemed a cliché if anyone but Rose had been involved, but he knew she was the genuine article.

She'd bewitched him, he concluded as he towelled down roughly. No woman should be allowed to do that. Hadn't he made a pledge not to draw anyone close? Yanking on his jeans, he pulled on the first top that came to hand. It wasn't just the fact they were flying home this morning that made him eager to start the day, but the thought of working alongside Rose that drove him on. Raking impatient fingers through his still damp hair, he left the room, slamming the door behind him.

And then he got a call.

Preparing the ponies for their flight was one of Rose's favourite jobs, but she couldn't help listening out for Raffa. Where was he?

As soon as she finished work, she went to the tack room to grab a glass of water before the flight, to find a new notice pinned up on the board.

Señor Acosta regrets leaving before thanking the grooms for their hard work during this trip.

Raffa had left without saying goodbye? So much for enjoying himself last night! Thank goodness she'd had the good sense to go to her own bed alone, instead of inviting him to join her. Imagine how she'd feel if she had slept with him.

Worse than now? Was that even possible?

Now she noticed something glinting on the floor. Swooping down, she recognised the sparkling black stone encased in white metal as one of the cufflinks Raffa had been wearing last night while they were dancing. Later in the stable, he'd been in shirtsleeves, she recalled.

The find was not a glass slipper, and Rose was no Cinderella, but she'd have to get it back to him somehow. Tucking it safely inside the breast pocket of her shirt, she returned to work.

'Rose, have you seen this? It's addressed to you.' Rose's friend and fellow groom Adena excitedly handed over a note. 'How was the wedding?' Adena asked with a grin.

'Spectacular,' Rose admitted.

'I thought as much,' Adena said. 'Looks like a letter from the boss,' she added, leaning over Rose's shoulder.

So, he hadn't forgotten her. Ripping the envelope open, Rose found an invitation to spend the following week on Raffa's yacht! *Incredible. Exciting. Terrifying.* Then reality hit. This was no romantic billet-doux, but a call to action by her boss. She read it again.

> *I have to know you're confident enough to handle all the responsibilities of Head Groom, including entertaining royalty.*

For a moment Rose was panic-stricken. Royalty? Could she even curtsey? She couldn't do it—not a chance!

Why not? Hadn't she made the successful transition from a small farm in Ireland to Raffa's fabulous facility in the heart of Spain? Surviving six brothers meant she was no shrinking violet, and a working life was all about exploring possibilities. So long as entertaining royalty didn't involve feathers or veils, she was up for it.

'On board his yacht,' Rose murmured thoughtfully.

'He uses the *Pegasus* as a floating office and entertainment centre,' Adena explained.

'I see,' Rose murmured, wishing she had more experience to draw on. It wasn't her ability to adapt to these new demands that concerned her, but her naivete where men were concerned. Flirting at the wedding was one thing, but being enclosed on a yacht for a week with a man she found so devastatingly attractive...six brothers looking over her shoulder and a drunken father in the background hadn't exactly given Rose much chance to learn about men.

She'd done okay so far, Rose reasoned. She'd just have to rise to the occasion, and hope Raffa didn't do the same.

Landing by helicopter on a swaying deck in the dark was quite an experience. There was no sign of Raffa in the welcoming committee, which consisted of two uniformed stewards who had obviously expected Rose to arrive with a great deal of luggage.

Shouldering her backpack, she smiled her thanks as a man who introduced himself as the purser helped her down. To say the ground was shifting beneath her feet was an understatement, but she was determined to make the most of this new adventure.

Try telling yourself that when you can't get a signal on your phone, or your balance on the deck! Clinging to the rail, she smiled brightly at the purser as he waited patiently for Rose to follow him. This was the experience of a lifetime, she reminded herself, not a trial by ordeal.

Once they were inside the spectacular interior of the mammoth yacht, Rose began to relax, though another shock was waiting when the purser showed her into her quarters. She had expected something small and cramped in the bowels of the ship, but he had just opened a pair of grand double doors on the most amazing suite of rooms.

'All for me?' She breathed like a muppet as she took in what looked more like an upscale penthouse than a cabin on a ship.

'Yes, ma'am,' the purser replied. 'All for you.'

Two very different worlds had just collided. She knew horses could often cross the boundaries of race, wealth and class, and Rose had always been comfortable working alongside Raffa on his ranch, but here she felt…completely at sea?

'I hope you'll be comfortable,' the purser said as he showed her around the most sumptuous accommodation imaginable.

'Are you sure this is where I'm supposed to be staying?'

'If you'd prefer another suite—'

That wasn't what she'd meant at all. 'This is absolutely perfect.' If entirely over the top for a groom. Alarm bells started ringing when she stared at the emperor-sized bed.

'You'll find the dressing room is stocked with most things you'll need,' the purser continued, 'but if there's anything else you can think of that's missing, we can have it flown in by helicopter.'

Of course they could, Rose marvelled. 'Well, this is wonderful.' And miraculous. How did they even know her size?

Leading her through to a dressing room with the dimensions of a conventional lounge, the purser opened drawers and cupboards on an array of high-end goods.

'Sorry to repeat myself,' Rose said, frowning, 'but are you sure all this is for me?'

'Señorita Adena was asked to fill out a list of things you might like.'

Adena? Ah, that solved the mystery, but why hadn't Raffa asked Rose straight out? Didn't he trust her to ask for the right things to fit with his lifestyle on board the yacht?

The thrill of looking around made Raffa's presumption fade away. Not only had Adena proved to be the best of friends, she'd done the most excellent job.

'You'll find a letter detailing plans for each day,' the purser informed Rose. 'In your free time, you may use the swimming pool on the sun deck, where you can call for drinks and snacks. Please enjoy the rest of your day.'

'You're very kind.' She had to force herself to walk slowly to the door as she showed him out, but the moment the door had closed behind him she rushed back to pounce on the letter. Ripping the envelope open, she pulled out a note. Embossed with the logo of a flying horse, it said in Raffa's bold black script:

> *You will be dining in the open-air salon tonight at eight o'clock. Dress: casual.*

Casual, as in banged-up jeans and an old faded top? She doubted it. Shower first, with the suit she normally wore for interviews hanging in the bathroom to steam out the creases. A fresh blouse later, and she'd be ready for whatever lay ahead.

The temptation to take a quick tour of the outfits in her dressing room proved irresistible. It would be rude not to. Adena had gone to so much trouble. These were clothes Rose had only seen in magazines before. Caution was not a word she would use in connection with them. Glamour was the watchword here.

'I miss you, Adena,' Rose murmured as she stared in awe. 'And I promise to wear at least one of these fabulous gowns, if only as a nightdress…'

Rose reckoned a swim before dinner might relax her. The way she felt—excited, aroused and bewildered at the thought of seeing Raffa again in these extraordinary surroundings—threatened to take her mind off the reason she was here. Plus, she had to brace herself for disappointment when he treated her not as a dance partner, or a woman he wanted to spend time with, but as his head groom—which should have been enough for her, but really wasn't. Selecting her armour, she chose a bright green swimming costume with matching cover-up. This was no time for blending into the shadows.

A sense of urgency pervaded his work the moment Raffa learned Rose was on board. Finishing the last of his video calls early, he found it impossible to concentrate on anything else until he'd seen her. A head groom gained unique insight into his life, meaning the position called for the utmost discretion, along with encyclopaedic knowledge about horses, together with the ability to communicate that knowledge to all types of people. This week would prove whether Rose was ideally suited in the long term for the job.

She was certainly suited for his bed, he reflected before he could stop himself as he pulled on his swimming shorts. The purser had informed him that Rose was in her stateroom, so he planned to swim and clear his head before meeting up with her. Having spent the morning behind a desk, he was eager for exercise.

He arrived at the pool to find Rose had settled in before him. The surprise of seeing her there was a punch to his senses. With her back to him, and a large-brimmed hat hiding her spectacular hair, it was clear she'd gone for impact, rather than discretion, by choosing an emerald green swimsuit that outlined her spectacular figure. A matching cover-up was draped across the chair, but she made no attempt to reach for it as she turned to face him.

Rose.

Grabbing a swim towel from the stack on the side, he slung it around his neck.

Removing her hat, Rose placed it carefully on the sun-bed at her side. With a graceful action, she reached up to free her glorious hair from the colourful scarf containing it. As she raked her fingers through the waist-length tumble, the effect it created was, to Raffa's mind, a fiery cloud to compete with any sunset.

'Raffa!'

'I'm sorry if I startled you.'

She clutched her chest. 'It's good to see you,' she said. 'Thank you for inviting me to your yacht. Not as a guest, of course,' she added quickly, as if wanting to reassure him on that point.

'I hope my purser has made you comfortable?'

'If I had to walk the plank anywhere, I guess this is the best place to do it.'

He raised a brow. 'Let's hope that won't be necessary.'

His body urgently demanded one thing, while his mind demanded another. He required the best of the best in the role of Head Groom. Rose was that individual. There'd be other women he could have in his bed.

But they wouldn't be Rose.

'The *Pegasus* effortlessly covers vast distances, allowing me to entertain at short notice. No hotel can compete with the facilities here.'

'I heartily confirm that,' Rose agreed.

Something had to give. How could she be so cool when the wolf inside him was howling with impatience? 'Swim?' he suggested curtly, willing his body to behave.

'Why not?' Rose replied eagerly.

'You do swim?'

'I do,' she confirmed, with what he thought was a glint of amusement.

Rose accepted the invitation gladly. Having seen Raffa in black swimming shorts that revealed more than they concealed, she badly needed cooling off. Her senses were in free fall, but wanting him was dangerous to both her heart and mind. How to stop wanting him was the problem. Raffa was her boss. Rose was here to prove she could handle all aspects of the job. Expanding her working life was an exciting prospect, and one she embraced with enthusiasm…but there was nothing to stop her having a little harmless fun along the way.

The water was deliciously cold against her overheated skin. Rising to the surface, she drew in air before slicing through the water as if racing her brothers. Within moments a form appeared beneath her. It was Raffa, swimming underwater on his back. She kicked even harder, but, the wretch he was, he pulled ahead.

'You cheated,' she accused when they reached the far end, by which time she was laughing with sheer pleasure.

'I cheated by swimming underwater?' Raffa queried with a frown. 'You should have set the rules before we began. You're a great swimmer. Fast,' he approved.

'Six brothers, remember.' She spoke with the broadest of smiles, appreciating her brothers more in that moment than she ever had before.

'And a competitive spirit,' Raffa added. 'You'll need that to go far in your career.'

'I won't disappoint,' she promised fiercely, loving the way they could switch from play to work and back again.

'This experience will be good for you, Rose. You don't know how strong you are until you're tested.'

'Prophetic words?' she queried as Raffa placed his big hands on the side of the pool and sprang out. 'Not up for a race, then?' she shouted after him.

Stopping dead in his tracks, he turned. 'Is that a challenge, *señorita*?'

'*You* mentioned competitive spirit,' she reminded him.

The wait of a few short seconds felt endless to Rose, and then Raffa turned slowly to face her. 'Race me?' he queried.

'Why not? I race my brothers.'

'Head start?' he offered.

'If you think you need it.' Without waiting for a reply, she launched herself backwards in the water. Raffa followed and, in a stroke or two, overtook her.

'You should have mentioned you swam for Ireland,' he teased when they reached the far side.

'Good race,' Rose gasped.

When Raffa sprang out, he dipped down again to take hold of her hand.

'Thank you,' she said as he hauled her out of the pool as if she weighed nothing.

'You're an excellent swimmer,' he remarked as he tossed a towel in her direction.

'And you're an excellent liar. You beat me by half a pool's length.'

'Only because I was going slowly,' Raffa teased, with a look that heated her from the inside out.

'I'm challenging you to a rematch,' she shouted after him.

'I look forward to it.'

'So long as you don't allow the result of that swim-off to affect your judgement when it comes to my job?'

'I enjoy swimming with you,' he said, displaying the power in his formidable torso as he opened his arms wide. 'We can have that race any time you like.'

'I'll take you up on that,' Rose promised.

He grinned.

'This is a fabulous way to spend your time,' she remarked as they settled down on the sunbeds.

'It is a great way to travel,' Raffa agreed. 'Efficient,' he concluded with a thoughtful nod.

An incredulous laugh burst out of her. 'Only a billionaire could say that. The rest of us catch the bus, or hope it doesn't rain when we take the bike out of the shed.'

She was never quite sure how far she could push it, and it was a relief when Raffa laughed too.

Seeing his life through Rose's eyes was like seeing it through a new and extraordinary prism. As he followed her gaze across the pristine deck, he noticed, for perhaps the first time, what she meant. Their surroundings were spectacular. And so was she. Unaffected by wealth or status, Rose was one of those truly rare things: a very nice person. And as such, he should give her a swerve. There was too much darkness inside him, too much unresolved anger and grief. Bad things happened to people he cared about, and it would be ridiculously easy to become involved with such an intriguing and attractive woman.

Was Rose so different beneath the surface? Didn't she have shadows too?

He wouldn't add to them. 'Dinner's at eight o'clock sharp,' he reminded her.

'Don't worry, I'll be there.'

He held her stare a dangerous beat too long, before springing up and walking away. 'I have business calls to make,' he called over his shoulder.

'And I have swotting up to do, in case you feel like testing me this evening on the names of all those people you want me to meet.'

'Later,' he confirmed.

She watched Raffa disappear down the companionway and had to resist the urge to chase after him, but that would be entirely unprofessional and, thankfully, sensible Rose knew it.

Back in her own suite, she took a shower then tugged on jeans and a top before sitting down at the desk to glance over the notes she'd made. She was usually a fast study, but that was before Raffa invaded her mind.

I must not screw this up.

The words banged about in her head. It would soon be eight o'clock, but the touch of Raffa's hand on hers when he'd helped her out of the pool with a grip so firm and sure and safe... And with that look in his eyes that had been the complete opposite of safe. She must not screw this up, indeed!

The next problem was not what to wear. The contents of Rose's luxurious dressing room might be tempting, but temptation was the last thing she needed tonight. Securing her hair in a sensible ponytail at the nape of her neck, she considered doing without make-up. After all, what was make-up but cheese in a mousetrap, when the look she should be aiming for was dry biscuit? But Adena had worked so hard to make sure Rose lacked for nothing. It would be churlish to throw those efforts back in her friend's face. Adena would be hungry to hear about everything…including the high-end products still in their cellophane wrappers.

A flick of mascara, and some nude lipstick later, and Rose was ready to meet her fate.

Glancing at her phone out of habit, she grimaced and shut the door again. The press was still discussing the mystery woman seen dancing with 'The World's Most Eligible Bachelor' at his sister's wedding. Gossip had already identified the woman as none other than Rose Kelly, a groom from Ireland who worked in Raffa Acosta's stable. 'The deadly Acosta charm works its magic again.'

'Not on me,' Rose pledged out loud, but she couldn't resist reading on.

'Yet another willing victim sacrificing herself on the altar of lust. And who could blame her?' the journalist asked archly.

Rose wasn't given to cursing. She heard enough of that language at home, but tonight she made an exception. Had Raffa read this too? Were these few column inches in the press all that her hard work added up to? It was naive to think she could keep the encounter with Raffa at the wedding a secret when everyone with a phone was an amateur paparazzo, but to suggest she'd jump into bed with a man simply because he was sex on two hard-muscled legs was…

Not going to happen, Rose determined as she smoothed the skirt of her serviceable suit.

Worse luck.

CHAPTER FOUR

IF SHE'D BEEN worried about Raffa's reaction when he read the articles about them in the press, it was nothing to Rose's reaction when she saw where she was about to eat supper. The scene on deck was like something from a film set. She couldn't help exclaiming, 'Do you eat like this every night?'

Raffa swung around, and so did her heart. In fact, it lurched in each and every direction at once, and it took all she'd got to bring it back, to adopt a friendly but serious expression as she walked towards him.

'Good evening, Rose.' Pulling away from the rail where he'd been lounging, Raffa advanced with a steady, purposeful step.

'I didn't expect this,' she admitted with a long glance at the dining table. Dressed with crystal and silver beneath a gently rippling white canopy, the area was lit by flickering candles, which suggested a lot more than a business dinner.

'You thought we'd eat burgers, and hang with a couple of beers?' Raffa suggested dryly, before explaining, 'My chef wanted to test some of the recipes for my champagne reception—'

Rose's heart jumped alarmingly once again. She'd somehow managed to park the socialising element of the week in an underused part of her mind. Not that she didn't party in Ireland, but a ceilidh down the village hall would hardly compare with a celebration on board the *Pegasus*.

'—so I told the chef this would be the ideal occasion,' Raffa continued smoothly.

'Of course,' Rose agreed. 'Who are we receiving? At the champagne reception, I mean.'

Raffa had already turned away to speak to the steward. 'No champagne, thank you. I'll call if we need anything more. His Serene Highness, for one,' he said, switching back to Rose. 'Don't look so worried. My champagne reception is nothing compared to the Prince's annual charity ball the following night.'

'And when is the champagne reception?' Rose asked.

'Tomorrow night.'

'As soon as that?' Rose's throat dried. 'You'll be busy.'

'And so will you,' Raffa assured her. 'There won't be a better opportunity to launch you into society. You haven't been long in the job, and these events will give me the chance to introduce you around and see how well, or not, you're received.'

As the World's Most Eligible Bachelor thief, Rose didn't imagine she'd be welcomed with open arms.

'Aren't you pleased?' Raffa prompted.

Rose reminded herself that this was El Lobo, the Wolf, as Raffa's black stare stabbed into hers. 'It all sounds very exciting,' she lied, doubting six great hulking brothers had prepared her for the type of high-society individuals she would meet on Raffa's superyacht. 'I'm looking forward to it enormously.'

'Is that why you've lost your appetite?'

Raffa missed nothing. Laden platters had been placed in front of them, and Rose couldn't face a thing. 'It all looks delicious.' Her stomach grumbled right on cue. When had she last had something to eat?

Finally, she ate, and the food was indeed delicious. She told Raffa so in a series of appreciative moans. She could do this. She had to do this if she wanted to progress in her career. When he began to talk about the ponies they both loved, she knew it would be possible, because this was once again the serious-minded man she worked for and respected, the man whose unparalleled equine knowledge had drawn Rose to work for him in the first place. It wasn't long before her enthusiasm for the topic spilled over, and the glamorous occasions ahead of her lost their power to intimidate.

Rose continued to impress him over dinner. The press had been less than kind to her since the wedding, suggesting she was an opportunistic gold digger, making the most of her surprise inclusion in his sister's wedding. He was accustomed to being picked over by the press, but it was new for Rose, yet she made no mention of it. Even when he broached the subject, she brushed it aside, and got back to talking about the animals she loved.

'Rest easy, where those articles are concerned,' he said as she continued to weave the magic of unaffected charm over him. 'They won't influence my thinking on your work. The post of Head Groom is too vital for that.'

'Thank you for the reassurance,' Rose said as she dabbed at her mouth with a napkin. His gaze followed her movements. The evening had grown chilly while they'd been eating, and when she reached for the throw on the back of her chair, he leaned forward and draped it around her shoulders.

'I've learned so much while I've been working for you,' she admitted, staring up at him with the frankness in her eyes that made her irresistible. 'I adore my work, and I'm open to any and all developments where my career is concerned. I've got such wonderful colleagues. We wouldn't be the team we are without them, and I've made so many friends.'

As she talked, he saw the passion in her eyes, and suddenly wanted that same passion directed at him, but relationships outside his immediate family had proved impossible since the tragedy. He could go so far and no further, before his concern to protect others from his darkness kicked in. So many things had become impossible on the night he saw his parents perish in front of him. His mother used to say love is beautiful, but he thought it agonisingly cruel.

Something in his thoughts must have communicated to Rose and triggered a surprising response in her. 'Tears?' he queried. 'Does your job mean so much to you?'

'It means everything to me,' Rose confessed fiercely, pulling herself together fast. 'When my mother fell ill, she made me promise to take her place and look after the family. My brothers have flown the nest, but my father's still a constant worry, so I have to succeed, to be in a position to support him, just as my mother asked.'

Hostage for life, he thought, realising that Rose would never believe she'd done enough. He was glad she'd confided in him. It explained the shadows in her eyes, and her constant drive to be the best. He could relate to those emotions.

'Everything I do is geared to keeping the family afloat,' she continued. 'And please don't feel sorry for me. Remember, I chose this path.'

Had she, or had Rose's direction in life come from a desire to break free from what must have been a difficult childhood? 'Thank you for your company tonight,' he said formally, bringing the evening to a close. 'You've got a big day ahead of you tomorrow, so try to get some sleep.'

Rose stood and thanked the stewards, who reappeared at exactly the right moment to hold her chair and open doors. 'Goodnight, Raffa. Sleep well.'

He doubted that would happen with Rose lying in a bed only a few yards away from his.

Rose was determined to keep things upbeat the next morning at breakfast. She and Raffa had trodden a tight-rope over grief the previous evening that could alter the course of this week, if she dwelled on it. Working in a top stable was tough for all concerned, which meant a good-humoured, purposeful attitude was essential.

'Good morning,' she said brightly, joining Raffa at the table. The only problem now was Raffa in cut off jeans, revealing rock-hard muscles in his deeply tanned legs, and a top that showed off everything, including his infamous wolf tattoo.

But this was not the time for feasting on Raffa, who launched straight in with the news that he had more conference calls to make that morning. 'Meanwhile, you will liaise with the galley staff and everyone else on board the *Pegasus*, to ensure the champagne reception runs smoothly tonight. I have some additions to the list of people I've asked you to talk to at the event. It always helps to have a plan.' His black stare lingered on her face, unreadable and inconveniently arousing. 'Rose?'

'Sorry.' Moistening her lips, she quickly refocused. 'I'm delighted to help in any way I can. I'm so looking forward to meeting your guests.'

'No careless revelation of trade secrets,' he warned.

'You can rely on me for discretion.'

'We'll heave to in the ocean off the coast of Monte

Carlo. My crew has entertained like this many times before, but I'm looking to you to add something more...an extra dimension, if you will.'

'Of course.' Excitement gripped Rose as she switched on the part of her brain that delighted in organising the heck out of things.

Raffa went on to explain that the *Pegasus* would be dressed for the reception as well. 'Pennants, lights, champagne, music, and, of course, you'll join me in welcoming His Serene Highness on board.'

'Of course,' she agreed, imagination running riot at the thought of sharing the occasion with Raffa.

'The event starts at eight. Things move fast in the Acosta world,' Raffa cautioned.

'I think I already know that,' she pointed out good-humouredly, 'and I promise not to let you down.'

'Excellent,' Raffa said briskly. 'The following night, as I mentioned to you yesterday, I will be the Prince's guest of honour at his most important charity event of the year. There'll be more people for you to meet at the ball, so I suggest you mug up on the names I've given you.'

To hear the brazen invitation to sin sitting next to her coolly detailing plans for upcoming events made Rose want to smile at the unlikely clash of sex and heat and business.

'It's an opportunity to start building relationships at the very highest level,' Raffa explained, staring straight into her eyes. 'You'll be adding to your knowledge of how deals are done in the horse world. Your reputation in Ireland was second to none, and now you're going global, Rose.'

'I'm excited,' she admitted, and not just by the professional opportunities Raffa was putting her way. 'I'm guessing formal dress will be required?'

'Just bring your quick wits along,' he advised, lounging back in his chair.

'I will,' she vowed, eager to make a start on her homework for the night.

Trepidation successfully quelled, Rose was bouncing off the ceiling with anticipation in her dressing room later that same afternoon at the thought of the night ahead. A champagne reception *and* a prince. Thank goodness Adena had arranged for such an amazing selection of fabulous gowns for Rose to choose from. Slipping into the green silk sheath she'd selected for the event, she gasped at the transformation in the mirror. She looked so elegant she could almost believe she belonged in Raffa's very different world.

The phone rang, distracting her. It was Raffa wanting to know Rose had checked up on everything she was supposed to.

'You sound breathless,' he remarked. 'Are you sure everything's all right?'

Learning to walk in high heels with a skirt that wrapped around her like a mummy's bandage wasn't the easiest thing she'd ever had to do. 'Perfect,' she lied, steadying herself on a handy table as she kicked off the perilous heels.

'You can't be tense tonight,' Raffa warned. 'My guests will sense it, and they won't relax if you don't, which means no one will have a good time. Did you find something you're happy to wear? If not, I can always arrange for the helicopter to take you to Monte Carlo to select something else.'

If that didn't knock the air out of her chest, nothing would. 'That won't be necessary,' she managed with studied calm. 'Thank you for the offer, but there's more than enough choice here—'

Rose stared at the receiver in her hand as the line cut. What would Raffa think when he saw her in this? Was it too much? She smoothed her hand down the sleek silk clinging to her body like a second skin. No reaction from Raffa would be a slap in the face, while even the smallest reaction might steal her attention from the only thing that mattered tonight, which was promoting Rancho Raffa Acosta. No place-filler tonight, she would instead be co-hosting a party with a billionaire. And yes, it would be nice to have Raffa look at her with something more than speculation in his eyes, but there could be no loitering in the shadows this time. It would be full-on guest-hosting from the get-go.

Hair down, make-up on, and a spritz of scent later, she was ready to embark on the next stage of what she was coming to think of as Rose's Remarkable Journey.

Glamorous evening? Bring it on.

Dressed overall, and with all lights blazing, the *Pegasus* looked fabulous tonight. Rose stood in awe for a moment in the entrance to the grand salon, the main reception area on the yacht, staring past all the trimmings to where one man stood alone on the deck. She didn't need hand holding, which was just as well, as Raffa's life was one long line of business discussions, so he'd doubtless have his own itinerary for tonight. The *Pegasus* wasn't so much a billionaire's folly as a floating necessity that allowed him to move his office around the world. No wonder he was such a polo fanatic. Playing the game was the only downtime this titan of the business world allowed himself.

She stopped in her tracks, hearing the first of the tenders approaching. Moments later the chatter of excited partygoers floated across the water. Changing direction, she prepared to greet the first of their guests.

It was accepted etiquette that everyone must be in place before the Prince arrived, and Rose was gripped by the same excitement as the rest at the thought of a royal visitor, but even that paled in comparison to watching Raffa circulate amongst his guests. He eclipsed everything and everyone around him. As distinguished as a prince, he was as sexy as humanly possible, having dressed for the occasion in an immaculately tailored white jacket and slim-fitting black trousers. With midnight blue sapphires flashing at the cuffs of his crisp white shirt, he was hot and hard, and heading her way. Fumbling in her evening purse, she cursed softly, only now remembering his missing cufflink was in another bag. *Next time!* She'd get it back to him tomorrow latest.

'I see you found a dress,' he commented.

Did that slight angling of his chin, and that look in his eyes, denote approval? 'I did,' she confirmed.

'Great choice of gown,' he said with the lift of a brow.

Sound faded as they stared at each other, until all she was aware of was Raffa. 'I'm glad you approve.'

His lips slanted, as if to let her know that, whatever he thought of the dress, he knew she'd have worn it anyway. 'You've also done a good job with the details.'

The flowers in her hair, or the addition of bite-sized canapés to accompany the flutes of champagne?

'The guests you'll meet tonight know how to enjoy themselves,' Raffa informed her. 'You'll find the party achieves a momentum of its own.'

Like so many things, Rose thought, basking in awareness as Raffa placed a hand in the small of her back to guide her across the deck to the first of the people he'd like her to meet. This turned out to be a prominent professor at the forefront of animal therapy, and he and Rose were soon deep in conversation. She thanked Raffa silently with a warm glance. 'You're welcome,' he murmured before moving away.

When Raffa returned, Rose and the professor were still talking animatedly. 'You'll have to excuse us, Professor,' he apologised. 'The Prince's helicopter is due to land, and we must be there to greet him.'

'Of course...' The professor bowed over Rose's hand. 'I hope we have the chance to talk again very soon.'

'You seem to have made a good impression there,' Raffa remarked as they made their way to the helipad. 'I'm glad. The professor's important to me. He saved me at a time when I had so much anger inside me, it threatened to consume me. He made me see that animals could help to soothe the human spirit.'

'They have an innate healing quality I've always been interested in pursuing,' Rose confessed.

She could guess when Raffa had been at his lowest point, and was glad the professor had been able to help him. She only had to think back to how her own emotions had run the gamut after her mother's death, from despair to hollow emptiness, and on to anger at the injustice of random fate, to understand the turmoil that so often accompanied grief. This was the most insight Raffa had given her, but now was not the time to draw him out even further. He'd tell her more when he was ready to—or, not at all.

He felt a jab of something unexpected as he watched the Prince talking to Rose. Had he ever experienced jealousy before? The Prince was charming, and Rose was easily the most attractive and interesting woman at the party, but she was no Cinderella, waiting for a prince to sweep her off her feet. She was a hard-working woman, who knew her job, and whose natural charm and ability to listen and be genuinely interested put everyone at ease. When the Prince moved away, Raffa watched Rose work the crowd with all the flair of an accomplished host. She made everyone feel special, and had quickly become the hub around which his party flowed. His one complaint was that the food had turned from savoury to sweet by the time she returned to his side.

'You've arrived just in time to gorge on chocolate,' he said as a steward offered them a plate full of sin.

Rose laughed. 'Don't tempt me.'

'Dive in—one for each hand,' he advised.

She glanced at him and blushed. 'I'd love to, but I'm guessing our guests won't appreciate a chocolate hand-shake—'

'Allow me...' Selecting a delicious-looking treat from the tray, he touched it to her lips.

Rose's gaze flashed up and darkened, almost as if he'd made a move to kiss her. The temptation to do so over-whelmed him, especially when her tongue crept out to lick her lips, but she turned in response to the chatter of their guests, and quickly excused herself to introduce some newcomers around. That was what he wanted, of course. A successful party depended on the swift reac-tions of the host.

It should be what he wanted, he amended, as Rose charmed yet another group. She was careful not to leave anyone out—except him, apparently. With an amused huff, he pushed away from the rail and set out to work the other side of the deck.

Guests took precedence over anything else. Even Raffa, though her gaze kept straying to him. He could turn on the charm at parties, but Rose had glimpsed the darker side of their glamorous host. It would be good for both of them to let some light into the darkness, but Rose had never had the time to properly deal with the past, and guessed Raffa was in a similar position. Maybe one day they would manage it, but, with the party in full flow, tonight was not the right occasion. She had stewards to help and food to bring out, as well as what seemed like a constant stream of misplaced items to find for various guests.

When the evening finally drew to a close, and the Prince thanked them both for a most wonderful party, Raffa was quick with his praise. 'You worked hard tonight,' he told her as they stood watching His Serene Highness's helicopter lift off the deck. 'Thank you, Rose.'

'Thank you for the opportunity,' she replied with genuine warmth. 'It's been a wonderful evening. I didn't expect to enjoy it quite so much.'

'You were the hit of the night,' he reassured her, 'and you've another big day ahead of you tomorrow, so you'd better get a good night's sleep.'

'I will,' she assured him.

They stood facing each other, Raffa with his head dipped in Rose's direction. Something in his eyes made Rose raise her chin. There was a moment, a very long moment, when she was absolutely certain Raffa would kiss her this time, and Rose was equally sure she'd kiss him back.

Seconds ticked by, and when—once again—nothing happened, oddly disappointed, she turned to go. 'You get a good night's sleep too,' she called to Raffa over her shoulder.

Thoughts of Rose plagued him throughout the night. Reliving the moment when the thought of kissing her had crossed his mind and taken hold made an ice-cold shower a necessity.

The ice-cold shower was no help at all. Lifting his face to the spray, he attempted to banish lustful thoughts from his mind.

That went well.

Cursing viciously, he cut off the stream of water, stepped out and grabbed a towel to dry off. This was why he never allowed himself to feel. Feelings only got in the way. Sex had been his saviour in so many ways. It brought physical relief and blanked out the emotional pain of the past for however long it lasted. Planting clenched fists on the marble surface of the washstand, he stared at his reflection in the mirror. A hard man stared back. Rose Kelly had no place in his mind. He had nothing to offer her, apart from employment opportunities on his ranch.

Raking his hair with stiff, angry fingers, he grimaced as memories of the past came flooding back. When he'd discovered the pilot had been drunk, he'd cursed himself for not boarding the private jet to check it out himself before it took off with his parents on board. He'd learned a vital lesson that night. Love was not invincible. It could be destroyed by something as simple as a bottle of whisky in the wrong hands.

Impatient at this lapse back into a past he couldn't change, he scowled and left the bathroom. Rose's soothing balm was what he needed—her laughter, her challenges and an enlivening dose of her cheek. Admittedly these were all a poor substitute for sex, but something had to help him relax.

Only, seeing Rose in person would have to wait. Business meetings were stacked up in front of him, and it was the charity ball tonight. Texting Rose, he reminded her of her itinerary. There must be no slackening off from the standard she'd set last night.

I have meetings all day. You have hairdresser, beautician, etc. at noon. Report to the helipad eight p.m. sharp. R

He thought about adding a few encouraging words, but Rose had done very well without them so far.

Rose was still rubbing sleep from her eyes when her phone pinged. 'I should have put it on silent,' she muttered, squinting to read the short note. Seeing it was from Raffa, she sat bolt upright, instantly awake. Touching her lips, all she could think about was their almost kiss. Was Raffa thinking about her, and remembering it too?

Heart in her mouth, Rose scanned the text fast. And frowned. Clearly not. No mention at all of last night, just a list of appointments she was expected to attend. Crushed, she was in no mood to comply. Hairdresser? Beautician? What was she—a show pony? Then a worse thought occurred: Had she made a fool of herself last night—misjudged the look with that gown? No. Even in such a glamorous frock, she'd been dressed down in comparison to some of the women.

Sitting cross-legged on the bed, she pulled faces at her reflection in the wall mirror. She scrubbed up as well as the next person. It wasn't as if she were planning to attend the ball in her pyjamas. Hairdresser? Hadn't she been doing her own hair all her life? As for needing a beautician? You couldn't correct a face full of freckles without a bucketful of Polyfilla, and no one was coming near enough to slap on a face full of that. And what exactly did 'etc' mean? A stylist perhaps? That could be useful, Rose concluded with a frown. She could do with someone to teach her how to walk in high heels.

Raffa would apparently be busy until he attended the ball, but at least that spared her the usual interrogation over breakfast this morning. He was not an easy taskmaster. She had studied hard at equestrian college, but Raffa had obviously eaten and fully digested the texts. There wasn't a thing he didn't know about horses.

Not seeing him wasn't all good. Apart from the obvious basking in the glow of a flame that burned so bright, the lack of Raffa meant losing her anchor in this sea of plenty, and there was no guarantee he'd be her rock tonight. Raffa would be seated with the Prince, while Rose would be so far away, she'd probably be sitting out in the yard.

A flutter of apprehension gripped Rose, until she reminded herself that she'd managed pretty well last night, and would manage again. The one thing she'd never had a problem with was standing on her own two feet, and any expansion in her duties signalled a welcome progression in her career.

A knock on the door jolted her out of the reverie. Was it Raffa? He'd look great carrying a breakfast tray. She smoothed her hair. 'Come in...'

It was a uniformed steward with a smiling explanation. 'Señor Acosta thought you might like breakfast in bed today.'

With Raffa, yes, Bad Rose suggested. 'That's very kind of you,' Good Rose said politely, lapping up the sight of a tray laid so perfectly it was fit for the Ritz.

'Your beautician and hairdresser arrive at noon,' the steward said, as if he'd been asked to reinforce Raffa's message. 'Señor Acosta suggests you relax for the rest of this morning.'

Suggests? Unless Rose was mistaken, that was an in-struction. Raffa wanted her to be fresh tonight, and out of his way today. Had that 'almost kiss' affected him too—in a way that made him determined to stay away from her—or was she making too much of it?

'Breakfast looks delicious,' she called tactfully after the steward as he left the room, though her appetite had all but disappeared.

Releasing her death grip on the butter knife, she started to prepare herself mentally for the palace ball. The first thing—the most vital thing of all—was to fi-nally remember to return Raffa's cufflink. She couldn't entrust it to anyone else.

Searching out the evening bag she intended to use that night, she secured the black jewel in the small zip-up pocket. Her next task was to remind herself how much she enjoyed meeting new people, and how she relished di-verse topics of conversation. What was so different about tonight? A ball at the royal palace would be daunting for anyone, though for Raffa it would be all about business. Networking was a crucial part of his life. And now, for some annoying reason, a parade of unfeasibly beautiful females, all with the world's most eligible bachelor in their sights, plonked itself in her mind. She tried reas-suring herself that her only task was to choose a dress to wear, while those imaginary women, in competition for Raffa, would be at it tooth and claw.

Closing her eyes on that unfortunate image was no use at all, for there they were, taunting her as they sashayed up and down behind her eyelids.

Where the choice of gown for tonight was concerned, glamour the heck out of it was the only answer.

CHAPTER FIVE

HIS TRANSFER FROM ship to shore was seamless, but he couldn't relax until he knew his team had arrived at the palace. Until he knew Rose had arrived at the palace. Infuriating woman! Why was she always in his head? No matter how many times he told himself that caring for anyone outside his immediate family might attract fate to take an interest, he appeared unable to stifle his concern for Rose. The evening would be dull without her. Even if she appeared in her interview suit she would light up the room.

He'd gone ahead of his team to meet the Prince in private to discuss some upcoming polo matches, and now he was pacing the ballroom like a youth on his first date. *Where the hell was she?*

Glancing at his watch, he spat out a curse. It was only two minutes since the last time he'd looked. He had skipped a reception after his business with the Prince to make sure he was here in time to reassure Rose that this vast space, with its ceiling painted by some protégée of Michelangelo, glorious marble floor, stately pillars and glittering chandeliers, was merely top dressing for what really mattered, which were the charities that would benefit from the after-dinner auction tonight. He was confident the stuffed shirts present would be captivated by Rose's warmth and charm, and he couldn't wait for them to meet her. What a surprise they'd have, in the form of a spirited Irishwoman with laughter in her eyes and kindness in her heart.

Kindness was perhaps Rose's greatest asset, he reflected, that and her voluptuous body, which was outstanding. His thoughts jumped to what she'd wear for such a dazzling occasion. It was impossible to predict anything where Rose was concerned, apart from the fact that she'd be true to herself, and that in itself set her apart.

Spying His Serene Highness making directly for him forced him to concentrate on the here and now. There could be no more glancing up the sweeping marble staircase to see if Rose had arrived, or staring at his watch, willing the hands to move, but he found it hard to concentrate on what the Prince was saying, and could only trust he dipped his head and nodded in all the right places as the Prince went on. 'I'd like to discuss the details of our polo matches with your head groom present—'

A flurry at the top of the stairs distracted them both. They weren't alone in inhaling sharply. The palace ballroom had hosted many beautiful women, but none could compare to the woman at the top of the stairs.

Rose had paused in a halo of light, to take in her surroundings and get her bearings, he guessed. The impulse to leave the Prince, mount the stairs and escort her down the sweeping staircase was overwhelming, but this was Rose. This was her moment. No hiding in the shadows tonight, she was obviously determined to put on a good show for him, and if that meant dressing like a queen, and lifting her chin to warm the room with her smile, then that was exactly what she would do.

'I have to say, you have impeccable taste,' the Prince observed in a discreet murmur.

'Rose is an exceptional horsewoman,' he replied, re-

fusing to besmirch Rose's reputation with even the slightest hint of impropriety.

As he had expected, Rose didn't wait for anyone to
escort her down the steps. Several contenders tried, and
were all charmingly but firmly dismissed. Chin up, eyes
smiling, Rose appeared to float down the stairs wearing
the highest of heels. How long before she kicked them
off? he wondered with amusement.

Leaving the Prince with a gracious bow, he waited at
the foot of the stairs. Rose's exquisite green eyes smiled
into his, but the enchantment of her presence was infectious, and the Prince lost no time in joining him to welcome Rose.

'You'll sit with us on the top table,' His Serene Highness insisted with his customary charm.

'I'd be honoured, Your Serene Highness,' Rose replied engagingly.

Only the swift blush that pinked her cheeks told him
how surprised she was to receive this invitation. When
she glanced at Raffa and raised an awestruck brow, he
smiled and nodded with genuine pleasure for Rose.

'You look stunning,' he whispered when the Prince
left them to join his wife. He recognised the peach-co-
loured dress with its illusion underskirt as one he had
particularly favoured. The close fit did more than hint at
the perfection of the body underneath, while the colour
brought out the highlights of gold and copper in Rose's
ravishingly beautiful hair. She had chosen to wear her
hair down tonight and looked amazing.

'Stunning?' she queried in the same discreet tone.
'You mean, I'm not wearing breeches smeared in mud?'

'I mean,' he said, 'you look beautiful tonight.'

'You're blinded by the jewels I'm wearing,' she teased,
referring to the spectacular diamond earrings and neck-

lace he'd had couriered to the *Pegasus* especially for tonight. Everyone was clearly wearing their best pieces,
and he hadn't wanted Rose to feel left out. 'I wondered
what *etc* meant when I read your text,' she added with
an impish smile, 'and now I know.'

'I'm pleased you chose to wear them,' he admitted as
he escorted her to the Prince's table. 'I was by no means
certain that you would.'

'I couldn't leave them rusting away in that old jewel
case. I'll never get the chance to wear things like this
again,' she added, touching her fingertips reverently to
the intricate diamond necklace. 'So, I thought, why not?'

'Why not, indeed?' he agreed, enjoying the novelty of
a woman who would never take such extravagant jewels
for granted. 'Enjoy them while you can.'

'There is another possibility,' she suggested.

Her words made him tense. Was Rose about to disappoint him like all the rest by being so overcome by the
obvious value of the jewels, she'd see no further than his
bank balance? 'What's that?' he queried mildly.

'I agree to become your mistress,' she said, perfectly
straight-faced. 'Then, I can wear jewels like this all the time.'

Disappointment slapped him in the face, to the point
where he almost missed what she said next.

'Even when I'm mucking out,' she added with a grin.
'In fact, I'd like to order a tiara to complete the set. As
Head Groom, I should have some sort of badge of au-
thority, don't you think…?'

There was a moment of stunned silence and then he
laughed as such a strong sense of relief flooded through
him. He'd certainly met his match in Rose. 'I think that's
an excellent idea—'

'Hold on!' She held up her hand. 'I've thought of an
even better one.'

'What's that?'

'You donate the jewels to the charity auction tonight.'

'Donate the jewels?' he exclaimed with surprise. 'I had intended for you to keep them—to wear on occasions like this.'

Rose gasped, hand to chest. 'What a responsibility! Where would I keep them—in the hay store? Look, I don't mean to be ungrateful, but there are some fabulous fakes out there at a fraction of the cost, if you think it's important for me to wear jewels. Personally, I just can't see why they're necessary. Either people are interested in what I have to say about your ponies, or they're not. And, just think about it,' she confided, bringing her fragrant head close to his, 'the proceeds from the sale of these gems could be put to far better use.'

He shrugged. 'You make a good argument. Auction them, by all means. I'm only sorry I didn't think of it myself.'

'That's what a head groom's for,' she teased.

'Do you take anything seriously?' he asked as Rose's eyes fired with an engaging triumph that had nothing to do with her going one better than him, and everything to do with Rose's generous nature finding an outlet tonight in the charity auction.

'Oh, yes,' she told him with a level stare. 'I take my job very seriously indeed.'

'Which is exactly why I brought you here.'

'Then I'd better get to work,' she said, breaking the spell.

Their lips had been close, stares locked, as the fate of the jewels was decided.

Feelings he'd ruthlessly subdued for years continued to bombard him as he stepped back. 'The Prince is already seated. We should join him.'

'Is that you hinting I've said enough?' Rose asked with a twinkle.

'More than enough,' he confirmed mock-sternly as he took the greatest pleasure in escorting Rose to the Prince's table. Lavishing extravagant gifts on a woman had always been his way of easing his guilt at feeling nothing for them, but Rose needed no such gifts or grand gestures. She thought with her heart when it came to riches, and had touched him deeply with her suggestion to auction the jewels.

'You look happy,' she remarked as they approached the Prince's table.

'I am,' he admitted. Rose made him look outwards, instead of brooding on the past. How could he not feel happy about that?

Dinner, as expected, was excellent, and it was further enhanced by Rose, who once again played her part to perfection, charming everyone. When the plates were cleared the auction began. There were some big-ticket items, attracting huge sums of money, but when Rose was introduced, and stood to offer her stunning jewels for the charity, there was a collective gasp. The Prince, who had already been informed of the donation, had invited Raffa to take the rostrum, to handle what was confidently expected to be a record-breaking sale.

The first bid was a million, and it went on from there. At one point, Raffa jokingly reminded his audience that Rose was not part of the deal. She smiled sweetly at him, to a chorus of groans, but it was the look that passed between them that briefly stilled the crowd. The magic of a supposed liaison between them had the added bonus of driving bids even higher.

'Congratulations!' The Prince stood to applaud them both as Rose's jewels were sold for an astonishing amount. 'You make a great double act,' he remarked. 'Thank you both for your most generous donation.'

Rose handled the praise with her customary modesty, and soon had the Prince laughing at some quip she'd made. Later, when His Serene Highness had left the table, she reached across to hand Raffa something. 'What's this?' he asked. Instinct drove him to close his fist around Rose's pale, cool fingers.

'If you let go of me,' she whispered discreetly, 'you'll find out.'

'And if I don't?'

'You'll have one cufflink, instead of a pair. You dropped it at the wedding, when we were in the stable.'

Shock and a bittersweet sense of relief shot through him with the force of an arrow. 'And you've waited until now to give it to me?'

'Thank you is enough,' she scolded him lightly.

'Thank you,' he gritted out ungraciously.

Making his excuses to their table companions, he pushed back his chair and stood, indicating that Rose should do the same. For once, she complied, almost certainly because his face was so thunderous and she feared a scene.

'What have I done wrong?' she demanded as he ushered her at speed in the direction of the French windows leading on to the palace gardens. He stopped short on the veranda at the top of the steps. Losing the cufflink had devastated him, but his carelessness wasn't Rose's fault and he shouldn't take his self-recrimination out on her.

'You kept it safe for me all this time,' he confirmed gruffly.

'Of course I did.' Rose looked at him with concern. 'I didn't realise it meant so much to you, or I'd have made sure to get it back to you right away.'

'You kept it as a talisman instead.'

'Yes…it did feel like one,' she admitted with a puzzled frown. 'You think that too?'

'The cufflinks are special. I've always believed they carry a special magic. I've been kicking myself for being so careless ever since one disappeared.' Holding the jewel tightly in his fist for a moment, before stowing it safely in an inside pocket, he explained, 'They were the last gift from my mother.'

'Oh, Raffa…'

Rose was right. There were no words. After a silence, she led the way down the steps. His uncertain mood must have left her wondering if he'd follow, but as always Rose was both undaunted and sensitive to what was needed most, which was distance between them and everyone else at the Prince's ball.

She carried on through the subtly lit gardens, without attempting to speak, or comfort him. She didn't need to. An understanding had sprung between them, based on their shared grief.

How Rose wished she could reach inside Raffa and drag out all his pain. She felt so frustrated as they walked along. A determined woman didn't like to admit defeat, nor find it easy to accept there was a problem she couldn't solve, but so much of Raffa remained hidden. The only way forward, Rose decided, was to look at the small part of his grief he had shared with her as the first step on a long journey. Would she be a part of the rest of that journey? There was no way to tell. They'd be returning to the ranch soon, where life would return to normal. Rose would be fully occupied in the stable, while Raffa resumed his busy life. Their sole connection would be work, with chances to be close as human beings nigh on impossible. Determined to change that for a time, she dipped down to slip off her shoes. 'We're both due a night free from guilt and the past. A night to run free,' she declared, and with that, she was off.

Picking up her skirts, she ran across coarse European grass that pricked her feet, but it was damp and refreshing, and with each step she took, the sense of freedom increased. An ornate fountain dominated the centre of the lawn. It held the promise of cooling spray, as well as shade and privacy behind its elaborate stonework. The scent of flowers was intoxicating, and so was the thought of the man stalking her. She ran faster and faster into a situation of her own creation, knowing she could be risking everything on an impulse.

She skirted behind the fountain and held her breath. Closing her eyes as she rested back against the cold stone, she knew what she ought to do, when Raffa found her, and that was thank him for a wonderful evening and politely say goodnight, but if she didn't want to take things to the next level, what was she doing here? And if Raffa didn't want the very same thing, why was he coming after her?

Every moment seemed to stretch into an hour, and she almost jumped out of her skin when he finally rounded the fountain. Even in the dark, she felt his black stare on her face. It scorched its way through her body, heating every erotic zone she possessed, but, instead of yanking her into his arms as she'd halfway hoped, Raffa kept his distance, and stared out to sea. Had she misjudged this chemistry between them? Perhaps he didn't feel the same way she did. Maybe she was in danger of making a fool of herself. Upfront as always, she went ahead to find out. 'Kiss me,' she whispered.

'That isn't sensible, Rose.'

'I don't care,' she replied stubbornly.

CHAPTER SIX

THEY DIDN'T KISS right away. Instead, they shared the same breath, the same air, teasing by promising contact, only to pull back. When Raffa finally drove his mouth down on hers, delay and anticipation had built to such a crescendo the outcome was inevitable.

'What, here?' Raffa murmured with surprise as Rose drew him with her to the ground.

'Why not? Or, are you afraid of grass stains?'

He laughed as he joined her, and she sank into an embrace so firm, yet gentle, she had never felt so safe in her life. 'Don't stop?' he confirmed.

There was no stopping, no calming her, either, until she heard a peal of laughter.

'Relax,' Raffa soothed. 'It's only another couple enjoying the fruits of the night. They don't care about us.'

'A fruit of the night?' Rose repeated with a grin. 'Is that what I am?'

Cupping her buttocks in one big hand, Raffa nudged the fine mesh of her gown aside. Exposing her breasts, he suckled each nipple in turn. Thrusting her fingers through his hair, she kept him close. 'Touch me. Touch me here… Show me… Show me what to do.'

'That would be my pleasure,' Raffa whispered as he set about undressing her.

'You really don't care if we're discovered?'

'I really don't,' he admitted in the half growl she loved.

Rose was perfect. Everything about tonight had been perfect. Knowing every inch of Rose intimately was inevitable and right. Planting kisses on her neck, he abraded her skin very gently with his stubble. The thong she was wearing was composed of the finest Swiss lace and yielded easily to his strong fingers. She was so aroused the flimsy fabric could barely contain her. Trailing his fingertips over the site of her arousal, while denying Rose any real pressure, made her fierce. 'Don't tease me,' she warned, attempting to guide his hand to where she wanted it.

'But I enjoy teasing you,' he admitted as he shook her off to continue his lazy exploration.

Thrusting fiercely against his hand, she clung to him, almost in desperation. A complex mix of strong and vulnerable, Rose was unique in his experience. He enjoyed the contrast, but refused to take advantage of it. 'Relax,' he soothed. 'You don't have to rush this or do anything. Leave it all to me.'

She obeyed, moaning in pleasure as he gradually increased the movements of his skilled fingers until she had to stifle her cries of completion.

Having made sure she was completely satisfied, and knowing he'd always remember the look on her face as she came, he reached for his phone.

'What are you doing?' Rose asked, frowning, still panting with the force of her climax.

'Telling my people to have the helicopter ready to leave right away.'

'You'd leave without saying goodnight to the Prince?' Rose sounded scandalised. 'I should thank him for a wonderful evening,' she insisted. 'I feel bad—'

'There's no need to thank him. The Prince is fully occupied with matters of his own. If it helps you to feel better, you can send him a note tomorrow.'

'I will,' Rose assured him with feeling.

He helped her straighten her clothes. 'We'll pick up your shoes on the way,' he promised, reminding Rose of the high heels she'd discarded.

'I still feel bad, leaving like this,' she admitted with a glance towards the brilliantly lit ballroom.

'The one thing you don't feel is bad,' he said, wrapping a protective arm around her shoulders.

'You could be right,' Rose conceded with a mischievous nod.

Raffa directed the pilot to the second officer's seat, and he flew the helicopter from the palace to the *Pegasus*, while Rose sat in the second row, wondering if it was possible to be any more aware of her body and its needs than she was now. It seemed the more Raffa introduced her to this forbidden pleasure, the more she wanted. She was so greedy for him.

He was tough, rugged and hot-as-hell sexy, and an excellent pilot too. Their landing was barely discernible. One moment they were in the air and the next on the swaying deck of the superyacht. It could have been a metaphor for her life, Rose reflected, now she'd had the chance to quietly and calmly reflect on the events of the night.

'You can take your headphones off now,' Raffa prompted as the second officer bid them goodnight and left.

Not wanting the fairy tale to end, Rose gave herself another blissful moment, before reluctantly doing as Raffa said. She knew that the clock had struck midnight and

Cinderella's shoes were now firmly in place. 'What time would you like to meet up tomorrow?' she asked, to demonstrate her understanding that they were back on the boat where things would have to change between them.

'Tomorrow?' Raffa sat back in his seat to shoot her a quizzical look.

'I thought—'

'What did you think, Rose?'

Opening the door, he came around to help her disembark. Moving into his arms felt so right. It was moving out of them that felt wrong, but now they were safe on deck, she imagined they'd be heading off to their own accommodation. How their hands touched, brushed, until finally they linked fingers, she had no idea. It didn't do to examine things too closely sometimes.

'Do you want to call by your room first?'

'No need,' she exclaimed breathlessly.

They almost didn't make it as far as his suite. The moment they were inside the *Pegasus*, Raffa swung her around and thrust her back against the wall. Lodging his fists either side of her face, he kept her in place for a kiss as hungry and as fierce as any she could dream of. The pressure of his body against hers was exciting and arousing, and it was only moments before she was moaning again...noisily.

Raffa was laughing when he released her. 'My security guards will come running.'

'Good! Kiss me again,' she demanded, high on Raffa wanting her.

Their kisses grew increasingly heated until she took Raffa by the hand and dragged him through the ship, laughing, excited and breathless. This was what had been missing in her life, this ability to feel without counting the cost of everything. If she could just have this—him—Raffa—for one, single night, she'd take it, no question.

Shouldering open the door to his suite, Raffa swung Rose into his arms and carried her to the bed. The only thing clear in his head was Rose. She was his focus, and he was determined to make every moment special for her—

But she could still surprise him.

'How d'you do that?' he asked as she gasped out her pleasure. 'All I've done is lie you down on the bed.'

'Maybe it's enough,' she suggested, laughing. 'I really don't know,' she admitted. 'Nothing like this has ever happened to me before, so it's you who must have the knack.'

He drew back. 'Are you saying I'm your first?'

'Not technically,' she admitted, shyly, he thought, for Rose. 'But in every way that matters—' she lifted one shoulder and let it fall again '—you are my first.'

'You'd better explain.' He sounded harsher than he'd intended, but he had no intention of taking Rose if he was her first and there was even the smallest chance that she'd regret it later.

'All right,' she conceded, reading his expression with her usual ease. 'You want the truth? Here it is. You can laugh at me all you like. I'm sure you're going to think me a real country bumpkin, compared to the women you usually date.'

'Stop right there,' he warned. 'I don't think that at all.'

She gave him an assessing look, and then explained. 'Fumbles in the back seat of a car, with someone who knew even less than I did, could never match up to this.'

'That's it?' he pressed, frowning.

'That's it,' she confirmed.

He wanted nothing more than to fold Rose in his arms

and kiss her to reassure her, but Rose hadn't finished with her surprises. Reaching for him, she began to deal with the buttons on his shirt, until she lost patience and they went flying everywhere. Tumbling her back on the bed, he kicked off his shoes, unbuckled his belt and snapped it from the loops. This short break gave Rose the chance to leap into a kneeling position in front of him.

'No,' he said firmly. 'This first time is for you.'

'And the next ten thousand are for you?' she teased, breathless with laughter and excitement.

'If you're lucky,' he teased her back. 'But, seriously, Rose,' he murmured after a long, consuming kiss, 'no second thoughts?'

'Are you joking?' she demanded, looking at him with surprise.

'I'm being perfectly serious,' he assured her.

'Resisting you would take more power than I possess.'

'That's what I'm afraid of,' he admitted.

'Let me repay some of the pleasure you've given me,' she implored.

'We'll be here all night.'

'Isn't that the purpose of this?'

Rose's chin was angled as she asked the question, and her eyes were sparkling emerald green. Making her move, she took matters into her own mouth, and he needed every ounce of his self-control to pull back from the intense pleasure that provoked. The answer was to turn her beneath him, before he lost it completely. Removing her dress, he pulled away to admire her naked body, while Rose, indolent and relaxed, rested her arms above her head in an attitude of absolute trust.

'Not so fast,' he warned when she wrapped her legs around him. 'We've got all night.'

* * *

Did they? Rose wondered. This week on Raffa's yacht would soon be over, then they'd sail back to Spain, where the realities of life were waiting. But it was hard to argue when Raffa was moving steadily down her body, dropping kisses along the way.

Slipping a pillow beneath her buttocks, he raised her even higher. Resting her legs on the wide spread of his shoulders, he dipped his head. Every inch of her ached with desire. 'Surely, it's your turn soon?'

'Your pleasure comes first for me.'

'But you're equally important,' she insisted fiercely, before he found a most effective way of silencing her.

'Use me,' Raffa encouraged.

'Like this?' She shivered with extremes of sensation as she tried touching him to the most sensitive part of her body.

'That's not so hard, is it?' Raffa murmured, smiling down.

'It's extremely hard,' she approved, taking him a little way inside her.

'Like this,' he husked against her mouth.

The initial ecstasy of Raffa sinking deeper gave way to frustration when he pulled back. 'What are you doing?'

'Protecting us both,' he explained as he quickly sheathed himself.

He was so gentle and patient, which was good, as he was big and she was small. It didn't seem possible for such a mountain of a man to be so tender, but when he finally sank inside her to the hilt and rotated his hips, she was drawn into a deliciously unavoidable vortex of pleasure.

Much later they threw themselves down on the bed. As they turned to face each other in silence, it was as if they'd both accepted that something more than sex had just occurred.

But the sex had been truly astonishing, Rose silently conceded as she rolled closer to Raffa simply for the pleasure of having him wrap her in his arms. She dozed off for a while, but woke with a start.

'You okay?' Raffa murmured. Drawing her closer, he brushed Rose's tangled hair away from her face.

'I'm fine,' she whispered back, snuggling into his muscular chest as scenes from the past flashed behind her eyes. The thrill the Kelly family experienced whenever her father came up with another of his crazy schemes. But as sure as night followed day, crashing disappointment always followed. The tin on the mantelpiece, where Rose's mother kept her scant savings, would be emptied, and there'd be a call from the pub to say someone was bringing her father home. Was all closeness fated to end that way? Was this bliss she was sharing with Raffa an illusion? Could she trust it? Could she trust anything? What about Raffa? Was all the publicity about the perfect family he'd been a part of before his parents died all a sham too?

And was Rose being selfish, only thinking of herself right now?

'If you're okay, why are you so tense?' he asked, pulling his head back to stare into her eyes.

'Tell me about your parents,' she said.

There was a long pause, and then Raffa began to speak. 'I drove them to the airfield that day. I even helped them with their luggage. I stood and watched as their plane took off. It was our private jet, so there was nothing to stop me going on board to speak to the pilot.'

'Why would you have done that?'

'I don't know—I just...' Raffa shook his head, at a

loss for words. 'If I had visited the cockpit, I would have smelled the drink on the pilot and realised something was badly wrong. I could have stopped that flight.' He grew more heated. 'I should have stopped it—told them to get off—'

'But you had no reason to go on board in the first place,' Rose pointed out gently. 'How many of us live with guilt, and what good does it ever do? I could have stepped between my father and mother when they were arguing—snatched the bottle from him, searched out the rest of his seemingly endless supply of booze. He even hid the bottles in the rubbish bin outside, and that was one of the more obvious places. I could have made more effort to find help for both of them, but instead I did as my mother asked, and stayed quiet. I was much more obedient in those days. Only when it was far too late did I learn to speak up.'

'You were young, at school, and then laying the foundations of your career,' Raffa reminded her. 'A career your mother surely wanted you to have.'

'She did,' Rose confirmed. 'But, d'you see what I'm getting at? We can both blame ourselves endlessly, but what good does it do? We've learned from our mistakes, and now it's time to move on.'

'Says you,' he teased as he drew her back into his arms.

The emotion Rose stirred inside him was almost too extreme. Feelings, memories, everything he'd brooded on for years, threatened to escape the carefully built dam. What had really changed was that he suddenly wanted to confront the past head-on, rather than banishing it to some forgotten part of his mind. Rose had done that. Her determination to love and protect those she cared for touched him. He was the instigator, the protector, the hero, and occasionally the villain, the man who had never needed support from anyone, but, in the high-octane setting of a professional polo ranch, someone with heart, as well as an organised mind, was ideal. Rose was that person. He was right to have appointed her Head Groom. Fearless when it came to brushing convention aside, Rose had passion and fire that matched his.

It was only a matter of time before that passion distracted them both once again, and what started out as gentle, soothing caresses turned fiercely demanding. Lavishing attention on her breasts, he teased her nipples into even tighter buds, while Rose writhed against him, seeking the release they both craved. Taking hold of his hand, she brought it down, her intention clear. Rose knew what she wanted, and how to get it too. At his first touch, she claimed her explosive release, and very soon wanted more. 'I'll be quiet this time,' she promised with a teasing grin, forcing him to remember his comment about the security guards.

'Make all the noise you want.' Sex was an exercise at which he excelled, but with Rose it was so much more. He'd never laughed so much, nor found a woman so appealing. They ended up on the floor laughing, and the next minute things turned wild and raw. Every rule went out of the window. Between them, they had rewritten the rules. All he cared about was Rose's pleasure—and all she cared about was his.

It was only later when they were quiet again, he noticed that she was studying him intently. 'Is something wrong, Rose?'

How to tell this man what she was thinking? Rose stared silently into eyes that weren't bloodshot with booze, or narrowed in anger...into a face that was strong, but not cruel.

'Nothing's wrong,' she lied with a gentle smile. Raffa had helped her to understand that sex could be deeply meaningful, as well as fun. To think those fumbles in the back seat of a car had left her with the impression that sex was a waste of time, and why bother? She knew why now. Raffa had shown her what sex could really be like, and how close it could bring two people.

But for how long nagged at the back of her mind.

Pulling his head back, he stared her directly in the eyes. 'Unhappy thoughts? Hey, come on, or I'll worry about you.'

'Worry? After that?' She laughed to reassure him, but was she as strong as he thought her? Her father's situation was getting worse, and for all he'd done wrong in the past she would never desert him. If she confessed that, Raffa was bound to question Rose's long-term commitment to his team.

'If you need to talk,' he pressed.

'Here? Now?' she teased in an attempt to distract him.

'At any time,' Raffa said, emphatically. 'I'm not so busy that you'll have to come to bed to talk to me.'

'If that's what it takes,' she murmured, resting her cheek against his warm, hard chest.

'I love that you stop at nothing,' Raffa admitted on a smile. 'But if there's something you want to say, I'm listening.'

Like Rose's fear that her father's condition might worsen suddenly? Loyalty to her family prevented her from saying more. 'Nope. I think you've covered it.'

'I'd rather cover you,' Raffa growled as he tumbled Rose on to her back.

Resting on her elbow, Rose watched Raffa sleep. She marvelled at how close they'd become. That was a precious memory to keep safe when their very different worlds split them apart.

A ping on her phone distracted her. Reality had come calling in the form of a text from her brother Declan. Reading it, she frowned.

Go home now, Rose. You're needed in Ireland.

Rose typed furiously.

Where r u, Dec?

Rome. But Dad needs help right now—before I can get there.

Everything inside Rose tensed. Whatever had happened must be bad.

What's happened?

It's serious, Rose. Only you can drop everything and go right away.

Whether she agreed with that last statement or not, there was no point wishing things were different. She had to leave now. A few more exchanges with her brother proved even more alarming. It turned out that their father was currently cooling his heels in a police cell after rampaging out of control.

Pressing her lips together until they hurt stopped the tears. Everything she had to lose was right here in this room. Tonight was nothing more than stolen time, an indulgence she couldn't afford. Rose's father couldn't look after himself, and both she and Raffa could. That didn't mean that the affection, the laughter, the trust and the care they'd shared meant nothing. She'd never forget it.

Never.

But there was no time for tears—no time for anything but booking a ticket to Ireland.

Don't worry, Dec. I'm on my way.

CHAPTER SEVEN

WITH THE FAIRY TALE well and truly over, Rose slipped out of bed, grateful that Raffa slept on while she debated what to do. Should she wake him and tell him the news? Didn't he have enough on his plate? Leaving a note was better, she decided, but how to explain in a few dry words what last night had meant to her? There weren't enough words—or enough time, she realised with a glance at her watch.

Hunting around, she found pen and paper in the night-stand, and wrote a quick note.

Please forgive me. I didn't want to disturb you. A text from my brother says there's trouble at home. Don't worry, I'll be fine. In touch as soon as possible. R

A member of the crew, accustomed to ferrying strangers of one ilk or another, took her to shore in one of the small, fast boats stored in the hull of the superyacht. From there it would be a cab ride to the airport, and a swift journey home. Fretting as she stared back at the sleek, shadowy form of the *Pegasus*, Rose wished she'd said thank you on the note to Raffa for the opportunities he'd given her...for everything.

She should have known the roller-coaster ride she'd seen her parents take was pretty much the same for everyone. Tightening her hands around the frigid steel rail, she determined to find her way back to the upside of that ride. Wallowing in self-pity was a complete and utter waste of time. What she needed now was resolve and the strength to turn things around.

If you'll have me back once I've found a solution for my father, I'll see you in Spain.

She cast this thought into the wind whipping her hair about, which was about as effective as trying to stem the tears pouring down her face. Action was what was needed now.

A curse of regret, of frustration, of determination, flew out of her mouth. Knuckling her eyes, she stemmed the tears. No way would she stop searching, until she found the answer for her father's addiction, and a way forward for herself.

He woke slowly, basking in sensations of complete satisfaction from the previous night. Reaching for Rose, he found her side of the bed cold. Instantly alert, he sat up to see the sheets had been straightened. The entire suite was silent. Was she back in her stateroom, swotting for that morning's interrogation, as Rose liked to describe his probing into her experience with horses? No one was more dedicated to her work than Rose, and he had yet to find a gap in her knowledge.

Rolling over on the bed, he picked up the phone to call her room. It rang out. His next call was to the purser. It shot him out of bed. Add resourceful to Rose's list of accomplishments, but in this instance, she'd taken things too far, leaving the *Pegasus* by motor launch some time shortly after dawn. His first response was stone-cold anger. How could she leave him without a word after all they'd shared? Was it possible he'd misread her character so badly? He'd told Rose things he'd never told another soul. And she'd trusted him. He had believed the confidences they'd shared had connected them on a deeper level. Obviously, he was wrong.

Had she thrown away the chance to work on his ranch? Was that all it meant to her? *'Gran Dios en el cielo!'* If this was what it meant to have feelings, feelings could go to hell!

He showered and dressed, and only then saw the note. Snatching it up, he read it quickly, then brought it to his face.

What the hell am I doing? Do I think it might contain a trace of her scent?

He gave a bitter laugh at his foolishness.

Trouble at home? What did that mean? Rose had cut him out when he could have helped her. Obviously, she didn't agree. Was this anger the result of a blow to his pride? If Rose was in trouble, she needed him. As a concerned employer he had a duty of care to his employees.

To hell with that! Rose came first, employee or not.

Whatever nightmares the past had held, Rose would never abandon her responsibilities without good reason. She had put her family first, which was exactly what he would have done in her place. Making a call, he filed a flight plan to Ireland.

How would Raffa feel when he read her note? Hurt? Puzzled? Angry?

Rose ground her jaw as the cab took her to the Garda station where her father was being held, knowing it would likely be all of the above. He'd trusted her, and confided in her, and she'd walked out on him, as if the things they'd shared had meant nothing to her. She'd tried texting him, but for some reason the texts wouldn't send. Was Raffa blocking them? Who could blame him? He could only think the worst of her.

She had to put those thoughts aside as the cab slowed and parked up. She'd promised her mother to look after the family, and that was exactly what she'd do.

Spain seemed like a distant dream when Rose learned how bad things were. The officer in charge explained that her father, who was currently sleeping it off in a cell, had assaulted his carers during a drunken rage, and it had taken two strapping members of the Garda to subdue him.

'You can't expect anyone to take care of him outside of a hospital facility,' the officer insisted. 'It's not safe to be around him.'

'I'll take care of him.'

How? How?

The question banged in her brain. This was so much worse than she had imagined. She'd been thinking she'd have to find new carers, now it seemed she might have to take their place, which meant giving up her career— never seeing Raffa again. But, what else could she do, when family was everything?

Lifting her chin, she stared into the officer's eyes. 'He's my father. I love him, and I'm here to take him home.' The how, when and where would have to wait. The deathbed promise Rose had made to her mother would always come first.

She would sort this out, whatever it took, although the bank manager she'd called from the cab had said there was no money in the farm's account. There were no magic wands, either, so she'd begged him for a couple of weeks to sort things out. Thankfully, he'd agreed, but she had two weeks and no longer.

The irony was that Rose had left Ireland in the first place in order to earn enough to keep the farm afloat and pay for her father's care, but now— Her heart lurched with pity and love as her father shambled along the corridor towards her. Everything would have to change, she realised. 'Come on, Dad. Let's take you home.'

Piloting an aircraft calmed Raffa. Learning to fly as a teenager had been a revelation. He'd become a better planner because of it, thorough and more meticulous. Logical decisions became instinctive, when patience was vital, rather than a virtue. The circumstances of his parents' death had brought out the worst in him. Flying had improved his angry resentful clay, fashioning it into something close to a decent human being. Forgiving himself for leaving them that day would never happen, but becoming a pilot had given him the calm he needed to go on. He'd need those qualities in Ireland. His team had supplied more information about her father, which made him even more concerned about Rose.

His jet sliced through the brightening sky on autopilot, giving him the chance to reflect on their time together. Not just the sex, but the quiet times in between, when they'd talked and shared and listened. That was new to him. Zany, beautiful, unique and caring, Rose was a completely new experience for him. She'd willingly sacrifice everything she'd worked so hard for to take charge of her father's care, and she had opened a window on the part of him that had been shuttered for years. Far from regretting the feelings she'd stirred up inside him, he understood why she was racing back to save her father. Family was everything to him too. What that meant for his ranch, and Rose's unparalleled work as his head groom, was something he'd soon discover.

* * *

Love was a strange and indelible curse, but overall it was a blessing, Rose concluded, feeling the warm glow of familiarity, with all its upsides and downsides, as the cab splashed through the mud in the yard to pull up outside the familiar ramshackle farmhouse. It had taken all her powers of persuasion to get the driver to take them anywhere with her father still marinated in booze.

Love didn't rely on being fed with regularity, or even handled with care, Rose concluded as she glanced at her father slumped in the corner of the cab. Love just was, and she loved her father. He wasn't a bad man. He was a weak man. What made it easier to face the future ahead of them was remembering the man who'd cried in her arms when her mother died, the man who knew full well how sick he was. That was the man she'd come home for, the man she'd search heaven and earth for to find him a treatment.

Not that a moment of panic didn't grab her as the taxi driver helped her to manhandle her father out of the cab. But then she remembered Raffa's words. *You don't know how strong you are until you're tested.*

'Come on, Dad. We're home.'

Rose opened the farmhouse door with her father trailing behind. It was hard to know whether to follow his bleary stare and discover where he was hiding the bottles, or go straight on in. Feed him first, she decided, and then go and hunt the bottles.

There could have been no bigger shock when she opened the door. Far from the neglected, cold stone hearth she'd been expecting, a fire was roaring, and the ancient scrubbed table in the centre of the room was loaded with food.

The noise that greeted them was tumultuous. Half the village seemed to have turned up to welcome them home. The warmth of good neighbours embraced her, her father too, and not as the local drunk but as someone in need of compassion and love.

'Ah, you didn't think we'd leave you on your own,' Máire, the warm-hearted owner of the local bakery, exclaimed as she wafted away Rose's thanks. 'I knew your father when we were at school together, before the drink turned him bad. I'll be taking him to live with me and my boys when you go back to Spain.'

'I can't let you do that,' Rose exclaimed. Her best guess was that Máire's five strapping lads ate the profits of the bakery as it was, and if her father was as violent as the Garda said he was, would any of them be safe?

'But you are going back to Spain?' Máire asked with a worried frown.

'I don't see how I can,' Rose said, shaking her head. 'He's my responsibility—'

'You've got your own life to lead,' Máire said firmly. 'Your father won't get into trouble with me,' she added, wrapping a capable arm around Rose's shoulders. 'My boys will keep him in line. If we can't be neighbourly in a small place like this, what hope is there for the world? And my lads will be only too glad to help you with the horses.'

Great riders, all of them, and kind to their animals, Rose quickly assessed. 'That would be wonderful—' All of Máire's suggestions would be wonderful, but Rose had never turned her back on a problem yet. 'Maybe in the short term,' she reluctantly agreed. 'And I can't tell you how grateful I am, but I'll be paying for your time—'

'That won't be necessary.'

Everyone turned to face the door.

'Raffa?'

Stunned rigid, Rose's brain simply refused to compute the fact that Raffa Acosta was framed in the doorway of the ramshackle farmhouse where she'd grown up.

Her face heated up in response to his level black stare. The last time she'd seen him, he was sprawled naked across the bed they'd shared. 'You're here,' she managed lamely.

'Evidently,' he agreed blandly.

Private jet. Fast car waiting on the tarmac, Rose's brain rapidly deduced. The sight of him, hair rumpled as if he'd got out of bed and come straight here, not even bothering to tuck in his top properly, sent a bolt of lust straight to her core. Jeans, boots and a leather jacket with the collar both up and down completed the picture of a man whose world could shift at the speed of light.

'Let me get you a drink,' Máire offered, stepping in between them to break the awkward moment. No one else spoke. They were too busy staring at superstar Raffa Acosta, a man of myth and legend in a village where horses, and everything connected to them, were practically a second religion.

'Would coffee be possible?' Raffa suggested, his gaze not wavering from Rose's face for a moment.

'Why don't I get you a glass of water while you wait for the coffee to brew?' Rose suggested, glad of any excuse to escape that burning stare.

'Did you know he was coming?' she whispered discreetly to Máire.

'Declan said—'

'Declan?' Rose interrupted with surprise. 'Raffa's been speaking to my brothers?'

'There's no law against it, as far as I know,' Máire told her with a shrug. 'Apparently, your man has business in Ireland.'

'He's not my man,' Rose whispered hotly, and just as fast she regretted the outburst. 'Sorry, Máire—I just didn't expect to see him here.'

Was she that business, or did Raffa have other plans? Rose wondered, conscious of his stare on her back. When she handed him the water, he was careful not to touch her, she noticed. She couldn't blame him. Lifting her chin, she confronted the harshness in his eyes. 'Well, this is a surprise,' she murmured.

'Isn't it?' he bit out.

'You read my note?'

'I wouldn't be here otherwise.'

'I'm sorry for the way I left.'

'Why didn't you wake me?'

Rose opened her arms in a helpless gesture. 'What could you have done?'

'I could have brought you here, for a start,' Raffa ground out as he backed her into a shadowy corner, out of earshot of the rest.

'I can—'

'Manage very well on your own?' he suggested with impatience. 'Can you care for your father, when he's in one of his drunken rages?'

Raffa knew everything, Rose realised. His team must have filled him in. How it must have hurt him to be reminded of the dangers of drink. The fury she could see in his eyes was that of a much younger man. He was remembering a tragedy from years back. The incident with her father had only increased his pain tenfold.

'Will you stay home twenty-four-seven to make sure he doesn't hurt himself—or you?' he raged. 'Are you prepared to sacrifice everything you've worked so hard for? How do you intend to magic up the money for his care? And he will need care. Your father needs professional help, Rose. You can't help him, or you'd have done it long before now.'

'I can love him,' she countered fiercely. 'And Máire's offered to help—they were at school together. She's one of the few people he trusts, and her sons can handle him until I find him the type of care he needs.' Touching Raffa's arm to reach him, to offer him consolation, only resulted in him shaking her off.

'That's a very kind offer from a neighbour, but you know it's only a short-term solution. What about your job with me, Rose?'

'Can we talk outside?' She understood why Raffa sounded so harsh, and why there was no warmth in his eyes, so it was a relief when he agreed.

She led the way, and didn't stop walking until they'd left the farmyard behind, and were at least half a mile down the road. There was a tree that looked a bit like an umbrella. It acted as a sunshade in the summer. Today it was a leaky umbrella, and Rose hadn't thought to bring a coat.

'Here. Take this,' Raffa growled when she hugged herself and shivered. Shrugging off his jacket, he draped it around her shoulders. It still held his warmth.

'I will need time off,' she admitted, dragging the jacket closer, 'but I promise to make it up to you.'

There was no reaction from Raffa. This was worse than talking to the boss. It was like talking to a stranger. It was impossible to believe she'd been wrapped in his arms only a few hours before, when he was as remote and aloof as this.

The past had done that. It had damaged them both, and now she was hanging on to her career by a rapidly fraying thread.

'What if I take my holiday leave to try and sort this out?' she offered. 'Would you allow me to do that?'

'And you'll restart, when?' Raffa asked, still without a shred of warmth in his voice. 'At *your* convenience?'

'No,' Rose protested. 'I'll stick strictly to schedule.'

'And how will you make that happen? You can give me no guarantees,' he exclaimed angrily. 'A few lines on a scrap of paper to explain your sudden departure? Why should I trust you?'

'I promise I'll return as soon as I can.'

His look chilled her. 'You say that now,' he rasped.

The distance between them had never seemed greater. The closeness they'd shared seemed to have completely disappeared, but she couldn't let it go without a fight. 'How long are you staying in Ireland?'

Raffa's brow furrowed. 'Why do you want to know?'

She had no right to know, but having him close to her was like having a rock to moor her ship to. A ship that had been well and truly holed beneath the waterline. She'd picked herself up many times before, but not like this, not with her heart in tiny pieces.

'You should go back to the house,' Raffa insisted in the same emotion-free tone. 'Your neighbours have gone to a lot of trouble to welcome you home.'

'You're not leaving already?' Rose's voice hitched on the words.

'No, but the party isn't for me, and I'll only distract you from the welcome your friends want to give you, and that wouldn't be right.'

'We'll speak again, though?' She'd be begging next.

'We will,' he confirmed.

Where and when was never mentioned, leaving nothing but doubt in Rose's mind. Career or family? Those were her choices, and family won through every time. There'd been a glimmer, just a glimmer of possibility that she could finally live her own life, love, and thrive, and...

Do what? *Live selfishly?* Was that what she wanted? No. Of course it wasn't. She'd sacrificed all thought of romantic relationships in the past, and that was what she'd do again now.

Is it the right thing to do, or is it cowardice? Am I frightened of risking my heart? My parents' relationship turned into a living hell. Am I incapable of believing I can do things differently? Where's my courage gone? Where's the determination that brought me to Spain, to support that very family and further my career? Is that all spent now?

'You'll find me at the inn,' Raffa said, shaking Rose back to reality. 'If you need me, call.'

I need you now, thought the woman who'd always managed everything on her own. 'I have your number,' Rose confirmed.

'And meet me tomorrow. Nine o'clock at the inn.'

Raffa raised a hand as he walked away. He didn't turn around.

CHAPTER EIGHT

'*Dios!*' HE WAS pacing his room at the inn like a caged
animal. From having no feelings to *this*?

The moment he'd seen Rose with her father, any anger
he'd felt at her desertion had swung to concern for a
valued member of staff. A drunken father—a drunken
pilot—the connection was unavoidable. This was his
worst nightmare come true.

But he wasn't standing by helpless this time. He'd
summed up the situation at the farmhouse in a glance. The
old man needed more help than either Rose or her neighbours could give him, which was all the more reason for
Raffa to bring forward his plans. He glanced at his watch.
Rose was due shortly. The inn was close to her farm. Sleep
had eluded him, but that was no fault of the warm-hearted
landlady. The accommodation was more than adequate.
Bed. Bathroom. Desk. What more did he need?

He'd reserved a private room downstairs for his meeting with Rose. This was no romantic tryst, but the venue
for a serious talk. She couldn't just take off whenever she
felt like it. There was a process to be followed, as Rose
well knew. He relied on his staff, particularly someone
entrusted with one of the most vital jobs. The only reason he was prepared to cut Rose some slack was because
no one understood loyalty to family better than he. Hear-

ing a door open and close, and the murmur of voices, he headed downstairs. Rose brought the chill of morning with her, along with her familiar wildflower scent. She looked tense. He barely had a chance to say hello before the landlady he'd struck a deal with to buy the inn bustled forward.

'I've prepared the room as you asked.' She beamed. 'Your room now, Señor Acosta. If there's anything else I can get you?'

'Nothing,' he said briskly. 'Thank you. I'm sure everything will be fine.'

He'd planned to tell Rose about his purchase of the inn at a more appropriate time. Now she looked shocked. It couldn't be helped. In his world things moved quickly. In this instance that speed could only benefit Rose. 'Come in,' he invited, noting how pale she looked.

'This is *your* room?' Rose challenged the moment the door was shut.

He allowed himself a moment of pleasure at the fact that a fire had been lit and two battered leather armchairs, made more inviting with the addition of handsewn cushions, had been drawn up either side. These were good people, full of good intentions. 'I'll answer your questions later,' he promised, indicating one of the seats. 'Have you had breakfast?'

'I don't want to eat,' Rose told him in a clipped tone. 'I'd rather get this over with. If you're going to fire me, please don't draw it out.'

'I've brought you here to discuss your future on my ranch.'

More colour drained from her cheeks.

'Rose, listen to me before you draw any conclusions. I'm going to call for coffee, toast and eggs. You're no good to me in pieces. I know the situation at home is hard, but you don't have to battle through this on your own.'

'And then you'll fire me,' she said confidently.

'There's a process to follow on my yard, as you well know. I'm not firing you. Gross misconduct would call for instant dismissal, and I hardly think leaving my bed in the early hours fits the bill.' Rose's jaw worked, but she said nothing. 'You'll get through this,' he promised, 'but you can't disappear on a whim. If something important happens outside work, all the more reason to come to me and explain why you're worried. That's what I'm here for.'

Her green eyes turned dark with emotion. 'So, you're not sacking me.'

'I just said so. This is simply a reminder that the position of Head Groom can't be left empty for long.'

'I don't expect it to be. Adena will cover for me. And, please believe me, I didn't anticipate any of this.'

'But you must have known how sick your father was, and yet you didn't tell me.'

'How could I tell you under these particular circumstances, knowing I'd only add to your grief over your own parents?'

'I think I can handle it.'

'Can you?'

She looked so concerned, he couldn't be angry with her. Everything she did, all she had ever done, was always for the good of other people. On that thought he called for breakfast. She looked as if she hadn't eaten properly in days.

'It's been a race against time,' she confessed. 'Save enough money for my father's care, or stay here to care for him without any money. Those were my choices. I foolishly thought I'd have sufficient funds in time to save him.'

'You can't live your life playing catch-up, Rose.'

'Tell me about it,' she agreed with a humourless laugh.

Straightening up, she raised her chin bravely. 'So, the pub belongs to you now?'

'It does,' he confirmed.

'There's just so much to take in. I couldn't believe it when you arrived last night. What are you up to, Raffa?'

'I'm here on business.'

'Buying up the village, and fitting in some pastoral care at the same time? I'm sorry,' Rose added quickly, with a gesture suggesting she'd do anything to undo those words. 'I've no right to question you. It's just that our situation is so complicated.'

'No, it isn't. If I can keep my personal and professional lives apart, so can you. I'm offering you a way forward. Take your holiday entitlement if you need to, but don't shut me out. As your employer, I'll support you any way I can, but the position of Head Groom must be filled—if not by you, then by someone else.'

Dios! What was he saying? This wasn't about business, it was all about Rose. He wanted to help her as much as he could, but she wouldn't let him.

'I appreciate you giving me a second chance,' she said, matching his formal tone. 'I'd like to take you up on the offer.'

With that, she got up and left the room, leaving him to smash his fist into the table with frustration.

'I hope I'm not too late,' the landlady announced within moments of Rose leaving as she backed into the room with a loaded tray of food.

'Just leave it on the table, thank you.'

He could think of nothing but Rose—chin up, shoulders back, typical Rose, ready to take on the next challenge and the next. Her fighting spirit would see her through, but she couldn't go on like this forever. If she refused his help, he'd watch from the wings, ready to catch her if she fell. He would always care for Rose, even from a distance.

Care was a strange word, very close to love…

And didn't he destroy those he loved?

Not this time. He couldn't fix everything, but nothing on earth would stop him caring for Rose.

Rose went straight from the meeting with Raffa to check on her father, who was living with Máire and her boys at the bakery. Rose was looking forward to seeing him, and dreading it too. She never knew what to expect, and it was impossible to be in his company without feeling such regret for the man he might have been. Máire had said he was responding well to the discipline her sons imposed, but, as Raffa had pointed out, that only was a temporary solution. Relationships were rarely straightforward, she reflected as she walked down the village street. With the threat of dismissal removed, Rose was relieved, but not comforted. Nothing could compensate for losing the closeness she'd so briefly experienced with Raffa, and his new formality had left her feeling she'd lost something precious that she might never get back. *You can't have everything,* she told herself firmly as she knocked on Máire's door. That would be greedy.

'I've given your father the small bedroom directly above the bakery,' Máire explained as she welcomed Rose inside. 'It has its own bathroom, and there's no access to either exit without going past my room,' she added with a wink. 'But he's out with my boys at the moment. You'll stay for a mug of tea?'

'Will they be long?' Rose asked with concern, picturing the wreck of a man she'd brought home from the police cell. News that her father was out with Máire's strapping lads might either herald a turning point or a chance for him to escape the bakery to sneak off for a drink. Whichever it was, Rose had good cause to worry.

'They'll walk him to death, if they don't work him to death first,' Máire confided. 'And they're on top of his drinking. They got their own father sober, remember?'

Rose hummed diplomatically. She remembered Máire's husband stopping the drink, but she also remembered him running off with the vicar's wife afterwards.

'Your father had too much time on his hands to think about your mother, and he'll not get a drink here,' Máire reassured her. 'So, you go find that meal of a man, and ask about his plans for the hall—'

'The *hall*?' Rose tensed. 'Don't you mean the pub?'

Máire laughed as if Rose had just said the funniest thing. 'Pub, the hall—who knows what else he's bought up in the village? By the time Señor Acosta's finished here, we'll all be dancing the flamenco and snapping our castanets.'

His team was well on with the purchase of the Old Hall. He hadn't mentioned it to Rose, as he didn't want to raise her hopes until the deal was done. The large baronial-style building was perfect for one of his sister's retreats. He couldn't wait to tell Sofia what he'd found.

'You do know I'm still on my honeymoon?' Sofia complained with her usual good humour.

Hearing a steel band in the background, he drew his own conclusions. Her husband, Cesar, had never stinted on exotic hideaways. He'd probably bought a new island for his bride. 'This won't take long.'

'Just don't buy up everything in the village,' Sofia said with concern when he explained his plan, 'or Rose might think you're taking over. Don't hurt her, Raffa. She's got more than enough to put up with.'

Sofia and Rose had enjoyed some quiet time in the run-up to the wedding, with plenty of chance to unload. 'I've no intention of hurting anyone. I'm helping by—'

'Buying up everything?' his sister suggested dryly. 'May I humbly suggest that might not work where Rose is concerned?'

'The Old Hall will make an excellent retreat.'

'My first in Ireland,' his sister reflected thoughtfully. 'Why not?'

Sofia was forced to agree. 'For once, I can't think of a single reason to argue with you.'

'Which must mean it's time for you to get back to enjoying your honeymoon, while I put these ideas into action.'

'Explain your plan carefully to Rose. She won't thank you for throwing your money around, unless she understands why you're doing it. Rose is determined to stand on her own two feet, and I admire her for it.'

'You like her?'

'I like her a lot,' Sofia confirmed, 'and I want you to be happy, but that means taking off your blinkers to see things from Rose's point of view. Can you do that, Raffa?'

He refused to be drawn on the subject of Rose.

'You want me to butt out of your love life?' Sofia suggested.

'I don't need your advice,' he confirmed.

'True,' she said. 'You need crowd control.'

Ice rushed through Rose's veins as she clutched her phone to her face. Her oldest brother, Declan, was on the other end of the line, telling Rose that Raffa Acosta had indeed bought the Old Hall. What next? she wondered, though in fairness the building had been derelict for some time, with no sign of anyone with either the money or the inclination to restore what had once been a thriving estate. 'How do you know this?'

'He phoned me. The man himself,' Declan explained, sounding as pleased as Punch.

'Raffa Acosta phoned you?' Rose's brow pleated in puzzlement. Raffa hadn't said a word to her. 'What else did he say?' she asked suspiciously.

'He'll be making an offer for the farm next,' Declan said, in what Declan would call his 'only half joking' voice.

There was no joke about it, as far as Rose was concerned. 'And you think that's a good idea?'

'It would be a solution,' Declan confessed. 'It would let you off the hook, for a start.'

'I don't want to be let off the hook.'

'Why do you keep on supporting our father, after the way he treated you and our mother?'

And my brothers, Rose thought, taking a moment to revisit the past before returning her attention to the call. 'He's ill, Dec. Alcoholism is an illness. Our father needs help, not blame. If we did sell the farm, I'm frightened the shock might tip him over the edge. I can't just let that happen, and then walk out on him.'

'That's easy to say when he's not trying to knock your teeth out.'

'He'd never do that to me,' Rose declared. 'All that bluff and bluster was just the drink talking.'

'He'd only have to fall on you, to knock you out flat.'

'I think I'm a bit nimbler on my feet than he is. Look, I'll get back to you, Dec,' Rose soothed, knowing Declan was remembering things in the past that couldn't help either of them now. 'I'll let you know what I find out,' she promised.

Raffa was buying up the Old Hall as well as the pub? Rose's heart pounded like a jackhammer at the thought.

What was he up to? He'd admitted he was in Ireland for business. That had stung at the time, but now the possibility of selling the farm had entered her mind, she was forced to consider it. The money it raised would allow her father to have the best treatment, while her brothers would each get a stake to plough into a business of their own. With Raffa at the helm, the farm animals would have the best care, and the land would be maintained to the highest standard. Was it such a bad idea? There was no point dwelling on it now. She had to speak to Raffa.

'A new era unfolds!' the landlady at the pub exclaimed the moment she heard Rose's voice. 'Señor Acosta is not only keeping us all on, he's increasing our wages. What a marvel he is, Rose. The man hasn't stopped all day.'

No, Raffa had definitely been busy, Rose reflected tensely as she replayed the conversation with Declan. 'If he's still there, I'm coming over to speak to him. See you soon—' Before the landlady had a chance to answer, Rose had cut the line, grabbed her battered waxed jacket from the hook behind the door, and was on her way to confront a man causing more uproar in the village than if aliens had landed.

There was no doubt Raffa could do a lot for the area. Equally, trying to stop him doing anything people in the village disagreed with would be like trying to stop a juggernaut in its tracks.

Ideas flooded Rose's mind. Digging out her phone with frozen fingers, she placed a call, and hurried on. She'd barely walked half a mile when she heard a powerful engine approaching. Pressing back into the bare twigs of the hedge, she gasped with shock as the vehicle roared past, shooting filthy water into her face. There was only one man who could afford to drive a car like that around here. Boss or not, she shook her fist at the disappearing tail lights. The SUV screeched to a halt. Raffa must have seen her through the rear-view mirror. Good job he hadn't heard her swearing at him. Mud-drenched, she stalked towards him. Not only was Raffa Acosta a control freak, who thought he could buy up Rose's home town, he was also, she reluctantly noted as he opened the driver's window, the hottest guy this side of hell.

'What do you think you're doing?' she blazed on a breath tense with anger.

'I wanted to see you.'

'Well, now you've seen me, what d'you think?' She held out her arms, to reveal the extent of her soaking.

'You need a bath?' Raffa suggested in a husky drawl that would have made her toes curl, if they hadn't been frozen solid in her boots.

'Hop in, Rose. You'll be warm in here.'

'You'll be seared to a crisp if I climb in beside you. Where do you think you are? A racetrack?'

'Truce?' Raffa suggested, with a look in his eyes and a curve to his sinfully sensuous mouth that brought a rush of inconvenient memories of the hot kind flooding back. 'Truce as far as the farmhouse, at least,' he amended. 'I'm here to repent.'

Rose hummed.

'When you're clean and warm again, I'll explain. Meanwhile...' leaning across the cab, he opened the passenger door '...jump in.'

She was freezing cold, covered in mud and still furious, but the draught of warm air from the interior of the cab was fragrant with the spicy aroma of Raffa. 'There'll be a surcharge for valeting the vehicle,' she warned.

A smile flickered at one corner of his mouth. 'I think I can cover it. Get in, Rose...'

Sometimes it was better to admit you needed help and just say thank you. And if ever there'd been a time to be swept into the rock-solid warmth of Raffa's world, however temporary a stay that might be, this was it.

CHAPTER NINE

HE DROVE SLOWLY to the farmhouse with the heater turned up high. It felt good to cross swords with Rose again, good to have her close. He hadn't forgotten anything, not the way she felt in his arms, or how generous she was in bed, in life, in everything. Or how she'd annoyed the hell out of him by leaving the *Pegasus* so abruptly.

Things were moving faster than expected on the acquisition front, and, from the tense way she was holding herself, he guessed Rose had already spoken to her brother. It wasn't just the shock of a soaking making that chin jut out or those emerald eyes blaze like jewels. He had wanted to be the one to tell Rose of his plans for the village, but only when everything was settled. Raising her hopes would be cruel. He'd hoped his plans for Declan would reassure her. No one knew the land, or how to care for it, better than Declan Kelly. He'd moved fast to secure her brother's services.

He glanced across at Rose, sitting bolt upright in her seat. He'd do anything to persuade her not to sacrifice her life for a duty that no longer existed. Rose's father was going to receive the best possible care, and her brothers could take care of themselves.

Drawing to a halt outside the front door of the farmhouse, he jumped down to help her out. She didn't wait for that, and pushed past him to the front door. He lingered behind for a moment to give her a chance to compose herself before following her inside.

'Do you mind?' he asked, peeling off his jacket. He glanced at the drying rack in front of the hearth.

'Be my guest,' she told him in a clipped tone.

'Shall we sit down?' he suggested.

'Of course,' she agreed. 'Tea?'

'Coffee, if you still have some.'

'Tea it is, then.'

Lifting her chin as she went about her business, Rose reminded him why he was determined to keep this strong, dependable, amusing, quirky and impossible woman in his life.

'What are you doing here, Raffa?' she asked him bluntly as she placed a mug of tea in front of him, so strong he was sure the spoon could stand up in it. 'What are you really doing here?'

'I'm here on business. If you want to take a shower,' he added with a relaxed gesture towards the staircase, 'go right ahead. You must be uncomfortable soaked in mud, and I'm happy to wait.' The tip of her nose was red, and her cheeks were whipped scarlet by the wind. She had never looked lovelier to him.

Ignoring his suggestion, she launched straight in. 'Buying the pub, and then the Old Hall. Is the farm next?'

I thought I could trust you, but now I know I can't.

That was what blazed from her angry expression.

'I haven't done anything underhand, Rose. The Old Hall was for sale, and it's perfect for our needs.'

'*Our* needs?' she queried suspiciously.

'I didn't want to raise your hopes until everything was in place.'

'Raise my hopes about what?' she demanded, frowning.

'I believe, as does Sofia, that the Old Hall would be perfect for one of my sister's retreats.'

Rose looked shocked. 'A retreat in Ireland?'

'Why not? Extra accommodation at the inn for patients attending for assessment, or for staff coming here for interview. I'd say the set-up is perfect,' he confirmed.

Rose's expression was utterly transformed. 'Are you serious?' she asked, as if hardly daring to hope.

'Yes.' He sounded calm, but inwardly he was in turmoil. Nothing mattered more to him than Rose. The thought of not seeing her again was unacceptable to him. Somewhere along the way, between the humour they'd shared and the verbal battles they'd indulged in, as well as their night of passion, a change had happened, but she wasn't ready to hear that yet, any more than he was ready to say the words she wanted to hear. 'I need a head groom,' he said instead. 'You need a solution for your father.'

'You'd build a retreat in Ireland to get me back to Spain?'

'Yes,' he admitted with a one-shouldered shrug.

'So, I'm another of your charities.' She bristled. 'I don't mean to be ungrateful, Raffa, but I know how you love a good cause.'

'Your father won't be the only one to benefit from it, Rose.'

'I'm sorry.' Mashing her lips together, she turned her head to avoid his gaze. 'I shouldn't get so het up. It's just that I don't know what to say.'

'Don't say anything—except, "I'm coming back to Spain."'

'Is this leading to an offer for the farm?' she asked suspiciously.

'Declan does have an interest in selling the farm,' he admitted.

'So, it's all been decided without any input from me?'

'No. Of course it hasn't. You and your brothers would all have to agree to sell.'

'How many have you talked into the deal so far?'

'There's just you to persuade now,' he admitted.

'So, I'm the last to hear.'

'You've been through so much—'

'Don't—don't do that!' She held up her hand as if warding him off. 'Don't say you're protecting me. I'm not the baby sister. Treat me as I deserve to be treated, with the same respect you show my brothers.'

'That has always been my intention, which is why I'm here to talk about it in person.'

'If you approach it the right way, selling the farm could be an answer to our problems,' she conceded. 'It's not what I want, but I have to be pragmatic. My father needs money spending on his care, and the farm could provide that.' Lifting her chin, she stared him in the eyes. Beneath the bravado, he saw a young woman struggling to hold everything and everyone together. Crushed beneath the weight of perceived duty, Rose had yet to come to terms with the fact that she was no longer needed by her brothers as she had been in the past.

'Whatever happens in the future, the Kelly name will remain above the farm,' he pledged.

'With the Acosta brand on every horse, man and dry-stone wall?' Rose suggested as the enormity of the sale of her family's farm overwhelmed her.

'Don't think of me as a wrecking ball. These purchases are the fastest way to help you and your brothers, as well as your father, and others like him. All I ask is that you see the broader picture and take your feelings for me out of it.'

But she couldn't. Some sort of dam had burst inside

her, and a wall of pure emotion hit him square in the
chest as Rose sprang up and shoved her chair back so
hard it crashed to the floor. He'd never seen her like this
before, hands shaking, face drawn. Trapped between a
past she couldn't change and a future she couldn't see
her way clear to reaching, Rose was as close to a breaking point as anyone could be. He stood in the same instant, ready to catch, soothe or deflect blows, if that was
what it came to.

'You don't have to do everything on your own, Rose.
Accept help when it's offered. You have no difficulty accepting help for your father. Why can't you accept help
from me?'

'Because my father's situation at the bakery is temporary until he starts treatment, while your suggestion
means permanent change.'

'Is that such a bad thing?'

'It narrows down my options, and my brothers' options too.'

'What if I told you that I've asked Declan to manage
the farm?'

Rose's lips turned white. 'So, it is all decided. I was
going to ask you who would pay for Declan to come
home, but there's no need for that, is there? Because
you've already arranged it. You're like the hub of a wheel,
directing us all around you—how fast we move, where
we go, and when.'

'No. That's not what I'm doing. Forgive me, Rose,
but I thought you wanted to work on my ranch. Clearly,
I was wrong.'

'I did—I do.'

Rose clutched her head as if that were the way to shake
an answer into it. He longed to take her in his arms, to
offer her comfort, but he knew that would only make

things worse. 'Go take your shower,' he said instead. 'Don't rush. I'll still be here when you come down.'

It took Rose a good minute to regain her composure, then, firming her jaw, she nodded in agreement. She was on her way across the room to the staircase, leading to what he guessed would be spotlessly clean but basic facilities, when she caught her foot on the edge of a rug. Launching himself across the kitchen, he snatched her into his arms before she hit the ground. Steadying her on her feet, he gave her a chance to recover from the shock.

'Thank you.'

Her voice was shaking, and he flinched inwardly to see Rose so utterly at a loss. 'There's no need to thank me. I'm here for you.'

'Are you?'

She searched his eyes in a way that took hold of his stone-cold heart and fired it into life. Feelings they had both fought so hard to subdue suddenly overwhelmed them, and they crashed together with longing and urgency. But this was Rose. He shouldn't have been surprised when she pulled back.

Raking her hair away from her flushed face, she said calmly, 'Welcome to Ireland, Raffa. I hope you find everything you're looking for here.'

'I have,' he gritted out.

Cupping her face, he drove his mouth down on hers. When he pulled back, the look that blazed between them had nothing to do with employer and employee—or whether or not he was interested in buying property in Ireland. It was primal and deep, and easily eclipsed his desire to plant a stake in Rose's beautiful homeland. 'You taste of mud,' he commented wryly when they paused for breath.

'And you taste of everything I should avoid,' Rose fired back.

'You don't want to avoid me, or why are you here?'

'Because this is my home?'

But Raffa was right. This might be the most misguided thing she'd ever done, but who was going to stop them? Life was measured in moments, some good, some bad, and Rose had learned to grab the good ones and hold on tight. Practical problems could wait. She didn't want tender or teasing. She wanted hot, hard and now, the type of sex that blotted out everything in an explosion of furious passion.

Bodies collided as they cleaved to each other again. Hooking one leg around hers, Raffa thrust her back on top of the kitchen table. Moving between her legs, he undressed her with his usual efficiency. Unfastening his zipper, he used one arm to pillow her head, while his black eyes blazed a promise into hers. That promise of forgetfulness and oblivion was enough for Rose to cry out and claim it right away. Swept into a vortex of pleasure, she rejoiced to be lost. This was appetite pure and simple.

Consumed by arousal, the decision had moved out of their hands. Rose's senses took the lead, while Raffa's experience proved the route map. Even when she begged him for release, he knew how big he was and how carefully he must proceed. That wouldn't do for Rose, not when her heart, soul and body were so utterly his. Grabbing his biceps, she groaned her approval in response to the silky pass of something warm and smooth between her legs. Closing her eyes to concentrate on sensation, she exhaled on a shaking breath when he made a second pass, allowing the tip to catch inside her.

'Again?' he suggested.

'And again,' she agreed, plunging into an abyss of pleasure that left her gasping for breath as he finally took her to the hilt.

One powerful release could never be enough—not when every inch of Rose was tuned to Raffa's frequency. *'Yes!'* she breathed out again, moving fiercely with him.

Sweeping everything off the kitchen table, he lifted her legs and wrapped them around his waist so he could move more freely, and with even greater force. The vibrations rocked the table halfway across the room, while Rose exclaimed rhythmically with pleasure each time he dealt her a firm, effective stroke. Even the sounds they made were arousing, as was the sight of Raffa staring down at her, clearly enjoying himself. 'Don't stop!' she warned. 'Don't—' He didn't give her a chance to finish before upping the tempo, which drove her straight over the edge.

'Are you okay?' he asked as she dragged in some noisy breaths. Cupping her chin, he stared into her eyes. 'Rose... I didn't hurt you, did I?'

'Hurt me?' His question touched her. Reaching up, she rasped the palm of her hand against his stubble-roughened cheek. 'Of course you didn't hurt me. That was... amazing.'

'Watch the flattery,' he warned with a smile.

She loved the look between them that said they understood each other again. The problems hadn't gone away, but nothing could get in the way of these precious moments.

'Your face is smeared with mud,' she observed, smiling into his eyes.

'I'll take that as a compliment, as yours is too. Is it time for that shower now?'

'Could be,' Rose agreed, grinning as Raffa swung her

into his arms. 'It won't be the type of facility you're used to,' she warned as he jogged up the stairs.

'Running water's all we need.'

Apart from each other, she thought.

Shouldering the door to the bathroom, he turned on the shower. Only now did Rose remember she'd forgotten to flip the switch to heat up the water. 'We're going to freeze,' she warned as Raffa stripped off his clothes.

'Not a chance.' Lifting her into the small cubicle, he secured her arms above her head, nudged his way between her thighs and proved he was right.

If everything could be solved by sex, they'd have the answers to all the world's problems, Rose reflected the next morning. If she had the answer to the doubts etched on her heart by the past, she'd make nothing of the fact that Raffa had already left, leaving his side of the bed cold. Picking up the note he'd left on the pillow, she hardly dared read it. Man up! He was hardly the type to sneak off in the night.

As she had?

Rose growled with impatience, hoping that wouldn't be something else to plague her for the rest of her life. She'd had her reasons. Raffa must have his.

She read the scrawled note.

Not tit for tat. Time to get back to business. R

What had she expected? A declaration of love?

Her body was still throbbing from the attentions of an extraordinary lover, but fabulous sex did not a relationship make. A future between billionaire polo player Raffa Acosta and Rose Kelly, penniless groom? How likely did that seem? Fairy tales didn't happen in real life. And it was a bit too late to worry about getting in too deep where Raffa was concerned. She was already in over her head, with her heart and soul fully engaged. If there was some way to stop that, it remained a mystery to Rose.

Showered and dressed, she made her way down to the kitchen. Expecting the room to be cold, and the fire to be out, she was surprised to find logs blazing in the hearth, and a fresh pot of coffee on the table. And another note.

This is to help you break that tea habit. I can't stand the stuff. R

Smiling and crying at the same time, she brought the note to her chest. She already missed his sense of humour and Raffa's caring ways most of all, but she didn't have a clue where he was, what he was up to or how long he'd be away.

Closing her fist around the note as a torrent of longing and uncertainty overwhelmed her, Rose knew, whatever Raffa was planning, her father had to take priority over her feelings.

Crossing to her mother's desk, she selected a piece of writing paper and began to write. Then stopped. It took time to deliver a letter. Raffa could be halfway across the world. She'd send a text instead. Even that took an age. Could they ever resolve the gulf between them? Rose doubted it. She refused charity, while Raffa liked to handle the reins, not share them. She could only be sure of one thing as she placed a call to Sofia. Telling her heart to forget Raffa Acosta was a waste of time, when her heart remained set on having him.

CHAPTER TEN

THE SKY WAS dark when he left the farm. Being with Rose last night had only spurred on his plan. The past controlled Rose, as it had controlled him, and he was determined they would both move forward. Fate had always seemed his enemy before, but fate had brought him Rose. As Head Groom, she could travel with him, be with him, sleep with him too.

That might make a sad sort of sense, but he couldn't see Rose in the role of convenient mistress. He'd seen her with the children on the ranch—playing with them, teaching them, spending time with them out of choice. Rose wanted more than to be any man's plaything. And she deserved more too. Saving her father while shoehorning in a career was an impossible ask. Plus, she'd be a lousy mistress, he concluded with amusement as he jumped into the SUV. Weren't mistresses supposed to be compliant? Good luck with that! Rose would have her say whatever the situation. His smile broadened at the thought.

Rain lashed the windscreen, throwing up plumes of mud behind the vehicle. The rotten weather matched his mood. Nothing was the same without Rose. She entertained him, touched him, moved him, as no one had. He had to find a way to make this work without promising more than he could offer. It would be far easier to walk away and keep his emotions safe under lock and key, as he always had, but Rose had already made that impossible.

A chord from his phone distracted him as he pulled up in front of the pub. Switching off the engine, he scanned the text.

Rose was offering her resignation? Not on his watch. He texted back.

I don't accept this. I offered you two weeks' holiday leave to sort things out. Use them. R

Every detail of how Rose had tasted when he'd kissed her, and how eagerly she had pressed her body against his, crashed into his mind. Thundering his fist down on the wheel, he gave way to the force of his frustration in a roar. So much for keeping his emotions under lock and key! One thing was certain: Rose stayed in his life. She was too important for anything else. Okay, so the details were sketchy, but details could wait. He'd think about the pros and cons later. Kicking the engine into life, he wheeled the vehicle around to drive back to the farm.

After a successful call to Sofia, Rose hugged her phone close, knowing she should be thrilled at the chance for her father to recover drawing closer. And she would be thrilled, if overshadowing that hadn't been the knowledge that Rose couldn't have everything. Implementing her plan for animal therapy programmes, a plan she hoped would help her father find a renewed sense of purpose, would take longer than two weeks of holiday entitlement, which left her with no alternative but to resign from her post on Raffa's ranch. The thought of breaking from him, disappointing him, was crushing. She'd do anything to avoid hurting him, but she had to be upfront about her decision so he could get on with appointing the next head groom.

When it came to writing a formal letter of resignation, which would have to follow the text, however long it took to arrive, she ended up scrapping three attempts. Tears spoiled the rest. Raffa meant everything to her. He'd been an exceptional boss. She'd learned so much from him. The chance to work with his top-class horses was a gift she would never be able to repay, but the faster she could get the animal therapy courses up and running at Sofia's new retreat, the sooner she'd have something concrete to offer her father.

And Raffa?

Dreams should be confined to childhood where they could do no harm, Rose concluded as she bit down on her kiss-swollen lips.

'Raffa!' She jolted upright as the door flew open. Glorious and powerful, he was also absolutely steaming mad. Gathering her scattered wits, she stood to confront him. 'Did you forget something?'

Ignoring the question, he held out his phone. 'What is the meaning of this?'

'So you've read my text.'

'D'you think?'

Skirting around him, she closed the door he'd left open. When she turned back, he was facing the fire. She didn't need to see his expression to read the tension in his back. How could she explain to a man as driven as Raffa Acosta that loyalty was as complex as love, and that Rose's duty lay with her father because he couldn't help himself?

He swung around abruptly. 'Well? Would you care to explain your text?'

His unwavering stare held her in check for a moment, but she rallied fast. 'It's only fair to you and my colleagues to give someone else the chance to be Head Groom.'

'What about your chance, Rose?'

'I can look after myself.'

His expression darkened. 'And is this what you really want?'

'It's not what I want,' she tried to explain, 'but it's what's possible.'

'So, you're determined to stay on in Ireland. And do what?'

'Work for your sister.'

Raffa couldn't have looked more shocked. 'You're going to work for Sofia?'

'It's the only answer,' Rose insisted. 'My father needs me. I must stay here. I have to earn money. How else can we live? Even if I have to stand alone on this, I'm rejecting your offer to buy the farm. I'll find another way— talk my brothers around—'

'Your father needs professional help,' Raffa interrupted, 'which will be more effective if he's left to focus on his therapy for a while. I need you in Spain to fulfil the contract you signed—the contract I countersigned in good faith. Do you even have a plan going forward?'

'Yes, of course I have a plan.' She could only hope it wouldn't shatter when she put it out there, as the warmth, trust and openness she'd shared with Raffa had. 'I'm going to run animal therapy sessions at your sister's retreats, beginning with the one in Ireland.'

'Nice of you to discuss this with me first.' Raffa's

sarcasm was more cutting than the coldness on his face. 'Does our recent past mean nothing to you?'

'Of course it does.'

The words were ripped from her soul, but Raffa remained unconvinced. 'Is this you being stubborn?' he demanded, frowning. 'Because surely you can see that you stand to lose more than you gain.'

'I'm not trying to gain anything,' Rose attempted to explain. 'I'm trying to help.'

'You're not getting back at me for my "buying spree" in the village, as Sofia puts it?'

'I would never be so petty,' she defended hotly.

Raffa exhaled slowly. 'I need you, Rose,' he admitted grimly. 'My ranch needs you.'

'You can easily find another head groom.'

'Not like you. Your father and brothers don't need you to oversee their every move. You're finally free, Rose. Can't you see that?'

'I must see my father settled.'

'Are you creating work for yourself? Or are you too frightened to come back to Spain?'

'Frightened?' Rose asked with surprise. 'I apologise for firing off that text without proper thought, but I won't change my mind. My father has this one chance, and, with your help and Sofia's, I hope things will improve for him. Only then can I consider what I want to do.'

'What do you want, Rose?'

She frowned as she thought about it. 'The chance to be me, I suppose.'

'You've got that chance now,' Raffa said fiercely. 'Why don't you take it?'

Rose slowly shook her head. 'I know I've hurt you, but I could never have predicted how quickly my father's condition would descend into violence.'

'Given your father's volatility, you must have known from the start that accepting a position on my ranch held a degree of risk, but you took that job with all it entails. I don't accept your resignation. You're a courageous woman, Rose, but you still have to learn that it takes more courage to step forward than back.'

Raffa's words echoed in Rose's head long after he'd slammed the door behind him. Was she destined to spend the rest of her life frightened that love might leave as it had when her mother died? Raffa was so special, was the thought that he might live up to his formidable reputation and walk away holding her back? He was doing everything in his power to help her. Why was she ranging herself against him? Was he right in saying she was holding on to a cause that no longer needed her? If that was true, it could only be to avoid the risk of breaking her heart

He hammered the gas all the way back to the pub. Rose was strong enough to make her own decisions. If they excluded him, so be it. No woman had ever put so many obstacles in his way, but easy was boring. He was always seeking new challenges, but he hadn't expected one to come in the form of a woman who checked him every step of the way.

Springing down from the vehicle straight into a pothole of mud, he cursed in a variety of languages, but ended up laughing at yet another example of how Rose could distract him beyond reason. It made no sense to keep her close when she was determined to follow her own path, but what had common sense ever had to do with him and Rose? Each time he brought logic into play where Rose Kelly was concerned, logic let him down.

* * *

The silence was deafening. She'd heard nothing from Raffa in the week since their last encounter at the farm, but she'd thought about him night and day, wishing she'd left the door open instead of sending that text, and then compounding it by insisting she intended to follow her own path. Even the progress she'd made with drawing up plans for the animal therapy programmes couldn't close the yawning gap left by a man with expressive black eyes and a will as strong as her own.

Was this love?

No, this was pig-headed stubbornness. That was what it was. So, suck it up, Rose. She was ready to fire the starting gun on recruiting staff and identifying animals for the Irish retreat—there were others who could do that, but Rose must oversee it.

Must she? Did she execute every job on the ranch, or were others quite capable of handling things on their own without her close supervision? Wasn't the idea of a team just that—each part knew what it had to do and got on with it?

With a growl of frustration—who liked to hear the truth, especially when it came from herself?—Rose picked up the phone to confirm with the applicants she'd chosen that the status of the project was full steam ahead.

There was still the achingly hollow hole left by Raffa. If Rose had thought distance would soothe her where that was concerned, she was wrong. He might have ignored her letter of resignation, but the urge to share every tiny detail of the progress at the retreat with him was eating away at her. There were some things he did know. Raffa had visited her father, which had shocked Rose to the core. Facing up to the truth, that she was no longer the crucial element without which her family would crumble, left her feeling calmer, and ready to speak to Raffa. It was long past time to talk things through with him face to face.

'He's not here, love,' Sylvia, the landlady at the pub, informed Rose. 'I thought he would have let you know that he flew back to Spain this morning.'

'Right. Yes.' Having anticipated a rational discussion with Raffa, Rose was completely thrown. She puckered her brow as if recollecting. 'I must have got the days mixed up.'

She trembled all the way home—from shock at Raffa's leaving. There was nothing to be done about it, she told herself fiercely. Lifting her chin, she strode on.

There was a parcel waiting for her at the farmhouse. Rose's heart turned over when she identified Raffa's bold black script. Backing into the kitchen, tearing the package open as she went, she pulled out the note inside.

Thought you might need this. R

It was the notebook Rose had been keeping since the day she started work on Rancho Raffa Acosta. It was thoughtful of Raffa to send it on, but it felt like the first step in a long goodbye. She guessed it had been found on the jet and one of his people had sent it back to him. Rose was never careless with things like this, and had to accept that a world full of Raffa Acosta was a world full of distraction. Turning the notebook over in her hand, she imagined him thinking about her as he sent it on, maybe hoping she took it as a sign to move on.

That was what she wanted, wasn't it?

Then why did she feel so bad?

* * *

A few days later another delivery arrived from Raffa. She didn't open this one right away. Instead, she placed it on the kitchen table, where it sat like a silent visitor, waiting to be acknowledged. The packaging was neat, the handwriting unmistakeable. What was it this time? A scold's bridle to stop Rose speaking her mind, or maybe a potion for removing mud from her clothes? She braced herself for hurt as she glanced at it. Still, it was thrilling to know Raffa was still thinking about her—in a purely professional sense, of course. He was noted for his concern for staff members.

Walking around the table, she trailed her fingertips over the packaging, imagining him holding it, lifting it, writing her name. Sitting down at the table, she finally reached out to grab it and rip off the paper. It was an academic book on the study of animals and their great value in helping those with addictions. What broke her was seeing the name on the spine. Having met the author on board the *Pegasus*, and admired his work, Raffa had given her the most precious gift possible. She hugged it close, as if that could transmit her gratitude. Then she read the message on the flyleaf.

Thought you might need this too. R

If this was Raffa's blessing for Rose to go her own way, it was the most thoughtful goodbye she could think of. There was no reason to feel sad. So why was she crying? What good were tears when there was work to be done? Her first job was to thank Raffa for the gift. Finding paper and pen, she took a moment to think, then wrote.

Thank you for such a thoughtful gift. I will need this.

I need you too. She didn't write that bit down.

Please tell the professor I'll treasure every word.

Another pause followed and then she wrote more.

Until we meet again. R

She was effectively saying goodbye to her dream, a dream that had changed beyond all recognition when she became emotionally and physically involved with Raffa.

Had that dream changed? Was she incapable of compartmentalising work and romance? She didn't exactly sit around daydreaming on hay bales, or waste time in bed, discussing the respective merits of various horse liniments.

Too much time had been spent worrying about planning and logistics, Rose concluded. Could she do this or that, while she was here or there? What about risking her heart for a change?

CHAPTER ELEVEN

'A CALL FROM ROSE? Put it through.'

A slow breath pealed out of him when he heard the familiar voice. It was like a cooling draught in an overheated desert, where playing polo for his friend the Sheikh was more of an endurance test than a pleasure. Propping his hip against an ornate gilded console table, Raffa longed for the simplicity of Rose's kitchen. He'd just kicked off his boots, after returning to his opulent, air-conditioned suite in the Sheikh's palace to shower and dress for dinner. But speaking to Rose was far more important than donning a tux.

'Are you okay? Is something wrong? Do you need help, Rose? Money?'

'I'm fine, Raffa. Honestly. I just wanted to thank you for the package you sent.'

'It was nothing.'

'It was everything to me,' Rose argued firmly. 'I learned so much from my short time with the professor, and to think you went to the trouble of getting hold of a signed copy of his book with that lovely message, saying our chat was the highlight of his evening. Of course it's important to me. I'll treasure it.'

Silence could be as intimate as speech, he discovered. He'd discovered a lot of things with Rose. Neither of them rushed to break that silence as he remembered how pleased he'd been to see a professor he respected deep in conversation with Rose.

'I'm sorry if I've kept you from your work.'

'You haven't,' he assured her. 'Are you sure you're okay?'

'Honestly, Raffa, don't worry about me.'

Someone had to. He pictured Rose and dragged in a breath, as if the air around him carried her wildflower scent. 'Are you busy?' he asked, wanting to keep her on the line.

'Yeah.' She laughed. 'Mucking out.' There was a pause, and when he laughed, she added, 'Did I say something funny?'

Apart from the fact that he had to get it through his head that Rose was no shrinking violet, or precious princess, but a stand-up woman who was almost certainly leaning on a pitchfork surrounded by dung. 'Mucking out?' he repeated. 'Can't you find someone to do that for you?'

'Why should I?' Rose sounded perplexed. 'No one makes my horses more comfortable than me. They've missed me while I've been away, haven't you?'

He recalled the ancient ponies on her farm, and wondered if Rose would use them for the animal therapy project. Almost certainly, he concluded. Rose thought of everything for everyone, including her horses. The old-timers would love nothing more than having renewed an interest in their lives.

'I really have to go now,' she apologised. 'These babies are waiting to be fed—'

'You called me,' he reminded Rose, frowning. Why would she do that, unless she had something more important to say than thank you? 'Rose?' He stared at the dead receiver in his hand. They knew each other well enough for him to know when she was holding back. But why? Was it because whatever Rose had wanted to say couldn't be said over the phone?

Concern leapt inside him. What was going on?

He called his sister, who confirmed his concern was well founded. 'Rose is working all hours, trying to do everything herself. She won't listen to me,' Sofia told him with concern. 'It's as if she's in a race to get everything in place for her father. I've never known anyone to work so hard. She needs you to slow her down, Raffa. You're the only one she'll listen to—'

He'd heard enough. His next call was to the Sheikh. Making his apologies on the basis of an urgent family matter, he booked a flight plan to Killarney and Rose.

Rose was in the middle of interviewing potential staff for the new retreat when Raffa appeared at the door. Surprise shot her out of her seat. 'Your timing is terrible.'

'My timing, as always, is impeccable,' Raffa argued with a long, assessing look. 'I've sent the candidates for lunch, so you can take a break. Have you eaten anything today?'

Rose's heart started thudding. Raffa was taking control again. 'You had no right to dismiss the applicants. I plan to eat as soon as I finish the interviews.'

'You look tired, Rose.'

'I'm not tired,' she fired back. 'Aren't I allowed to be surprised to see you? If I'd known you were coming—'

'You'd have made yourself scarce?' he suggested dryly.

'I would have carried on as usual,' she insisted, straightening up, 'but with a bigger break so we'd have a chance to talk. As it is?' She shrugged. 'I can't spare the time.'

Ignoring that, he scanned the room. 'Is this your bag?'

'Yes,' she said hesitantly. 'What's this leading up to?'

'You might want to bring it with you. My assistant will continue the interviews, leaving you free for the rest of the day—' He held up his hand when Rose began to interrupt. 'The man taking over from you is Sofia's trusted colleague. It was Sofia herself who—'

'Sent in an enforcer?' Rose suggested with an accusatory look.

He ignored that too. 'When did you last eat or sleep? And don't tell me you're fine. I can see the exhaustion in your eyes. I'm here to help, Rose. I have resources. Use them. Allow others to pick up the slack before you fall asleep on the job.'

'I can't just walk out of here,' she protested.

'Why not? Delegate the rest of your work, and come back stronger and fresher.'

A wave of tiredness hit, making Rose sway in her seat. Just the mention of taking a break was so tempting. As was the concern in Raffa's eyes. She couldn't take much more of caring Raffa, before she ugly-sobbed and clung to him. And he did have a point. The retreat was well on its way to completion. They'd open soon, which would allow Rose to pull back from devoting every waking hour and most of the night to the project.

'Ready?' he asked from the door.

'This won't take long, will it?' she asked, imagining a quick bite at the pub.

'That depends on how long you're going to take.'

The hint of a smile on Raffa's face drew her out of the seat like a magnet. 'I suppose I can take my lunch hour now.'

'No suppose about it,' he insisted.

But they didn't stop at the pub. He took her in the

car—she thought they were going to the Old Hall, to take a look at how things were going on. He drove straight past, continuing on to a destination unknown. 'Where are we going?' She glanced around as she sifted through the various possibilities in her mind.

'To Spain,' Raffa said casually.

'What? I can't go to Spain! I'm needed here.'

'If I leave you here,' he said calmly, 'you'll collapse with exhaustion. Thanks to your hard work the opening of the retreat has been brought forward. I see no reason why you can't supervise the rest of the project remotely, as I do with many of my business concerns. Your father's in safekeeping until he takes up his place at my sister's retreat in Ireland, so there's no reason why you can't take a break. I can't be sure you'll do that, unless you come home with me.'

Home. Home with Raffa? Rose glanced around. 'This is my home,' she protested.

'You can't have two homes? You can supervise the therapy programmes remotely. Come back for a rest. Give yourself a chance to think clearly.'

If she was honest, for once in her life she was almost glad to be offered the chance to take a breath. 'So, I shouldn't worry about you trying to control me?'

Raffa huffed a laugh at that. 'I control my work and my horses. I have zero desire to control you—that's even if I could, which, I'm happy to say, I can't. I wouldn't change a thing about you—apart from your stubbornness when it comes to refusing to think about yourself.'

He wanted the best for Rose. Having seen her so free in his arms, he wanted her free all the time. She was working herself to death, trying to save everyone and everything, when it was as clear as day that what Rose needed was saving from herself.

'The airstrip,' she exclaimed as they passed through the gates. 'But my letter of resignation's in the post.'

'So? I haven't read it yet,' he said with a shrug. Nor would he. 'This isn't about work, Rose. It's about you taking a well-earned rest.'

She gave him one of her looks. 'You have to kidnap me to make me rest?'

'Appears so,' he agreed.

The look on Rose's face pierced his heart in a thousand different places. She was too tired to think straight, but his thoughts were all in order. 'I want you back, Rose. You don't belong behind a desk, organising schedules.'

'There's a lot more to my job at the retreat than scheduling.'

'Training therapists?' he suggested. 'Trying to pass on the fairy dust that makes you so special? Come on, Rose, you're a hands-on woman with exceptional skills. Are you happy to throw all that away?'

Rose couldn't pretend she didn't have doubts about the direction her career was taking. Once she'd set up the therapy programme there'd be very little hands-on work for her to do. Was it the loss of control or the loss of Raffa that was turning her upside down? There'd been no controlling her father in one of his rages. Had that left its mark? Was Raffa trying to control her, or was he trying to help?

'You don't have to devote every waking moment to work,' Raffa insisted.

'Says you, who's mired in work,' she pointed out.

'I would never stop you leaving if you got a better offer, though I'd fight like hell to keep you—'

As his head groom?

Of course as his head groom. What more did she expect? She didn't want that to be her future. What Rose longed for more than anything was a proper work-life balance, and for that balance to include Raffa on both sides of the equation. She just didn't know how to achieve it. Work had always been her safe space that allowed her to shut out everything else—the arguments at home, and the grief at the loss of her mother, and then, more recently, her ever deepening feelings for Raffa.

'I'll do anything I can to stop you making a fatal mistake,' Raffa insisted as he swung the wheel to bring the SUV to a standstill at the steps of the Acosta jet. 'But I refuse to stand by and watch you take a disastrous path that can only lead to a dead end. I know your potential, Rose, and I can't let you squander it. Your father's future is secure. What he needs now is space, so the professionals have the chance to help him. He's at a stage where guilt is his main enemy, which is why it's important for him to know that you have a life too.'

Rose exhaled and shook her head. 'You know just which buttons to press.'

'I have no ulterior motive here. I'm simply being honest with you, Rose. It's time for you to let go. It's your turn to fly.'

'Taking my foot off the pedal at work doesn't come naturally,' she admitted, wondering if they were still talking about work. Was this polo superstar Raffa Acosta making his bid for the woman he believed was the best head groom, or was Raffa asking Rose to stay for another reason? This wasn't a movie with a happy-ever-after ending guaranteed. Life was tougher than that.

Yes, Rose's inner critic agreed, for once. When you want something, you have to go for it. You have to take risks—not all of them calculated. Sometimes it's necessary to act on pure instinct.

And if that means returning to Spain?

Raffa hadn't made a fortune in tech only to live in the Dark Ages. She could still be in touch with her father's therapists and with the programmes at the retreat, as well as with her brothers and anyone else Rose needed to contact. There was actually no excuse for her to stay behind in Ireland. She could work anywhere in the world and still keep her foot on the pedal. But there was something to sort out first. 'Even after a letter of resignation, you'd have me back?'

'What letter of resignation?'

When he stared at her like that, Rose knew exactly what she had to do.

CHAPTER TWELVE

ROSE SETTLED STRAIGHT back into life on the ranch. After a week of rest, during which Adena took over as Head Groom, Rose began to feel refreshed. Sleeping late, and eating her fill of the delicious food on offer, together with swimming in the river when she wasn't riding flat out through the lush green meadows with the wind in her hair, all contributed to her growing sense of peace. There was only one thing missing, and that was Raffa, who'd said she needed space.

Not this much space, Rose reflected as she paced the office he'd set aside for her. It wasn't all bad. Máire had contacted Rose out of the blue to say she'd like to be involved in the new retreat. Working with friends was a gift Rose had found on the ranch, and she was thrilled to think it could continue in Ireland.

Her thoughts returned to Raffa and she sighed, missing everything about him—the chat, the laughter, the banter they'd shared, as well as their closeness. At least she could concentrate on work while he was away. Well, that was the theory, until she left the office to go to the tack room, where she found her friends clustered around the TV. The feature they were watching showcased a man who lit up the screen.

'Romance?' Raffa was querying in answer to one of

the reporter's questions. 'Romance is for those with too much time on their hands.'

Rose flinched.

'So, you're not a romantic person?' the reporter stubbornly persisted to a background of Raffa and Rose dancing at Sofia's wedding.

'I'm a practical man who believes in chivalry,' Raffa said with a shrug. 'An outdated quality, no doubt—'

'Would your groom have dared to refuse you?' the young woman interrupted with a simpering laugh.

'The person in question knows where to draw the line—something I suggest you embrace.' Ripping off his microphone was the producer's cue to cut quickly to Raffa whacking a ball across a polo field with the force of a bullet to a chorus of good-natured cheers from the tack room.

'With all that talk of chivalry, he does belong in another era,' one of the young male grooms proposed, with a cheeky sideways glance at Rose. 'When men were men and women did what they were told,' he added recklessly, to the accompaniment of a bucket full of pony nuts being tipped over his head by Adena.

While chaos ensued, Rose watched a montage of Raffa on the screen. He hadn't needed her on this business trip, as he'd only played one match. Her heart ached with longing. No amount of common sense could deal with that. The camera loved him. She loved him, and it was getting harder by the day to hide that fact from her friends.

'There's a letter for you, Rose,' Adena announced as the good-natured scrum in the tack room broke up, and everyone returned to their duties. 'I recognise the handwriting. I wonder what it is this time.'

Since the day Raffa had embarked on this latest trip,

he'd been in contact with Rose constantly, not on a romantic level, of course, for which, if she had an iota of that common sense she was supposedly famous for, she should be grateful.

She was not grateful. She missed him like hell. Each delivery had contained something practical connected to her job. If there was ever a signal that it was time for Rose Kelly to get real and finally accept that Raffa Acosta had no wish to embark on a long-term relationship with his head groom, then surely, that was it? Shutting off the screen, she blanked her mind to every taut and tanned muscle.

'Aren't you going to open the letter?' Adena pressed.

'Not here.' Rose smiled apologetically. She craved the privacy of her room. 'It's probably just a list of instructions to add to those I already have,' she said as she tucked the envelope into her pocket.

Once her door was closed, she ripped the envelope open. And gasped. It was an invitation to spend her birthday on board Raffa's superyacht.

As fast as surprise and elation swept over her, gloom set in. The accompanying note was hardly romantic.

This will be an ideal chance to discuss business. I'm inviting some people I'd like you to meet. R

'That sounds like fun,' Rose murmured, pulling a face.

But why not? Why the hell not? Socialising was part of her job, and for as long as it lasted she'd do that job to the very best of her ability. And if she didn't wear those fabulous clothes hanging in her dressing room on board the *Pegasus*, who would?

Don't even go there, Rose's inner critic advised. *Just reply to the invitation and accept.*

* * *

Raffa sent a helicopter to the ranch to pick her up. As it hovered overhead Rose hoped with all her heart he'd be at the controls. He wasn't. A cordial older man in uniform came to help her board. There was scarcely any conversation on the way, bar the information that they would be joining the *Pegasus* off the coast of Spain. Would Raffa greet her when they arrived, or would he be too busy? He might not even be on board, she reasoned sensibly. Helicopters were nifty taxis for the super-rich. He could be anywhere.

With anyone.

And that was none of her business.

How could her heart be so wrong? Rose wondered as the pilot helped her down on to the deserted deck. No welcoming committee this time. Just the instruction to report to the grand salon. Thankfully, the sea was smooth today with just the slightest hint that the ground was shifting beneath her feet. How apt, she thought as she opened the doors to the grand salon.

'Surprise!'

She gasped with shock. There were banners everywhere, wishing Rose a happy birthday, and so many people she knew—some she hadn't seen for ages. *And all her brothers!*

'How—'

Sofia was at her side in moments. 'Come with me.' Raffa's sister linked arms with Rose to draw her deeper into the crowd. 'You deserve this,' she shouted above the cheers, as Rose shook her head in bewilderment. 'This is our chance to say thank you, for all your hard work on the new retreat, for the programmes you set up and for… well, just being you.'

'I don't know what to say,' Rose shouted back.

'You're going to enjoy this,' Sofia promised. 'Kellys *and* Acostas, as well as a prince or two. If that isn't a chilli-spiked mix, I don't know what is. I'm a respectable married woman, but even I'd have to be wood from the neck up not to think lock up your daughters when the Kelly brothers are here.'

'I can't believe they're all here,' Rose marvelled. 'How on earth did you find them?'

'Thank Raffa, not me,' Sofia explained. 'There isn't a thing that man can't do when he puts his mind to it. And don't mind your brothers—look at the cake!'

A snowy white damask tablecloth set off a towering edifice of chocolate and cream. 'Six entire feet of chocolate heaven,' Sofia enthused. 'I can't wait for you to cut into it.'

Rose stared ruefully at her rumpled travelling clothes. 'I'm not dressed for this.'

'None of us are, but we will be,' Sofia promised.

'Happy birthday, Rose...'

The familiar deep husky tone thrilled its way through Rose's body. Raffa's eyes finished the job. His expression was such a mix of brooding purpose and delicious promise, her words came out jumbled and all in a rush. 'Just seeing my brothers again—I can't express—I don't deserve this.'

'Sofia assures me you do. Please accept this as our birthday gift. Can I interest you in a glass of champagne?'

'Oh, no, I should keep a clear head, but thank you. I imagine there are people you want me to meet.'

'You do as you please tonight. This is your birthday party.'

'I'd like to say hello to my brothers.'

'What are you waiting for?'

She glanced up, thanks blazing in her eyes. The last time she'd had a birthday party her mother had been alive.

* * *

Rose, Rose, Rose, Raffa reflected, thumbing his stubble as he watched Rose's exuberant reunion with her brothers. Everyone enjoyed spending time with Rose. The entire impossible-to-please Acosta clan appreciated what Rose had accomplished, both on his ranch, where she had improved rotas and training regimes, and at Sofia's retreats, where her programmes were already making a difference.

And then there were his personal feelings for Rose.

If he'd been a different man, things might have moved faster with Rose, but protecting her from his darkness took priority. That said, it was becoming harder each day to be apart from her. Imagining Rose with another man was totally unthinkable.

'I've got an announcement to make,' Sofia declared in her usual fizzy tone as she tapped on a glass. 'Your Royal Highnesses, lords, ladies and gentlemen—'

He might have known several jokers would insist there were no gentlemen present.

'To honour our friend Rose Kelly,' Sofia continued the moment order had been resumed, 'we're going to take a short break to get changed into our finery. And no shenanigans while you're below decks,' she warned with a mischievous twinkle, 'or the party will never get started.'

This remark brought about a fresh bout of good-natured laughter, during which Raffa asked the purser to make sure a steward accompanied Rose to her suite. He was determined she would feel at home on the *Pegasus*, not as his employee, but as a valued friend of the family.

Closing the door on the now familiar sumptuous accommodation, Rose rested back against the wood with relief. She needed a few quiet moments to get her head around everything that had happened in the past few hours. The birthday party was such a lovely thing for Raffa and Sofia to have arranged, but Raffa's appraising stare had told her nothing beyond his concern. Trying to be businesslike and sensible about this, she reasoned, pulling away from the door, was impossible where Raffa was concerned, when just seeing him again was enough to flood her mind with images of his impossibly powerful body pressing hungrily against hers.

Heading for the dressing room to pick out something to wear for the party, she wanted to impress him. What was wrong with that? Today was her birthday, and this year she was gifting herself Raffa.

He was as stunned as everyone else when Rose returned to the party. Bathed in moonlight, she looked like an old-time movie star in a slim column of night-blue silk, with a split up the side that revealed her flawless legs. But, once again, it was her hair that took the prize. She had chosen to wear it loose, and it tumbled to her waist in a fiery profusion of shimmering waves. Lust fired inside him. Rose Kelly fired him in every way possible. There were many beautiful women on board the *Pegasus* tonight, but none compared to Rose, because her inner beauty, fired by a generous heart and a loving nature, meant she could not be outshone.

'Will you dance with me, *señorita*?' he asked, bowing over Rose's hand, marvelling at how pale and slim it was, and yet how strong.

'I'd love to,' she said in her customary unaffected way.

Rose's delectable scent and quick smile intoxicated him, as did the sparkle of challenge in her bright emerald eyes. This promised to be an outstanding evening.

'You dance well, *señorita*,' he said, relishing the brush of her body against his.

'I have an excellent partner,' she replied with a grin and the lift of a brow.

Rose might be in the mood for teasing him, but tonight she looked like a queen—a queen who moved in his arms as if she belonged there. The acid stares from her brothers suggested the attraction between them was glaringly obvious. Don't hurt her, their looks said, as clearly as if Rose's brothers had bellowed the instruction in his ear.

'What can we do about this?' he reflected out loud.

'About what?' Rose asked.

Sweeping her brothers' concern from his mind, he voiced his own. 'I haven't got a birthday gift for you.'

'What's this?' Rose demanded, glancing around. 'Isn't this party the most wonderful gift? Not to mention the gown I'm wearing,' she added, smoothing an appreciative hand over the tailoring.

'These are such small things, Rose.'

'Not for me,' she assured him with a reproachful look.

At a loss to know how to please a woman who expected nothing from him, when he wanted to do so much for her, he drew Rose close again and they danced on. But not for long. 'I really should go and look after the guests,' she told him during a brief pause in the music. 'My brothers will never forgive me if I don't introduce them around.'

And with that she was gone. He filled the gap left by Rose by making sure everyone was enjoying themselves. They caught up later at the cake table, where Rose, surrounded by a crowd of well-wishers, was telling everyone that she'd been spoiled tonight.

'No more than you deserve.'

She turned at the sound of his voice. 'Raffa!' Her glowing eyes told him everything he wanted to know, and he was glad when her companions took the hint and melted away.

'This is such an amazing night,' she enthused. 'Just look at this cake...'

The lightest touch of Rose's hand on his arm was a thunderbolt to his senses. He followed her stare to the towering mountain of chocolate icing, festooned with various horse-related candies attached to each layer of the mammoth structure. On the topmost layer, the figure of a woman riding a horse was supposed to represent Rose, but the sculpted hair on the marzipan figurine was bright orange, while the horse was a dull, chocolatey brown. Neither did justice to Rose, or to her favourite pony. It was a good attempt by his chef, but now he wished he'd sent for a master patissier from Paris. The hair should be glittering gold, and the pony should have its ears pricked and its head turned towards Rose.

The ceremony of cutting the cake was a welcome break from the growing sexual tension between them. Rose made a big play of wielding the knife in a way that made everyone laugh, but then she grew serious and made a short speech. Thanking both him and Sofia, for the opportunities they'd put her way, as well as the chances they'd given to so many more people, she also thanked her guests for taking valuable time out of busy schedules to join the celebration.

'There's no one more deserving than you,' his sister called out.

Sofia's comment was received by answering cheers as Rose cut the cake. He took a glass of champagne to Rose so they could toast her birthday. 'You still haven't told me what you'd like for a gift,' he reminded her.

'Being here with my family and friends is enough,' she assured him.

'Some small token, surely?' he pressed.

She thought about it for a moment, then held up the

untouched glass of champagne in her hand. Like all the crystal on board the *Pegasus*, the image of a flying horse was etched on the side of the flute. 'How about this, so I can remember tonight forever?'

He pulled his head back with surprise. Even for a woman he knew could not be bought with riches, this was a disappointingly modest request. 'I'm sure I can think of something better than a champagne glass for you to remember tonight by.'

Her eyes filled with longing, but only for a moment, and then, Rose being Rose, she reverted to her usual cheeky self. 'You just don't want to break up a set,' she said, eyes dancing with amusement.

CHAPTER THIRTEEN

'BROODING?' ROSE ASKED Raffa towards the end of the evening.

A helicopter beating a noisy retreat overhead spared him the need to supply an answer. It would have been necessarily brief. If he couldn't explain to himself why his past failings still haunted him, or how he woke in the night, believing he'd effectively killed his parents, how could he put into words how he felt about Rose, or how he feared losing her, as he'd lost others he'd loved? Watching Rose's reunion with her brothers had brought it all back to him. Seeing his own brothers—some married now, and seemingly free of the past—had made him question whether he deserved that same level of freedom.

'Your guests are leaving,' Rose prompted. 'Shall I report to the helipad, or to the stern where the small boats are leaving?'

'You're not leaving,' he exclaimed with surprise. 'You're my guest.'

'That's why I plan to go back with the rest of your guests. This has been one of the best nights of my life. I don't know how to thank you.'

'By not thanking me,' he insisted, frowning. 'There's no need.'

'Raffa?'

'Yes?' He stared down, then tensed as Rose put a comforting hand on his.

'I'm happy to stay, if you're feeling...'

As she searched for an appropriate word—one that wouldn't cause offence, he guessed—he changed his mind about having her stay. It would only lead to more hurt for Rose. 'You should leave on the last tender.'

'At least you're not saying I must leave,' Rose qualified with a glint of humour in her eyes. 'Can I be honest with you, Raffa?'

'Of course,' he said stiffly.

'I don't think you should be alone tonight.'

He laughed as he made a dismissive gesture. 'Do you seriously think I'll be alone?'

She followed his glance around the still crowded deck. 'You know what I mean. Sometimes I think we're like two lost souls, grieving and hurting, then shrugging it off, which solves nothing. We heal nothing,' she stressed in a soft yet intense tone. 'If you and I don't talk to someone—and for me, I'd like that someone to be you—we'll never move on. Don't,' she begged when he began to disagree. Reaching up, she placed her fingertips against his mouth. 'Please don't say there's nothing wrong, or that you're fine. That's been my mantra for years now—for all the good it's done me.'

There was another long pause, and then he suggested, 'My study?'

The chance to share quiet time with Raffa was the only birthday gift Rose craved, but with each step closer to Raffa's study, she worried that by the time they arrived in the privacy of his room he'd have changed his mind about opening up. Keeping things locked inside him was such a habit, there was no easy way to start talking.

He switched on the light and closed the door behind them. 'Sit,' he invited, indicating an easy chair. She perched on the edge, while he crossed the Persian rug, with its long history and muted shades, to a spectacular glass unit where he kept his drinks. Pouring two generous measures of brandy, he offered one to Rose. She accepted the fine crystal balloon, but even the smell of the alcohol was enough to put her off. 'Do you think I could have a glass of water instead?'

'Of course. Don't drink the brandy if you don't want it.' Filling a tumbler with ice, he topped it up with pure spring water.

'Won't you sit too?' she asked, knowing this was the best chance she had to stop Raffa strapping on his guilt even tighter. No one liked to admit to an Achilles heel. How much harder must that be for a man like Raffa Acosta? She knew what haunted him, because she felt the same need to fiercely protect everything and everyone she cared about. 'I build barriers,' she admitted with a shrug. 'So do most people until they're sure of their ground.'

'What are you trying to say, Rose?'

'That I understand you.' She paused. 'I respect you. You're a great boss, and, of course, I want to have everything—my job with you, my place in Ireland and more besides...'

'What more besides?' he demanded, frowning.

'Don't you know?'

'If you insist on talking in riddles, I'll never find out.'

As he began to pace the room, she took the chance to open up a little more, in the hope of encouraging Raffa to do the same. 'The past made me afraid to show my feelings—afraid to risk my heart. I thought I couldn't live through the pain of losing my mother, and decided it was better not to feel anything ever again. Now I realise that nothing can erase the past, so I think of the good times—the fun we had—baking together, the laughter and charades at Christmas before she became sick. When I confronted the alternative, which was to stay home with a drunken father, getting nowhere, doing nothing, I finally came to terms with my mother's death, and realised that what she'd wanted for me was not to stay home and take her place, but to assume a moral responsibility for the family, so I could keep her purposeful, upbeat spirit alive. But to do that meant leaving home, so I could make enough money to keep things afloat.'

'You can see that now,' Raffa interjected. 'But you're just as guilty of beating yourself up. Deathbed promises can be misleading, and it's only natural you worry about letting your mother down.'

'That hasn't changed,' she admitted, 'but I'm equally sure your parents wouldn't expect you to hold yourself responsible for their deaths. Forgive me, Raffa,' she added gently. 'I don't want to step on your grief, I'm just trying to say, in my rather clumsy way, that we're fighting the same demons, you and I.'

Raffa remained silent for so long, she began to wonder if it was a hint for her to leave. She decided to test the theory. 'I apologise if I've overstepped the mark tonight. After such a great party, I should keep my mouth shut, and only open it to say thank you.'

Raffa's short, humourless huff wasn't much, but it was a start, and Rose clung on to it with relief. 'Forgive my silence,' he said after a few more tense moments had passed. 'I haven't talked about my feelings to anyone. The shock of losing my parents was overwhelming. There was no chance for a last hug, or for me to tell them how much they meant to me.'

'There's never enough time for that.'

Another pause, and then he met her concerned stare head-on. 'You've never had a problem being forthright, have you, Rose?'

She smiled ruefully. 'Isn't that why you hired me?'

'I hired you because you're the best,' Raffa confessed with a shrug. 'There was nothing more to it than that, until…'

'Until?' she pressed.

'I don't like fate to notice those I care about.'

'Fate's pretty busy, and can't be mean all the time,' she countered in an attempt to lighten his mood.

'Trust you to put a positive spin on fate's intentions, Rose.'

'Whatever fate has in store for me, I'll cope. I'm here for you, if you need me, but if you've just brought me here to say the sex is great, but you feel nothing for me—'

'That is not why I brought you here.'

They stared at each other for a long moment, and then crashed together, two powerful forces colliding. There was no submission or mastery, and no holding back, either. There was only matching hunger and equal need. Raffa swept his desk clear. Clothes went flying everywhere. Nudging his way between her thighs, he sank deep with a roar of satisfaction, only equalled by Rose's cries of release. There was no finesse, none needed. They strove with full concentration towards the next staggeringly intense release. It wasn't once, twice or even three times that Rose's rhythmical cries of pleasure echoed around Raffa's study, until finally she lay utterly spent in his arms.

'Again?' he teased.

She dragged in some much-needed air. 'What do you think?'

When they were quiet again, Raffa mused huskily, 'I only wish there were more time to spend with you.'

'So, you've no time for sailing on your yacht, or having sex with me in your study?'

'You deserve more than that, Rose. As for the yacht?' He gave a casual shrug. 'It's useful for business.'

'My bike's useful for getting to the village from the farm, but I don't make it an excuse for living in the past. I've seen you torment yourself, and I've felt the repercussions. I understand you, because I spent years being stoic, and thinking I could take it. And it was true to some extent. I could take pretty much anything until you came along and opened up a well of feeling inside me. But you helped me too, because now I know I'd rather feel and bleed and cry than remain numb and sensible. I'm hungry to experience life, with all its challenges, and learn every step of the way. And if I can eventually raise a family to do the same, I'll count that as the greatest achievement of my life.'

'I can't offer you what you hope for, Rose, and I won't take the risk of you being hurt.'

'Isn't that up to me?' she demanded, frowning. 'It sounds to me as if you've decided to take the easy option and quietly back away.'

'Quietly?' Raffa raked his hair. 'There'll be nothing quiet about it.'

'Then open up,' she challenged. 'Offload some of your guilt. You're always telling me to share the load. You won't be free from the past until you do the same.'

'I would never do anything to hurt you.'

'Coward!' she flung at him with frustration. 'What do you think you're doing now, if not hurting me? Why can't you be honest with both of us? You refuse to risk anything but your body, and that will never be enough for me. Am I wasting my time?' she demanded.

'Rose—'

She brushed his comforting arm away. 'Lots of people live busy lives and still find time for love. What I need is you, constant and unchanging, not holding back emotionally because you think you're going to hurt me. Let me decide about that. We find it easy to laugh together, and challenge each other, why can't we turn that into something deeper? I'm not made of rice paper. I won't break if we go at it hammer and tongs. I'll come back fighting. You know I will.'

Raffa inhaled and drew himself up. 'I decided some time back that I would never have a family, because I don't have the time a family deserves. I'm a busy man with global interests. No one benefits from being dragged from pillar to post across the world.'

'You have your yacht,' Rose pointed out with exasperation. 'You can take your family and your home with you. Why can't you adapt your life like everyone else? Haven't you seen your brothers do that?' Something flickered in Raffa's eyes that drove Rose to press on. 'Or are you just too damn selfish to compromise? I refuse to believe that. A man who cares so deeply for his siblings must, in some deep part of him, want to recreate that same sense of warmth and love.'

'Children deserve parents who have time to lavish affection on them,' he argued stiffly.

'The same affection you lavish on your horses?' Rose suggested. 'Are you saying you can find time to do that, but you won't be able to show your children that same level of attention?'

'Aren't you getting ahead of yourself, Rose?'

'Maybe I am,' she admitted. 'And maybe I don't care.

You'll marry someone one day—if only to hang on your arm at events. I care about you, Raffa. Can't you see that?'

He shook his head slowly. 'I have responsibilities towards the people who work for me. The families that depend on my companies for their livelihoods. What will they do if I'm distracted by a family of my own? How can I possibly—'

'I don't know,' Rose flared, all out of patience. 'Why don't you ask your brothers? These excuses are weak. You'd find ways to make things work. Love *is* hard, and it can be cruel. It can hurt like nothing else, but when it's right, it's wonderful and transforming for those with sufficient courage to claim it.'

'Are you calling me a coward again?' Raffa said hotly.

'Where romantic love is concerned? Yes.' Maybe he wasn't the man she thought he was. Maybe the infamous Raffa Acosta was just too selfish to spare any part of himself. 'When I choose someone to spend the rest of my life with, it will be a man who shares everything with me, as I share everything with him—and on every level, not just sex. I don't want some big spender who can put on a show, but who balks at the small things that really matter.'

'Is that how you see me?'

He looked shocked. If Rose could have taken back her angry words, she would have done. Emotion so often prompted exaggeration, and right now she was drowning in the stuff. Heat flooded her face as she remembered the small, thoughtful packages Raffa had sent while they'd been apart, and then tonight, the wonderful birthday party. Maybe the fault wasn't all with him. Maybe she was guilty too.

'No,' she admitted. 'That's not how I see you. You're generous to a fault, and always thoughtful. I didn't mean to sound ungrateful—'

'I don't want you to be *grateful*,' he roared. 'I didn't throw tonight's party to impress you. I arranged it because I care about you.'

Raffa cared about her. Shouldn't that be enough? What was wrong with her? Did she have to try and spoil everything? The last thing she wanted was a fight. Why was she constantly building obstacles between them as fast as Raffa dismantled them? Would it be such a terrible thing to work for him *and* sleep with him?

Yes. Worse. It would be a disaster. When Raffa married, as one day he would, Rose would be left pressing her nose against the glass, and that would be the end of her. She'd have to leave her job, and then what would become of her father?

Turning her face away so he couldn't see her expression, she spoke in a false bright tone. 'Well, I'd better be going. I don't want to overstay my welcome. Don't worry about me getting back. I'm a seasoned campaigner when it comes to taking small boats to shore.'

'You'll do no such thing,' Raffa stated firmly. 'It will be more time efficient to fly back on the helicopter.'

He sounded as if he were solving a minor transport hitch for one of his employees. She'd asked for that—begged for it, by mentioning romantic love, when Raffa couldn't have made it clearer that that was the last thing he wanted.

She hugged herself close to hide the fact she was shivering as he called up the pilot, to warn him there'd be another flight tonight. Well done, Rose. She'd ruined a perfect evening. Perhaps Raffa was right to keep his feelings in check where she was concerned. Perhaps Rose should try doing the same thing herself. He was already scanning documents on his desk, so she couldn't see his expression, but she didn't need to see his face when the tension in his back told its own story. 'I'll say goodbye, then...'

Silence. 'Thank you again for a wonderful evening,' she tried again. 'I'll never forget it—'

'I'll never forget you. Rose—'

She almost jumped out of her skin when Raffa swung around. 'Go,' he prompted with a glance at the door. 'You don't want to be late for your lift.'

Moving restlessly on her cosy bed in her cosy room at the ranch, feeling anything but cosy, Rose knew she had no one to blame but herself. Thanks to Raffa, her birthday celebration had been perfect, and she had to go and spoil it, by trying too hard to unlock him, while selfishly holding back on her own feelings. She wouldn't know the extent of the damage she'd caused until he returned to the ranch. Waiting only made things worse. Why hadn't she thought to ask him when he'd be back?

The peal of the phone shook her out of her dismal thoughts, and in one of those rare cosmic moments, she knew who it was. 'Raffa?'

'I'll be home tomorrow.'

Home? He made it sound as if they lived together in an altogether conventional way. How nice would that be?

'Call a full meeting of grooms for tomorrow at midday in the stable block.'

She shot to attention immediately. 'Yes—' He didn't give her time to ask if he needed anything else, before cutting the line.

That was not a call from brooding Raffa, or sensual Raffa; that was a call from her boss. Well, at least she could get one thing right. She had a fantastic team. The stable block ran like a well-oiled machine. Noon tomorrow, they'd all be on parade.

* * *

Having delivered Raffa's message to the other grooms, she set about cleaning out the stables. The rhythmical application of a scrubbing brush was great for ordering her thoughts. She scrubbed harder than usual today. Having parted on such bad terms with Raffa, she'd do anything she could to restore some ease between them. His phone call hadn't been exactly reassuring on that point, but even hearing his voice was better than nothing. She was glad she'd handwritten a note to thank him for the party. Her mother would countenance nothing less. Some things from the past should be cherished, Rose had learned, while others were best discarded. It was just sorting out which was which that was the problem…a problem she and Raffa shared. It would be nice to sort that problem out together, but that was clearly a dream too far.

If she became his mistress, Rose's inner niggler insisted, she could still have a career, and advise on Sofia's projects. She'd be in a far better place to help her father with Raffa's private transport at her beck and call.

Sell her soul for a free ride on a private jet? No, thank you! She wanted more than jewels and a jet. She wanted Raffa's heart. If he still had one to give.

Dios! What was Rose Kelly doing to him? No woman had ever got under his skin like this before. He was piloting the helicopter from the *Pegasus* to his ranch, not even waiting long enough that morning to pack a bag, and all because of Rose. He'd called the meeting to arrange a rota to exchange staff between Ireland and Spain. Rose was crucial to both set-ups. He wanted her to be flexible and not feel trapped. Business was not the only reason he was returning to the ranch. Rose was the main reason. Rose, and the unfinished business between them.

As he hovered over his vast estate, snow-capped mountains glinted in the distance. A rip of adrenalin surged through his veins. The thrill never diminished. This was his kingdom, his passion, his life's work.

So you are capable of feeling emotion. You just don't want the inconvenience of anyone laying their emotional needs on you. Land just is. It doesn't answer back. Right?

He hummed thoughtfully. Landing smoothly, he released his harness. Instinct told him where she'd be.

He found Rose exactly where he'd expected to find her, in the stable talking quietly to one of his ponies. Standing in a beam of light, she looked otherworldly, sensual, lush, ravishingly beautiful. 'D'you mind if I join you?' he asked.

She started at the sound of his voice, but just as quickly recovered. Her eyes analysed his manner in an instant, and a slow smile lit up her face. 'Hello,' she whispered. 'Welcome back. Come on in. Be my guest.'

'Too kind,' he murmured wryly. 'How are things, Rose?'

Better now, her kind eyes told him, but there was a shadow behind Rose's eyes that spoke of something else. They'd parted badly. His fault. Wanting to protect Rose from himself was not going so well. As she began to detail everything he needed to know about the ponies, he let her continue for the sheer pleasure of watching her mouth form the words, when what he really wanted was for Rose to break off and fling her arms around him, tell him that she'd missed him. He wanted those capable, work-worn hands on him now.

This was agony, way beyond frustrating, Rose thought as she chattered away. All she wanted was to tell Raffa how much she'd missed him and loved him.

And suspected she might be pregnant with his baby?

No. Not that. Not now. Not yet. Let them have this moment first.

Rose was as regular as clockwork, never late…never two weeks late, as she'd realised last night. She'd rushed out first thing this morning and bought a pregnancy test to confirm or discount her suspicions, and would use it as soon as—

The pony standing between them in the stall stamped its hooves as if impatient for them to get on with it. Forced to blank her mind to what might or might not be, she swooped down to collect up her grooming kit. Standing up brought her face to face—or, more accurately, face to chest—with Raffa.

He stared down. She stared up. He reached out first, but his fingertips only had to brush her skin for her to launch herself into his arms. Their kiss was fierce and reassuring. She wanted it to last forever, but her fellow grooms, reliable as always, chose that same moment to arrive.

'Wipe away those tears,' Raffa whispered against her mouth. 'Or they'll think I've sacked you.'

'You wouldn't dare,' she whispered back.

'Try me,' he challenged with a bone-melting smile.

They weren't healed, but this was a giant step in the right direction. To hear humour from Raffa made happiness surge through every part of her. They were back. He was back. *It* was back—the humour that connected them.

He'd need that sense of humour if she was pregnant.

He turned serious. 'Have you eaten yet?' he asked with concern.

'I will when I've finished my work—and then there's the meeting, don't forget.'

'You never finish work,' Raffa remarked dryly, 'and there's just enough time before the meeting—'

'To eat?' she queried. No. She thrilled, reading Raffa's expression.

'Leave that now,' he insisted.

Rose doubted anyone noticed them leaving. They crossed the yard hand in hand, fingers entwined as they walked purposefully in the direction of the cookhouse, and then on past the door.

CHAPTER FOURTEEN

SLAMMING THE RANCH-HOUSE door behind them, he turned and lifted Rose. She sprang up and wrapped her legs around his waist in the same instant. A few swift adjustments later, and they were joined. Relief overwhelmed him.

'More— Now— Harder,' Rose gasped as she clung to him.

He couldn't speak. His energies were employed elsewhere.

After their first noisy release, he carried her up the stairs to his bedroom. They were both laughing with relief as he lowered her on to the bed. 'What are you waiting for?' Rose asked.

'I'm drinking you in,' he admitted as he stared into emerald eyes bright with fire and laughter.

'Don't take too long,' she warned. 'Remember, we've got a meeting to go to.'

'Practical to the last. Before you say it, I know what you're going to say—that's why I hired you.'

Stripping off his clothes while Rose did the same, he pulled her into his arms on the bed. 'Did you take a shave this morning?' she asked, cupping his face in her hands. 'I could file my nails on that stubble.'

'You like it.' Statement, not question.

'You know I like it. I like you.'

'Only like me?'

'Do you deserve more than a like?' She gasped as he took her firmly and deeply. 'You most definitely do.'

'So?' he queried with amusement.

'So, don't you dare stop. Remember the meeting. Time's short.'

'Less time for speaking, then.' He smiled, loving Rose's nerve and her courage, and the fresh wildflower scent that was so unmistakeably hers.

'Whatever happens now, or in the future,' she told him when they were quiet again, 'I want you to know how I feel. I love you,' she said plainly, 'and that won't change, whatever you think of me. I hope my telling you this doesn't change anything?'

It changed everything. The look on Rose's face, the concern and the warmth, and the love, tinged with anxiety, touched something deep inside him. Reaching for her, he brought her close. Turned out, that was entirely the wrong thing to do.

'Don't pat me like your bloody pony!' she exclaimed, yanking herself free. 'I don't want your reassurance only for you to push me away in a few hours' time. I've told you how I feel about you. At least have the good manners to let me know how you feel about me.'

Rose sprang up. He did too. Passion ran high between them, as usual. There was never a time when Rose backed off. That was one of the things he admired most about her, but she seemed additionally driven today.

'Tell me,' she insisted fiercely. 'If I have the courage to lay my heart on the line, don't you think you should too? If you don't want me, you only have to say.'

'Of course I want you—' Only now did he realise quite how much. But what could he offer her? A heart of stone?

A driven life? Constant travel? No respite? None of the simple things Rose longed for, like a family of her own. Bringing her into his arms, he kissed her and, to his unbounded relief, Rose kissed him back.

'Kiss me like you never want to let me go,' she whispered against his mouth.

He should be saving her from a man who, by his own admission, was incapable of giving Rose what she really needed, but instead he kissed her until no barrier on earth could keep them apart.

They fell back together on the bed, embracing as passionately as if they'd just invented sex. 'I've missed you so much,' Raffa admitted hoarsely. 'I never thought I'd feel this way about anyone.'

'I missed you too,' Rose confessed, arching her back in ecstasy as he took her again.

This time their lovemaking was slow and tender and deep. Raffa stared intently into her eyes as he took her with as much care as if she were made of the rice paper she'd teased him about.

'Don't wait for me,' he whispered. 'This is all for you.'

She rode the waves until they subsided, and then lay nestled in his arms, waiting for a sign from Raffa that she wasn't wasting her time loving him as much as she did. Could a man who'd made love to her as he just had feel nothing for her? He found words difficult, she reasoned. Rose had always been upfront with words and actions, but not everyone was the same. Each touch, breath and gentle consideration Raffa had shown for her pleasure had to mean something, didn't it?

She hated feeling so vulnerable, but being with Raffa had stripped her soul bare. Feeling more emotional than usual, as if there really was far more at stake, she remembered the pregnancy test in her bag. 'It's nearly time for the meeting. We should go—' Grabbing a throw, she headed for the bathroom with her bag. No doubt she appeared purposeful, but she was crying inside. Whatever the test showed, Raffa had been given every chance to tell her that he loved her, and he'd let that chance go.

Rose excused herself from the meeting early, looking pale. When she returned, Raffa noticed the change in her right away. 'Are you all right?' he asked as soon as their colleagues had left them. 'Rose?'

'I must have eaten something,' she fudged, avoiding his stare.

'Get the doctor to check you over.' There was a full medical team on-site. 'Now,' he prompted when Rose hesitated. 'I can't allow you near the horses if there's the slightest chance you're under par.'

'I'm not sick,' she flared, turning around to face him.

'How can you be sure?'

'Because I'm pregnant.' She let the silence hang for a few moments, before adding, 'I took a test and it's positive.'

His logical mind accepted this calmly. They hadn't been exactly abstemious. Even using protection there was always a risk.

Rose's face betrayed nothing. It was as if all the progress she'd made in expressing herself freely had taken cover behind a protective shield. There was nothing to compare with a mother's instinct. Rose would protect that child above herself.

That was the logical side of things, but something else was happening that he couldn't ignore. Feelings were erupting inside him faster than he could control. He was going to be a father. His own father had been the most wonderful man, and Rose would be the most wonderful—

She broke into his thoughts. 'You don't have to say anything. I know this won't work for you.'

He held up his hand. 'Give me a chance to take it in. It isn't every day I get the news that I'm going to be a father.'

'I don't expect you to become involved,' she continued as if he hadn't spoken. 'I can handle this on my own. You made it clear from the start that this sort of thing isn't something you'd want to be part of, and I accept that—'

'This sort of thing?' he interrupted blankly. A lifetime of telling himself that he would never have a family— that he didn't deserve a family, after the way he'd stood helpless as his parents had perished—had been turned on its head, firing his thoughts in all directions at once. He could hardly keep track of what Rose was saying, for wondering why he hadn't declared his happiness right away. Why was he selfishly keeping these thoughts to himself? Was it because a man locked in some ridiculous eternal struggle with guilt believed he had nothing to offer a child?

'I'll do what every single mother does,' Rose was saying as he refocused. 'I'll keep on working and juggle my commitments. I still have some savings left—'

'Stop.' His command was fired by anger at himself. Surely, he was better than this? 'Why would you struggle when I can help you?'

'Is that you saying you want to take over? Because, if it is,' she warned, 'I'm telling you now that I won't let you control every aspect of this pregnancy. I won't join the mares in your breeding block to be cosseted and guarded for the duration. I'm a healthy woman who doesn't need to be smothered by expert attention. All I ask is to care for my child.'

'Who says you can't?' He was beginning to see his

way through the maze. Rose needed more than reassurance, she needed proof that he would care for her, whatever her decision. 'I get that you're up in the air right now, with hormones racing, but please give yourself the chance to think things through calmly before you turn me down. There are consequences I'm not sure you've considered.'

'Like what?' Rose demanded defensively.

'Like the fact that you can't continue to work as you do—'

She paled. 'Are you firing me?'

'Of course not.' Her question had shocked him. 'But I must lay out the facts. You can't have close contact with my horses. This is a professional stable, housing spirited, highly bred and occasionally unpredictable animals. I'd be derelict in my duty as your employer if I allowed you to take any risks. Let alone the fact that my insurance won't cover you in your current condition.'

The effect of his speech appeared on Rose's face in tension lines and pallor. 'I hadn't thought about that,' she admitted quietly.

'Why would you? You haven't given yourself a chance to consider anything properly.'

She frowned. 'But I should have thought things through…'

'In the time it took from taking the test to now? Don't be so hard on yourself, Rose. This is as new to you as it is to me, but we'll find a way. We'll make this work with plans that suit both of us, and, more importantly, that secure our baby's future happiness.'

He meant every word to reassure her, but they seemed to have the opposite effect on her. It was a shock to see Rose, strong, resilient Rose, the woman who challenged him every step of the way, drop her face into her hands and cry.

* * *

Rose blundered out of the room, barely knowing where she was heading. How could she have overlooked something as vital as insurance cover? A policy for a pregnant woman working in a professional stable? She doubted such a thing even existed. Wrapping her arms protectively around her waist, she headed off down the road from the ranch to the vast acreage beyond. The urge to find space surrounded by nature was the only thing she could think of to soothe her mind. What she didn't want was Raffa outlining his cold-blooded plans. For once in her life, Rose Kelly, the biggest planner of them all, wanted something far more elusive and precious—Raffa's love, for their baby, for Rose and for the family she longed for. She longed to share this overwhelming joy with him. She'd wanted Raffa to pull her into his arms and say he was the happiest man alive.

Piercing bird calls drew Rose's gaze skywards. There were eagles in this part of Spain. She loved to see them wheeling and jousting, coming together only to fly apart again, before yielding to some mysterious force that brought them back to fly together.

Was that love?

Whatever it was, watching the magnificent birds calmed and healed her. Any child would be lucky to be brought up here, but Rose had many things to consider—her father, the family, the farm, the programmes for Sofia and the fact that she couldn't stay here indefinitely, watching from the wings, trying to explain to a child why its father wasn't around all that often.

They'd move forward with or without Raffa, Rose vowed silently. Like every single mother on the face of the earth, she'd find a way. Hadn't she taken care of her brothers since her mother died? She wasn't exactly a novice when it came to running a home.

She was about halfway back when she spotted a rider. Only one person rode as fast and fluidly bareback on such a highly bred horse. *Raffa.* Why was he coming after her?

Bringing his horse to a halt in front of her, he stared down at her face with concern. 'Come on,' he encouraged, holding out a hand. 'You can ride with me.'

'I thought you didn't want me near your horses?'

'Without me to keep you safe, that still holds fast.'

'Where are you heading?'

'To the river, so Duque can cool his heels while we talk.'

If he wanted to talk she wouldn't turn him down. Taking hold of his hand, she sprang up behind him on to the horse. 'Arms around my waist,' he said as they took off at a steady canter. The temptation to rest her face against his back made her sit up straighter than ever.

Raffa dismounted first and then lifted her into his arms. 'I was worried about you,' he admitted. 'You looked so pale. Thank goodness you look a lot better now.'

'The fresh air helps.' As did he. 'Don't worry, I'll stay on for a while to make sure Adena feels confident enough to take over from me, and I'll call Sofia. Babies are supremely portable, so—'

'And you, Rose?' Raffa interrupted. 'What about you?'

'Me?' She stared into his eyes. 'I'll be fine, of course.'

'Living where?'

'Here, in the short term, if you'll have me, and then I'll go back to Ireland, I suppose.'

Doubts crowded in, but if she couldn't work with Raffa's horses, there was nothing here for her. 'Maternity benefits will kick in eventually,' she reflected out loud.

'We have an excellent plan in place,' Raffa confirmed,

'but I don't see you resting as you should if you return to Ireland. When I brought you back to Spain, you were on the verge of exhaustion. A repeat of that would be dangerous, both for you and the baby.'

'I'll be sensible,' she promised.

'Until you have a thorough check-up, you don't know what is and isn't possible. Everyone's different, Rose. You're safer here.'

'Your mares carry some of the most valuable stock in the world, and you keep them in regal splendour, but I don't want to be indulged to that degree. I'd feel uncomfortable. I'm not used to being plied with things I don't need.'

'What I have in mind will take all the worry out of pregnancy for you.'

'A magic wand?' She laughed bitterly. Raffa didn't join in, and they strolled the rest of the way to the riverbank in silence. When they sat down, Rose took the opportunity to reassure him. 'This isn't your problem. It's mine.'

'There is no problem to solve, there's a child. And this is *our* situation, Rose. You're not alone.'

All the right words, but he sounded so matter-of-fact. You couldn't force someone to love you, no matter how much you wanted it, Rose reflected as Raffa went on, 'It makes sense for you to stay here. You'll have the best of care. Doctors can fly in. You can have anything, and anyone you want around you. You'll still be able to work remotely without coming into contact with the horses.'

'What about my father, and everything else in Ireland?'

'Your father's safe at Sofia's retreat, and I have a team in place to manage the rest, remember?'

His team. His child. His plan. Rose hugged herself, wondering about her place in all this, and if Raffa could ever unbend enough to welcome a baby into his heart.

CHAPTER FIFTEEN

ROSE SURPRISED HIM by springing up from the riverbank, saying she could do with a rest. His protective instinct kicked in right away. Pregnant women needed lots of rest, he'd heard, though Rose didn't look tired, she looked determined. What was she planning now?

He took her back to the ranch at a steady pace, and saw her safely into the grooms' accommodation with the instruction not to go anywhere near the horses. Mounting his stallion once again, he took a long, fast ride, only slowing when the sun began to dip behind the mountains. The doting uncle—a position he had happily espoused—was destined to become a father. His brother Dante hadn't stopped talking about the wonderful transformation in his life since his wife, Jess, had a child. Could Raffa feel that way too? Did he have the capacity to show a child the love it deserved? And what about Rose? He'd held back from sweeping her into his arms when she'd told him the news because that might have led her to believe that he could be everything she needed when he still wasn't sure himself. The most important thing now was to persuade Rose to change her mind about accepting his help.

Warp speed described Raffa's reaction to Rose's news. Before the end of the day, Rose had received calls from

the secretary of a surgeon-gynaecologist to the royal
household in London, as well as from a famous London
college where nannies were considered the best in the
world. A brief text from Raffa confirmed that he had
asked these various individuals to get in touch with her,
and that they would be liaising with him once they had
spoken to Rose.

And so it begins.

Perhaps he was just being protective, Rose allowed as
she waited for Raffa to pick up the phone. Remembering
how defensive she'd been when it came to him buying
the farm, the pub and the hall back home in Ireland, seeing everything Raffa did as an attempt to control her, she
wanted this to be different. It was only natural for him
to want the best for his child, and that included looking
after the mother. Their baby was all Rose could think
about, so she could hardly blame him for that.

'Rose?'

Feeling calmer, she released her vice-like grip on the
phone. 'You sound distracted.'

'I'm riding.'

Riding hard, Rose gathered. To get her out of his system? Or maybe to help him come to terms with the news
of her pregnancy? 'Can you stop—or rein in, at least?
Don't fall off on my account.'

A bark of laughter greeted that remark, followed by a
few moments of noisy silence, during which she imagined
him reining in and springing to the ground. She waited
a beat or two, to give him the chance to get organised,
before continuing. 'I've been fielding a lot of phone calls
from medical professionals and others.'

'That's down to me,' he confirmed. 'Making sure you
have the best care.'

'You know, I could have handled that myself.'

'Let me get back, settle my horse, take a shower, then we'll talk.'

'I'd like that.'

'We'll meet in the yard. Say, half an hour?' he suggested.

She frowned. 'Won't it be dark by then?'

'Full moon tonight. Use plenty of bug spray.'

She wanted to laugh hysterically at his mundane remark, but mostly she fretted that he'd get back safely in the failing light.

There was no fretting when she saw Raffa in the yard...no anger or angst, either, just a wave of deep, overwhelming love. He looked amazing in nothing more than a pair of banged-up jeans and a top that sculpted his freshly showered body. There was a night-blue sweater slung over his shoulders, and his thick black hair was still damp and unruly, as if he hadn't wasted a moment raking it into place before coming to meet her.

'Warm enough?' he asked.

Before she had a chance to answer, he swept the cashmere sweater from his shoulders and draped it around hers.

'The people I asked to contact you come with cast-iron recommendations,' he explained as they strolled in the moonlight in the direction of the distant pastures. 'The recommendations come from my brother, and his wife, Jess. I wouldn't have suggested these particular professionals otherwise.'

'What's wrong with my family doctor?'

'He's in Ireland.'

'While the specialists you recommend are in London and Madrid?' Rose guessed.

'They're not there now,' Raffa told her with obvious satisfaction. 'They're on their way here as we speak.'

'Don't you think that's a little high-handed?'

He looked puzzled. 'They're the best. They took care of my sister-in-law.'

'And here was me thinking parents decide these things together,' Rose said lightly, not wanting to sour the mood. 'There are two of us involved in this,' she reminded him.

'I don't know what more you want of me, Rose.'

'I don't want you to box off this pregnancy like one of your many projects,' she explained. 'I appreciate you taking the trouble to arrange things, but it would have been much better to discuss it with me first.'

'I've done everything I could think of,' he admitted with a frown. 'I don't understand why you're upset.'

'You're micromanaging me within a few hours of learning I'm pregnant. How did you expect me to feel?'

'That I care about you.'

His words hung in the silence between them. Was she at fault? Was Raffa showing her how much he cared and how keen he was to be a part of this? 'So long as you're not trying to control me.'

'Control you?' He huffed a laugh. 'I stand as much chance of controlling you, Rose Kelly, as I would performing dressage on a wild stallion.'

'But you'd break the horse in eventually...'

He gave this some thought. 'I'd begin by winning his trust, and then I'd train him in the ways I prefer.'

'Wow. Is that what I should expect?'

'And when persuasion failed,' Raffa continued as if he hadn't heard her, 'I'd be forced to think of something else.'

Rose stilled when she saw the look on his face. 'You wouldn't kiss him?' she exclaimed.

'Not like this,' Raffa agreed as he took her in his arms.

What was she doing?

She belonged here.

Why was she kissing him back?

Because there was no other way.

This was hopeless. She was hopeless. How could she resist a man who made her feel as if she had everything to lose and gain in his arms?

Raffa raised a brow when they pulled back briefly. 'But if you'd rather not?'

'I'd rather,' Rose exclaimed, happiness surging inside her. If there were a world of men to choose from, this was the only man she would choose to father her child. Her next and most vital task was to banish the shackles that tied him to the past.

Sex could be wild and fun, or it could be tender and intense. Either way was perfect with Raffa as her lover. His care of her on the riverbank brought tears to her eyes. Release was sweet, complete and draining. But had it changed anything between them? Rose wondered as they lay replete in the sweet-smelling grass. When it came to relieving tension, there was no greater cure than sex, but it didn't always supply a solution.

They walked back to the ranch house together, side by side, but not touching, which led her to wonder, if she wanted things to change, why didn't she do something about it?

They were approaching the grooms' accommodation block when Raffa frowned and asked, 'Why don't you move in with me? It would be so much simpler.'

'For you, or for me?' she asked good-humouredly.

'Everyone on the ranch respects you, and I've come up with the perfect solution to all your concerns.'

'Of course you have,' she teased lightly, loving Raffa for his rock-solid conviction that he was always right, even though it drove her crazy at times.

'Marry me.'

'What?' Rose's mouth fell open. She couldn't have heard him correctly.

'Marry me,' he repeated, as if that were the most obvious statement in the world. 'You trust me. You trust me with your body. You've already admitted that you love me. It can't be such a giant step to agreeing to marry me.'

'Am I expected to take this seriously, or is it another of your jokes?'

'No joke,' he assured her. 'When I think back to my sister's wedding, all I remember is the most bewitching woman I'd ever met putting me firmly in my place. Now that same woman is carrying my baby, and I want to provide for that child—more than provide. I want to see it grow up. I want to teach it to ride, to read, to swim—it's only logical to ask you to marry me.'

'Logical?' Rose interrupted stiffly.

'I won't ask anything of you,' Raffa explained, as if this was what he thought she wanted. 'I'm laying out the most sensible plan.'

'Logical *and* sensible?' Rose's Celtic temper flared. 'Why not add capable to that, while you're at it?'

'Marriage would solve all your problems,' Raffa insisted, as if he had come up with the only possible way forward for them.

Bracing herself, she flashed an angry stare into his eyes. 'I don't have any problems. I'm expecting a baby. Oh, wait. I do have a problem—the baby's father, who speaks every thought in his head without thinking about the hurt he causes.'

'Hurt?' Raffa was clearly taken aback. 'Marriage to me is the perfect solution for you.'

'Because I don't have your means?' Rose challenged.

'I can find a good doctor all by myself, and I'm not afraid of hard work, remember. I was born practical.'

'But you deserve to be loved.'

Everything crumbled inside her. He couldn't have said anything worse. Yes, she deserved to be loved, but he wasn't offering to love her, was he? He was offering a logical solution to her problem. Now she felt like a charity case, with the great Raffa Acosta offering her marriage as a convenient way out. 'I deserve to love too,' she fired back. 'And I will be loved.' As she spoke she instinctively cradled her stomach. Her baby would love her, and she would love it, fiercely.

'You should be thinking about the baby, and what's best for our child.'

'I think about nothing else. I'll provide for our child, and I'll keep you informed—'

'But I love you, Rose.'

She stopped dead. 'What did you say?'

'I love you,' Raffa repeated, meeting her gaze. 'I want to be part of your life. You're the other half of me, the half that completes me. I love you,' he said again. 'My life is empty without you, Rose. If I don't have you to share everything with, it means nothing to me. Wasn't it you who said we're the same? Well, you're right. We're both fighting a past that haunts us—not all at once, we stumble sometimes, and get things wrong, but each time we fall back, you and I, we get up again, and march forward.'

These were the words she'd longed to hear. 'You're serious, aren't you?' she breathed hopefully.

'Never more so,' Raffa assured her fiercely. 'I love you with all my heart, and I'm begging you to be my wife. With you in my life, it will have meaning and love, and hope and dreams for our future. You won't deny me that, will you?'

'You are the most exasperating man,' Rose replied lovingly.

'And you're the most impossible woman on the face of this earth. A good match, I'd say. So, stop asking yourself, can I trust this man? Can I trust what's happening? Those doubts belong in the past. Look forward and know you can trust me, Rose.'

Rose didn't even know why she was crying. This should be the happiest day of her life. When Raffa took her in his arms, *he* knew. 'Did you ever cry for your mother, Rose? Are you thinking right now how much you wish you could tell her your news?'

Her chin shot up. 'How do you know that?'

'I know you. I've taken the time to get to know you, so I understand how well you've learned to hide your feelings, just like I knew, as you know about me, that one day those feelings would have to come out.'

'It isn't easy...'

He huffed a short laugh. 'Don't I know it? *Dios*, Rose, it's such a gift to be able to tell you how much I love you.'

She exhaled shakily. 'You're right.'

'Always,' Raffa teased. 'Your mother would be so proud of you,' he added softly. 'She'll be singing at our wedding.'

That broke the dam. Rose cried, and not in a pretty way. Raffa had unlocked something inside her that she had been unable to do for herself. Longing for things she couldn't have, like her mother's comforting arms around her shoulders one last time—to hear that gentle voice advising her to be strong, almost as if her mother had known what lay ahead. While she sobbed, Raffa held her, and he waited until she was quiet before producing a familiar red bandana from the back pocket of his jeans.

'Better now?' he asked as he mopped her face.

'You won't be able to wear that again.' It was a weak attempt at humour, but it was something.

'I have plenty more,' he reassured her.

Lifting her face to his, she confronted him with what she knew could only be bright, red-ringed eyes. 'And you?' she challenged softly. 'Can you be as open and honest with me as I've been with you?'

Open and honest? Honour was everything to an Acosta, but he knew what Rose was getting at. Giving way to grief was never the easy option. It took strength to reveal sadness and regret as Rose had. Revealing more of himself had been impossible before Rose arrived in his life, because his task had always been to inspire confidence in others. His staff deserved the best of him, and the vast youth following that fame had brought him demanded nothing less.

'You've been as bottled up as I have, but we're both changing for the better, and we'll change faster with a baby coming. If you can't express your feelings, what use are they to anyone?' Rose's question pierced the armour he'd spent a lifetime building, but her next words stripped it clean away. 'I love you completely and utterly, Raffa Acosta. I have since Sofia's wedding when you came out with your outrageous suggestion that we go to bed. I believe you and I have something really special to offer a child, and that's honesty when it comes to feelings and deeds.'

'You're always thinking about other people, Rose. It's time you thought about yourself. I've been heavy-handed in the past, but all I care about is you and this baby. Forgive me?'

'There's nothing to forgive,' she said with the warmth that made Rose so special. 'You blame yourself as I do for things that happened in the past, but could we have done more for our parents? I doubt it. You were a youth, thrilled to be taking them to the airstrip. When that unspeakable tragedy unfolded in front of you, it was bound to leave its mark, but you weren't in a position to instruct your parents what to do, any more than I could stop my father drinking. Hindsight is a great thing, but you can't blame the young man you were, any more than I can be afraid of risking my heart, because I witnessed such a sad version of love at home. We're different people now, you and I.'

'I can't let you be on your own tonight. You're coming with me.'

'Where are you taking me?' she asked as he linked her arm through his.

'To my bed. But not for sex,' he added when she shot him one of her direct looks.

'Not for sex?' she repeated. 'What do you plan instead? A bedtime story?'

The return to the humour they'd always shared was the greatest relief. Cupping Rose's face in his hands, he asked her, 'Do you remember what I said to you that night at the wedding?'

'Every word,' she assured him. 'It isn't every day I'm invited to have sex with a man just to relieve his boredom.'

'Well, now I'm asking you to come to bed with me because I'm madly in love with you, Rose Kelly. I can't live without you. I don't want to try. Give me the chance to hold you in my arms and keep you safe.'

A smile started slowly on her mouth until finally it lit up Rose's eyes. 'And in the morning?' she prompted.

He shrugged and smiled. 'Tomorrow's another day.'

CHAPTER SIXTEEN

ROSE WOKE SLOWLY, unsure for a moment where she was. She only knew as she stretched and rubbed her eyes that she'd enjoyed the best and deepest sleep she could remember.

In Raffa's bed?

She shot up to find him slumbering beside her, spread across every spare inch of the bed. She'd never seen him so relaxed. Running inventory on her sleep-warm body proved they'd slept and nothing more. They'd lifted a huge burden before they'd settled down to sleep together last night. Grief wasn't easily dismissed, but they'd found ways to deal with it. Everything was easier together.

How her mother would have rejoiced at the news of this baby, Rose reflected as she reached for her phone. She'd downloaded an app that showed a child in various stages of development in the womb. Theirs was the size of a blueberry, soon to become a plum, with a lemon and a grapefruit to follow. A fruit salad of joy, she reflected happily as she rested back on the plump bank of pillows.

'What are you doing?' Raffa grunted sleepily.

'I didn't mean to wake you.'

'What's so urgent you had to use your phone? Do you have a problem, Rose? Is it something I can help with?'

'No. Here. Take a look.' She passed the phone.

'What am I looking at?' Raffa asked, perplexed.

'That's the size of our child,' Rose explained.

'Are you giving birth to a blueberry?'

She laughed with sheer happiness. 'No, to a beautiful child.'

Leaning over to share the moment, she felt a tear on her hand. 'Raffa... So, you have no feelings?' she said gently.

No feelings? Raffa was drowning in them. That it had taken the graphic of a blueberry, showing the approximate size of a baby at around six weeks old, was ridiculous—but true. Wherever his feelings had been hiding, Rose had released them. Having started the process last night, she'd delivered the coup de grâce on the small screen of her phone.

'What have you done?' he whispered, accepting and welcoming the emotion overwhelming him.

'I don't know,' Rose responded in the same gentle tone. 'What have I done?'

A wave of regret hit him. 'I wish my parents were alive to see this.'

'And my mother,' Rose agreed softly.

'Life can be cruel.'

'No,' she argued with a firm shake of her head. 'Life is wonderful. Just when you think you've lost everything, you stumble across something new that lifts you to the sky and makes you see the possibilities.'

'You see the bright side of everything,' Raffa commented huskily.

'Not always,' she reminded him. 'I see what there is to be seen. You can see it too. We owe this child of ours to be open and happy, and free from guilt. Let's not burden the next generation with our regret.'

'How did I get to be so lucky?' Raffa growled.

'You asked the wrong woman to go to bed with you?' Rose suggested.

'I asked the right woman,' he insisted. 'I just didn't know it at the time.'

'I only know that I love you, and I understand you, Raffa, and I'll spend the rest of my life proving that you're not to blame for anything, if I have to. When grief and guilt is so deep-seated, it takes time to ease, but we'll keep chipping away until it gets better. I'll always be here for you.'

'Whether I want you or not?' he said.

'Quick study,' Rose approved. 'Even if you send me packing, I'm on the end of a phone.'

'I won't be calling, because you'll be here at my side. I love you with all my unworthy heart. Maybe I should have started with a marriage proposal at Sofia's wedding, and saved myself a lot of trouble.'

'You know I wouldn't have said yes,' Rose countered.

Turning her beneath him, Raffa loomed over her. 'As I'm on one knee at the moment, this seems like the perfect moment for you to answer my question. Will you do me the great honour of becoming my wife?'

'This is not the perfect moment,' Rose argued on a laugh. 'You'll have me saying yes for another reason altogether.'

'I'm prepared to risk it—but hurry up, you're stretching my patience.'

'That's not the only thing that's stretching,' Rose observed wickedly.

'Is that a yes?'

'Yes, I'll marry you,' Rose confirmed, feeling as if her entire world had turned in the right direction at last. 'Of course I will. My answer's...*yes!*'

* * *

News that Raffa Acosta, the world's most eligible bachelor, was off the market spread like wildfire. Sofia was the first to congratulate Rose, with Rose's friend Adena hot on Sofia's heels. Some of the publicity regarding Raffa's previous reputation was unkind, but Rose brushed it aside, because she knew the man beneath the hype, the man who was so much more than his press suggested.

Raffa made sure they had plenty of private time to build on the deeper connection that was growing between them every day. They understood each other on so many different levels. When it came to sex, which it so often did, Rose remarked that if she hadn't been pregnant, she would have been by the time they got married.

Their wedding was to be held at Raffa's beach house on the beautiful Spanish island of Ibiza, where their guests could bathe in gin-clear water beneath a cloudless sky. Raffa arranged for the Acosta jet to fly everyone over. It would include a mystery guest, he revealed to Rose this morning in bed. 'I love a good mystery,' he teased, 'but I'm not going to discuss it now, when we have so many better things to do—'

'Like…?'

Rose's question was lost in a shriek of laughter as Raffa brought her on top of him. 'I love you,' she whispered later, when they were both lying contented on the bed.

'Not as much as I love you and our child,' Raffa assured her as he moved down the bed to lavish kisses on the gentle curve of her stomach, before moving even further down, to kiss Rose in the way she could never get enough of, no matter how long they spent in bed.

Sofia and Adena were Rose's attendants at the wedding, with Máire in the role of high-spirited matron of honour.

'Never has so much chiffon and lace been put to better use,' Máire declared as she turned this way and that to admire herself in the mirror. 'You don't look too bad, either,' she told Rose, with a cheeky grin.

Rose's gown was a simple sheath of ivory silk that revealed a hint of the curve of her belly. Rose had no intention of hiding the evidence of her pregnancy, any more than she would try to hide the depth of her feelings for Raffa and her friends on this special day.

Those friends shrieked in unison as Raffa strode unannounced into the room.

'You shouldn't be here,' Sofia scolded her brother.

'Rose?' Switching his demanding gaze to Rose, Raffa only had to raise a brow for Rose's senses to sharpen.

'Could you give us a few minutes?' she tactfully asked her friends.

As soon as they'd gone, she held Raffa to account. 'Must I stand here all day with only a robe covering the dress you're not supposed to see?'

'There's an easy solution,' he advised. 'Take it off.'

Reduced to a quivering mass of love and lust, she slipped out of the dress, and managed to hide it from sight beneath the robe she'd been wearing. 'You're overdressed,' she complained as Raffa took her in his arms. 'Not only that, you have the tang of the stable about you. Have you come here straight from riding?'

'I have an important duty to perform.'

'Call that an excuse?' she asked as he unbuttoned his fly and pressed her back against the wall.

'No. I call this an excuse,' he said as he reached into the breast pocket of his shirt, at exactly the same moment as he took her deep.

'Am I supposed to be able to concentrate?' Rose gasped out.

'Enough to recognise there's no room for a velvet jewel box in my breeches,' Raffa groaned out.

'There's no room for much else but this,' Rose remarked on a half moan, half sigh as he twisted his hips skilfully in the way he knew she loved.

Thankfully, by this time, Raffa had put the box down on the dressing table, all the better to concentrate fully on what he'd come to do. Efficient to a fault, he was fast and firm, and soon had Rose gasping out her pleasure just before he found his. When they were both calm again, he reached for the velvet box.

The wedding ring he'd chosen was a perfect circle of diamonds. 'A symbol of our love,' he explained. 'Fiery, constant and unbroken. But, of course, totally impractical for a hands-on woman like you.'

Rose shook her head in bewilderment. 'So…?'

'So, these are our forever rings.'

He delved into his shirt pocket again, producing another velvet case, this one containing two plain matching platinum bands. 'I've changed the insurance policy,' he explained, 'to accommodate your not-so-secret visits to the stable, and I guessed diamonds would get in the way.'

'Diamonds never get in the way,' Rose protested on a laugh.

'You've changed your tune,' Raffa teased.

'I may be practical, but you've taught me never to be ungrateful,' she said, 'and I promise not to take risks. Our child is too important for that. In fact, I insist you accompany me on all my visits to the stable.'

'Deal,' Raffa agreed with a breath-stealing look.

Holding up the glorious diamond circlet to the light, so it flashed blue fire from its prisms, Rose smiled her delight as Raffa drew her into his arms. The kiss lasted perhaps longer than it should have done, but no one was battering down the door yet, and some things couldn't wait.

'As you're so pleased with your diamond ring,' Raffa remarked as he rearranged his breeches, 'I hope you like this one too.'

Rose could only gape with astonishment as she stared at the magnificent diamond ring he was now holding up. 'What's this for?'

'High days and holidays?' he suggested with a shrug.

The huge, flawless emerald-cut diamond on a slim, diamond-studded band was exquisite. 'I can't possibly,' Rose protested.

'Of course you can,' Raffa insisted. 'Part of our deal demands that I spoil you.'

'Why haven't I seen that clause?' Rose demanded with a teasing smile.

'Put it on,' Raffa prompted softly. 'The diamond is one of a kind, just like you.'

'But I'm not flawless,' she pointed out.

'And I am?' he challenged with a sideways look.

'No, thank goodness, you're not,' she agreed as he reached for her. 'Raffa! No! We can't. There isn't time,' she protested.

Putting one tanned finger over her lips, he proved her wrong.

'Don't shave,' she begged afterwards as he gently rasped his stubble across her neck.

'And look like a ruffian on my wedding day?'

'Just don't,' she begged.

Raffa's black eyes stared into hers, and then he lifted Rose's ring hand to kiss her palm. 'Whatever you say, Rose Kelly.'

There was nothing complicated about love, Rose concluded. When two people were meant to be together, nothing, not even fate, could intervene. She'd place her hand in Raffa's with total confidence when they joined their lives forever.

Rose and her attendants were escorted to the beach by a Spanish guitarist. The tunes he played moved everyone to tears, or maybe the emotion was due to the mystery guest Raffa had included in the ceremony, as he'd promised Rose.

The reunion with her father, who was waiting for Rose on the beach, to walk her down an aisle composed of white rose petals, came as a complete surprise, and almost threw her. Regaining her composure as fast as she could, she was made up by the change in him. His eyes were clear and his bearing was proud, and he was obviously moved to see his only daughter. 'How can I ever thank you?' he began.

'Don't,' she begged in a whisper as she linked her arm through his to bring him close. 'You don't have to thank me for anything. Your recovery is all down to you. You had to want it, and you had to find the strength to make it happen. I'm so proud of you, Dad, and so glad that you're here. It could never be the same without you.'

'D'you mean that, Rose?'

There were tears in her father's eyes. 'I do,' she stated firmly.

Everything took on a new and brighter aspect as everyone stood to greet the bride. Rose was proud of her father, and so very thrilled to have him walk her down the aisle. In a few short words, he'd explained that Raffa had arranged for her brothers to bring him over. Leaving the retreat was a wrench, he explained, as now he was responding positively to therapy, he was able to help others, which was a much healthier focus than thinking about his next drink.

'Just so long as I don't have to leave the retreat, Rose. I've made my home there now. It's somewhere I truly belong.'

'According to Sofia Acosta, you have a job there for life, if you want it.'

'I do want it,' her father confirmed with feeling. 'I love you, Rose. You've made everything possible, and I know I don't deserve you.'

Raffa had made everything possible, Rose thought as she fixed her gaze on the man she loved, standing unshaven beneath a bridal arch lavishly decorated with flowers as delicate as he was strong.

'Happy?' Raffa whispered as her father placed Rose's hand in his.

'Always and forever when you're around,' she pledged with deep love and trust.

EPILOGUE

Four years later

LOOKING BACK ON the last four years, since what had been termed in the press 'the most romantic wedding of the year', Rose wouldn't have changed a single thing. Two gorgeous rosy-cheeked babies later, she had not had one moment of regret for marrying a man it seemed the entire world lusted after.

Family meant everything to him, Raffa said as he lifted three-year-old Ava Grace into her basket saddle, while baby Luke, who had already perfected the knack of making Acosta-style demands, waited impatiently for his turn.

'And it's great news that Máire wants to take on more responsibility for the retreat in Ireland.'

'Now that I have more responsibility in Spain,' Rose agreed as Raffa led the small Shetland pony while Rose walked alongside.

'The good your father is doing, by helping others at the Irish retreat through his own experiences, is remarkable,' Raffa commented with obvious pleasure.

'Just my brothers to sort out now,' Rose confirmed with feeling. The Kelly clan had gained a new notoriety in the press, thanks to their connection with the Acostas. Rose suspected her brothers weren't altogether displeased about that. It had certainly upped their tally of conquests. They were creating havoc amongst the female population everywhere they went.

'They'll come to their senses eventually,' Raffa soothed, reading her mind.

'As you should know,' Rose remarked wryly.

If it hadn't been for Raffa insisting they could make it together far more successfully and enjoyably than they ever could apart, what would have happened to them? Raffa might never have transformed into the most caring husband and father, and she might have become a slave to her work, but now their happiness was infectious. *Let's hope it stretches to my next announcement*, Rose thought.

'Twins?' Raffa exclaimed, pretending shock at the prospect.

'Not man enough to cope?' she teased, knowing full well that Raffa would be besotted by the new arrivals, and the very first to help out.

'I couldn't be happier,' he assured her. 'Anything and everything to do with you brings me more happiness than I could ever have imagined. As well as the best luck,' he added, referencing a recent huge contract for the Acosta tech company, as well as the fact that Raffa had been voted polo player of the year for the third year in succession. 'Or perhaps my luck's due to this,' he added, kissing Rose. 'The more I kiss you…'

'The more babies we make?'

'Well, if you're already pregnant I can't do any more harm now, can I?' he pointed out with a wicked smile.

Raffa stared deep and long into her eyes.

'You're all I'll ever need, Rose Acosta. You're the love of my life, the mother of my children, and I adore you, now and forever.'

* * * * *

COMING SOON!

We really hope you enjoyed reading this book. If you're looking for more romance, be sure to head to the shops when new books are available on

Thursday 28th October

MILLS & BOON

THE HEART OF ROMANCE

A ROMANCE FOR EVERY READER

MODERN

Prepare to be swept off your feet by sophisticated, sexy and seductive heroes, in some of the world's most glamourous and roma locations, where power and passion collide.

HISTORICAL

Escape with historical heroes from time gone by. Whether your passic for wicked Regency Rakes, muscled Vikings or rugged Highlanders, the romance of the past.

MEDICAL

Set your pulse racing with dedicated, delectable doctors in the high-p sure world of medicine, where emotions run high and passion, comfc love are the best medicine.

True Love

Celebrate true love with tender stories of heartfelt romance, from th rush of falling in love to the joy a new baby can bring, and a focus or emotional heart of a relationship.

Desire

Indulge in secrets and scandal, intense drama and plenty of sizzling h action with powerful and passionate heroes who have it all: wealth, sta good looks…everything but the right woman.

HEROES

Experience all the excitement of a gripping thriller, with an intense r mance at its heart. Resourceful, true-to-life women and strong, fearle face danger and desire - a killer combination!

To see which titles are coming soon, please visit

millsandboon.co.uk/nextmonth

MILLS & BOON

Coming next month

UNWRAPPED BY HER ITALIAN BOSS
Michelle Smart

'I know how important this maiden voyage is, so I'll give it my best shot.'

What choice did Meredith have? Accept the last-minute secondment or lose her job. Those were the only choices. If she lost her job, what would happen to her? She'd be forced to return to England while she sought another job. Forced to live in the bleak, unhappy home of her childhood. All the joy and light she'd experienced these past three years would be gone and she'd return to grey.

'What role do you play in it all?' she asked into the silence. He raised a thick black eyebrow.

'Are you part of Cannavaro Travel?' she queried. 'Sorry, my mind went blank when we were introduced.'

The other eyebrow rose.

A tiny dart of amusement at his expression—it was definitely the expression of someone outragedly thinking, *How can you not know who I am?*—cut through Merry's guilt and anguish. The guilt came from having spent two months praying for the forthcoming trip home to be cancelled. The anguish came from her having to be the one to do it, and with just two days' notice. The early Christmas dinner her sister-in-law had spent weeks and weeks planning had all been for nothing.

The only good thing she had to hold on to was that she hadn't clobbered an actual guest with the Christmas tree, although, judging by the cut of his suit, Cheekbones was on a huge salary, so must be high up in Cannavaro Travel, and all the signs were that he had an ego to match that salary.

She relaxed her chest with an exhale. 'Your role?' she asked again.

Dark blue eyes glittered. Tingles laced her spine and spread through her skin.

Cheekbones folded his hands together on the table. 'My role...? Think of me as the boss.'

His deep, musical accent set more tingles off in her. Crossing her legs, thankful that she'd come to her senses before mouthing off about being forced into a temporary job she'd rather eat fetid fruit than do, Merry made a mark in her notebook. 'I report to you?'

'*Si.*'

'Are you going on the train ride?'

Strong nostrils flared with distaste. 'It is no "train ride", lady.'

'You know what I mean.' She laughed. She couldn't help it. Something about his presence unnerved her. Greek god looks clashing with a glacial demeanour, warmed up again by the sexiest Italian accent she'd ever heard.

'I know what you mean and, *si*, I will be on the voyage.'

Unnerved further by the swoop of her belly at this, she made another nonsense mark in her book before looking back up at him and smiling ruefully. 'In that case, I should confess that I didn't catch your name. I'm Merry,' she added, so he wouldn't have any excuse to keep addressing her as 'lady'.

His fingers drummed on the table. 'I know your name, lady. *I* pay attention.'

For some unfathomable reason, this tickled her. 'Well done. Go to the top of the class. And your name?'

'Giovanni Cannavaro.'

All the blood in Merry's head pooled down to her feet in one strong gush.

Continue reading
UNWRAPPED BY HER ITALIAN BOSS
Michelle Smart

Available next month
www.millsandboon.co.uk

LET'S TALK
Romance

For exclusive extracts, competitions
and special offers, find us online:

- **f** facebook.com/millsandboon
- 🐦 @MillsandBoon
- 📷 @MillsandBoonUK

Get in touch on 01413 063232

For all the latest titles coming soon, visit
millsandboon.co.uk/nextmonth

JOIN US ON SOCIAL MEDIA!

Stay up to date with our latest releases, author news and gossip, special offers and discounts, and all the behind-the-scenes action from Mills & Boon...

 millsandboon

 millsandboonuk

 millsandboon

It might just be true love...

MILLS & BOON
Desire

Indulge in secrets and scandal, intense drama and plenty of sizzling hot action with powerful and passionate heroes who have it all: wealth, status, good looks…everything but the right woman.

MILLS & BOON
MEDICAL
Pulse-Racing Passion

Set your pulse racing with dedicated, delectable doctors in the high-pressure world of medicine, where emotions run high and passion, comfort and love are the best medicine.

Eight Medical stories published every month, find them a